Sarah Vaughn's voice, sweet and strong, filled the room singing a ballad. Without warning, Anthony pulled Michelle away from the bookcase and led her in a slow dance. For a time, a very short time, Michelle strained to keep him at arm's length. Though she couldn't remember how or when, the song ended to find her body pressed against his and her head resting on his shoulder. As she lifted her head, to step back, his mouth caught hers. Another song began as they clung to each other kissing deeply, eagerly.

"Anthony, this isn't a good idea." Michelle's protest, murmured between tender caresses from his lips, sounded weak even to her own ears.

"Feels like a very good idea." Anthony flattened his body to hers, his hands gripping her hips. "Chelle, I want you. I can't settle for being just a friend."

"No, wait." Breathless, Michelle pulled back from him. "This is too much, too soon."

With a tremulous breath, Anthony let his arms fall to his sides. "We've been lying to each other for weeks, Chelle."

Michelle closed her eyes. "Things haven't changed, I'm afraid."

"I have." Anthony took her hand and led her to the sofa. "I'm willing to talk and I think you're willing to listen."

"You mean we should talk about us and what happened without anger or accusations?"

"It's what I wanted for a long time, Chelle. Can we try?"

Michelle's heart raced as she looked at the soft, imploring expression he wore. Could she be making another mistake? A tiny voice whispered not to give in. But his touch awakened a long dormant yearning. "Yes," she murmured.

SENSUAL AND HEARTWARMING
ARABESQUE ROMANCES FEATURE
AFRICAN-AMERICAN CHARACTERS!

BEGUILED   (0046, $4.99)
by Eboni Snoe
After Raquel agrees to impersonate a missing heiress for just one night,
a daring abduction makes her the captive of seductive Nate Bowman.
Across the exotic Caribbean seas to the perilous wilds of Central America . . . and into the savage heart of desire, Nate and Raquel play a
dangerous game. But soon the masquerade will be over. And will they
then lose the one thing that matters most . . . their love?

WHISPERS OF LOVE   (0055, $4.99)
by Shirley Hailstock
Robyn Richards had to fake her own death, change her identity, and
forever forsake her husband, Grant, after testifying against a crime syndicate. But, five years later, the daughter born after her disappearance
is in need of help only Grant can give. Can Robyn maintain her disguise
from the ever present threat of the syndicate—and can she keep herself
from falling in love all over again?

HAPPILY EVER AFTER   (0064, $4.99)
by Rochelle Alers
In a week's time, Lauren Taylor fell madly in love with famed author
Cal Samuels and impulsively agreed to be his wife. But when she
abruptly left him, it was for reasons she dared not express. Five years
later, Cal is back, and the flames of desire are as hot as ever, but, can
they start over again and make it work this time?

*Available wherever paperbacks are sold, or order direct from the
Publisher. Send cover price plus 50¢ per copy for mailing and
handling to Penguin USA, P.O. Box 999, c/o Dept. 17109, Bergenfield, NJ 07621. Residents of New York and Tennessee must
include sales tax. DO NOT SEND CASH.*

AFTER ALL

Lynn Emery

Pinnacle Books
Kensington Publishing Corp.

http://www.pinnaclebooks.com

PINNACLE BOOKS are published by

Kensington Publishing Corp.
850 Third Avenue
New York, NY 10022

First Printing: November, 1996

Printed in the United States of America
10 9 8 7 6 5 4 3 2 1

One

Michelle watched the blinking red light in fascination. Years of hard work and sacrifice had led to this moment. She thought of her days slogging away at a small town newspaper editing copy; the day she finally got a byline; then the first time she went on the air at a local radio station reading headlines fed from a news service. Every step she had taken in her career was with an eye on one goal: television news reporting. Still, her stomach muscles tightened as the camera moved closer. Was she ready for this?

"Just got a hot tip from my source at the police department. Councilwoman Wilson's son just got arrested for possession of pot. At least we've got something hot to lead with now. So dump that snoozer on the new community center opening." Jason Brett, the producer's assistant, spoke in rapid-fire delivery as he lifted the top sheet from the neat stack in front of her.

"Give me that back!" Michelle snatched the paper from his hand.

"Thirty seconds," Bob, the cameraman, barked at them. "You kids play nice now." Even with most of his face hidden behind the camera, his impish grin was visible.

"What do you think you're doing?" Jason's face turned several shades of red.

"Those people sold chicken dinners and washed cars to get that center open, and I'm going to see that they get recognized." Michelle's large brown eyes glittered with ire as she stared him down.

"Fifteen seconds," Bob called.

"Why you—"

"Ten seconds." Bob stuck his head clear of the camera. "You planning to make your debut on the six o'clock news, Jason?"

A fuming Jason scurried out of view but stood glaring at her. Bob raised his hand as he silently counted down. Within a split second, he pointed at Michelle. The red light winked out and a green light came on.

"Good evening. Welcome to Channel Twelve, the News Leader. I'm Michelle Toussaint filling in for Steve Stroder, who's a little under the weather. Leslie Gravier has the night off. Among our stories tonight, through hard work and without government assistance, folks in the crime-ridden community known as Easy Town provide an alternative to the streets for neighborhood kids. And our school board grapples with a serious budget shortfall. But first, our lead story. Randall Wilson, son of local councilwoman Hazel Wilson is again in the news—"

Michelle concentrated on her delivery and poise, determined to appear as though she had been born reading the news in front of thousands of television viewers. Yet when Fred Cambre began his weather report, she couldn't refrain from taking a deep breath. It was as if she had been under water for the first fifteen minutes of the broadcast. The rest would be easier than having to carry the whole load. Just her luck the chance she finally got to co-anchor in Leslie's place, Steve came down with the flu.

"And that's it for sports. Join us later tonight for Sports Spotlight at eleven. Michelle." Gary Twill, dapper in his deep green jacket, nodded crisply. The former college football star flashed his famous smile at her.

"Thanks, Gary. Finally, a grassroots effort by parents and several small churches pays off. After a lot of hard work, residents in one of the toughest neighborhoods here in Baton Rouge finally opened the doors of a renovated house that had been a haven for drug dealers and users. Now that house will provide services to uplift young people. Channel Twelve salutes the Highland Street Community Center as the newest beacon of hope in a place that sorely needs it." Michelle rapidly read the story omitting several lines since time was short. Bob even rolled twenty seconds of the videotape.

"That's it for the news at six, join us at ten o'clock for a complete update on these reports and more." Michelle felt comfortable and relaxed.

"Smooth, Michelle. Real smooth." Bob winked at her. All three cameras were now off. "Uh-oh, shark approaching," he said in an undertone.

"Jason tells me you have the idea that you decide what stories get on." Weston Lockport, tall with gray touching the temples of his black hair, walked up close to Michelle as she stood sipping from a tiny paper cup of water.

"I read the story on Randall Wilson." Michelle knew better than to smile or make excuses. Fighting the urge to step back, she merely tilted her head up to gaze into intense black eyes.

"But you don't argue with the news producer."

"I didn't argue with you."

"Jason acts on my instructions, something you know very well."

"I didn't refuse to do the story. Do you think I'm crazy? I just told him I had enough time to do the community center piece, too." Michelle kept a straight face. She knew that an anchor had little if any say-so in what stories got on, and to buck the producer or news director was professional suicide.

Lockport arched his thick eyebrows at her. "That's not exactly how he described it." The studio went quiet while he studied her for several moments. "Solid presentation though." He nodded curtly before he strode off. That was high praise indeed from the usually taciturn producer.

"Whew, you dodged that bullet." Kate, the short, plump production assistant, waited until Lockport was off the set before approaching Michelle. They walked to the newsroom together.

"I know. That little weasel Jason really grates on my nerves. Every time I've tried to get on a story that's positive about our community, he slams it with Lockport."

"Listen, I'm just a lowly production assistant, but I say be careful. Jason can be a spiteful weasel, and Mr. Lockport listens to him for some reason," Kate warned.

"Yeah, well. It was worth it to see him change more colors than the fall leaves in New England," Michelle snickered.

"He was so steamed, I swear he was whistling like a teakettle." Kate covered her mouth to smother a giggle. The amusement left her round face. "Uh, I gotta go. Hello, Jennifer." She hurried off.

Jennifer Callaway, tall and blonde, never even glanced at Kate, let alone acknowledge her greeting. Ruthless in her pursuit to win more awards than any other reporter, she had little time for those who could not further her career. Wearing a blue pants suit that showcased her fabulous figure, she did not enter a room as much as she took possession of it.

"Well, you didn't screw up. This time." Jennifer gave her a frosty smile.

"So gracious in defeat. An attitude befitting a former Miss Dunghill, 1984." Michelle made a small curtsy.

"Miss Springhill," Jennifer hissed at her with a scowl.

"Whatever. And no, according to Mr. Lockport I definitely did not screw up, as you so delicately put it." Michelle strolled to her desk.

"Don't get too used to it. I mean affirmative action can take you only so far." Jennifer followed her.

"What?" Michelle whirled around.

"You heard me. Lockport has his marching orders, sugar. Having you on-screen is politically correct. But that's only a fad. Real talent and ability will win out." Jennifer tossed her hair.

"You're right. So where does that leave you? I know, Bingo the Clown is up for grabs on the afternoon kiddie show. You can handle that. They print his cue cards in words of three syllables or less." Michelle's eyes smoldered with anger.

"Ha-ha. We'll see if your smart mouth doesn't get you in big trouble. If that stunt you pulled tonight is any clue, all I have to do is wait until you self-destruct." Jennifer flounced off.

"Damn her." Michelle slammed a desk drawer. Hard as she tried, the suggestion that she was being given breaks for anything but her ability really touched a nerve.

"I heard. She's just green with envy and willing to say anything to hurt you." Gracie gave her shoulder a pat.

"But she could be right. For years this station has been lily-white. With all the industry emphasis on diversity, token gestures are being made all over the country." Michelle stared at the computer screen in front of her morosely.

"Listen, you're good. We know it and they know it. So what if their motives aren't pure? Success is the best revenge, I always say."

"You know, for a redhead you're all right." Michelle smiled mischievously.

"Hey, cuz, us Irish gotta stick together."

"Shoot, I never should have told you about that distant branch of my family tree."

As Michelle joked with her friend, she began to wind down from the tension of her debut. Though they rarely saw each other after work, she and Gracie were close colleagues. With her easygoing style, Gracie was a perfect balance for Michelle, who tended to take herself too seriously. Though only four years older, Gracie had more experience under her belt and none of the ego usually found in the business. She had helped Michelle with valuable advice during her first year at the station.

The newsroom still hummed with activity as the evening shift of reporters bustled in and out, gathering material for the late newscast and stories to be presented on Monday.

"Look who's here." Gracie tapped Michelle on the shoulder and pointed.

Michelle felt a hard thud in her chest. Even six years later, the sight of Anthony Hilliard made her heart beat faster. But now she was twenty-seven and should have better sense. Still, Anthony the man brought on the same reaction now as he'd caused when they met at age fourteen in the lunchroom at Glen Oaks Junior High.

"Mr. Hilliard, it's so nice to meet you." Jennifer purred as she held the hand of the tall handsome man in a somewhat less than businesslike handshake.

"This could be a new horror movie, Lizard Man meets the Incredibly Annoying Woman." Michelle snorted in disgust before turning back to her computer.

"With that face and body he could stick his tongue out at me anytime." Gracie sighed.

"Take a cold shower," Michelle retorted. "Thought you were so in love with your husband, Hal the hunk."

"Just 'cause my plate is full don't mean I can't look at the menu." Gracie winked.

"I ought to call your reverend daddy. And a Black man at that." Michelle shook a finger at her.

"Now, Daddy has mellowed these past few years. Why, he even invited a Black pastor to worship at his church. Hel-lo, good-looking man at two o'clock," Gracie whispered.

Anthony Hilliard moved across the room with the same agility he was famous for on the basketball court and the track field. His six-foot-two frame formed a triangle, with broad shoulders narrowing down to his trim waist. Though clothed in an expensive brown suit, it was still easy to see that his arms and legs were thickly muscled. With skin the color of brown sugar and dark brown hair, he caused female heads to turn. Anthony flashed a winning smile that melted almost everyone. Michelle folded her arms. Her expression meant to convey she was not bowled over by his mere presence.

"Hello, Michelle." His deep baritone voice rolled out like a velvet carpet. Anthony extended his hand.

"My, my," Gracie breathed.

"Oh, grow up," Michelle hissed in her ear. "Hello, Anthony." Michelle gave his hand a weak shake before pulling hers back.

"Congratulations on a fantastic job. You haven't lost any of your style when it comes to public speaking. You didn't ace speech class in our senior year for nothing."

"Thanks. Oh, this is Gracie O'Hannon. Gracie—" Michelle began to straighten the teal jacket then stopped. Why should she care what he thought of her appearance?

"I know," Gracie broke in. "Pleasure to meet you, Mr. Hilliard." She pumped his hand all the while grinning widely.

"Good meeting you, Ms. O'Hannon. That story you did on our church last week was outstanding."

"Gee, thanks. It was great learning its history. A hundred and twenty-five years and still going strong. Christ the King Baptist Church is something you can all be proud of."

"We are. And thanks to your story, we've gotten more support to expand our after-school programs for kids."

"Oh, wow. That's just wonderful." Gracie blushed.

"So what brings you here?" Michelle tried not to make a face at her friend. She would not to be taken in by his cheap attempts to win brownie points.

"I'm being interviewed for the 'Sunday Journal' show."

"Really? Isn't that . . . nice." Michelle kept shifting her gaze from those intense dark brown eyes. But she found herself staring at his shoulders, then his broad chest. Finally, she decided she was better off looking at his face. She shuffled her weight from one foot to the other.

"I . . . just thought I'd say hello since I saw you." Anthony's eyes held a question. "I've been back in town almost two months now, you know."

"Yes, I knew." Michelle had spent those first weeks taming the urge to call him. But she had been determined not to give in.

Looking from one to the other, Gracie began to back away from them. "Good-bye, nice meeting you, Mr. H—." She bumped into Kate, who was startled out of staring at the scene before her.

"Anthony, please." Anthony's smile lit up his handsome face.

"Anthony." Gracie gave a short laugh. Turning she bumped into Kate again. "Isn't that your desk over there? Move." She spoke through tight lips as she pushed Kate ahead of her.

Anthony turned back to Michelle. "Like I said, I've been back home for a while now. Working in Atlanta was a great experience for me."

"I heard you were working for Darryl Beshears. Pretty impressive learning from one of the top African-American architectural and construction empires in the country." Michelle was sincere. Darryl Beshears was as famous for building community centers and youth sports gyms for a song as he was for making million-dollar deals to build large corporate structures.

"It was invaluable. I learned more about the business than I could ever learn in a classroom. But it was demanding. I had little or no social life." Anthony raised his left hand to smooth his hair, even though it was perfectly in place.

"Really?" Michelle noticed that he wore no wedding ring. Her pulse quickened.

"What about you? I suppose your career has kept you very busy, too."

"Pretty much, yeah." Michelle was careful to keep her face blank, her arms still folded.

"But I guess you have to eat dinner sometime, right?"

"Mostly on the run."

Michelle allowed herself to take him in from head to toe for the first time. Being this close to Anthony again brought back a rush of memories and, disturbingly, old feelings. Their separation and the demands of her career had done much to dull the ache caused by their breakup. But now, with him so near, she found it hard to feel the rancor that had sliced through her six years earlier. Here he was, just as handsome but with a confidence that made him even more attractive. She smiled in spite of herself seeing his tie a tiny bit crooked.

"Pull it a little to the left." Michelle tugged at her own collar.

"Still happens from time to time. You always did have to get me straight." Smiling, he arranged the silk paisley tie.

"How's your mama?" Michelle asked. Unfolding her arms, she leaned against her desk.

"Better. She's taking her medicine now. I see to that." Anthony's face softened into an expression of tender affection.

"That's good. High blood pressure is nothing to play with, especially for us. And make sure she eats right."

"I do. Speaking of eating, maybe we could grab a bite sometime. Lunch or dinner?"

"I don't know. I keep really busy and—" Michelle looked down at her pumps.

"I would very much like us to get together. Please, Chelle." Anthony moved closer.

Michelle felt a rush of warmth hearing him use her nickname in a way only he could. "Wednesdays I finish up early, around four."

"Anthony, here you are. Sidetracked by a beautiful woman, eh? I understand." Ike Batiste strolled up.

Michelle stiffened at the appearance of Anthony's uncle. The thud of her heart now signaled a very different reaction, one of loathing and suppressed wrath.

"Uncle Ike, you remember Michelle Toussaint. We went to school together. McKinley High and Southern University."

Anthony placed a hand on the arm of the tall man who joined them.

"Ah, yes. Our star reporter. How are you, honey?" Tall and distinguished, Isaac Batiste was handsome in a hard way. His hair was a salt-and-pepper gray. His tan-brown skin shone as if polished. Leaning forward to kiss her, he blinked when she stepped back.

"Mr. Batiste. Of course you remember me. I'm sure you remember my father, too." Michelle's expression hardened.

"Of course. Well, Anthony, they're waiting for us, son. Hurry along. Bye, now." Ike smiled at a point over her shoulder before walking away.

"Be there in a minute." Anthony turned back to Michelle. "So Wednesday is a good day, huh?"

"I don't think so. I forgot I'm working on a big story that's going to keep me tied up for quite a while." Michelle stood erect and unyielding.

"Come on now, Chelle."

"I said I'm going to be too busy."

"Listen, this is about us, not Uncle Ike." Anthony's jaw tightened.

"He's still the same. Still oozing greasy charm." Michelle grimaced as though the taste of something sour was on her tongue.

"Michelle, don't start that again. Uncle Ike is a good person. He's been like a father to me, more than my own father." Anthony's tone was a plea to forget the past.

"And you still have on those blinders, don't you? You think I can just forget the past? After what he did to my family? Not likely. You breeze in here asking me to have dinner with you after the way you slammed me when I was down. Man, you both have egos the size of the Grand Canyon. Forget it."

"Talk about people not changing. You see only what you want to see. It was all in your mind, Michelle. I cared about you. You pushed me away."

"I was sick of hearing you be a one-man cheerleading squad for that slime bucket. He tried to ruin my father."

"Your father was having financial problems that had nothing to do with Uncle Ike. You know that."

"What the hell do you know about my father's finances? Look, I'm not going to debate this with you. We went through this six years ago. Good-bye." Michelle picked up a stack of files and stormed off. She almost crashed into one of her best friends.

"Whoa! Don't run over me, child." Laree's eyes grew big as she looked past Michelle. "Hey, there's Anthony. Hi—he's leaving. Man, I didn't get a chance to speak to him."

"So what? You're late, Laree. If you'd had your butt here on time I'd have been outta here." Michelle pursed her lips in annoyance. She threw the files down on Earl's desk, then realizing she still needed them, picked them up and marched back to her desk.

"Get up off my back, girl. You said eleven. It is now ten minutes past the hour. I was on time. It's just that you was into your thing with Anthony. Don't take it out on me."

"What's up? Let's celebrate. Girlfriend did a job on the news. Go on with your bad self, Chelle." Shantae did a little dance in front of Michelle.

"Careful, honey. She just dumped on me." Laree sat on the edge of a desk.

Laree Holland and Shantae LeJeune had been Michelle's best friends since the fourth grade when all three jumped rope in the playground. Laree was the office manager at a local plumbing supply business, Shantae a sales manager at a local department store with an ambition to become a buyer. They had planned to treat Michelle to dinner in honor of her Saturday debut as anchor.

"Say what?" Shantae eyed Michelle. "Why is your mouth all stuck out. We're supposed to be on our way to par-tee, and you look like somebody sucking on lemons." Shantae flipped back her long red braids.

"Anthony's here," Laree said, her eyebrows raised almost to her hairline.

"Oo-wee, you mean I missed the fireworks? Damn!" Shantae snapped her fingers.

"There were no fireworks. I don't want to discuss it. Let's just go and have a good time. Now come on." Michelle unlocked her desk and jerked her purse from a bottom drawer.

"Oh, yeah, I can see we're on our way to havin' a real blast." Shantae shook her head as she and Laree followed Michelle out.

"You've been mighty quiet for the last hour, son. Anything you want to talk about or ask me?" Ike Batiste wheeled the big midnight-blue Lincoln onto the interstate highway.

"Nah, I'm just thinking about some stuff I've got to take care of at work." Anthony stared out of the car window at the tops of buildings sliding by.

"That Michelle is pretty as ever. Thick curly hair, big brown eyes you can get lost in, just like her mama. A real lovely lady for sure." Ike glanced at Anthony sideways.

"Yeah." Anthony had thought of little else since learning he would be at the station where Michelle worked. And seeing her had crashed through all his defenses, making his reassurances to himself that he was over her a joke. But he had been a fool to hope they could . . . what? Be friends, or more? Michelle had made it clear what she thought of him. He flinched remembering the cold distance in those beautiful eyes.

"Don't let it get to you, boy. With everything you've got going for you, there are beaucoup women waiting to get next to you." Ike seemed to read his thoughts.

"She simply can't forgive me for defending you. Michelle is so damn stubborn." Anthony's fists were clenched in his lap.

"I tried to help the guy, but he fell on his face because of his own bad judgment. Then he tries to ruin my reputation. Forget it." Ike reached out to give Anthony's arm a quick squeeze. "Tell you what, let's stop off at Luther's Bar-B-Q. I'm starving. Okay, champ?"

"Sure, why not." Anthony gave him a forced smile. Uncle Ike was right, it was best to forget it. He set about trying to repair the damage to the wall he had built around her memory. The wall that kept her from dominating his thoughts and helped him make it through so many long, lonely nights.

"Hi, Mama. How have you been?" Michelle planted a kiss on her cheek.

Michelle had cut short her dinner with Laree and Shantae, pleading the need to turn in early. Though it was after ten, she'd promised to visit her mother before going home. Annette would sulk for days if that promise was not kept.

"Your father isn't home yet as usual. Working late." Annette refilled her glass of wine.

"How are you?" Michelle insisted on steering her away from familiar complaints.

"Fine. Your father embarrassed me as usual. Marvin Cato phoned to ask why Thomas hadn't paid his alumni dues for Alpha Phi Alpha. I mean for God's sake, all the balls are coming up. You know what your father said when I asked him about it?" Annette plunged ahead before she could answer. "He said he was tired of putting out that kind of money, and he needed it for some business expenses. Now I have to face Carolyn and Shirley at the Delta meeting Thursday. Oh, they won't say anything, just give each other significant looks. Damn that man!"

"Maybe he's right. I mean, he's had a rough time these last few years."

"Now you're defending him to me? You of all people. Knowing what he's put me through." Annette took a deep gulp of her drink.

"Yes, Mama, he's kind of cold and stays away a lot. But this won't help." Michelle gently pried the wineglass from Annette's fingers.

"Well, he's mistaken if he thinks I'm going to take this. I've got the money, I'm going to pay the dues. That'll show him up for the cheapskate he is. He'll do a slow burn for days then give me back the money. Ha!" Annette threw back her head.

"Mama, please—"

"Don't bother trying to talk to her. By noon she's knocked back so much wine, she sloshes when she moves. There's no reasoning with her." Thomas came into the large den and shrugged off his coat. Powerfully built, Michelle's father looked easily ten years younger than his age at fifty-five.

"Home before two in the morning. My goodness, and it's not even a school night for little Gloria," Annette said.

"Go sleep it off, Annette. I'm not in the mood."

"Go to hell, dear." Annette walked out on unsteady legs. "Michelle, come to my room before you leave?" Her voice was plaintive.

"Be there in a minute, Mama."

Thomas rubbed his eyes with a weary gesture. "She gets worse every year."

"Why can't you at least try to treat her with some respect?" Michelle chided him.

"Who do you think you're talking to, girl? What's between your mother and me is personal," Thomas snapped.

"Staying gone all the time doesn't help whatever your problems are. And your ongoing battles didn't do much to make things easier for Brian, Dominic, and me." Michelle tried to maintain her bold tone but withered under his scrutiny. Even to her own ears, her voice took on a little-girl sound.

"You don't understand and I'm not going to explain." Thomas held up a hand to forestall her. He started up the stairs then stopped. "I hear Anthony is going to be on Channel Twelve. He's done well with his business. Have you talked to him?"

Michelle twisted a lock of hair, more than ever feeling like a child caught being naughty. "Yes, but only for a minute. I don't want anything to do with him," she said with force.

"He was a fine boy, and he's become a fine young man. Got a good reputation as a fair businessman. Like I told you six years ago, don't judge him by what his uncle does. His mama's done a fine job balancing Ike's influence."

"He thinks Ike hung the moon. No way do I want any part of either of them. Since Ike ruined your business, you and Mama have—" Michelle bit her lip. The dark look on her father's face stopped her.

"You have no right to interfere, Michelle. I will not discuss my marriage with you."

Michelle looked down, unwilling to let him see how close she was to tears. "I'm sorry, Daddy. It's just I hate to see you so unhappy."

"I know," Thomas spoke softly. He stood for several seconds looking as if he wanted to say more, then seemed to decide changing the subject was better. He started back up the stairs and spoke over his shoulder. "By the way, I saw you tonight. Not bad, but don't talk so fast next time."

"Thanks for your support," Michelle mumbled at his retreating back.

She chafed at the grudging compliment. Just once she wished her father could unbend, give more of himself than in small doses. But Michelle was as tough as Thomas. She minded more for her mother, whose stinging remarks masked her deep need for constant reassurance she was loved. Once she was in her car driving home, she felt relieved to be out of the tension-filled house. Then she felt guilty for feeling relieved. Had her parents ever been happy together? Seeing them now, it was difficult to believe. Yet Michelle remembered those times, years ago, when they shared laughter easily. Those precious days when they were all together as a family, before Ike Batiste almost destroyed her father's business. Michelle gripped the steering wheel thinking of his arrogance. Worse still, she could hear Anthony's voice, his defense of what she saw as something indefensible. No handsome face or ingratiating smile could make her forget. Anthony Hilliard had no place in her life. And she would never allow herself to weaken again.

"I just got a call from a source in the DA's office. There's something fishy going on with the Housing Authority. Some big names have come up." Nathan, the assignments editor, sat forward frowning in concentration, his bushy white eyebrows an unbroken line above his bloodshot blue eyes.

Ten reporters sat around the table in the conference room. Every day at ten in the morning, it was Nathan's job to decide who followed up on what story. A task that some days won him friends, other days earned him scorn. But he was good at his job. His decisions almost always proved to be on target, even if the admission was made grudgingly. And he had the right temperament. It was seldom he cared what the reporters thought of his decisions.

"Didn't you talk to some angry housing project residents last year, Michelle?" Gracie spoke around the donut in her mouth.

"No, they lived in houses with subsidized rent. It's this program where landlords get a portion of the rent paid by the government and the renter pays whatever they can afford based on income," Michelle said. "But they're administered by the Housing Authority."

"The Section Eight Housing Program." Wayne, the reporter who mostly went after white-collar crime reports, spoke up.

"Right. Anyway, they were complaining that the landlords weren't following the rules for repairing the houses or keeping them up. After a couple of interviews minor repairs were made, but nothing really changed. The staff at the Housing Authority clammed up." Michelle got up to refill her coffee mug.

"Have you still got contacts there?" Nathan rubbed his chin.

"Yeah, a couple of the women have left. But I think at least one guy is still there. What was his name?" Michelle tapped a polished nail against the ceramic mug. "I'd have to look at my notes from back then."

"Nathan, I interviewed the mayor's Human Services Department director only a few months ago. We even met with Charlotte Kinchen, the executive director of the Housing Authority," Jennifer said.

"For a story on the Arts and Humanities Council's Annual Gala." Gracie snorted. "Not exactly the same thing."

"The point is I have access to the powers that be. If this thing is big, then you need someone who can talk to them." Jennifer stared at her coldly.

"Gracie's right, Jennifer. This story starts with the people who have to live in these low-rent houses and apartments. And the staff who deal with them every day. Those are the important contacts right now." Earl, a short wiry Black man, tilted his chair back on two legs.

"Sure, you build it from who gets hurt the most." Rexanne Chauvin peered at them over her large round eyeglasses. She was older than most, in her early forties, and a respected investigative reporter.

"Michelle, get to work on it. Now, the chlorine leak at Shaw Chemical—" In his customary style, Nathan listened then made his ruling quickly before moving on.

"Nice going, Chelle. You scored on poor old Jennifer again." Gracie wore a malicious grin. They sat at their desks again after the meeting.

"Cut that out. If Nathan hadn't thought it made sense for me to do the story, I wouldn't have been assigned. It's not about scoring on other people as you put it. It's about informing the public and doing the best job we can." Michelle pulled out an old spiral-bound notebook.

"Uh-huh. Go on," Gracie urged.

"Okay, beating out Jennifer is the icing on the cake." Michelle giggled.

"And how sweet it is," Gracie agreed. She pointed to a folder. "What's that?"

"My trusty notes from last year. Ah, here it is, the maintenance supervisor was the guy I talked to. I always had the feeling he wanted to say more than he did." Michelle began dialing the phone. "Yes, may I speak to Greg Matthews. Really? Do you know where he works now? Thank you."

"Gone, huh?" Gracie began stuffing items in her bag in preparation for going out on her assignment.

"Yeah, but I've got his home number somewhere."

Michelle spoke to his elderly aunt, who proudly told her that Greg was working at a local real estate management company and would be home after five in the evening. Since she had plenty of other tasks, Michelle put a note on her phone to remind herself to call Matthews later. A busy day followed with background research at the library on several features coming up and chasing after people who would rather not be on camera but would give assistance on other stories. By five thirty that evening, she was back at the station.

"What a day." Gracie half fell, half sat in her chair. "Two hours of having these really obnoxious little poodles climbing on me. Gee-whiz."

"Anna Belle May, right?" Michelle kept writing without looking up.

"How did you know?"

"Because you've been working on that Historic Preservation thing for two weeks. Anna Belle has been in on beautification and restoration projects in this town since the dawn of time."

"And you can't talk to her at their offices. Oh, no. You have to go to that huge old house where she holds court. What about that Housing Authority thing?"

"Just talked to him. I'm meeting him at his house in—Oops, five minutes! See ya." Michelle dashed out.

"Thanks for seeing me on such short notice, Mr. Matthews." Michelle settled onto the flowered sofa, her notebook balanced on one knee.

"It's okay. Look, I'm not sure how much help I can be. I left the place almost eight months ago." Greg Matthews was a compact five foot eleven with a barrel chest and muscular arms. His skin was the color of copper.

"There are some rumors floating around about under-the-table deals. Maybe connected to the maintenance of public housing or the rewarding of contracts for repairs. As the maintenance supervisor you would have been in a position to know a lot about how things were handled."

"I just sent men out to do the work. I didn't have nothing to do with that stuff." Greg shifted in his chair and rubbed his hands together.

"But you know who did," Michelle prodded.

"Charlotte Kinchen. But like I said, I didn't make none of those decisions."

"Charlotte Kinchen, right?" Michelle began writing.

"Now hold on. I don't want my name mentioned in this." Greg waved at her notes nervously.

"These will only be read by me."

"Sure," he said derisively.

"Okay, I won't use your name, just a code. Now tell me about Charlotte Kinchen."

"She coordinates daily operations like rent collection, calculating how much rent people pay, supervises the apartment managers, stuff like that."

"I see. So she decides what companies get the contracts?"

"There's supposed to be a bid process, but a company other than the lowest bidder can be used. For instance, if they're trying to use more minority or women-owned firms. Or if they feel the work done by a particular company is better and would save costs in the long run."

"So what companies usually get picked, Greg?" Michelle cut right to the bone.

"Charlotte got some heavy friends, you know what I'm sayin'? And they got friends. I got four kids to feed."

"Who are her friends? Just tell me. I'll get the rest myself."

Greg twisted a key chain for several moments before answering. "James Bridges . . . and Ike Batiste. She tight with them. People that you don't wanna get mad at you. That's all I can say."

Michelle fought to keep her face from showing the excitement she felt. Ike Batiste and James Bridges had been among the most prominent Black businessmen in Baton Rouge for over twenty years. James Bridges had a thriving janitorial business frequently hired by Ike Batiste to clean up his newly constructed homes and vacant properties. Greg was right, both had powerful connections locally and around the state.

"Close enough to break the rules?" Michelle looked at him.

Greg nodded. "Real good buddies."

"And they get a lot of business from the Housing Authority? Are you saying they get a lot of business because of this friendship?"

"I told you that's all I'm gonna say." Greg shook his head.

"That's enough, Greg." Hooking the ink pen through the wires at the top, Michelle slapped the pad against her palm. "That's more than enough."

Two

Anthony sat at his desk head down, the blueprints spread in front of him. He had been sitting in this position for thirty minutes.

"What're you doing, man, trying to memorize 'em?" Cedric lifted one corner of the paper.

"Just looking to make sure everything's okay." Startled to see his partner standing in front of him, Anthony began to fold the blueprints.

"Hey, we still need those out." Cedric held the blueprints. "Your head is definitely somewhere else today. What's up?"

"Nothing. I'm okay. The new library on East Boulevard is the biggest job we've gotten yet. I want everything to be done just right." Anthony took a sip of coffee then frowned. "Cold." He got up to refill his cup from the pot in the small kitchen down the hall.

"Well, I ain't buying it. I've known you long enough to know that sitting around with a stupefied look on your face means one thing—you saw Michelle," Cedric called out.

"Bull. And lower your voice." Anthony hurried back down the hall looking over his shoulder. "Keisha is supposed to be here any minute. She's taking me to lunch."

"So? She should have gotten the message by now. She's been chasing you for months, and you haven't even been on a date." Cedric clasped his hands to his chest and batted his eyes. "Oh, Anthony, do you like my hair like this?" He pretended to fluff his hair.

"I know, but we've been working really close on the City wide Church Committee. And she does have feelings. I jus have to let her down easy."

"Okay, okay." Cedric stretched his tall lanky frame in on of the black imitation leather chairs opposite Anthony's desk "So how is Michelle these days?"

"What makes you think I know?"

"Quit playing games with me, man. I know you saw he at the station and she let you have it with both barrels."

"So you went over to Shantae's house to visit little Devonne, right? No doubt to give the little tyke some lessons on baseball, or is it football?" Anthony tried changing the subject.

"Don't even try it. Yeah, I'm seeing Shantae. And Devonne plays on both of the peewee teams I coach. The boy is gonna be an all-round athlete. Now back to Michelle."

"Damn! I should have just said hello and walked away. No, I had to make a fool of myself trying to be friendly. She still blames Uncle Ike for her father's business problems," Anthony said in a voice tight with exasperation. "And me for not agreeing with her."

"You still got a thing for that woman. Course I don't blame you. She's got the look."

"I don't have a thing for Michelle. I just hate that we broke up the way we did. All through high school we were so tight, remember? We even had a five-year class reunion. Almost everybody showed except Michelle."

"Man, some of those bourgeoisie girls did give her the cold shoulder when her dad was having financial problems. Y'all was kinda stuck up." Cedric stuck his chest out. "They only accepted me cause I was the star of the football team and so good lookin'." He chuckled.

"We weren't stuck up. Maybe we were into our own clique, but that's normal for teenagers."

"All the same, she got treated differently after that."

"But not by me," Anthony blurted.

"Well—"

"I didn't turn on Michelle, Cedric."

"Let's just say you kinda backed off when she started talking about your uncle Ike being a crook." Cedric examined his fingernails.

"We had a couple of big arguments about him, sure, but I wasn't going to stop seeing her because of it. We could have worked through that. She was just too angry to listen."

"And you were too proud to beg. I still say you ain't lost that lovin' feelin' yet, my brother."

"I moved on long ago." Anthony refused to look him in the eye.

"Hello, Anthony, dear." Keisha swept in. She wore the long deep purple cape that matched her dress as though it were a queen's robe.

"Hi, Keisha. How's tricks?" Cedric stood up.

Keisha seemed to notice him for the first time. "Hello. I'm just fine." She honed in on Anthony, ignoring him. "Lunch time. We're going to Angelle's. You love their seafood gumbo."

Cedric made a face behind her back. "Nice seeing you, too. Later, Anthony. You gonna meet me out at the subdivision around two, right?"

"Sure. See you then." Anthony waited until he was sure Cedric had left. "That wasn't very polite."

"Cedric doesn't like me and I don't care for him. Now let's have lunch." Keisha smiled sweetly, her tone saying the subject was closed.

Angelle's was crowded as usual. Its location close to the downtown area and near the river made it ideal for working people. Keisha and Anthony waved at several acquaintances as they were led to a table on the second floor overlooking the Mississippi River.

"We're lucky to get this view as crowded as they are." Anthony sat down.

"Luck had nothing to do with it, sweetie. Mr. Early over there reserved this table for us." Keisha waved at the head-waiter, an older Black man who nodded, smiling.

"What's so special about today?" Anthony opened the menu.

"We never officially celebrated your winning the bid last month to build the new library. Since I neglected you so, I'm making it up to you now." Keisha put her hand on his.

"You're too good to me, Keisha." Anthony sighed. Looking over her shoulder, the smile froze on his face. Anthony's jaw muscles tightened. The sight of Michelle entering the restaurant on the arm of another man was an unpleasant shock.

"You're welcome. What's wrong?" Keisha turned to follow his gaze.

"Hmm? Oh, nothing's wrong. I, uh, thought of a detail at work that needs to be taken care of.

"Isn't that Michelle Toussaint, the news reporter on Channel Twelve? I don't recognize that handsome man with her."

"Dosu Lemotey, he has a large export business. I guess Michelle is interviewing him for a story." Anthony looked out of the window.

"Not the way they're laughing and carrying on. Say, you know her, don't you? You have got to introduce us. Oh, look, they're coming this way. Hi!" Keisha waved vigorously, determined to get their attention.

"A friend is speaking to you." Dosu touched Michelle's arm, causing her to look around.

"Goodness, she must know me but I have no idea who she is." Michelle smiled and headed for their table.

She stopped short when she realized the man with his back to her was Anthony. Dosu reached for her thinking she had lost her balance. Just as his hand came up to Michelle's waist, Anthony looked at them. He turned away sharply.

"How are you?" Michelle stood awkwardly not only because she was trying to guess who Keisha was, but because of Anthony.

"I'm Keisha Grant. You know Anthony, right?" Keisha extended a hand.

"Yes, hello. Dosu, this is Anthony Hilliard."

"How do you do?" Dosu said in his softly accented English as he reached out to shake hands.

"I watch your news show almost every day. I just love those reports you do. Are you going to the Black and White Ball this year? I hear it's going to be fabulous." Keisha scanned Michelle from head to toe. "Lovely outfit. Saw something just like it in the Neiman Marcus catalogue."

"Really?" Michelle ignored the less than subtle attempt to find out where she shopped.

"I believe we have mutual acquaintances." Dosu spoke to Anthony. "Clarence Burrell and Darryl Beshears speak highly of your work, Mr. Hilliard."

"Thank you. I learned a lot from them. Have you known them long?"

"Clarence and I met when I came to this country to attend Tuskegee Institute. We have been friends since then. Here is my card. I understand you may be building more homes and offices in the future. I import many items that can be used to furnish and decorate them." Dosu handed him a gold-lettered business card.

"It may be another year before we get to that point, but I'll certainly keep you in mind. So how have you been, Michelle?" Anthony wore a stony expression as he looked at her.

Michelle stood awkwardly between the two men. She twisted the long strap of her purse. "Good. And you?"

"Just fine."

"You two practically grew up together, I hear." Keisha grinned. Suddenly the light went out of her face as she looked from Michelle to Anthony.

"We've known each other for a long time, yes. Michelle and I met in the seventh grade." Anthony's gaze wavered from Michelle to the scene outside the window. A moment of uneasy silence followed.

"It was nice meeting you, Ms. Grant." Michelle nodded at them both before moving away, ahead of Dosu.

Anthony was lost in thought for the rest of their extended lunch. Keisha vainly tried to engage his attention, but his conversation was perfunctory and distracted. So Dosu Lemotey was the reason Michelle had given him the cold shoulder. Apparently getting over him had been easy. When they pulled up in front of the office, he got out of Keisha's Volvo without speaking.

"Good-bye." He waved to her, a vacant look in his eyes.

"Hey, is that all?" Keisha pouted.

"Hmm? Oh, sorry. Thanks for lunch. It was nice. I better get going. It's almost two and Cedric will be waiting for me." Anthony seemed to shake himself awake.

"Okay. See you tonight?" Keisha's voice dropped low.

"I'm going to be working awfully late. I'll call you later."

Anthony left before Keisha could say anything more. In the mood he was in, he did not think he could stand too many questions. He was angry that seeing Michelle with another man could shake him so. Not seeing her at all was bad enough, but now he knew there was someone else in her life. Anthony plunged into work for the rest of the day in an attempt to wipe the picture of Michelle smiling at another man from his mind.

"How long were you together?" Dosu spoke softly, breaking into her thoughts.

"What?" Michelle blinked. She realized that she had hardly spoken since they had left Angelle's.

"The way you so carefully avoided paying very much attention to him was very revealing." Dosu's handsome face wore a gentle, wise smile.

"We've known each other since we were about fourteen." Michelle tried to dodge the real question.

Dosu cocked his head to one side. "The tie between you is strong." He seemed to be looking straight into her heart.

"Anything we had ended some time ago. He stabbed me in the back."

"I think maybe you and he have hurt each other yet would like to mend that hurt. It is in his eyes, and yours." Dosu parked in front of the station.

"Our . . . problem is much deeper than you think, Dosu. It was more than a quarrel. We've both moved on since then, believe me," Michelle said in a firm tone.

"There is an African proverb, 'Love is like young rice: transplanted, still it grows.' "

"Love? No way. More like contempt. He defends and supports a man that tried to hurt my family. A man who has the morals of a vulture. Anthony Hilliard is beneath contempt. Be careful doing business with him." Michelle's voice rang with animosity.

"I will remember, Michelle. But you remember what I said also." Dosu gave her a brotherly kiss on the forehead.

Michelle sat at her desk going over the old notes, or at least she appeared to be. Dosu had become a good friend whose counsel she greatly respected. That he saw something in her that reached out to Anthony filled her with anxiety. Thinking back, she still felt the burning pain that seared through her six years ago. A pain caused by Anthony's betrayal. She remembered the look on his face as he defended Ike Batiste. As things became increasingly worse for her father, there was a distance in his voice and manner whenever they met. No, she was not that green college girl anymore. Anthony would never worm his way back into her life only to tear it apart again. Gritting her teeth, determined to push away thoughts of him, Michelle doggedly forced herself to focus on the words before her.

"Well, here she is. Lois Lane, ace reporter." Jennifer stood next to her desk, a smug look on her face.

Michelle glanced up only briefly. This was the last thing she needed right now. She pulled the keyboard to her and began tapping out a rough draft of a report.

"Working on the big story, I suppose." Jennifer had something to say and would not be discouraged.

Michelle pushed the keyboard aside. "Okay, let's get this over with. What is it?"

"Nothing really. That is, if you think my getting two plum assignments Nathan was leaning toward giving to somebody else nothing. I'll be covering the city council meetings for a while."

"Big deal. Everybody is happy to have that rotated."

"And Weston," Jennifer said, pausing dramatically. "After discussing it with Nathan, of course, he has decided that I'll be doing a regular feature on good news type stories. We decided to call it 'Beacons of Hope.' "

"What?" Michelle sprang from her chair. "That story on the community center was supposed to be only the first in a series! It was *my* idea."

"There was quite a positive response. Weston felt we should definitely go with it. And Jason felt you had your hands full, especially with this Housing Authority thing." Jennifer waved her hand at the papers on Michelle's desk.

"Where is Nathan? I have a few things to say to him, and Jason, too."

"I think they're both in Jason's office. But you're wasting your time, dear," Jennifer called after her as Michelle stormed out.

Without knocking, Michelle pushed through the door to Jason's office. She was so angry, she stood seething for nearly thirty seconds unable to speak until they noticed her.

"Not only didn't I hear you knock, I don't remember telling you to come in." Jason sat back in his chair.

"What the hell is this about Jennifer getting my feature?" Michelle managed to blurt out.

"Mr. Lockport made the final decision, but I suggested it. Problem?" Jason raised an eyebrow.

"You know damn well that I put in extra hours lining up interviews, tracking down sources for that idea." Michelle stood feet apart, jabbing an accusing finger at him.

"Jennifer has been doing these little 'feel good' pieces for a while now. Besides, we decided to throw in some public appeals to help people who need assistance. We need to compete with Channel Seven's Madeline Mason with her 'We're on Your Side' segment. I figure the combination will give us the edge. And viewers respond very well to Jennifer." Jason wore a superior smile.

"Oh, I get it. We're going to have a battle of the blondes. Play it safe, right? After all, minorities make up only twenty percent of the market share. I was going to spotlight efforts by poor people to change things in their communities. Jennifer is going to spend her time hopping from one society club soiree to the next."

"May I remind you that some of our largest advertisers give very generously to many worthy causes. Are you suggesting they don't deserve recognition?" Jason said.

"They get plenty of press now, and you know it. Most of the time when we have film from places like Easy Town it's showing young Black men being led away in handcuffs." Michelle threw up both hands in a gesture of frustration. "There is more to those neighborhoods than that. I think we have a responsibility to show it."

"Jennifer will spotlight the minority community. In fact, she has a story on that African-American sorority that contributes thousands every year to the Sickle Cell Anemia Foundation." Jason shrugged and spread his arms wide.

"Nathan, you know that's not where I was coming from. Michelle turned to him, dismissing Jason.

"What can I say, Michelle? I gave it a shot, but Weston thought his idea was stronger for the station. More broad in scope I think was the way he put it."

"But, Nathan, the closest Jennifer will get to poor neighborhoods is to speed past them on her way to the tanning salon," Michelle retorted.

"I'll review leads and make sure we get some of those stories, too. I promise. But this isn't my call, you know that." Nathan cupped her elbow and led her out to his office.

"Thank you, Nathan." Jason waved them out of his office in a gesture that indicated no further discussion was warranted or desired.

Back in Nathan's office, Michelle paced the narrow area between his desk and the door. "I worked hard for this. I deserved to be given a shot."

"I know you did, but calm down. You've got some pretty good assignments, remember? That Housing Authority story for one. My gut tells me it's going to be big. A career maker. The kind of story investigative reporters dream of." Nathan sat heavily in his old swivel chair.

She gave a sigh. "You may be right." Michelle stood still and rubbed her chin, wearing a thoughtful expression. "But it's going to take time to dig it out. It's like an iceberg—most of it's hidden beneath the surface." She switched gears as the spark of her ambition was fanned.

Nathan leaned his elbows on the desk. "Yeah, but think of the payoff. My guy at the DA's office says they just put another investigator on it."

"Sure, but they could decide there isn't enough evidence to move on. So while I'm chasing a possibility, as promising as it may seem now, Jennifer will be flashing her pearly white fangs once a week like clockwork." Michelle let out a dispirited groan.

"Yeah, but with the inside track you'll have on the Housing Authority story, you could get an exclusive from the DA. Now, stop bitching, Toussaint. Get out there and do your job." Nathan had spent more time being supportive than he usually was with reporters, but now his patience was exhausted. He crossed to the door and swung it open.

"You're right. After all, tomorrow's another day." Michelle parodied Scarlet O'Hara's last line.

"That's the spirit. Now go." Grinning, Nathan jerked a thumb toward the newsroom.

"Thanks for coming with me to this thing." Michelle pulled the shawl up around her shoulders. Despite the cool October night, it kept her warm.

"Are you kidding? This place is gonna be ground zero for all the fine-looking African-American professional males within a fifty-mile radius." Laree tugged at her form-fitting dress as she struggled to get out of Michelle's sporty Mustang.

"They will be with their wives, fiancées, and girlfriends. So don't get your hopes too high."

"Get real, relationships begin and end every day. Just step back and watch me work my magic." Laree pulled the matching coat to her dress around her shoulders.

"You ought to be ashamed, girl," Michelle said, laughing as Laree swung her hips.

As they entered the banquet hall, both scanned the crowd. The tickets purchased were to benefit the local Big Buddy program sponsored by a coalition of African-American churches and businessmen.

Laree let out a low whistle of appreciation. "I have never seen so many furs and diamonds in one room. Look, there's Maureen Clarence-Harrington. Oh, and Shirley Aucoin. Making the rounds so everybody can see their jewelry."

"Yeah. These kinds of see-and-be-seen happenings really bore me. If it wasn't to benefit such a great program, believe me I wouldn't be here," Michelle muttered in an undertone so as not to be overheard by the others seated at their table.

"Sugar, I'm sorry Dosu had to be out of town. But I'm happy for me. Hi there. Hello." Laree waved gaily at several acquaintances at nearby tables, one of which was a handsome man who was quite dashing in a dark gray tux.

"Laree, don't you see that woman next to him? She's giving us a dirty look," Michelle whispered.

"That's Theron Mackey. He's been divorced for a year and he's fair game. Like my grandmama says, if you can't hold your man, hold your hand." Laree patted her long black hair.

"How is Miss Hannah doing?" Michelle smiled at the waitress, then frowned at the bland plate of food before her.

"Going strong. Got a new boyfriend, child. He's a younger man, sixty-nine. She just turned seventy-seven. Mama and my aunts and uncles are too embarrassed." Laree giggled.

"Good for her," Michelle said.

"Hell, yes. I wanna grow up to be just like my gramma."

A distinguished gray-haired woman wearing a heavy gold necklace with matching dangling earrings approached. The blue sequined top she wore glittered as she walked beneath the chandeliers suspended over the banquet hall.

"Ms. Toussaint, so glad to see you. Wonderful turnout isn't it?"

"Hello, Mrs. Harrington. Yes, it is. This is my friend, Laree Holland."

"Nice to see you. I hope you're going to do a report on us. We need more positive exposure." Mrs. Harrington flashed a professional smile.

"Yes, we will." Michelle drummed her fingers then realizing it, she put her hand in her lap.

"Marvelous, dear. Now you enjoy yourselves." Mrs. Harrington floated on to the next table, leaving behind a strong whiff of expensive cologne.

"Geez, that woman has a personality like a fingernail across a blackboard. She's a self-important, upper-class snob." Michelle spoke in a low, tight voice.

"I thought she seemed okay." Laree was busily devouring the chicken marsala, all the while checking out the other guests.

"Mrs. Maureen Clarence-Harrington is in one of my mother's social clubs. Believe me, those women are more interested in status and appearances than the work these charities do in the community." Michelle glanced around with distaste.

"Lighten up. The people who are dedicated do-gooders need money, the people with money need to think they're doing their share. It all balances out, right? Now let's get back to the important stuff. You know Theron Mackey, introduce us." Laree was again favoring him with a big smile.

"No way. That lady isn't going to come after me with her butter knife," Michelle hissed at her.

Their good-natured argument was cut short when they realized they were attracting the attention of the other guests at their table. To Laree's disappointment, and Michelle's relief, they had been joined by an elderly couple and two middle-aged women. For the rest of the evening they made small talk with them. A jazz quartet provided music, and a portion of the banquet hall had been cleared for dancing. Laree was soon on the dance floor with a succession of men. Michelle turned down all requests preferring to observe.

"May I sit down?"

Michelle started at the familiar voice behind her. Turning, she saw Anthony standing next to an empty chair. The middle-aged ladies had decided to call it a night after the speech.

"Please?" Anthony took a deep breath.

"Fine, sure." Michelle looked away.

Anthony cleared his throat several times. "We raised a lot of money selling tickets. And the raffle was a big hit, too." He tapped the table with a spoon.

"You helped organize this?" Michelle began to turn back to him, then stopped herself.

"Yes. I'm an honorary board member. I started being a Big Buddy in my senior year of high school, remember? 'Course with the business and all, I don't have the time since I got back home."

"That's right, I'd forgotten. I wonder how Jamal's doing." Michelle sat a little less rigidly next to him. She remembered the young boy Anthony had devoted so much time to help. Jamal was fourteen and Anthony nineteen when they were paired by the program. They had been so close that all their friends had teasingly called Jamal Anthony Junior. Neither Anthony or Jamal had minded one bit.

"Pretty good actually. His mother says he finished at the vocational school. He's working for an air-conditioning and refrigeration repair shop in Lake Charles. Hey, he's getting married in about three months."

"Married? Little Jamal?" Michelle stared at him in surprise.

"Michelle, he couldn't stay fourteen forever. He's almost twenty-four now."

"Time flies." Michelle shook her head with a smile. "Remember that time he punched you in the stomach when you tried to take him back to school? He was something else."

"Yeah, we had some rough times in the beginning."

"Then there was the time you brought him to the Friends and Family Day picnic at our church, and he called that other kid a— well, let's just say he accused him of unnatural relations with his mother."

"Sister Stansberry grabbed him by the ears and shook him until his teeth rattled." Anthony chuckled.

"Yeah, then she made him clean up by himself, and you had to bring him to her house for private Bible lessons once a week for a month."

"That was as much punishment for me as him. Sister Stansberry had that little street-tough kid jumping every time she called his name. All she had to do was say 'Jamal!' in that alto voice of hers."

"You should have seen your face when Jamal asked why y'all couldn't go back to Sister Stansberry's house after the month was up," Michelle teased.

"He still visits her. Can you believe it?"

"Sure. His maternal grandmother died when he was just five years old, and he never knew his father's family."

"Never knew his father," Anthony corrected and started tapping the table again.

"But between his mama, you, and good old Sister Stansberry, he had lots of love." Michelle's voice softened. She also remembered why Anthony felt so strongly about reaching out to help other boys.

"Knowing somebody cares whether you live or die certainly helps." Anthony studied her face. "That's what Uncle Ike did for me, Michelle. I know he's not perfect, but when my father left us he was there for me."

"Listen—"

"I'm not asking you to feel the same as I do about him. And maybe he's done some wrong things. Just try to understand. I cared for you and him, but I never chose. I swear to you, I never chose him over you."

"Anthony, I don't know what to say." Looking into his eyes, Michelle felt a flutter in her chest. In that instant, the over two hundred other people in the room disappeared.

"Say we can at least be on speaking terms. I miss our friendship." Anthony reached for her hand.

Keisha appeared suddenly. "Here you are. Anthony, Representative Benson has been asking for you." Her lips pursed at the sight of his hand covering Michelle's. "Saying hello to an old friend, I see. Ms. Toussaint."

"Good seeing you again, too," Michelle muttered. Michelle was irritated at her possessive attitude.

"I'll be there in a minute," Anthony broke in quickly.

"You've already been gone almost twenty minutes. Now, come on." Keisha's voice took on an aggravated, nagging tone.

"There are quite a few people here I've known all my life, friends and acquaintances, Keisha." Anthony's voice was strained.

"Keisha, dear. How are you?" A short, plump woman with

obviously dyed red hair and large ruby earrings said as she fluttered painted fingernails at her.

"Dr. DeLousse, how are you?" Keisha smiled winningly before turning a stern face back to Anthony. "Anthony, are you coming?"

"Keisha, I'd like you to meet someone." Dr. DeLousse beckoned to her.

Michelle feigned an expression of being impressed. "My, the Dean of Women at Xavier University is a friend of yours."

"She and my mother were roommates at Spellman." Keisha lifted her chin just a bit.

"Really? Isn't that something?"

"Yes, well, I attended Spellman also. Anthony, I'll see you shortly?" Keisha stared at him pointedly. When he nodded, she flounced off gushing a flowery greeting as she approached the others.

"Guess it's time for you to go."

"Right." Anthony frowned for a few seconds watching Keisha. Turning back to Michelle, he placed an arm around the back of her chair. "Listen, let's start over. Lunch maybe one day next week?"

"Give me a call." Michelle's mind was in a whirl with that simple invitation.

Anthony gave her hand a pat before leaving. He was all grace as he wove his way through the tables to join Keisha. Michelle felt a warm stirring at the animal way his body moved. Her hand tingled where he had touched it. Well, surely one lunch was harmless. She was still absentmindedly rubbing her hand when Laree came back.

"Uh-huh, y'all can't stay away from each other. Soon as I spotted him over on the other side of the dance floor eyeing you, I knew he'd be over here." Laree plopped down and took a swig of iced tea.

"You wench. Why didn't you tell me?"

"You kidding? I wasn't ready to leave. You probably

would've jumped up hollering 'Let's go.' No way, sugar. Not with all these beautiful BPMs."

"What?"

"Black Professional Men. We got a bumper crop this year and it's harvest time, honey. 'Course you've got the one prize every woman in town is after." Laree nodded toward Anthony's table.

"We haven't even been on speaking terms for years." Michelle avoided her gaze.

"I notice you seemed to be getting along very well just now."

"I suppose it's time to let go of old grudges. It was a long time ago. We're both mature enough to, you know, look at things differently." Michelle gazed at Anthony, so dashing in his black tuxedo. He wore formal clothes as easily as a flannel shirt and jeans.

"Are you saying Ike Batiste is not so bad?" Laree gaped at her.

"Of course not. But I can't expect Anthony to turn on the man who practically adopted him and gave him the affection his father didn't."

"So you're saying Anthony is not so bad and you two are gonna heat it up. Go, girl." Laree gave her a playful nudge.

"Forget it. I'm only saying we could be . . . on better terms." Michelle still wouldn't look at her.

"This is me you're talking to, sweetheart. With you and Anthony, being on better terms is just the first step to Love Land. Watch what I'm saying."

"He won't get that close to me, not ever again." Michelle made it a point not to look in the direction of Anthony's table for the rest of the evening.

Sitting up in bed at three thirty the next morning, Michelle uttered a soft curse at the glowing blue numbers of the clock radio next to her bed. Hot chocolate, old movies, even a boring book, all her usual remedies for insomnia had failed. She had spent the better part of the night in a futile effort

to block thoughts of *him*. It was as if the image of his strong
jaw, those eyes, and that body was burned onto her eyelids.
Each time she closed her eyes, there he was. To make matters
worse, memories of being in his arms came flooding back.
And she kept hearing his voice. Yes, she too had missed their
friendship. But could she risk letting him back into her life?
His admiration for Ike Batiste disturbed her.

"Uncle Ike," Michelle said out loud.

Uncle Ike, who used people for his own gain. Who was
ruthless in business and, according to gossip, with women.
Even in high school, Anthony had emulated him. And when
her father's business went sour, everything about Anthony
seemed to reflect his uncle Ike. If what Greg Matthews im-
plied about his dealing with Charlotte Kinchen and the Housing Authority was indeed true, Uncle Ike had not changed
one bit.

Still, the happy memories of she and Anthony together
crowded out the negatives. Michelle rubbed her already reddened eyes and sank beneath the comforter. The warmth of
the quilts wrapped around her, reminding her of the way it
felt to be wonderfully enclosed in Anthony's arms and affection. Sighing, she dozed off feeling a tiny prick of longing.
A longing she thought had been successfully rooted out years
ago.

Three

"This is a hot one, baby. Ike Batiste is going down." Earl pushed a pile of books to the floor to sit in the chair at an empty desk next to Michelle and Gracie.

"Hey, it took me all day to round up those for one of my stories. If any of my bookmarks have fallen out, you're in deep trouble, buster." Gracie got up and began stacking them on the desk.

"What's this about Ike Batiste?" Michelle continued tapping her keyboard.

"His good buddy James Bridges was caught with his pants down, literally. His wife followed him to a fancy hotel last month. Listen to this: she pretended that she'd checked in with her husband but left her key inside. She got a maid to let her into the room." Earl wore a crooked grin. "Mrs. B. went into the bedroom and all hell broke loose. She's filing for divorce. From what I hear, she plans to bleed old Jimmy boy dry."

"Juicy stuff, but what's it got to do with Ike Batiste?" Gracie dropped the last book, satisfied that everything was as she'd left it.

"Mrs. Bridges wants to open up all his business dealings so that she can be sure he won't hide company assets or profits. Rumor has it that this will throw some very much unwanted light on his shady business practices." Earl leaned over Michelle. "Including his relationship to Ike Batiste."

Michelle stopped writing. "Doesn't he sell insurance and construction bonds, too?"

"Yep, does pretty well I hear." Earl nodded.

"That's real vague. I mean, people have been saying stuff like that about Batiste and his buddies for years. But it never amounts to anything that can be proven or even something the district attorney can use to make a case." Michelle shrugged and went back to her keyboard.

"Maybe so, but if anybody knows where the bodies are buried it would be his wife. She's bitter and wants revenge," Earl said.

"He's right. She's a woman scorned," Gracie agreed.

Earl stood up. "Anyway, I'm going to interview her. She claims there are folks high up in the mayor's office involved in some of the deals."

"Whoa, if you can pin that down you've got one helluva story. Those guys have been real cozy for the past four years." Gracie chewed on a pencil.

Michelle wore a look of pure skepticism. "Good luck. But don't forget, those guys have been sidestepping trouble for years without even getting close to a courtroom. Their double dealings are burrowed so deep, it would take major blasting to bring it to the surface. Hasn't been done yet."

"I'm counting on Mrs. Bridges having enough dynamite, babe. I'll keep you posted." Earl waved good-bye.

"You know, this could tie up somehow with your story. Gracie pulled a book from the pile and began thumbing through it.

"It's shaky. They could kiss and make up tonight. Mrs. Bridges would say she was making it all up out of anger and Earl's only lead would be a dead end. Still, it will be very interesting to see where it goes."

Michelle and Gracie went back to the work Earl had interrupted without mentioning Bridges again. Still, Michelle decided to file away the fact that Mrs. Bridges might be a good source for her later on.

It was a typical Monday for them. There were stories to
follow up from the weekend and new assignments handed
out for the week. Hard as she tried to deny it, Michelle's
attention was divided between work and anticipating a phone
call from Anthony. Arriving at her apartment, she changed
into her favorite oversized sweatshirt and old socks. Turning
on the radio, she started dinner. When the doorbell rang, her
heart skipped.

"Open up, girl," Shantae said through the door.

"Hey, now. What are you doing over this way?" Michelle
led the way back to her kitchen.

"I got off from work, you know, and just thought I'd stop
by and see what you're up to." Shantae picked up a piece of
carrot and began munching on it.

"Shantae, this is not on your way home or on the way to
your mother's house." Michelle leaned against the counter.
"What's up?"

"I stopped by to, you know, say hi and . . . you act like
I'm up to no good." Shantae's eyes were wide and innocent
looking.

"You're lying. Whenever your eyes get big and keep saying 'you know' you're lying."

Shantae turned her head so that her eyes were hidden from
Michelle's view. "No, I'm not. Honest, I haven't talked to
you in almost a week. I, you kn—, I mean—how's it going?
How was the banquet Saturday?"

"Ah-ha! You talked to Laree. The mouth of the south
couldn't wait to tell you." Michelle stabbed a finger at her.

"Tell me what, Chelle? I don't have any idea what you're
talking about." Shantae put down her purse and sat on the
stool at the breakfast bar.

"That Anthony was there and we talked."

"Oh, yeah. Now that you mention it, Laree did say something . . . I wasn't paying too much attention though." Shantae gave a careless wave of her hand.

"I see. The banquet was nice." Michelle continued cooking. Watching her friend with a sidelong glance, she changed the subject. "How was your weekend?"

"It was okay. So Anthony was at the banquest. What's he up to these days?"

"Nothing much. Say, you're welcome to have some of this, I've got plenty. I tell you, today was hectic—"

"Okay, so I'm lying. What happened with you and Anthony? Did he ask you out? Tell me everything." Shantae dropped her pretense of being interested in chitchat.

Michelle shrugged. "All he said was that we should at least be on friendly terms and maybe we'd have lunch this week . . . or sometime. It was no big deal really."

"Didn't call, huh?" Shantae clucked sympathetically.

"He didn't promise to call. And I didn't promise that I'd go out to lunch with him." Michelle banged the spatula into the sink. "Who cares? I have a life, thank you."

"This is Shantae you talking to, sugar. Let it out. Holding in that hurt ain't good for ya." Shantae came around to put an arm on her shoulder.

"Get off me, girl. I'm not holding anything in. I haven't seen the man in almost six years, and we weren't speaking then." Michelle shook Shantae's arm away.

"Sure, tell me anything. I was away at Jackson State when y'all were dating in college. But Laree told me how you were crazy for the dude. Couldn't get enough of his sweet stuff."

Count on Laree to remind her how intense her affair was with Anthony. They were together every day, holding hands or hugging. They shared a wonderful intimacy reserved for two people with a passion for each other.

Michelle scowled at her. "Don't be so crude. And Laree's mouth is going to get her butt in a whole lotta trouble."

"Come on now, we're your girls. Like the song says, lean on me." Shantae placed a hand over her heart.

"Will you stop," Michelle retorted. "I'm going to lean on you all right if you don't quit. Anthony is the past. I mean,

I was just being polite." The phone rang once and she grabbed it.

Shantae smirked at her. "My, eager to answer it, aren't we?"

Michelle stuck her tongue out at her before ducking into her bedroom with the cordless phone. She locked the door behind her.

"That answered my question," Shantae yelled. "You still want him."

Five minutes later, Michelle emerged from the room with the phone. The scowl had softened and she moved with more relaxed motions. Though she was careful to keep a bland expression, Shantae was not deceived.

"I have some iced tea if you'd like." Michelle turned quickly away from her scrutiny.

"I'll get it." Shantae got a glass from the cabinet and the pitcher of tea from the refrigerator. "When and where? And don't even try telling me it wasn't him. You've got a sparkle in your eyes that you didn't have before you got that call." Seeing Michelle's mouth open, she cut her off.

"Wednesday, Cheramie's." Michelle scooped up a large spoonful of vegetables and placed them on a plate for Shantae. "But it doesn't mean what you think." The soft, dreamy look in her eyes told a very different story.

"That shade of blue is perfect on you." Anthony gave her an admiring once over.

Michelle blushed, then felt like a silly teenager for it. Her embarrassment was made even more acute because of the two hours she had spent the night before deciding what outfit to wear. After much agonizing between her dark red suit and the royal-blue dress, the dress won. It made her hips look smaller she had decided after eyeing herself in the full-length mirror in her bedroom for the fifth time. She had agreed to

meet him, unsure that she was ready for him to pick her up.
That was too much like a date for her comfort.

"I'm really glad you said yes to lunch." Anthony sat forward. "I've been wanting to tell you how great I think it is
to see you on television. I knew you'd make it, though."

"What about you? Your own business. From what I
hear, you're building a reputation for some of the best work
around in the construction business. At least, to hear Shantae
bragging on Cedric."

"We've done better than even we expected. But it's been
a lot of long hours and putting most of the profits back into
the business." Anthony fidgeted with his napkin. "I wanted
to call you when I first got back, but I . . . wasn't sure what
to say."

"We didn't part on very good terms," Michelle said awkwardly.

Gazing at his face, Michelle did not want to say the reason
they had parted so bitterly. Though she had been fighting all
the old feelings, successfully as long as they did not meet
face-to-face, seeing him brought them vividly alive. A fact
that thrilled and frightened her. For weeks now she had tried
to revive the animosity that had filled her six years ago in
an effort to quell her attraction to him. Yet she could not
deny being with Anthony again, even though they were surrounded by people, felt good.

"Michelle, I didn't do a very good job back then of explaining myself or showing you how I felt. I can only plead
stupidity, and immaturity. It was a rough time for you, I
should have been more sensitive." Anthony still did not look
up.

"For both of us, I suppose. Your uncle Ike and my dad,
two men very important to us, clashed in a big way. It was
natural that we'd each defend family." Michelle lifted her
shoulders slightly.

"I don't agree with everything Uncle Ike does, but he
saved my life. When my dad walked out on Mama and me,

we both went through some bad changes. Mama struggled to make a living. We had our electricity cut off more than once."

"Oh, Anthony, I never realized it was that bad." Michelle felt a small shock.

Anthony's mama, Lizabeth, had always seemed in good spirits. Sure their house did not look as well-kept as the others in their middle-class neighborhood, but it had never occurred to her they had been on the edge of being destitute. Michelle now thought of herself as having been a self-involved, insensitive teenager not to have understood what should have been so plain if only she had been paying attention.

"And she had her hands full trying to keep me in line. I was heading for trouble when Uncle Ike stepped in. Some of the guys I used to run with are in prison now, one on death row."

"I know. It must be horrible losing friends." Michelle was moved he had shared something that was obviously so painful.

"Hey, I'm not looking for sympathy or making excuses for me or him. I only wanted to explain why I acted the way I did." Anthony looked up, his eyes intense. "I feel about him the way you feel about your father."

"You know, this is the first time we've talked about this without yelling at each other, me insulting your uncle, and you storming off. Maybe we've both grown up," Michelle said.

"Maybe so." Anthony's face relaxed as the troubled expression faded.

Michelle forced her gaze away from those eyes that held her. "Umm . . . everything on the menu looks so good it's hard to decide."

To her relief, the waiter appeared at that moment to take their orders. She needed time to sort out the torrent of emotions that threatened to overwhelm her. For the rest of the lunch, she kept the conversation confined to catching up on old friends, talking about their work, and other topics she felt were safe. Standing in front of the restaurant afterward, they smiled shyly at each other.

"Well, I better get going. I have a meeting later." Anthony didn't move.

"Me, too." Michelle shifted from one foot to the next.

"I've got tickets to a jazz recital on campus this Saturday night. Would you like to go? We could have dinner first since it doesn't start until eight."

"Things seem to be going so fast—" Michelle bit her lower lip. Somehow control of this situation was slipping from her. Or was it silly to think she ever did or could control her desire for him?

"Two old friends who enjoy jazz and love good food, that's all we're talking about." Anthony spoke quickly to ease the anxiety in her voice.

Michelle stared into his eyes for a long moment. Her heart jumped at the anticipation she read there. "Okay, I'd like that."

Driving back to the station, Michelle was in a bright mood. Turning up the radio, she bounced to the old rhythm and blues tunes being played. Tunes that she had once danced to with Anthony when they were in college. She smiled remembering how they all cherished their record collections, mostly oldies their parents had held on to from their college days. It would be so great to share the pleasure of hearing wonderful music with him again. Still humming an old Sam and Dave song, she entered the newsroom.

"Lunch was nice, huh?" Gracie winked at her.

"Not bad, not bad at all. What's up around here?" Michelle sat down.

"Be thankful you've been gone. Lockport is a very unhappy news director. Channel Six scooped us with an exclusive on the noon newscast. Seems there's a possible link with that councilwoman's son arrested for possession a while ago to a burglary ring. Jason's in hot water for not following up and getting a reporter out when Nathan asked him to."

"Hmm," Michelle said, her voice flat with disinterest as she turned on her computer.

"Jennifer is peeved because she got shoved around at the school board meeting, lots of angry parents about the latest busing plan. Her story is short by almost two minutes so Jason, poor thing, had to scramble for a filler so both the five and six newscast won't run short—"

"Serves 'em both right," Michelle said with a satisfied smirk.

"And Nathan is in a real foul mood and asking for you."

"Uh-oh." Michelle's eyebrows drew together in consternation.

"Exactly. Speak of the devil," Gracie mumbled then hustled off in the opposite direction from which Nathan was approaching.

"Why are you still here, O'Hannon? Aren't there two stories you should be out on?" Nathan's growl rolled across the room.

"On my way now, boss." Gracie vanished around a corner.

"Hi, Nathan. Love that shirt. Is it new? Nice fabric." Michelle rubbed a corner of his cuff between her thumb and forefinger.

"Save it! Toussaint. Where the hell have you been all morning?" Nathan was like a hungry lion that still had not been fed.

"Why, doing my job, of course. The school bus stop safety thing you sent me out on, remember?" Michelle said.

"Oh, yeah." Nathan lost some of his thunder.

"I had an appointment with the head of the school transportation department. What's wrong?" Michelle, patting his arm, gave him a look of concern.

"Don't mess with me today, Toussaint." Nathan scowled at her, but his voice had lost some of its gruffness. "That guy Greg Matthews called. Sounded kind of jumpy. Maybe he's decided to tell you more after all. But don't wait too long. Like I said, he could lose his nerve any minute. Said to call him at home cause he's off today."

"I'm on it." Michelle flipped open her small personal phone book.

"What's the occasion?" Nathan pointed to her dress and pumps.

"No occasion. Met somebody for lunch, an old classmate."

"Oh, a lunch date."

"No, we just met for lunch."

"A guy?"

"Ye-es." Michelle squirmed under his steady gaze.

"You dressed up to meet some guy. That's called a date." Nathan walked off.

"Was not!" Michelle yelled after him, then was abashed when several people turned to stare at her. Nathan kept walking.

"What changed your mind?" Michelle sat next to Greg Matthews at a McDonald's restaurant near his house.

"This is owned by Theo Lazarus, a Black man." Greg swung his arm wide. "Gave jobs to a lot of poor kids 'round here, you know? Got college students from Southern tutoring the ones he finds out are having problems with their lessons. He's made it and doing something good. But not all of them are like that." He sighed deeply.

"I know." Michelle stared out of the large glass window at the poor neighborhood.

"Couple of days ago, a little three-year-old baby pushed right on through a door. He went out on the balcony of his mama's third-floor apartment and ended up at the bottom of the stairs. He's in the charity hospital right now with a broken arm and two broken ribs."

"Terrible, but I don't understand what that's got to do with my story."

"His mother has been begging them to fix it for the last six months. They did a cheap patch job. I can't sleep nights knowing maybe I could do something to make things better. Fixin' up the projects ain't just a cosmetic thing, see what I'm saying? People are getting hurt." Greg stared at the untouched cup of cola in front of him.

"You think your friend would talk to me?"

"No way, she needs her job bad."

"Then I'm back where I was before you called. It doesn't help to hear all this but not be able to use the information. Charlotte Kinchen will just deny any of this is true."

"She won't talk to you, but she'll get copies of work orders stamped completed and the invoices showing the company that got paid for the work. Will that help?" Peering around, Greg leaned across the table, speaking in a barely audible voice.

"You bet! Oh, sorry." Michelle lowered her voice. "That would be a great way to start."

"Another thing, there's folks living in some of these projects won't mind talking to you. In fact, a couple have formed tenants groups. They've been complaining, but Miss Kinchen just ignores them mostly. I'll get the names from my friend."

"Thanks a lot, Greg. And thank your friend for me."

"We wanna see some change, Miss Toussaint. I won't lie, I'd enjoy seeing some of the so-called big shots get what's coming to them. But nobody should have to live the way those poor folks live."

"I'll do my best, Greg."

Michelle wondered later if she could live up to his expectations. The stakes seemed to be higher than just informing the public about a violation of their trust by officials being paid to manage a government program. Like Greg Matthews, she was reminded of the effects on those who had to endure the conditions in the government-subsidized houses and apartments. Had she been equally honest with him, she would have admitted that the prospect of exposing Ike Batiste was what really hooked her. Now she felt a little ashamed. On her way back to the office, Michelle began to outline a different approach. She decided to profile the lives of tenants trapped in what seemed like a merry-go-round of misery. Stories of their courage and struggles could stand in stark contrast to the obstacles they faced, including those thrown up by a system intended to aid them. The closer she got to the station, the more she was convinced of changing the direction of the story.

"Hey, you seem fired up." Earl peered over her shoulder.

"Umm. I just happened to see Mansur, our esteemed news director, a few minutes ago. I pitched the idea of beginning my series of investigative reports on wrongdoing at the Housing Authority with at least two reports on the conditions of public housing. Also, I'm going to profile some of the residents from a human interest point of view. Mansur gave me the green light." Michelle's fingers flew over the keyboard. "Brilliant, if I do say so myself."

"Scoring one with the big dog, smart move." Earl let out a long whistle of appreciation. "Of course, it's going to piss Jason off big time."

"How will I sleep nights?" Michelle snorted. Ending a sentence, she saved the text. "How've you been?"

Earl's face screwed up into a frown. "Awful. Cheryl is on this macrobiotic kick. Meals at home have become torture. She quit speaking to me for an entire day when she found an empty french fry bag in my car."

"Hang in there, next week it'll be something new."

"That's what scares me. Since she turned thirty-five, she's been obsessed with finding the secret to staying young and healthy." Earl sank down in a nearby chair.

"She looks fabulous, always has."

"I tell her that, but the fact that I'm five years younger bothers her now." Earl took a deep breath.

"Then keep telling her. And show her, too. Nothing elaborate, but compliment her on everyday things she does for you. Even those meals."

"I can't promise that." Earl laughed.

"Speaking of unhappy wives, have you talked to Mrs. Bridges yet?"

Earl moaned. "Oh, boy, have I. She spent the better part of an hour listing all his affairs, and everything he's done to mistreat her for the past fifteen years. It took all of my self-control not to cut her off and tell her I wasn't her marriage counselor. I'm going to talk to her again, but it doesn't look like she'll give me anything solid."

"More advice, domestic quicksand ahead. Don't get sucked in. A bitter spouse can be a curse as well as a blessing. If she spends the next one or two interviews ventilating about him without giving you something that could lead to a story, you're wasting your time," Michelle said.

"And it was so promising." Earl's face lit up with renewed eagerness. "But I have a plan. Maybe she'll give me the names of other people who might be willing to talk. Maybe somebody he's taken advantage of and wants revenge." He rose.

"Keep hope alive." Michelle waved good-bye to him. She hated to tell him how skeptical she was at his chances.

"Is Earl still dogging that James Bridges thing?" Rexanne strolled in and put her large leather bag on Gracie's desk. Sitting down wearily, she propped her feet on another chair.

"Yeah, he's got my sympathy. I think she's a woman scorned who wants to cause trouble for her husband, but doesn't have one piece of usable information." Leaning back, Michelle took a break from writing.

"If anybody knows something, it's her. It's a matter of how much she really wants to stick it to her husband. She may want to keep him awake nights worrying. She's probably made sure he knows she's talking to Earl. How's your big one coming along?"

"I'm on the right track." Michelle understood that she was referring to the one potentially big story she was working on.

"Count your blessings. I've been chasing my tail all morning with this follow-up on Senator Jeansonne. He is one slippery rascal." Rexanne raked fingers through her dark auburn hair.

Kate hurried over looking anxious. "Hi, Rexanne. Say Michelle, Jason's been asking me if you've submitted any footage for editing."

Michelle barely opened her mouth before Rexanne interrupted. "Jason, how are you?"

"Fine," Jason said warmly, smiling at Rexanne briefly. With her standing at the station, he was careful to always be cordial and respectful. Then he turned to Michelle. "We need to talk. My office." He walked away without waiting to see if she followed.

"Sure thing, Jason." Michelle spoke in a false light tone even as she made an ugly face at his back.

Looking back at Rexanne, she got a thumbs-up sign of encouragement from her. Kate tried a brave smile. Nathan was already seated in one of the fine leather chairs in Jason's office. Michelle raised a questioning eyebrow at him. Before he could speak, Jason began.

"It's been three weeks since you started on the Housing Authority story, yet you haven't had one report on air. Problem?" Jason settled in his large executive chair and crossed his arms.

Nathan spoke before she could respond. "Some pretty big names are being tossed around. Nobody is going to rush forward to spill the beans. As I've explained to you before, good investigative reporting takes time." His voice indicated his patience was being tested to the limit.

"What about the alleged solid contacts she had from a previous story?" Jason spoke to Nathan, but looked at Michelle.

"She can't go on the air without information that's been thoroughly checked out. Even then, Taylor and his legal minions will have to put it under their microscopes first," Nathan said.

"Since you're talking about me, and I'm so conveniently in the room, why don't I just speak for myself—thank you very much." Michelle's voice rose with each sentence. She looked pointedly at Jason. "It so happens I have a source inside the Authority who is going to make copies of some very interesting documents over the next few weeks. Since this person needs his or her job, this has to be done slowly and carefully. Furthermore, I was working on a series of preliminary stories about conditions in public housing—that is, until you interrupted me just now."

"Wait a minute." Jason held up a hand. "That's nothing but a rehash of the piece you did last year. I don't think so. Nathan, give her something else to work on. Maybe Jennifer can get an interview since she knows the director." Jason picked up his phone and punched her extension.

"When I spoke to Mr. Mansur this afternoon, he thought it was a great idea." Actually, Gerald Mansur had said it had merit and he was willing to review it.

"What?" Jason held the phone, ignoring the voice at the other end.

"He said he was looking forward to my report."

"How dare you go directly to Mr. Mansur!" Jason's face was flushed as he clutched the phone.

Jason never failed to remind the reporters that as Lockport's assistant, he funneled ideas for news stories and features to him for consideration. It was not practice to skip the chain and go to the news director. Skipping Lockport meant skipping Jason. And Jason liked control.

"He passed me in the hall and asked how it was going. He is the news director, he can ask those things, Jason." Michelle grinned at him.

"Then that's that. I agree with him, by the way. I've got

a lot of work, Jason. See ya." Nathan gave Michelle a pat on the shoulder as he sauntered out.

"Me, too," Michelle said to no one in particular. "I have to set up some interviews, schedule one of the guys to meet me at the Mason Housing Project to shoot some video; I tell you, it never stops." She followed Nathan out without looking back.

Michelle left work but had a mission to perform. She rehearsed her speech for the entire drive to see her older brother. She parked in front of the modern single-story suite of offices. Brian's gray Mercedes Benz was in his reserved space. Typical of him, he was working later than his employees. He exchanged the usual greeting and inquiries into her health in a perfunctory manner.

"What do you want from me, Michelle?" Brian, impatient to continue work, shuffled papers on his desk

"Daddy listens to you. Tell him to give Dominic a job. Mama is beside herself. You know how she gets, especially when it comes to Dominic." Michelle began to chew a fingernail, then caught herself when she realized what she was doing.

"Sure, Dominic could be standing over a dead body with a dagger dripping blood, and Mama would blame the dead man for soiling his precious hands." Brian's voice held a tinge of bitterness.

"Don't exaggerate."

"And you're just as bad. When will you both learn that bailing him out doesn't help? Dad's right, it's way past time for Dominic to stand on his own."

"I don't make excuses for everything he does, but Daddy won't give him a break. He treats his employees better than Dominic. He's the youngest and Mama went overboard spoiling him, it's true. But going to the other extreme is just as wrong. Brian, come on."

"Not this time, little sister." Brian went back to scanning the papers on his desk. "I've let you talk me into protecting Dominic for years, but no more. I've been burned too many times, especially when I get between him and Dad."

"But Dominic really wants to prove he can stick to something. You know how he feels about you. Your opinion means a lot." Michelle watched for some sign that he would relent.

Brian's head came up sharply. "Yeah, sure it does. Like the stunts he pulled in college. Using the money Dad was sending for tuition and books to party nonstop. It wasn't until the end of the second semester that we found out he wasn't even enrolled."

Michelle looked away. "Well, he shouldn't have—"

"Oh, and the time he took off for a fun-filled week in Jamaica with a young lady, leaving behind her very large, jealous fiancé. Who was it convinced Dad to give him money for the trip because Dom said he was going to an academic conference in San Francisco? Me, that's who. Who saved his butt from getting beaten by that seven foot tall psycho? Me, that's who."

"Listen, Brian, I know you've tried but—"

Brian cut in again. "As a matter of fact, Dad probably wouldn't listen to me anyway considering my track record as being such a sucker for the little con artist." He shook his head.

"Come on, all that happened a long time ago. Dominic says he's willing to settle down."

"Then if he's so grown up, why isn't he here speaking for himself?" Brian crossed his arms over his chest.

"Now that you mention it, he's outside now. He didn't want to come, or for me to try talking to you, either." Michelle jumped to her feet and went to the door as she spoke. "Dom, come in." Michelle pulled him into the room.

"Hey, big bro. What's up?" Dominic had their mother's facial features but with a masculine cut to the planes of his face. Where Brian had the rough handsomeness of Thomas,

Dominic had the boyish good looks that attracted all ages of women.

"Hi." Brian did not return his smile.

"This wasn't my idea. Before I knew it, we were here." Dominic, no longer smiling, glared at him.

"Look, don't you two start arguing. Brian, Dominic just wants Dad to give him a job. He's willing to work his way up from the bottom. Right, Dominic?" Michelle nudged him.

"Sure." Dominic stared at the floor.

"Then you go to him, Dominic. Stand up to him and show him you're ready to be a man," Brian said.

"I tried. He told me to go out and find a job on my own. If I could get and keep one for at least a year, he'd reconsider. He didn't even offer to help," Dominic complained.

"Sounds like a plan to me." Brian looked from him to Michelle.

"But Brian—" Michelle stamped her foot.

"No. Michelle, I won't baby him."

"To hell with it then, Brian. I don't need you or him." Dominic stormed out.

"You could have been a little more diplomatic, dammit."

"Michelle, stop. Stop putting yourself between Dad and Mama, between Dad and Dominic. Live your own life. I learned the hard way." Brian went to her.

"You mean be selfish. You've withdrawn into your own little world of wife, two kids, and a dog," Michelle spouted without thinking.

"That's not fair and you know it. We can't have normal family gatherings with Mama sniping at Dad, Dad sitting around not talking at all to keep from arguing. I enjoy the peace and quiet of my own home. So sue me. I notice you don't live at home anymore. And I know why."

Michelle held her tongue for a moment, then spoke. "I'm sorry. Okay, so their fights get to me, too. But a lot of it is Daddy's fault. Mama just wants to get his attention. Though why she bothers is beyond me. He's so cold and critical."

"Michelle, stay out of it. There are things between them that have nothing to do with you, things that only they can deal with." Brian went back to his desk.

"What things?"

"All I'm saying is, you can't play marriage counselor." Brian avoided returning her gaze. "And you can't make Dominic into a hard-working adult. He has to do that himself."

For as long as she could remember, Michelle felt a need to be the glue that held them all together. Maybe it was her craving for order. Or maybe her love for happy endings. But she would not stand by and do nothing. She never had in any situation, even as a child, and dealing with family difficulties was no different.

"Fine. I'll talk to Dad." Michelle took a deep breath.

"Chelle, I want things to work out as much as you do. But maybe Dad is right."

"I promised Dominic I'd try. Bye, big brother. As usual, I can't stay mad at you any more than I can at Dominic." Michelle gave him a fierce hug.

"You're too hard on Dad." Brian looked at her.

"For the last seven years, Daddy has been even more critical and withdrawn than he was before. I think he could do a lot to make things better." Michelle picked up her purse.

"Michelle, nobody is perfect. In any relationship, there are two sides to every conflict." Brian kissed her cheek lightly before opening the door.

The trip to her parents' home was silent. Dominic sat brooding, his chin propped on his fist as he stared out of the window. Michelle, already exhausted from a long day at work, was in no mood for conversation, either.

Something about her exchange with Brian bothered her. Try as she might, she could not put her finger on it. On the surface, he had said nothing in particular that she could remember. She replayed their discussion in her head as though it were dialogue from a play.

"Thanks for trying. Brian gets more like Daddy every day." Dominic continued to stare ahead morosely.

"No problem, cher." Michelle was still wrapped up in her own thoughts.

"What am I going to do, Chelle?"

"I'll talk to Daddy, Dominic." Michelle tried not to sound irritated.

But truthfully, defending him was practically a full-time job. The least he could do was make some effort to make it easier. Still, Daddy had been tough on Dominic since he was a little boy. Unfortunately, it had the opposite effect he was after. Dominic did not like following schedules or being on a timetable. Efforts to change him were a source of constant conflict. It got worse as Dominic got older. Now here they were adults and she was still fighting his battles. Brian's words came back to her. Maybe she was hurting him. Lately it seemed she spent a great deal of time and emotional energy on either Mama or him. Maybe it was time she spent some of that energy on her own personal life.

Anthony. That is what she meant, wasn't it? Until he walked into the newsroom and back into her life three weeks ago, all she thought of was her career. After all this time, a simple lunch was enough to set her dreaming like a lovesick teenager. Sure she had felt a strong infatuation for him, but that was a long time ago. As he said himself, they had grown up since then.

"What did you say?" Michelle snapped out of her reverie. Dominic's last words caused a kind of nebulous recognition, somehow associated with the puzzle of her older brother that had been nagging at her.

"I said, Brian doesn't think much of me, either. Though he doesn't say it outright the way Dad does. But you know Brian, most times it's what he doesn't say that counts."

That was it. It was what Brian hadn't said that troubled her. Brian had tried to tell her something without saying too much. Somehow she felt sure it was related to her parents and their unhappiness with each other. The vague disquiet caused by his words grew into a nameless dread that took root in the pit of her stomach.

Four

Michelle was enthralled with the saxophonist's masterful playing. The deep alto tones rolled out from him, a palpable force moving the entire audience and holding them all in the same magical place. The instrument spoke without words as the soulful rendition of an old Roberta Flack song, "The First Time Ever I Saw Your Face," seemed to touch everyone in a unique and powerful way. Michelle was acutely aware of Anthony seated so close to her. She shifted, trying to move a little farther from him. With each swell of the saxophone she felt a surge of heat. For a moment she was lost in the music, thinking of the real heat of his touch. The sweet taste of his mouth on hers. With a heart-wrenching last note, the performance ended to wild applause. Michelle's eyes flew open wide, startled out of her waking dream. She glanced sideways to find Anthony regarding her steadily. He smiled shyly before turning back to the stage. Michelle was mortified, sure the ardent images of her mind were mirrored on her face. She made a fuss of gathering her cape and purse to mask her flustered state. Anthony did not make her efforts any easier. His hands rested on her shoulders momentarily after helping to wrap the cape around her. Michelle moved away on shaky knees.

"That was really something else, wasn't it?" Anthony walked beside her in the crowd as they left the recital hall.

"Every note that guy played sent chills through me. And

the woman playing piano was just as fabulous," Michelle said.

"The trumpet solo was just as beautiful, don't you think?" He guided her gently toward his car.

"Great, the whole quartet was simply wonderful."

"It certainly was great." Anthony unlocked the metallic gray Honda Accord with the remote control.

"Yeah, it was great." Now seated behind the wheel, Anthony turned to her.

"Yes, indeed." Michelle smiled at him, then looked away.

"Say, why don't we go to Coffee Call for café au lait and beignets?" Anthony's face held a hopeful, anxious expression.

"Sure." Michelle quietly took a deep breath, relieved that the awkwardness of where they were to go next was resolved.

The café was brightly lit and crowded even at ten o'clock that night. The clinking of ceramic cups as hot coffee was being served layered the sound of lively conversations filling the room. The aroma of coffee and the hot, delicious doughy donuts hung in the air, welcoming all who came in from the crisp fall night. Threading their way through the tables, they finally found an empty one.

"Umm." Michelle took a long sip from her mug.

"This is the first time I've been here since I got back home. Man, I forgot how good these things are." Anthony shook powdered white sugar over the bowl of beignets.

"I stay away from this place, too much temptation. And the camera shows every pound." Michelle patted her midsection. "As it is, I could stand to lose a few."

"I don't see it," Anthony said after giving her an appraising look.

Michelle felt a glow of pleasure. "Yeah, well these hips are a bit too generous by industry standards. You know the saying, you can never be too rich or too thin." Michelle grimaced.

"Then the industry is wrong."

"I tell you, it's only been recently that the pressure to be a size four has eased up. You would be shocked at the number of women who ended up being treated for an eating disorder because of it." Michelle stared at a beignet.

"Here." Anthony pushed the bowl toward her. "You don't have anything to prove."

"What the heck, I'll just get rid of it later." Michelle sank her teeth into one.

"I hope you don't mean—"

"Huh? Oh, no—not me. I don't purge after eating. I mean I'll work it off at the gym. Don't worry, I refuse to let those skinny New York fashion mavens turn me into a basket case."

"You look fantastic and don't let anybody tell you different." Anthony waved his hand forgetting he held a beignet, showering her with powdered sugar.

"Hey, watch it." Michelle gave a yelp. Laughing, she brushed at the front of her dark red sweater dress. "What am I, a bowl of cereal?"

"Sorry. I'll pay to get it cleaned." Anthony reached out and began to rub the soft fabric. Realizing what he was doing, he snatched back his hand. "Uh, sorry. I mean I wasn't trying to— I was trying to get the sugar off," he mumbled.

"It's okay." Michelle paused in the middle of brushing crumbs from her lap. "Look at us. Fumbling and stumbling with each other, walking on eggshells." She threw down her napkin.

"I wasn't this nervous on my first date when I was twelve." Anthony grinned at her.

"And after the recital, we sounded like an echo; 'Wasn't it great?' 'Yes, great.' 'It was really great!' What was that all about?" Michelle chuckled, shaking her head.

"I'm just thankful I came up with the idea to come here or we might still be sitting in my car babbling 'great' to each other," Anthony quipped. They both laughed hysterically.

"That's one sound even sweeter than the music they were playing." Anthony gazed at her still smiling. "Know what I think? Neither one of us wants to say anything hurtful, even if it's unintentional. And you know what that means."

"What?" Michelle traced a line on the tabletop in a pile of sugar.

"That we still care something about each other. It means—" Anthony placed his hand on hers.

"I don't want to rush into anything, Anthony. The distance between us has been more than just miles and time. Maybe the best we can hope for is to be friendly acquaintances who speak politely if we happen to meet." Drawing her hand back, Michelle avoided his eyes.

"Why can't we be friends who get together occasionally for lunch or dinner? I know you're seeing someone. I'm not trying to get in your business, but if he has a problem with it I'll understand." Anthony's jaw tightened and he gripped his coffee mug. "I mean, if y'all agreed to not see other people."

"Dosu isn't like that at all. He's the most secure person I've ever known." Michelle had no intention of telling him that her relationship with Dosu was more of a trusted confidant than lover.

"Then what's the problem?"

"It's even more than that. Eventually we'll be arguing about your uncle Ike again." Michelle bit her lower lip. Anthony's bond with Ike ran too deep. Maybe deeper than his feelings for her?

"We're adults now. We don't need to keep fighting the battles of our families. If we concentrate on us, then we can get past it." Anthony tugged at her hand to get her to look at him. "At least give it a try."

"Let me think about it."

"Okay." Anthony held her hand for a few moments before letting go.

The rest of the evening was less tense and they talked about what each had been doing for the past six years. Watching him, Michelle was struck by how he had changed yet remained the same. Though he was more self-assured, he could be just as boyishly enthusiastic about his interests. His eyes lit up as he talked about his volunteer work with teenage boys. He totally lost all self-consciousness as he described the outreach programs his church had instituted. Michelle felt growing admiration for the man he had become. With a mixture of dismay and satisfaction, she admitted that she indeed wanted to be with him. But, she told herself firmly, only for friendship. Nothing else was realistic.

"Well, I had a really nice time." Michelle unlocked her front door and turned to face him.

The scent of his cologne beckoned to her tantalizingly, an invisible magnetic force she had to pull against. Michelle gave a slight shake of her head to clear it. His deep, rich voice sent a tremor through her.

"So did I. See you soon?" Anthony's eyes smoldered with fire.

Michelle could not move or break away from his compelling gaze. "Yes," she breathed. Realizing she was on the brink of promising much more, she shoved the door open behind her. "Good night." She had to get away fast.

"Good night, Chelle."

Shutting the door behind her, Michelle stood in the middle of her living room, trying to slow her breathing. With each passing minute, she tried to convince herself that she could keep him at arm's length. *No ma'am,* she told herself sternly. *You are going to stick to the original plan and keep him out of your life.* Even as the words rang in her head, Michelle felt a tickling of doubt that she could or truly wanted to be without him.

"Girlfriend, jump on it is what I say." Laree lifted a fork filled with salad. Waving her hand, the lettuce swung crazily.

"Honestly, I don't know why you even have to think about it."

"Amen. I mean, he's fine, successful, smart, goes to church. Honey, if you don't jump on it, somebody will." Shantae dabbed her mouth with a napkin before taking another bite of her shrimp po-boy.

"Y'all know perfectly well what happened. I called his uncle Ike a scumbag, more than once. It kind of put a strain on the relationship last time." Michelle picked at her salad.

"So? The man told you all is forgiven and apologized for the way he acted. What more do you want?" Shantae lifted a shoulder slightly.

"Yeah, what's the deal? Besides, all that stuff happened a long time ago," Laree said.

"The deal is Ike Batiste sucked my father into a business deal that almost ruined him. When the you-know-what hit the fan, Ike Batiste came out smelling like a rose. He didn't lift a finger to help him. Daddy paid a huge fine that sent him into bankruptcy, and Ike Batiste kept right on making money." Michelle put down her fork.

"Michelle, you won't be dating Ike Batiste. Anthony didn't have anything to do with what his uncle did," Shantae said.

"Shantae, I can't just pretend everything is cool. Every time I see the man, I get ticked off all over again. And Anthony is still real close to his uncle," Michelle said.

"Lots of people don't get along with their boyfriend's relatives. But you can get around it, girl." Shantae tapped the table with one long, fushia-colored fingernail.

"I doubt it." Michelle shook her head.

"Yes, you can. Naturally you can't attack the man every time you see him, but you can learn to put up with him." Shantae leaned forward.

"Michelle has a point." Laree screwed up her face.

"Say what? You just finished saying it was no big deal." Shantae's mouth dropped open.

"Yeah, but the more I think about it, the more I think

Chelle is right. I read this article in *Essence* magazine—"
Laree stopped eating.

"Here we go," Shantae blurted. "This woman plans her
whole life on magazine articles."

"No listen, this noted African-American clinical social
worker wrote about factors that contribute to a relationship
or marriage not working. High on the list was conflicts with
in-laws." Laree held up a forefinger.

"It just so happens I remember that article, thank you. She
also said that two mature adults committed to each other
should make it clear to both their families that their relationship comes first. And if possible, avoid subjects and situations that lead to arguments." Shantae smiled at Laree
smugly.

"I'm so confused," Michelle groaned.

"Bottom line, do you want him?" Shantae sat back and
eyed her intently.

"I—, we—" Michelle stammered.

"Yes or no," Shantae demanded.

"It's not that simple." Michelle turned to Laree for help.
Laree's eyebrows arched. "Don't look at me."

"Uh-huh, that's what I thought. Like I said, jump on it."
Shantae resumed eating, dismissing Michelle's attempts to
protest.

Michelle breathed deeply. "Thanks a lot."

"Michelle, you know what you want to do. You just don't
want to admit it." Shantae had not the slightest look of sympathy for her.

"She's right, girlfriend. If you didn't have strong feelings
for the man, we wouldn't even be having this discussion."
Laree changed sides again.

"Y'all don't get it. This isn't some Luther Vandross
lovesong video. This is real life. I don't think the past can
just be swept under the rug. No, friends maybe, but that's
all." Michelle stabbed a cherry tomato with force as she pre-

tended not to see the skeptical looks Laree and Shantae exchanged.

Michelle paced up and down. At his request, she had agreed to meet Greg Matthews at the Greyhound Bus Station. He had been reluctant to explain exactly why he needed to see her, which made her very worried. So far, she had done three stories profiling residents of public housing. She wasn't at all sure how long before even Gerald Mansur would begin to question her progress on the investigation into the Housing Authority.

Glancing at the large clock above the ticket counter, Michelle whispered a curse word. Greg was now twenty minutes late. She became uncomfortably aware that a group of three men were eyeing her movements. The oversized sweater she wore did not entirely disguise the soft curves beneath it. Michelle tugged at the hem to make it stretch wider. One spoke low to the others then came toward her. To her great relief, Greg came through the glass doors behind them.

"Hey, Greg. Over here, honey!" Michelle waved enthusiastically to him. As he approached, obviously puzzled at her reaction, she grabbed his arm. "Thank God, you finally showed up."

"Oh, yeah. Sorry." Greg gave the man a warning stare until he and his buddies retreated to a far corner. "My wife had to work overtime, which meant I had to pick my son up from football practice after school."

"Next time let's meet at the public library, okay? Now, what's going on?" Michelle sat next to him in the garish blue vinyl chairs. There were only a handful of people waiting in the large lobby.

"My friend says she's going to need more time before she can get the copies. Seems Ms. Kinchen has hired on some new office staff. They're always around since she's training them. My friend can't get to the files without somebody wondering what she's up to." Greg sat hunched forward as if cold.

"How much more time?" Michelle's heart sank.

"Maybe another week, maybe more. If Ms. Kinchen takes them out to the different housing sites, it could be next week, but my friend isn't sure when that's gonna be."

"Damn. No way she could do it after hours?"

"Nope. Could be she's a little paranoid 'cause of what she's planning, but she thinks Ms. Kinchen is watching everybody," Greg said.

"She may be right, Greg. I've done some reports on residents in the projects. They may suspect something else is coming." Michelle's brows drew together. "I don't want her to take any risks with her job. Guess I'll just have to be patient."

"Yeah, it's worse than that." Greg twisted his hands nervously.

"How?"

"There's some rough dudes working at the Authority now. James Bridges has been taking guys outta prison and getting 'em jobs there. At least ten of 'em working in maintenance now."

"Nothing wrong with giving brothers a break. Or is there?" Michelle was even more intrigued at this news.

"Yeah, except these guys are sorta like enforcers. I hear they been strong-arming people into giving them money, radios, and stuff to make sure they get repairs done. Ain't nobody talking 'cause they too scared. Maybe even dealing outta the apartment complex for old people on Gracie Street."

"Those no good— Tell your friend to take her time and get me everything she can. We're going to do this right so we can nail as many of them as we can." Michelle was angry and disgusted.

"I hope so. Nobody's been able to do it before. Listen,

ma'am, you better be careful, too." Greg's eyes were full of concern. "They can get pretty nasty."

"I'm not worried. They may get really mad about reporters, but even most criminals know it doesn't pay to bother us. It just makes reporters start nosing into their business." Michelle smiled at him reassuringly.

As it happened, Michelle had an interview the next day with LaWanda Sibley, a young single mother of three living in a subsidized apartment complex in the northern part of the city. LaWanda had struggled to finish a nursing assistant course at a local vocational school and was still trying to get a job. Greg had given Michelle her name. At LaWanda's suggestion, Michelle came in the mornings since most of the young thugs and drug dealers slept until early afternoon.

"Hey, girl. You was kickin' it on TV the other night. You gone be in charge down there 'fore long." LaWanda met her at the screen door with Relondo, her two-year-old baby boy, perched on her hip.

"Thanks, but I don't think so." Michelle grinned as she tickled the baby. His plump brown face dimpled with mirth.

"You know you will. Anyways, that was good. When you gone show me?" LaWanda put the baby down on the worn sofa next to her. He stood on wobbly legs, one hand clutching the front of her blouse, the other stuck in his mouth.

"Next Tuesday." Before sitting down, Michelle had to push a heap of toys from the sagging chair. She helped LaWanda toss them into an empty cardboard box that held other toys. "How've you been?"

"Same old same old. I got applications in at all the hospitals but I ain't heard nothin' yet. So I just been catchin' up on all my favorite soaps." LaWanda jerked a thumb over her shoulder at the television.

"Don't be discouraged. You'll get something."

"I guess." LaWanda brushed her hand over Relondo's bushy black curls. Her expression said she was used to disappointment. In her life, not getting a job barely above minimum wage was certainly not the biggest one she had experienced.

"You will." Michelle tried to sound hopeful. "LaWanda, remember I told you there are rumors that the district attorney is looking into wrongdoing in the Housing Authority?"

"Yeah, we coulda told 'em that a long time ago," LaWanda said.

"But they need proof to do anything about it. I've just been doing profiles of people like you. You know, where you work, what your goals are for the future, things like that. I was planning to report on how hard it is to get repairs done. Now I hear from somebody that ex-convicts are shaking down residents, even dealing drugs out of one of the projects. You heard any of that?" Michelle watched her closely.

"Keep your voice down, girl." LaWanda got up and went to the open door. She scanned the area outside. "Who told you that?"

"I can't say. Well?" Michelle spoke more softly as she followed LaWanda's gaze outside.

"Look, all I know is some of them maintenance guys done got to be good buddies with some of the dudes dealin' 'round here. And don't go askin' too many people 'bout it. Shirley lives one apartment down, and she's goin' with one of 'em." LaWanda sat at the end of the sofa closer to Michelle, speaking in a low voice.

"How long has this been going on?"

"It's gotten real bad in the past three months. Matter of fact, a coupla people got windows broke outta they apartments the day after they threatened to complain to the HUD office in New Orleans."

"Folks are scared, I bet. Maybe they won't be willing to talk to me, especially not on camera." Michelle began to get discouraged again. First the delay from Greg's friend, now this.

"I don't know." LaWanda drummed her fingers on the sofa cushion for several seconds, thinking hard. "Things gettin' kinda bad. Lemme talk to 'em. We organizin' our tenants association. We even been talkin' to some ladies over at two other projects."

"Don't do anything that might get them mad at you." Michelle leaned toward her, putting a hand on LaWanda's arm. She knew very well that LaWanda was not one to shy away from conflict.

"I ain't worried, honey. One good thing about having four brothers is they go after anybody that messes with one of us. Lots of folks know that, too. We gone get these places straight. We got to. Don't look like none of us gone be able to move no time soon. Just cause we poor don't mean we gotta live this way." LaWanda, forgetting her own warning, spoke in a loud, brash voice.

"Still, be careful. Your brothers aren't the most reliable characters. What if you can't find them?"

"Yeah, you right." LaWanda gave a grunt of disgust. "My luck they'd all be in jail on some charge. But it's no problem. I ain't in this alone. Now ain't you gone finish our interview? I don't want no excuses for my story not gettin' on TV."

For another hour, Michelle and LaWanda talked more like two women who met at the home of a mutual acquaintance and found they had much in common. Sam, one of the station's other video cam operators, showed up finally to get some footage of LaWanda, her apartment, and the project. LaWanda was only twenty-three, three years younger than Michelle, yet she had faced so much more. LaWanda had grown up in a succession of foster homes, either ignored or mistreated. Her mother was more interested in her string of live-in lovers than taking care of six children. LaWanda had loved and lost three men, all fathers of her children. Relondo's father had been killed in a drive-by shooting. Yet LaWanda still held on to the dream of a stable, safe life for herself and her children. Michelle liked her dry sense of humor. More than once LaWanda had Michelle and the cameraman laughing at situations that should have depressed them all. Finishing up, Michelle thanked LaWanda and gave the baby one last hug.

"Say, you gonna keep in touch, right? Come by anytime. You know, to just visit." LaWanda looked so vulnerable and young standing in the doorway. "I know we ain't nothin' alike. But talkin' to you is like, I dunno, I'm in your world. Sounds stupid, huh?" She looked away, embarrassed.

"No, it doesn't sound stupid," Michelle said with quiet assurance. "Not at all. I'll be in touch and not just about the story, either. We aren't as different as you think, not really."

Riding back to the station, Michelle began to rehearse her presentation to Lockport and Gerald Mansur on why the series was worth pursuing. She felt a growing determination not to disappoint LaWanda, Greg, and all the other people who had more to lose than she.

"For a while, I thought you weren't going to agree to see me again." Anthony kept his eyes ahead on the highway.

"I've really been busy. Honest." Michelle could feel his skepticism though he said nothing. "Beautiful day." She looked out of the window to her right.

It was a weak attempt to get on safer ground she knew. But she was sincere at least in her description of the landscape. After three weeks of putting him off, she finally agreed to a ride in the country. Still lounging in her pajamas with the Sunday paper spread all over the bed, his call had taken her by surprise that morning. Before she knew it, she had agreed that the weather was wonderful, and yes she would enjoy seeing the countryside. So after church, Anthony told her, he would change clothes and pick her up.

It was a glorious October day of cool temperatures in the early morning hours warming up to the seventies by afternoon. The low humidity, an infrequent occurrence in south Louisiana, made the mild temperatures even more enjoyable. Leaves a mixture of greens and various shades of orange waved in the light breeze, creating a gorgeous ripple of color in the sunshine. Yellow, blue, and lavender wildflowers bloomed along the highway and in the fields they passed. All this framed by a cloudless, blue sky made the day a splendid work of art not created by man.

"I see you brought a camera." Michelle lifted it from the seat between them.

"Yeah, sort of a hobby. I want to get some pictures. The water dropped in the spillway, leaving behind a temporary lake with fish trapped in it. They say the flocks of herons, egrets, and pelicans are a fabulous sight." Anthony turned onto the old highway leading into the little town of New Roads.

"I'll bet. I love this time of year." Michelle rolled down the car window a little more, breathing in deeply.

They passed fields of sugarcane not yet harvested. Large trucks loaded with the sweet stalks headed for the sugar mills. During this season, the mills operated day and night to produce the thick, sweet syrup so favored in Louisiana. As they rounded a curve, the lovely sun-dappled False River came into view.

"Have you done much fishing since you got back?" Michelle remembered how much he enjoyed the sport.

"Not nearly enough. Say, why don't we plan a day of fishing? We had some really good times back then." Anthony smiled though he kept watching the road ahead.

"I don't know." Michelle could have kicked herself for bringing it up. She had forgotten about the trips, dates really. Times spent alone growing closer, when their friendship blossomed into much more.

"Come on. Now that's something we can do at the spur of the moment when the weather's right. We've got until the middle of December before the water gets too cold. What do you say?" Anthony glanced at her.

"Okay, guess I'll have to dust off my old rod, reel, and

popping cork. I haven't gone very often lately. In fact, I left my fishing gear in my parents' garage," Michelle said.

"Then it's settled." He grinned broadly. "Let's say False River any Sunday after church, deal?"

"Deal." Michelle returned his smile, her heart skipping a little. She forced her gaze away from his, aware that she was in danger of doing something foolish like reaching for his hand.

Leaving behind the charming little town of New Roads, they turned onto Highway One leading to the even smaller town of Morganza, just north of which was the spillway. They drove for several miles in silence, enjoying the view and the soft jazz playing on the radio. As they approached the spillway, Michelle gasped with delight. Spread out on the water and perched on tree branches were hundreds of birds. Large gray pelicans spread their wings lazily as they bobbed in the gentle waves. Snowy-white herons circled above in graceful flight.

"Say, seems like more than the birds are going to feast on fish today." Anthony pointed. He pulled onto a dirt road leading to a levee.

There was a scattered crowd of fishermen and women. Some stood along the bank, a few were in bateaux in the water. Birds and people shared a peaceful coexistence as they pursued the same goal.

"This would make a fantastic picture." Michelle gazed around her lost in the scene.

"You're absolutely right."

For the next hour, they strolled up and down the levee, both happily discovering sights for Anthony to photograph. Like children at play, they scrambled down to the water's edge where Anthony eagerly snapped close-up shots.

"Look at that!" Michelle tugged at his shoulder, pointing to a pelican, its large wings flapping as it descended to the water.

"Got it. This new camera is great. That will be an awesome

picture. I can't wait to get it developed." Anthony checked the camera settings.

"You develop them yourself?"

"Yeah, it's as much fun as taking them. I've converted the extra bedroom in my condo into a darkroom. And today you can be my lovely assistant. Tell you what, let's have lunch at Thibaut's on False River. Then we can go down to Old River and take some pictures there. We can wind up the day seeing the results of our work." Anthony took her hand to help her climb the levee even though the slope up was gentle.

"Well—"

"Listen, if I promise to be on my best behavior and think only pure thoughts will you say yes?" Anthony, face solemn, held up one hand as if taking an oath.

"On your honor as a Big Buddy and role model to the youth of this great nation?" Michelle smothered a giggle trying to match his expression.

"I swear."

"Okay, but on one condition. I pay for my meal."

"We'll discuss that later." Anthony cupped her elbow and led her back to the car.

"Anthony—"

He bustled her into the passenger side of his car, cutting off further protest. "Now let's go eat. My stomach is talking to me."

The restaurant dining room had a wide view of the river and they were lucky enough to get a table near the large window. The long list of delicious choices made ordering difficult. After much discussion, they handed the menus back to the waitress and admired the scenery. Lunch was so enjoyable, they almost hated to leave. Yet the lure of more beautiful vistas to see and photograph was just as strong. For the rest of the afternoon they drove along the bayous and through small towns. Michelle forgot to question the wisdom of spending an entire day with Anthony. She was totally caught up in savoring the freedom of having no planned destination, no appointments, and no idea of what they might see around the next curve. There were no more awkward moments between them. Although there were long moments when neither spoke, it was a comfortable silence. They relaxed in a shared pleasure of their surroundings.

As the sun began to set, Michelle grew less sure that agreeing to spend the evening with Anthony was wise. Her anxiety increased when, after showing her around and getting her settled on the large sofa of his living room, Anthony switched on the compact disc. Strains of pulsating blues played softly. Muted lighting combined with the gray, blue, and dark green colors of the room to create an air of intimacy.

"Since it's only five o'clock, we can have dinner after we finish. I can whip us up something right here." Anthony poured a solution in a pan.

"Here? No," Michelle blurted out sharply. "I mean, don't go to any trouble dirtying up a lot of dishes."

"No problem, you'll be helping with the clean up." Anthony laughed.

"I'm not too hungry." Michelle cast about in her mind for other reasons not to stay longer.

"Not too hungry? You had a crab salad, I had a shrimp salad. Very satisfying for a few hours, but definitely not for the rest of the night. I make a mean pasta with mixed vegetables. Remember, I promised to be good." Anthony paused before turning off the light.

"All right." Michelle swore at herself silently. He had promised to behave, but could she?

The closeness of the dark room enveloped her. They worked together, Anthony explaining each step of the developing process. Michelle found her mind wandering from the task each time he stood near her. The companionable chatter between them felt right, as though they had never been apart.

"There. Now we let those dry," Anthony said. The prints hung on a wire strung across one corner of the room.

Anthony flipped the light switch and led the way back to

the living room. Pouring Michelle another glass of chardonnay, he kept up a steady stream of conversation from the
kitchen as he cooked. Michelle drifted from the kitchen to
the living room and back again. They talked about everything
from politics to religion, agreeing on some subjects and spar-
ring on others. Michelle did not know if it was the wine, the
music, or the cozy feel of their companionship, but suddenly
she became acutely aware that the warm flush she felt was
definitely not the wine. After dinner, Michelle washed the
dishes while Anthony dried. He shooed her out and put them
away alone. Michelle, after pausing to consider, sat in the
large chair. She pretended not to notice the amused half smile
Anthony wore briefly when he came out of the kitchen.

"You're pretty handy with a dishcloth." Anthony sat on
the end of the sofa near her.

"So are you. And unless you have a maid service to clean
up, you're not a bad housekeeper, either." Michelle glanced
around the tidy room.

"No, indeed. Mama taught me everything I know. She
always made it clear that keeping a house clean should be
shared by everybody that helped get it dirty."

"Smart lady, your mama. You'll make some woman a fine
husband."

"You think so?" Anthony gazed at her, a twinkle in his
eye.

Michelle hopped up from the sofa. To hide her discomfort,
she sorted through the stack of compact discs. "Very nice
collection."

"Thanks, I've been scouring record stores to get Louie
Armstrong, Billie Holiday, and Alberta Hunter recordings.
Listen to this." Joining her, Anthony switched off the music
to place another disc in the player.

Sarah Vaughn's voice, sweet and strong, filled the room
singing a ballad. Without warning, Anthony pulled her away
from the bookcase and led her in a slow dance. For a time,
a very short time, Michelle strained to keep him at arm's

length. Though she couldn't remember how or when, the song ended to find her body pressed against his and her head resting on his shoulder. As she lifted her head to step back, his mouth caught hers. Another song began as they clung to each other kissing deeply, eagerly.

"Anthony, this isn't a good idea." Michelle's protest, murmured between tender caresses from his lips, sounded weak even to her own ears.

"Feels like a very good idea." Anthony flattened his body to hers, his hands gripping her hips. "Chelle, I want you. I can't settle for being just a friend."

Michelle uttered a muffled moan as his tongue found hers. Yet somehow through the velvet haze of hunger that surged through her from head to toe, a tiny voice of caution sounded.

"No, wait." Breathless, Michelle pulled back from him. The room seemed to dip and sway. "This is too much, too soon." She waved him away with great effort as he tried to embrace her again.

With a tremulous breath, Anthony let his arms fall to his sides. "We've been lying to each other for weeks, Chelle. You don't believe we can just be *buddies* any more than I do."

"But we started growing up after high school, remember?" Michelle felt her equilibrium returning gradually as the days leading up to their final confrontation came back to her sharply. Those memories were like a dash of cold water in her face. She inched away from him.

"But not enough. We were still kids even then. Looking back on it now, I see myself not being able to talk about my feelings and you so angry you couldn't listen."

Michelle closed her eyes. "Things haven't changed, I'm afraid."

"I have." Anthony took her hand and led her to the sofa. "I'm willing to talk. And I think you're willing to listen."

"You mean we should talk about us and what happened

without anger or accusations?" Michelle said in a small voice.

"It's what I've wanted for a long time, Chelle." He brushed a stray tendril of hair from her eyes. "Can we try?"

Michelle's heart raced as she looked at the soft, imploring expression he wore. Could she be making another mistake? Having him look at her this way made the conviction to keep him at a distance begin to crumble. A tiny voice whispered not to give in. But his touch awakened a long dormant yearning. "Yes," she murmured.

Five

"Hello, Marcus." Anthony stood in his uncle's large family room. He eyed his cousin warily.

"What's up?" Marcus took a long pull from the beer bottle he held. Looking Anthony up and down, he gave a short grunt. "Nice clothes. Nice car, too. Living well, huh?"

"I'm doing okay. How've you been?" Anthony settled on the huge black leather sofa.

"Fine since I got out. The first few nights I had trouble sleeping though. Funny how even after just eighteen months in prison you can get so programmed to follow orders." Marcus tipped the bottle and, finding it empty, went to the small refrigerator behind the bar to get another.

"It's going to take some time, but you'll be all right."

"I'll do better than all right." Marcus looked up at him, frowning. "I've got plans."

"Yeah?" Anthony kept his voice and expression as neutral as possible. Marcus had always had plans, plans that generally led to big trouble.

"Yeah. I'm going to start my own business."

"Really? That sounds good." Anthony gave him a slight smile.

"You don't think I can do it, right?"

"If you work hard at something and stick to it, you can do anything." Anthony chose his words carefully.

"Maybe I'm not the big shot you are now, but wait and see. I intend to make it big."

"You always do," Anthony muttered.

"Say what?" Marcus glared at him.

Ike strode into the room, holding a small cellular phone. "It's always something. I tell you, Anthony, you were right not to get into rental property. It's one damn thing after another with tenants. Now, what are you boys drinking? Say, Anthony, Marcus looks pretty good, huh?" He was moving, talking, and fixing himself a drink, still energized from a long day.

"Yeah, sure." Anthony tried to put a lift into his voice that he did not feel.

"Yeah." Ike took a sip of his screwdriver and gave his son an appraising look. "Pretty good for a jailbird."

"If I was white, I wouldn't have gotten time for a little marijuana." Marcus frowned, his face showed bitterness.

"Lucky for you they only found traces of cocaine. Else your butt would've been sent up for twenty years. Not to mention you had violated probation four or five times. I couldn't talk or buy you outta that fix. Your color ain't had nothing to do with it." Ike spoke disdainfully.

"I'm through with drugs. I got too much going for me for that. It's not worth it."

"Yeah. How many times have I heard that before?" Ike waved a hand at him.

"I'm serious. I don't need it anymore."

"Uh-huh, we'll see. Say, boy, tell Anthony about your latest get-rich scheme."

Anthony grew uneasy with the direction the discussion was taking. "Hey, let's not talk about business now. What do you say we go out to Phil's for steak."

"No, no. You gotta hear this one first. Go on, Marcus. Tell him." Ike perched on one of the leather bar stools.

"Insurance. I want to open my own insurance company. It's a good idea, too," Marcus added defensively.

Ike ignored him. "Anthony, will you tell him how this

state is cracking down on insurance companies. They've got strict new regs."

"Maybe he should try it out. Besides, Marcus does well with selling," Anthony said, trying to support his cousin in the face of Ike's skepticism.

"The boy don't know a damn thing about the insurance business."

Marcus stared at Ike, his dark eyes flashing defiance. He spoke in a tight, controlled voice. "I worked for Mr. Trahan selling policies and helping his customers collect claims. I do know about insurance."

Ike gave a raspy grunt in derision. "When you showed up for work. Trahan did me a favor hiring you, boy." Turning, he spoke to Anthony. "He tolerated his foolishness because I got Trahan a lot of business."

"He was good though. Mr. Trahan said so." Anthony hated having to defend Marcus.

"Like I said, when he showed up for work. And where does he think he's going to get money to start his own business?"

"It wouldn't cost that much. Just a few thousand dollars. I could have a couple of offices in your building, I'll need to hire a secretary—"

"Forget it," Ike snapped.

"At least listen to what I'm trying to tell you." Marcus came from behind the bar to stand next to his father.

"Don't matter. I ain't spendin' none of my money on you openin' up no business. You can't stand getting up in the morning to work for somebody else. You got no discipline. To have your own business means you work ten times harder 'cause you gotta do it all yourself. What happened when I let you manage some of my properties? Huh, boy? Let's talk about that." Ike set his empty glass down with a bang.

"Uncle Ike, I think Marcus could maybe start by working for Mr. Trahan again. Then if he sticks to it, you might consider setting him up." Anthony searched for a way to head off a clash, to offer some middle ground that both could accept.

"I don't need you to speak for me! You stay out of this," Marcus growled at Anthony. He turned to Ike. "Ever since we were kids, you been putting him before me. Where did he get the money for his business? From you, that's who. But when I ask you for a few dollars, you start throwing up stuff in my face from way back. How come? Why can't you show me some respect?" Marcus shouted.

"First thing you gonna do is lower your voice to me, boy." Ike rose slowly to face his son. He stared at Marcus through eyes narrowed to slits, his rapid breathing audible in the deadly silence that followed his words.

"Daddy, I . . ." Marcus stammered, then stopped. Unable to take his eyes away from his father's, he backed away until he stood against the wall next to the fireplace.

"Come on, now. Everybody calm down." Anthony stood between them. He knew from Ike's expression that he could easily strike Marcus if further provoked.

"Sit down, Anthony. It's okay." Ike unclenched his fists. He turned around to fix himself another drink. "This is what you're gonna do, Marcus. I got you a job and you're gonna keep it. You better show up every day and be on time. Got it?" Not hearing a response, Ike looked at him over his shoulder. "I asked you a question, son."

Marcus nodded, his jaw muscles worked convulsively with the effort to keep silent. When he bolted from the room, Anthony went after him. Marcus sat in the kitchen at the breakfast table. He faced the bay window, staring through the pale yellow curtains into the dark.

"Say, man. You know how Uncle Ike is. He's doing what he thinks is best for you—" Anthony could see Marcus wiping his face.

"Leave me alone, man. Just get the hell outta my face." Marcus pushed the chair back so hard it fell over. He stomped out of the kitchen. Seconds later the front door slammed. The engine of his 280Z roared to life. With a sharp squeal of tires on pavement, the car shot off into the night.

"You were too hard on him, Uncle Ike," Anthony said to Ike when he walked into the kitchen.

"That boy had all the advantages. He wants the easy way out of everything. Always some excuse, always somebody else's fault for his screwups. He'll be all right and do what I tell him. Come on, let's go get that steak." Uncle Ike slapped him on the back. He pulled out the keys to his car.

"I'll drive." Anthony took the keys from his hand.

All through dinner Anthony could not help but think about his cousin. From the moment Uncle Ike had taken Anthony under his wing, Marcus had seen him as a rival for Ike's attention and affection. Anthony, one year younger than Marcus, had thought they could be like brothers. But Marcus made it clear from the beginning that he did not see Anthony as anything but an opponent. Nothing Anthony tried to do over the years could change this. And Uncle Ike did nothing to help. Instead of reassuring his son, he encouraged the competition by comparing the boys. Anthony loved his uncle, but he had to agree he could be ironfisted when dealing with others. Even his own family.

"Uncle Ike, try to talk to Marcus and smooth things out." Anthony got out of his uncle's car in the driveway and handed him the keys.

"I told you, he's gonna be okay. He'll mope around with his mouth stuck out for a few days, but that's all. Say, come in for a drink. I got some hot new videos." Ike winked at him, leering.

"No, thanks. You know I'm not into that stuff."

"That's right, you into the real thing. That's my boy." Ike punched him on the arm lightly.

"Look here, you've had more than a couple of drinks tonight. You should be turning in. I'll see you later." Anthony guided him to the kitchen door.

"Sure, son. I'll call you tomorrow." Ike found the key and unlocked the door. Light from the kitchen spilled out. "Anthony, I . . . Never mind. I'll call you."

"Good night." Anthony stood for a few seconds at the closed door before getting in his car and leaving.

The next two days were very hectic. Anthony was swamped handling details and problems associated with the three projects he was handling. He and Cedric spent as much time riding around to each site as they did in the office. Finally, things settled down somewhat and Anthony was able to spend a day on paperwork.

"Whew! I never thought I'd say this, but I hope we don't get any more business." Cedric set his coffee mug down on Anthony's desk and slumped back in the chair.

"You're right," Anthony agreed. "Being overwhelmed with more than you can handle is as much a disaster as having too little business. Which is why I turned down three jobs in the last week."

"Bless you, my brother. By the way, I just hired three more temporary workers, one your uncle recommended from that job training program. If things keep going this well, we might keep them on." Cedric smacked his lips after taking a big sip of coffee.

"Great. That was a very smart idea. We get good workers and take young men off the unemployment rolls." Anthony motioned his secretary to come in.

Rhonda, brisk and efficient, went around his desk to stand beside him. "Just need you to sign these, right . . . here. And here. How are you today, Cedric?"

"Tired but otherwise okay, Rhonda. What about yourself?"

"Fine." Rhonda cleared her throat and lifted an eyebrow at Cedric though she spoke to Anthony. "While you were out, Miss Toussaint called. She said she'll call you at home later."

"Thanks for mentioning that in front of Cedric, Rhonda," Anthony grumbled shoving the papers to her.

"Thank you, boss." Taking the papers from Anthony,

Rhonda turned her back to him to leave. She winked at Cedric as she passed.

"You and Michelle, huh? Y'all got it goin' on again. Man, that's nice." Cedric grinned at him.

"Don't give me that phony surprised look. Shantae has probably told you how often we've been out, where we went, and what we talked about."

"That's not so. I have no idea what y'all talked about." Cedric chortled. "Going good, right?"

Anthony lifted a shoulder. "You could put it that way." Despite his lowered eyes, the pleasure brightening them was obvious.

"Man, you're on the Love Boat and we both know it. Quit trying to sound so cool," Cedric needled him.

"Well, it has been a sweet three weeks. It's the same but different. Know what I mean?"

"Yeah, you're both older so now you've got grown-up love. I hear you."

"Hope everything else keeps going as well." Anthony sat forward again, the placid expression replaced by a slight frown.

"Why shouldn't it?"

"Marcus got out last week."

"Had to happen sometime, unfortunately. So what's the boy wonder up to now?" Cedric said.

"I could be wrong, but I think he really wants to change." Anthony tapped his ink pen on the desktop. "Uncle Ike doesn't buy it though."

"I'm not surprised. After the crap he's gotten into, who would?"

"Marcus has some serious problems, I have to agree on that." Anthony sighed.

"Damn right. His daddy has been bailing him out of trouble most of his life. Now he's an ex-con. Face it, if it hadn't been for Mr. Ike, Marcus would have been in jail a long time ago," Cedric said with brutal frankness.

"Could you let your only son go to jail if you could stop it? No, you'd try to save him. In his own rough way Uncle Ike did what he thought was right to turn Marcus around." Anthony rubbed his eyes.

"Why are you always making excuses for the little rat anyway? He's been treating you like a dog for years."

"Marcus sticks his chest out, but deep down he's hurting. Because of me partly. Uncle Ike has always tried to push Marcus into achieving by comparing us. I hate the way Uncle Ike rubs his nose in my successes," Anthony said.

"Unlike a lot of young brothers, Marcus had many opportunities. He didn't have to go the way he did." Cedric remained unyielding in his harsh assessment.

"Yeah. But even with all his advantages, in a way Marcus had it tough, too."

"If you say so. I don't see it though." Cedric stood. "Well, let me get a move on. For the first time in three weeks I don't think I'll be working late. I'm going home, take a hot shower, then cruise on over to Shantae's."

"Cedric in love with a ready-made family woman. Who would have thought it," Anthony teased him.

"Ah, man." Cedric fiddled with his sweater, eyes down.

"You were one helluva ladies' man. Talk about seriously into the singles party scene."

"I grew up, too. Kicking back with Shantae and Devonne—you know, the family scene—is real nice after a hard day out in the cold, cruel world." Cedric smiled sheepishly.

"When y'all planning to jump the broom?" Anthony enjoyed seeing him squirm.

"We talked about it. But we're in no hurry."

"You are hooked, my brother," Anthony crowed. He shook a finger at his friend.

"Okay, okay. Quit cackling." Cedric threw a pencil at Anthony's head.

"No, man. For real, I'm happy for y'all." Anthony picked up the pencil from the floor.

"It can happen for you, too. But—" Cedric shrugged.

"But what?"

"Michelle and your uncle Ike. What's going to happen this holiday season? I mean, you always have Thanksgiving dinner over at his house. You and your mama go over there for Christmas then to your grandmother's. May be best to keep the family stuff separate for now."

"Damn, you're right. I hadn't thought about it. But we've got plenty of time to work out where and how we spend the holidays." Anthony shook off the beginning anxiety.

"Don't wait too long to talk it over with her. Say, y'all coming to the Halloween party?"

"You bet." Anthony nodded.

"I'm going as Blacula and Shantae is going as a black widow spider."

Anthony smiled. "I'm going as Frankenstein and Michelle is going to be the Bride of Frankenstein."

"Uh-huh. The woman has got you to the altar already. Hoo—wee!" Cedric howled with laughter even as he ducked flying pencils.

"So what are you going to tell Dosu?" Laree stuck the straw in her mouth to suck some of her soft drink.

"And when are you going to tell him?" Shantae chimed in. Both stared at Michelle.

The three women had finally collapsed at a small restaurant to recuperate after three hours of intense shopping. Bags of all sizes and shapes had been piled in the fourth chair at the tiny wrought-iron table at which they sat. After ordering diet sodas and a large order of nachos, they gratefully rested three pairs of very tired feet.

"This evening." Michelle avoided their gazes.

"You should have told him three weeks ago, Chelle," Laree chided her for the umpteenth time.

"He's been really, really busy and we have talked only a

couple or three times on the phone. That isn't something you tell somebody over the phone." Michelle recognized the lame rationalization even as the words came out.

"You could have asked him to come over so y'all could talk." Laree was relentless.

"I needed time to figure out how I was going to break it to him, all right?" Michelle muttered defensively.

"I know what she means, girl. It was like that when I broke up with Tyrone." Shantae scooped up cheese on a chip.

"Shantae, pu-leeze! You showed that poor man the door so fast he was at his house across town before he knew what had happened," Laree said, cocking an eyebrow at her.

"Honey, when I finally found a mighty good man I didn't want to waste any more of my time." Shantae snapped her fingers twice.

"Besides, that was different. Tyrone was—" Michelle groped for a gentle way to describe him since Shantae had dated him for three years.

"A low-down, woman-chasing, blood-sucking parasite," Shantae jumped in to finish the sentence for her.

"Uh, right. But Dosu has been so sweet to me. He's kind, gentle, considerate—" Michelle took a deep breath.

"And wealthy, don't forget he has big bucks." Laree shook her head vigorously.

"Will you stop." Shantae poked her friend on the arm.

"He's a wonderful man. And he hasn't changed in the two years we've known each other. I know he hoped we could get into something deep but . . ." Michelle winced at the thought of hurting him.

"But he's not Anthony. It's like that song my grandmother loves to sing: 'It don't mean a thing if it ain't got that swing.' " Laree rocked from side to side.

"Girl, Miss Hannah is something else." Shantae giggled.

"I dread this conversation." Michelle took a sip from the soft drink in front of her. Sitting back, she rubbed her temples. Despite their attempts, her friends could not lift her spirits with jokes or silly antics. By the time her doorbell rang at six o'clock, the slight tension in her forehead had become a thudding pain. For two hours she had paced and rehearsed what she would say. Now her mind was blank with anxiety. Standing at the door, she took a deep breath before opening it. Dosu, handsome in a dark brown cashmere sweater and brown pants, smiled. Michelle forced a smile though she wanted to cry.

"Hello, Michelle." Dosu embraced her once the door was closed. "How have you been?"

"Good, pretty good. Would you like something? A cold drink or something hot? I could make us some tea. Or coffee. Whatever you prefer." Michelle started for the kitchen.

"Yes, coffee I think. It is quite cold out this evening."

"Oh, I have some cake my aunt made for me. Or maybe you'd like some cookies?"

"No, thank you. Maybe we will have dinner tonight," Dosu called from the living room.

"Oh, dinner. Coffee should be ready soon." Michelle stood uncertainly trying to decide where to sit. She decided to sit next to him on the sofa but not too close.

"You seem a little on edge." Dosu extended an arm across the back of the sofa. "Is everything all right?"

"Yeah, well, no, I mean—fine, things are fine. I'll see if the coffee is ready." Michelle darted into the kitchen. Cursing the pot for taking so long to drip, she stood drumming her fingers on the counter.

"You have something to tell me."

"What?" Michelle jumped at the sound of his voice right over her shoulder. She turned to find his eyes, soft with affection, searching her face. *I owe him the truth.*

"Come, let's sit down." Dosu took her arm and led her out of the kitchen. "Now, my Michelle, tell me what I think I already know."

"Anthony and I . . . have been seeing each other for the past few weeks."

"You still love him, yes?"

"I don't know if it's leftover puppy love, infatuation, or what. I honestly don't know." Michelle twisted her hands in her lap.

"But it must be something very special or else you would not be so disturbed. Look at me. From the moment I saw you two together, I knew that this thing between you was not resolved. Now I have a confession. I have not been too busy to call or visit, Michelle." Dosu patted her hand.

"I don't understand. You mean you didn't really go out of town and buy a lot of new merchandise?"

"No, that was true. But I could have seen you before now. To tell you the truth, I thought you needed space."

"Oh, Dosu, I—"

"There were no promises between us. We have been good friends. We still can be." Dosu kissed her forehead. "Now you can relax, okay?"

"You're a treasure, Dosu Lemotey." Michelle blinked away tears as she gave him a firm hug.

"Ah, now. I have made no great sacrifice. It is said that if you love someone, set them free."

"African proverb?"

"British rock star." Dosu smiled impishly.

Laughing with him, Michelle felt relieved she had not hurt someone dear to her. Noticing the inviting smell of the freshly brewed coffee, Michelle went into the kitchen. She prepared a tray and brought it into the living room. Over coffee, Michelle told him about Anthony and the cause of their rift six years before.

"His uncle, a man he looks up to, can be ruthless. My father worked for four years to rebuild his business and reputation." Michelle still felt the pain of those times.

"And for that you cannot forgive him." Dosu took a cautious sip from the steaming cup.

"We went through so much. My family hasn't been the same since. My parents have never been the same with each other." Michelle stopped short. This was the first time she had said it out loud, and the pain from that alone made it impossible to forgive Ike Batiste. "From everything I've heard, he hasn't changed one bit."

"Anthony was angered by your feelings, and you felt betrayed because of his loyalty to his uncle?"

"When we were younger, yes. But now maybe we can at least acknowledge that our feelings are legitimate."

"Yes. You must learn to accept his love for his uncle though you will never share it. He must accept that you cannot share it." Dosu summed up their task with his characteristic keen perception.

"I only wonder if we can." Michelle gazed into the coffee cup as if searching for the answer there.

"A challenge, I agree. I tell you this, you must at least try. Even if I won you away from him, I would always wonder if you were truly happy. And you, my Michelle, might always wonder about what might have been. Then neither of us would be happy." Dosu put down his cup.

"Thank you." Michelle felt the swell of affection for him once again.

"I do this for myself as well, you know. But remember these wise words: try this bracelet—if it fits you, wear it; but if it hurts you, throw it away no matter how shiny." He wagged a forefinger at her.

"Now, that is an African proverb." Michelle smiled.

"Of course." Dosu beamed. Standing, he extended his hand to her. "Shall we have dinner?"

"I swear, Daddy. You must stay up nights thinking of ways to make Mama mad." Sighing, Michelle looked around her father's office.

His was the largest office in a modest building built by him on property he owned. It was very organized. Three bookshelves contained neat rows of manuals and books. Michelle mused how much Brian was like their father. Both needed to have order in everything. She supposed it was what had gotten Thomas through those horrible days of watching his business collapse. Emotions always in check, Thomas pulled himself together and began to methodically rebuild his business. Unfortunately, his family did not respond quite as predictably. Never one to show affection, he became even more reserved. Annette's temperamental outbursts, at first merely annoying, finally disgusted him. Michelle could remember him lecturing her on how his mother stoically faced much greater hardships. To Michelle, her father was unfeeling. Annette needed to be hugged and reassured, something Thomas did not seem to understand or be willing to try.

Michelle had spoken to her mother the night before. As always, Annette made up ridiculous excuses for Dominic's behavior. Even Michelle had to admit she went overboard to defend Dominic. Hard as she tried to argue that it would be best to allow her father time to cool off from Dominic's latest escapade, Annette had worn her down until she agreed to see Thomas the next day. Not helping the situation, Thomas refused to give Dominic a job. Worse yet, he was going to take away his beloved Jeep Cherokee.

"No, she stays up nights nursing drinks and old resentments." Thomas did not seem the least upset.

"Do you have to fight her on everything? I know Dominic has made some mistakes."

"That's an understatement. Dominic is completely irresponsible. He's thrown away every chance to make something of himself."

"Dominic isn't like Brian. You're too hard on him. You have been since he was little," Michelle said.

"Look, I co-signed so he could get that Jeep. At the time I told him I had no intention of paying the note so he'd better keep a job. Well, he's missed three payments. Since I paid them, it's now my Jeep." Thomas continued signing and arranging the documents on his desk.

"You could give him a job here."

"The last time I did, it was a disaster. Remember?"

"He wants another chance, Daddy. I'd be the first to admit that Dominic has his faults—"

"Another understatement," Thomas retorted.

"But he tries hard. Maybe too hard. He just wants to please you. Why can't you see that Dominic operates on a different wavelength? He needs more space to be creative." Michelle was frustrated with her father's inability to be more forgiving with his youngest child.

"Creative? I suppose you could call changing plans with a customer on a whim, after my foreman and I spent days coming up with them, creative. His creativity doubled the price of the job, but of course Dominic assured him it was the same cost. I barely broke even," Thomas complained.

"Can't you be patient and teach him when he makes a mistake instead of jumping on him? He's not you or Brian. He's different." Michelle found herself saying the same things her mother had been telling Thomas for years. From the look on his face, she was no more persuasive.

"Patient? I have been patient. Dominic hasn't just had a second chance, my dear. He's had sixty chances with me because he's my son. No more. He'll make it on his own, or learn to do without." Thomas looked past Michelle, causing her to turn.

"Dominic. We were just saying . . ." Michelle watched her brother's stormy expression with a sinking feeling.

"I heard." Dominic faced his father. "I'll make it on my own, Dad. I've already got a job. A pretty good one."

"Dom, that's great! How did you get it?" Michelle hugged his arm.

"You mean who would be crazy enough to hire me." Dominic drew back from her. He came around to stand between them.

"No, I didn't mean that at all."

"Yes, you did. It's okay." Dominic stood straight and met

his father's scrutiny. "Dad, I'm sorry you had to pay the notes, but I'll need the Jeep to get to and from work. I promise to pay you back out of my first three paychecks. If not, I'll bring the Jeep back myself." He was not pleading, but spoke as one man asking a favor of another.

"All right." Thomas eyed him with mild surprise. He was clearly not used to this kind of approach from him. Reaching into his desk drawer, he handed him a set of keys.

"Daddy, isn't that great Dominic has a new job?" Michelle looked at her father. "Don't you think so?" Michelle dropped another hint that he was to be positive.

"Yes." Thomas seemed about to say more, but the tense expression on Michelle's face stopped him.

"So tell us all about it." Relaxing, Michelle turned to Dominic.

"I'll be arranging with contractors to do repairs and preventive maintenance on housing units." Dominic watched his father closely as he spoke.

"Hey, you have experience with that. You should do a real good job. Shouldn't he, Daddy?" Michelle prodded Thomas again with a slight movement of her head.

"I suppose," Thomas conceded. His expression remained impassive.

"So who are you working for?" Michelle smiled expectantly.

Dominic stood erect and paused before answering. "Quality Building Contractors."

"What! Have you lost you mind? That's—" Michelle spluttered. She faced him. Her voice shook with exasperation.

"Ike Batiste." Thomas spoke in a quiet voice of suppressed fury.

Six

The horror began in the parking lot. Bloody arms and legs were strewn around its perimeter. The sound of intermittent moans floated around them. Michelle kicked a head from her path causing it to emit a metallic squeak. Michelle shrieked and jumped back, almost knocking Anthony down.

"A truly sick mind came up with this," Laree twittered.

"Great idea though." Shantae looked around appreciatively at the spooky setting.

The three had decided to triple date. Laree was accompanied by a handsome gentleman she had met at the banquet. D'Andre met all of her qualifications: handsome, intelligent, and an employed professional. Shantae and Cedric brought up the rear, razzing each other about how they looked.

"Say, baby, I love that outfit. Why don't you buy it?" Cedric stroked the stuffed spider legs that hung from her diaphanous long black dress. "Yeah, wear it the next time I come over for the night."

"Sure, sugar. Just remember what happens to the male afterward." Shantae drew a finger across her throat.

The decorations were impressive. Tombstones lined the short hall leading to the large room where the party was going strong, giving all those entering the feeling of walking through a small cemetery. Inside the dance hall, orange and black balloons and streamers hung from the ceiling. The walls were also hung with fake skeletons, spiderwebs complete with huge rubber spiders, and more assorted body parts.

"Good evening and welcome to the Unique Social Club's Third Annual Benefit Monster Mash. May I have your invitations please?" A huge green monster cheerfully met them at the door. "Thank you. Your gift will help both the Baton Rouge Sickle Cell Anemia Foundation and the Highland Street Community Center. Have a good time."

"Man, this place is packed!" D'Andre, his gruesome mask pushed back from his face, surveyed the crowded dance floor.

"We're at table sixteen. This way." Michelle led them along the wall toward a section with tables.

Michelle seemed to glide along as she walked. Her figure-hugging ivory dress had a filmy, chiffon layer that drifted around her like a cloud as she walked. The neckline, cut low in the front and back, was made less revealing by a chiffon shawl. She wore her thick, dark hair piled high with a white streak painted up one side in front.

"Uh-huh, you look fantastic." Anthony let out a low whistle. His eyes glowed with admiration.

"Why, Frankie, you say the sweetest things." Michelle fluttered her eyelids at him as he held her chair.

"Come on, D'Andre." Laree, bouncing and snapping her fingers to the music, stood up. "Let's dance."

"Me, too." Cedric pulled Shantae from her seat almost the second she had settled into it.

Anthony headed for the refreshments. He returned minutes later with a tray of assorted bottles and glasses. "Okay. We have a strawberry daiquiri for Shantae, a piña colada for Laree, chardonnay for the young, upwardly mobile D'Andre." Anthony winked at Michelle causing her to snicker. "Coca-Cola for Cedric, the designated driver. And for us, Ballatore, a fine sparkling wine to celebrate our first month of togetherness." He tipped the bottle, pouring it into two plastic champagne glasses.

"Wonderful." Michelle sipped the drink, staring at him over the rim of her glass.

"The last four weeks have been very special." Anthony placed an arm around her chair and leaned close to her. "Thank you." He kissed her lips tenderly, then sat back with a sigh.

Michelle sat blinking rapidly, a wave of desire flooding her. With a trembling hand, she took another sip of the wine to buy time. But when the band began a slow tune, Anthony took the glass from her. He led her onto the dance floor. He guided her in a gentle swaying motion. Michelle tensed, trying to resist the strong force pulling her. It was useless. As the music swelled to a crescendo, Anthony began to hum soft and low, his lips brushing her ear. Michelle closed her eyes. Resting her cheek against his chest, she breathed in the spicy scent of him. She let go, allowing herself to be swallowed up in the delicious cocoon of being in his arms. Lifting her head, he kissed her again just as the song ended. They stood holding each other for several seconds before realizing that the couples around them were dancing to a livelier tune.

"Some song, huh?" Anthony gazed into her eyes.

"Some dance." Michelle made a conscious effort to slow her breathing as they returned to their table.

The others were already there laughing and joking about all the wild costumes around. That Anthony and Michelle were subdued did not go unnoticed by Laree. The men left to replenish their refreshments.

Laree poked Shantae in the ribs. "Did you see a certain couple heating up the dance floor?"

"Yes, indeed. If they had gotten any closer, she would have been wearing his costume," Shantae put in.

"We were dancing," Michelle popped back. "I think we would have looked stupid standing at arm's length from each other."

"That was more than a dance, honey. Y'all were making love." Shantae crunched on a cracker.

"Sho nuff. What happened to 'We're going to be just friends'?" Laree asked.

"I'll tell you what happened; once she got next to him, she couldn't fight the feeling. Woo-wee, didn't take my man long to melt the Ice Princess." Shantae turned to Laree.

"Uh-huh, that's right." Laree slapped her palm against Shantae's in a high five.

Michelle was trying to think of a stinging retort when the guys came back. As they set up fresh drinks, Michelle decided to accept the teasing with good humor. After all, how could she deny it? From the moment she saw Anthony in the newsroom, her feelings for him could not be ignored. Despite her best efforts and misgivings, the desire to be with him returned full force. Watching him smile, seeing the sensuous curve of his full mouth, hearing the rich deep tones of his laugh, caused her heart to pound. Still she had to keep in mind the dangers that came with giving too much, too soon. What if he turned on her again? Suddenly the merriment in his eyes disappeared. Michelle became alarmed that he could read the caution in her face. She looked up to see Marcus weaving his way toward them. The smile on Anthony's face was replaced by a guarded frown.

"Good evening, everybody. Seems like y'all havin' a good time." Marcus was dressed in a dark suit with tails and carried a mask. His eyes were abnormally bright. A petite woman stood slightly behind him wearing a vacant grin.

"Hello, Marcus." Anthony glanced away.

"My, don't the ladies look lovely tonight." Marcus stared down at Michelle. "Introduce me, cuz."

"Michelle, Laree, Shantae, and D'Andre, this is my cousin, Marcus. You know Cedric."

"What's happenin'?" Cedric nodded to Marcus and the woman.

"Damn, where are my manners? This is Nedra." Marcus jerked a thumb in her direction.

"Hey." Nedra giggled.

"Havin' a regular par-tee, eh cuz? Mind if we join you?" Without waiting for an answer, Marcus pulled up a chair next to Michelle. "Yeah—uh, grab that chair over there," he said over his shoulder. Nedra wandered off to sit down at another table, still giggling. "That's good. Cute but not too bright." Marcus leaned close to Michelle.

Cedric took a deep breath. "So what have you been up to since you got home?"

"Ain't nothin' to it. Just hangin', you know. Got a job thanks to Dad. Yeah, my old man always comes through for me, in his own way and his own good time."

"Well, congratulations." Cedric spoke quickly seeing Anthony begin to say something.

"Yeah, right. Maybe okay ain't enough, see what I'm sayin'?" Marcus blustered. "Now if I could get set up like my man here"—he thumped Anthony on the back—"everything would be cool. But I got a plan."

"Setting your goals is a step in the right direction." Michelle smiled at him.

"Oh, I've got goals all right. I'm going to get what I want, one way or another." Marcus lost his grin for a second.

"I wish you luck." Michelle's smile faded when she saw Anthony's expression. He was looking from her to Marcus.

"Why, thank you. Say, you're even more beautiful in person than you are on television." Marcus locked his gaze on her breasts as he leaned still closer.

"Back off, man." Anthony put his arm across the back of Michelle's chair as he stared menacingly at his cousin.

"Whoa, can't take the competition? The lady and I are just conversing, cuz. Where's the harm?" Marcus let his gaze wander the length of Michelle's body.

"You're pushing your luck with me, Marcus." Anthony started to rise from his seat.

"Come on now. Chill, man." Cedric reached across Shantae to lay a restraining hand on Anthony's arm.

"I think your lady friend might be getting a little lonely." D'Andre nodded toward Nedra. She was making kissing noises at passing men.

"Class act she ain't." Marcus snorted in disgust. "Cut that crap out," he shouted at her. "See y'all later. Bye, beautiful brown sugar."

With a laugh at the murderous expression on Anthony's face, Marcus slid his chair back from the table. He sauntered away with Nedra trailing him.

"Let it go, man." Cedric withdrew his hand only after Anthony was no longer staring at his cousin's retreating back.

For the rest of the evening, everyone worked hard to recapture the gaiety before Marcus crashed their party. Eventually Anthony loosened up and began to smile then laugh. When they were alone at the table while the others danced, Michelle was glad that all of his anger seemed to have evaporated.

"I'm sorry about getting so uptight a while ago. And I apologize for Marcus. I guess I shouldn't let him get next to me," Anthony said.

"He was just being silly because he'd had a little too much to drink. He didn't mean any harm." Michelle shrugged.

"I wish I could believe that. Anyway, I really am sorry."

"You don't have to keep apologizing. It's okay."

Michelle put her hand on his arm. Looking into his dark brown eyes framed by thick black brows, she felt that familiar warmth spreading across her body. When he placed his hand over hers, the warmth began a flame. The lights dimmed as the band began another love song. Their heads close together, they were locked in a world apart. A world reluctantly abandoned when the others came back to the table. They sat for another fifteen minutes drinking and talking, occasionally greeting friends who came over to say hello.

"Well, y'all ready to call it a night? Crowd's thinning out anyway." Cedric looked around.

"Fine with me," D'Andre said. Standing, he put Laree's jacket on her shoulders.

"Anybody want to go somewhere else? There's this really nice new nightclub on Third Avenue." Shantae held Cedric's hand.

"Nah, I don't think so." Laree moved close to D'Andre.

"Michelle?" Anthony looked at her, his eyes shining.

"I've had enough of crowds tonight." Michelle met his gaze.

"Ooo-kay, guess that's a wrap then," Shantae said as she winked at Cedric.

All were unusually quiet on the ride home. Cedric had a jazz cassette playing softly. The two couples seated behind in the van held hands and spoke quietly. Laree and D'Andre were dropped off first at her apartment.

"Good night. Thanks for driving us." Anthony helped Michelle out of Cedric's van. He fished the keys to his apartment from his jacket pocket.

"No problem. Later, Chelle." Cedric waved.

"Bye, Anthony. Good night, Michelle." Shantae took advantage of the fact that Anthony had turned away to give Michelle an exaggerated wink.

"Cedric, take her home please." Michelle gave an exasperated sigh.

"What was that all about?" Anthony hung up their jackets in a hall closet.

"Nothing. Shantae was just, I mean . . . It was nothing. Nice party, wasn't it?" Michelle definitely did not want to explain so she changed the subject.

"Yes, it was. Let's have some wine." Anthony put on some music then sat close to her on the sofa.

"Listen, don't go to any trouble. It's late and you're probably tired." Michelle began to fidget with her shawl, pulling it to cover her neck and chest. Her misgivings crept back now that they were alone.

"No trouble, and I'm not tired." Anthony fingered a tendril of her hair that trailed down her neck.

"Oh." Michelle avoided looking at him.

"You are one gorgeous Bride of Frankenstein. That dress makes you look like anything but a monster." Anthony laughed softly. His arm moved from the back of the sofa to her shoulders.

"Thanks. Hmm, gotta use the bathroom." Michelle stood abruptly.

"I'll be here when you get back," Anthony growled in his best imitation of a monster.

Finding the light in the hall bathroom, she closed the door. As she stared at herself in the mirror, she tried to come up with a credible excuse to leave. Work? Michelle cursed. *No, big mouth. You already announced to everybody how glad you were to finally have a weekend off.* Feeling ill?

"You all right in there?"

"I'm fine," Michelle answered as a reflex without thinking. *Idiot! Now you can't say you're sick.* Taking a deep breath, she flushed the toilet and turned on the faucet before returning to the living room.

"Here you go." Anthony handed her a long-stemmed wineglass.

"I better not since I'll be driving home." Michelle was mesmerized by the way his chest rose and fell underneath the shirt of his costume.

"If you wait several hours, the effects will wear off." Anthony took a sip from his glass, his eyes on her.

"Well I . . ." Michelle's voice trailed off. Absentmindedly, she drank deeply.

"Keep that up and you'll have to stay all night. Umm, have some more." Anthony refilled the glass.

"Oh, no," Michelle protested weakly even as she allowed him to pour the sparkling liquid.

"Oh, yes." Anthony pulled her to him. His mouth covered hers.

"I don't want to spill this on your sofa." Michelle drew away, her senses reeling from the waves of desire.

Without answering, Anthony put down his glass then took hers and set it on the coffee table. Using one finger, he lifted her chin slightly. He seemed to come toward her in slow motion. Michelle searched every inch of his face. The smooth brown skin. Dark cotton-soft hair framed his features. She closed her eyes and surrendered. The intensity of her response to his kiss surprised them both. Wrapping her arms around him firmly, she pressed her body to his. The chiffon shawl slid down allowing his hands to caress the smooth flesh exposed by the low-cut dress. Cupping one breast in his hand, Anthony traced kisses down her neck to the soft mounds. Michelle breathed a low moan as she arched her back to meet him. Anthony paused causing her to gasp with frustrated desire. But in moments he lifted her from the sofa to stand against him. Seeing no resistance in her eyes, feeling no attempt to extract herself from his attentions, Anthony took her hand and led her to the bedroom.

"Wait," Anthony whispered.

He went into the kitchen and returned with two large candles. Set on opposite ends of the large dresser, their flames were reflected in the wide mirror, giving the room a faint golden glow. With maddeningly slow motions, he unzipped her dress and eased it down over her hips. Pausing to kiss her, he then pushed it to the floor. Michelle stepped back to remove the strapless bra and pantyhose she wore. Never taking his eyes from her, Anthony rapidly yanked free of his costume.

Michelle sank down to the king-sized bed and Anthony lay beside her, gently stroking her thighs.

"Tell me what you want. Tell me." Anthony groaned as her hand sought to caress him into an even bigger erection.

"Here." Michelle guided his mouth to her breast. She cried out as his tongue touched her nipples ever so lightly.

Anthony shifted to get closer to the nightstand. Reaching into the drawer, he took out a condom. Tearing the foil packet, he removed the thin latex sheath. Michelle waited, anticipating his touch. Anthony pushed her back to nestle on the pillows. Burying his face in her hair, he tenderly entered her. For long, luscious minutes they matched slow movements. Teasing each other to heights of passion before pausing. But only for scant seconds. The sensation of their union compelled them to begin again, each time with more urgency.

"I love you," Anthony moaned. "God, I love you so much."

"Anthony," Michelle gasped, clutching his shoulders.

Lifting her slightly from the bed, he plunged ever deeper. Michelle felt an explosion of pleasure begin inside her at the probing of his hardness, then roll throughout her body, taking her breath away. Feeling his body shiver, she cried out, a cry of pleasure and abandon. Tired and spent, they lay together with arms entwined. Both remained silent and thoughtful for a long time.

"Are you sorry?" Anthony stared at her, a worried look shadowing his handsome features.

Michelle searched for regret and found none. "No, I'm not."

"Then talk to me." He rested his chin on her head.

"This scares me. It's so . . . intense." Michelle felt naked in more ways than one. Was the happiness worth the pain he could bring?

"I can't promise we'll never have an argument or be angry with each other. But I've cherished you for years, and I won't let anyone or anything keep us apart." Anthony gripped her tighter as if to prove his words.

"But your uncle is still who he is." Michelle drew back to look up at him.

"Yes, and though I love him, it doesn't mean I support

everything he does." Anthony caressed her cheek, his eyes soft with love. "I don't want to choose."

"I'm not asking you to." Michelle felt a surge of guilt at the thought of her investigative report. She struggled with her duty to the story and her desire not to hurt Anthony. "Just understand that I can't overlook some things," she said.

"Believe me, Chelle, I do." Anthony's voice was low and full of tenderness. They nestled back against the large fluffy pillows.

"What time is it?" Michelle murmured.

"Almost three."

"I should be getting home." Michelle made no move to leave the warmth of his bed.

"Might as well stay for breakfast."

"I can't drive home in broad daylight in that dress," Michelle said, her voice drowsy.

"Trust me, without it you'll attract a lot more attention." Anthony chuckled.

Michelle gave no reply because she was already asleep, her arms wrapped around his waist. Anthony pressed his lips to her forehead and dozed off to the sound of low music drifting in from the living room.

"Good morning, all." Michelle bustled in. "This cool weather is wonderful. I hope it holds up until Thanksgiving. Ahh, fresh coffee."

"Who's she?" Kate spoke in a stage whisper to Gracie.

"Someone doing a bad impersonation of Michelle Toussaint, who we all know is not a morning person." Gracie squinted at Michelle.

"What are you two chattering about? Why, Kate, you look stunning. That shade of green brings out your eyes." Michelle beamed at her.

"Thanks." Kate turned to Gracie. "Whoever she is, I vote

we keep her. I won't tell anybody if you won't. Bye, all."
She waved as she left.

"Guess I don't have to be Sherlock Holmes to deduce you
had a great weekend." Gracie sat forward eagerly.

"A perfect description." Michelle peered over her cup with
eyes that sparkled.

"That flush of joy means a man is responsible. And no
ordinary man. We are talking good old-fashion, bone-shaking
Doctor Feelgood."

"Well . . ." Michelle pursed her lips primly.

"You don't have to give me details. He left the evidence
all over you like fingerprints, darlin'. Just tell me who it is.
I won't tell a soul, cross my heart."

Michelle grinned at her. "Liar. Anyway, you met him."

"Yeah."

"He's kind, sensitive—"

"Yeah, yeah. Skip that and tell me who he is."

"Anthony Hilliard."

"Hello! Handsome and great in bed. What a combination."

"Gracie!" Michelle shushed her, looking around.

"Being handsome doesn't guarantee a man's got the right
stuff." Gracie shrugged.

"What makes you think we . . . you know." Michelle lowered her voice.

"Are you kidding? You've got so much afterglow you look
like a giant light bulb."

Michelle sighed and propped one hand under her chin. "I
know I'm wearing this goofy grin, but it won't go away. I
stood in the mirror for fifteen minutes trying."

"My oh my. Things certainly are racing along with you
two."

Earl walked up with a steaming mug of coffee. "What
things? Who are we talking about?"

"Girl talk. You wouldn't be interested. On my way to the
editing room. I'll be back in a few and we'll finish this discussion." Gracie left with a hand full of papers.

"Saw you at the Halloween dance. It was really nice."

"Why didn't you come over to say hello?" Michelle pointed to a chair for him to sit down.

"Y'all were on your way out by that time. I didn't know you were friends with Anthony Hilliard." Earl sat at the vacant desk.

"We've known each other for years."

"Pretty close then?" Earl stirred his coffee with a small plastic spoon still sticking up from his cup.

"You could say that. Why?"

"This story you're working on. It could hurt his uncle. Does he know about it?"

Her blissful mood vanished at the mention of Ike Batiste. "Of course not."

"I hear Jason is complaining long and hard that you aren't moving fast enough on it. If he finds out that you and Hilliard are involved, it could be trouble for your career," Earl said.

Michelle glowered at him. "Who do you think you are questioning my professional integrity?"

"No, I'm not."

"Yes, you are! Do you think I would compromise a story?"

"We've been colleagues long enough for you to know how I feel about you," Earl replied in a composed voice. "Calm down. I'm trying to tell you how Jason could use this to hurt you."

"Oh, come on, Earl."

"Stop and think. You and I both know he wouldn't hesitate to use this as a way to get you off the story, even question your credibility in general." Earl studied her for several seconds as what he was saying sank in.

Michelle breathed deeply. "Sorry. You're right. But I've thought about that. I started working on reports about problems with public housing long before Anthony and I started seeing each other again, for one thing. Plus, dozens of people know what Ike Batiste did to my family. No one would believe I'd go easy on him."

"Can you be objective though? Before you answer, think about the worst-case scenario. Batiste is in it up to his neck, you break the story, indictments are handed down. Could you go forward knowing it will hurt someone you care deeply about?"

"That would be tough, Earl. I'd be lying if I said otherwise. But knowing Anthony as I do, I honestly don't think he could support his uncle if it were proven he's harming people who can't defend themselves."

"Maybe not." Earl placed a hand on her shoulder. "Anyway, step carefully on this one."

Michelle mulled over their conversation after he left. Earl put her worst fears into words. Despite her confident speech to him, Michelle was unsure of herself. Earl had said nothing she had not said to herself dozens of times in the last weeks. It was the reason she held back from giving in to her passion for so long. The nagging voice in her head had been stilled only to have Earl wake it up again.

Gracie came back and plopped down in her chair. "Damn machine. More temperamental than a movie star. Now where were we?" She noticed Michelle's grave expression. "Say, the glow is gone. Don't tell me in the few minutes I was out of the room you two had your first fight?"

"No, I haven't talked to Anthony."

"Then what?"

"Anthony's uncle does business with the Housing Authority. He may be involved in some dubious transactions."

"So what? Listen, a reporter has to be cautious, sure . . . but we can't shape our whole lives around this job. Life isn't that simple. It's damn complicated in fact."

"Tell me about it," Michelle said.

"So do what you gotta do, champ. Go after the story. Nail whoever is dirty, and break it to your man gently an hour before the big story breaks. One hour, no more."

"What if he reacts badly?"

Gracie shook her head. "Honey, I didn't say it would be easy."

Michelle felt a cold, hard knot form in the pit of her stomach. "Just once I wish something could be."

Thomas sat brooding in front of the fireplace in his huge den. The big-screen television, sound turned down so that it was barely audible, played in the background. Thomas ignored the football game, staring instead into the flames. A tall glass of dark beer rested on his knee. When Annette came into the room, he did not speak or acknowledge her.

"How monotonous. Grown men crashing into each other for three and a half hours." She made a great show of changing the station in a bid for attention. Annette looked at him sideways. "You don't mind, do you?"

"No." Thomas still did not move.

"Good." Annette fiddled with the remote for several long minutes, glancing at him from time to time. "You've been home for all of two hours now. I mean waking hours, of course. Sleeping doesn't count. Are you well?"

"Yes."

"Just wondering. You seem not to be your usual vivacious self." Annette snickered into the tumbler she brought to her lips. She gulped a mouthful of its contents. "What gives?"

"I really don't want to get into it with you, Annette."

"Maybe I can help. Wow, I must be drinking too much to say that." She laughed as she held up the glass. "Come on, tell me." On less than steady legs, she crossed the room to sit beside him on the love seat.

"Dominic has a job."

"That's what you wanted, so what's the problem?" Annette drank again.

"With Batiste."

"Oh. Well, so what? You wouldn't give him a job or any

money. You told him to stand on his own. So he did what you told him to do."

"Typical."

"What does that mean?"

"Dominic goes to work for a crook like Batiste, a man who stabbed me in the back, out of spite. And you see nothing wrong with it."

"What happened was as much your fault as it was Ike's. You even said so at the time." Annette got up to refill her glass.

"Even knowing his reputation as a scam artist, I was gullible enough to think we could do business together." Thomas spoke in a voice raspy with anger. "Little did I know how badly he wanted to bring me down. You never said a word, did you?"

"This was years ago. Why keep raking it up?"

"Ike Batiste tried to ruin me because you left him to marry me. Well, he needn't have bothered. I got my punishment for it all right. You."

"I love you, too, sweetheart." Annette held up her drink in a mock toast.

"You and your friends must have had a good laugh over how you made a fool of me." Thomas stared at her hard, causing her to turn away.

"That isn't true. How many times do I have to say it? How many years before we put it behind us?" Annette slumped into a leather chair. "God, I'm so tired."

"Months of lying, sneaking to hotels. Then he dumps you like a piece of trash. Without missing a beat, you come home to play the loving young wife. I still remember that romantic weekend you pleaded for. We went to Houston and left the kids with your mother. Eight months later, Dominic is born."

"Stop it, Tommy." Annette covered her face.

"He patiently waited five years before he cleverly orchestrated my humiliation. Once again, I played the fool. Accepted a contract from him. He nearly succeeded in destroying the business my grandfather built from nothing, but he made sure I knew about your affair." Thomas stood over her, his voice steely with bitterness. "I'll never forget how he smiled when he told me the exact day you'd gone back to his bed."

"Please, stop it!" Annette jumped up to leave.

Thomas clenched her arm dragging her back. "But I stayed. I stayed because I couldn't bear the thought of leaving my children alone with you."

"They're gone now, so why are you still here?" Annette wiped her face with the back of her hand.

"Because I'll be damned if I see you get half of what I've got now. I worked too hard to get where I am." His eyes raked her with a contemptuous glare. "Like the song says, 'It's cheaper to keep her.' " He released his hold letting her fall back into the chair.

"You're crazy." Annette shrank into the cushions in a vain attempt to escape his cruel words.

Thomas stood over her. "Maybe so. But I don't intend to go anywhere. Somehow I'm going to find a way to knock some sense into Dominic before he's turns into a crook just like—" Thomas bit off the words.

Annette's defiance flared back when she saw his expression, a combination of pain and anger. "Just like who, Tommy? I dare you to say it," she hissed.

Thomas strode from the room.

"It isn't true. Why won't you believe me?" she screamed after him. "Thomas!"

Seven

"Screw the district attorney." Ike Batiste reared back in the expensive leather captain's chair behind his desk. Propping an ankle on one knee, he puffed on a cigar.

"I don't know, Ike. This time they say he's on to something. Word is out." James Bridges blinked in the cloud of smoke enveloping them.

"Ike's right, James. Connely has been sniffing around for years trying to get something on us," Buster Wilson said. His title of property manager did not begin to describe the varied tasks he was assigned. Having worked for Ike for twenty years, he handled those few delicate duties Ike trusted to no one else.

"But I hear he's been looking through invoices and work orders. Even records of rents collected over a four-year period." Bridges twisted his gold tie pin nervously.

"So what? He's done that before, too. Listen, there ain't no way he can find anything." Ike waved dismissively.

"You got Charlotte under control, right?" Buster cocked an eyebrow at Bridges.

"Sure. She knows what to do, but I still don't like it. We ought to do something about those ex-cons. Charlotte is even getting scared to say anything to them."

"I took care of that." Buster nodded.

"How?"

"Let's just say Buster had a little heart-to-heart with the

maintenance supervisor. He knows what to do with those men that can't get with the program." Ike smiled wickedly.

"He'll stop the drug dealing and strong-arm tactics, I hope." Bridges tugged at his collar.

"Bridges, be real. That stuff has been goin' on in the projects for years. Nah, Mason will keep it at an acceptable level so as not to unduly attract police attention. Long as it doesn't spill into the middle-class parts of town or make the news too regular, they would just as soon stay out of there." Buster brushed lint from his cashmere jacket.

"And you think the DA won't be able to come up with anything?" Bridges turned hopeful eyes to Ike.

"I'm tellin' you, man, relax. It's gonna end up like always: after a few months he'll be buried under a lot of facts that don't add up to anything." Ike sat forward. "Now what about this new contract? Charlotte tells me the feds are sending some money down to renovate old houses."

"Charlotte called you directly?" Bridges frowned slightly.

"We were talkin' about this other job I got for a friend of mine and she mentioned it. Now here's what I've been thinking. Those old houses I own downtown would be perfect. What with them developing down there, more and more of the young professionals are moving into those neighborhoods." Ike pulled out a map of downtown.

"But if you get that money, you're supposed to rent the renovated units to low-income, elderly, or disabled tenants," Bridges said.

"True, but the regs are so full of holes you can drive a truck through 'em. We can legally rent or sell those houses at premium prices." Ike looked up at him.

"I don't understand." Bridges stared at the map.

"The regs don't specifically say the elderly or disabled have to be low-income for one thing." Ike grinned.

"Yeah, and if the landlord can document that rentin' to a low-income family causes him a loss on the property over time, you can pay the money back at only nine percent interest." Buster shrugged.

"But listen to this. So many smart operators are taking advantage of the program that the feds don't have nearly enough staff to keep up with it all. So what happens? Nobody is checking to see if they're even following the regs. I got a pal in New Jersey who's rentin' houses for as much as $950 a month. No old people, no disabled people, damn sure no poor people." Ike grinned in admiration of his friend's cunning.

"Easy money." Buster ground out his cigarette.

"I don't know, Ike. Maybe we better not push our luck any more than we have to." Bridges shifted around in his seat.

"Settle down, James. Things are fine and they're gonna stay that way." Ike took his elbow and ushered him to the door. "You just go on back to your office and forget about Connely. Everything's gonna work out. Bye now." He beamed at a still frowning Bridges before closing the door.

Buster stood with his arms folded. "Ain't never seen James that uptight before. Think he's right? Maybe we should be worried about the DA."

"Nah, James just gettin' jumpy in his old age," Ike said.

"I dunno. Connely's investigators are askin' a lot of questions, but it's different this time. Sorta like they know what they're lookin' for, but they ain't gonna go directly to it. I can't put my finger on what it is though." Buster stuck a slice of gum in his mouth.

"They're fishin'. All we gotta do is keep our heads and don't do anything stupid. Besides, I got a little bit of insurance." Ike blew out smoke rings.

"What kinda insurance?"

"A certain young lady workin' in the DA's office is keeping me well informed. That's how I know what to tell Charlotte about her records."

"Damn, Ike. You better hope all them ladies don't ever get together to compare notes." Buster gave a short bark of laughter.

"Not hardly. Besides, my interest don't depend on either one of them. Remember what I've always said, Buster: don't get into anything with anybody that has less to lose than you, and always have a plan B." Ike tapped ashes from the end of his cigar into a large ceramic ashtray.

"Not another delay. I don't know how much longer I can stall my bosses, Greg." Michelle's finger tapped rapidly on the table.

"Can't you keep doing stories on people in the projects and houses? They've been real good." Greg stared at her apprehensively.

"That was okay for a while, but it's all about ratings. Scandal and criminal wrongdoing make for good ratings. Now what's the problem?" Michelle pushed back a section of her thick hair.

"For some reason Miss Kinchen has been real careful 'bout the records. She kept putting off letting anybody touch 'em but her. My friend says she was real tense for a couple of weeks, almost like she knew something was gonna happen. You didn't tell nobody what we were planning? With the work orders and invoices I mean," Greg whispered.

"Greg, please." Michelle gave him an admonishing look.

"Yeah, sorry. But something made Miss Kinchen nervous for a while. Anyway I'm supposed to call my friend at home now, so maybe we'll get good news. That's why I wanted to meet you later than usual. Be right back." Greg got a quarter from his shirt pocket and headed for the pay phone tucked in a corner of the restaurant.

Michelle sat sipping a small cup of coffee, staring out into the dark through the wide window. A steady stream of customers came in for take-out orders, leaving with bags of hamburgers and French fries. Michelle was not the least bit tempted. With Thanksgiving approaching, she fully intended to watch her diet now so she could indulge herself later. A

couple entered with their arms draped around each other's
waist. Michelle watched them scan the menu, faces close together as they decided what to order. Thoughts of the last few
weeks with Anthony filled her mind. She could almost feel
his arms pressing her body, smell the spicy odor of his skin.
Before, the sight of a loving couple would have caused her to
turn away, not wanting to acknowledge what she was missing.
Now she smiled in anticipation of seeing Anthony later.

Greg spoke into the phone quietly but gave her a thumbs-up
sign. He was nodding as he turned his back to her. Michelle's
bright, happy thoughts dimmed to foreboding. The information Greg's friend would give her might cool the blissful
warmth she and Anthony had worked so hard to restore.

Greg came back and sat down. "Tomorrow she's supposed
to start organizing all of the files, including work orders and
invoices. She says Miss Kinchen has been in a better mood
for the last couple of days. She asked my friend to work on
the files today. They'll be sending all of 'em over six months
old to be stored at the warehouse." Greg sat down.

"Oh." Michelle looked down.

"Hey, I thought you'd be glad. A few minutes ago you
were upset cause nothing was happening."

"No, I mean I am glad." Michelle smiled tentatively. "At
least now I can get Jason, the king of jerks, off my case."
Pulling on her large shoulder bag, she got up from the booth.

"I'll be in touch as soon as she tells me the first package
is ready." Greg waved good-bye as he drove away.

Later Michelle sat in the producer's office. Jason was behind Lockport's desk as though he wanted to make sure she
knew he was figuratively as well as literally closer to the
seat of power than she. Michelle made an effort not to make
a snide remark.

"Frankly, Mr. Lockport, I don't think we should waste any
more time on this. Obviously the DA hasn't come up with
anything. If they had, Connely would be moving forward
with a grand jury." Jason lifted a shoulder.

"The DA isn't stupid, Mr. Lockport. He's not going to blab about his investigation and give those folks a chance to destroy evidence or intimidate possible witnesses. Just because he isn't sending out press releases doesn't mean he has nothing." Michelle pointedly ignored Jason.

"Connely is a politician who loses no opportunity to show the public he's cracking down on crime. Believe me, he would have been talking by now." Jason propped a hand on the back of Lockport's chair.

"He's a smart man who knows that talking too soon or moving on a case with flimsy evidence means egg on his face. Not good for an elected official, especially with an election coming up in only six months." Michelle continued to look at Lockport.

"How much longer before you can look at those documents from your source?" Lockport's fingers formed a steeple in front of his face, partially hiding his expression.

"Two, three weeks at most." Michelle's lips twitched in an effort not to smile. He was hooked. But Lockport liked to think he made decisions based on his own intuition. It would not do to look self-satisfied now.

"And you feel confident about your source's ability to deliver?" Lockport lowered his hands. He regarded her with an iron gaze.

"Definitely." Michelle did not bat an eye.

"Go with it." Lockport nodded curtly then turned his attention to other matters.

Although Lockport began questioning him about a series on the police department, Jason's eyes were still on Michelle. Giving him a sassy wink, she left the room with a jaunty step. But out of his sight, her confidence sagged. There were long hours of hard work ahead without any guarantee she would be able to live up to her words. Michelle offered up a silent prayer that her source would not get frightened and fail to deliver.

For the next three days Michelle gathered information

about hazardous conditions in four of the largest low-rent housing projects. LaWanda, through her network of tenant groups, was able to provide her with more than a few good leads. Michelle had plotted out a grueling schedule by the end of the week.

Earl threw down his notebook in frustration. "Say, Michelle. You mind if the rest of us get video for our stories or is Bob under exclusive contract to you?"

"Don't whine, babe. It's so unattractive." Michelle continued to tap on her keyboard.

"Listen, ace reporter, some of us are working on important stories, too. My piece on riverboat casinos and river safety needs footage. How am I going to get it?"

Bob doubled up working the camera in the studio on some newscasts and going out with reporters with a minicam. He had the most experience of the three cameramen employed by the station. The least experienced and least liked, Robert C. Mansur, III, was working his way up to be their boss someday.

"Use Trenton—no, Gracie has him booked. I bet Junior is free." Michelle just managed to keep a straight face though she knew how he would react to her suggestion.

Earl threw up both hands. "Great. Throw me the crumbs. A wet-nosed kid that can't go two seconds without bragging that the owner is his grandfather, and he'll probably be our boss someday."

"He's not that bad. Just think of it as an opportunity to broaden his horizons. Introduce the lad to cultural diversity." Michelle chuckled.

"I'd like to introduce him to the guys at Boostie's Poolroom on a Friday night." Earl had a mean glint in his eye.

"Tsk, tsk. Be nice."

Earl craned his neck trying to read the text on her monitor. "Story heating up, huh?"

"Yep. Hey, get out of here." Michelle hit a button causing colorful tropical fish to appear on the screen. "Move along, sonny, and let grown folks get to work." She pushed him away.

"No problem. I have things to do. By the way, a friend of mine works at the New Orleans HUD office. But I guess you wouldn't be interested in anything I might contribute." Earl started to leave.

"Whoa! Hold up, home boy. You know I have the greatest respect for you." Michelle caught up with him, putting an arm around his shoulder. "In fact, let's sit down and figure out which day you can use Trenton or Bob. Right after we talk about your friend at HUD. Have a seat. Coffee?" She firmly turned him around and walked him back to her desk.

"Don't over do it, Toussaint." Laughing, Earl held up a restraining hand.

"So give it up." Michelle hitched her chair closer to his.

"Larry, my friend, goes around to the various federal public housing agencies monitoring compliance with regulations and laws. If he finds financial irregularities, he calls in the accountants and even lawyers. In some instances, he can get the Justice Department involved."

"You mean he's onto wrongdoing with our Housing Authority? The Justice Department is coming?" Michelle's eyes widened with excitement.

"Don't start writing your acceptance speech for the award ceremony yet. No, the Justice Department is not coming. But Larry has been concerned about Charlotte Kinchen for the last two years. Until now, he couldn't get a handle on what was up with her. Says she blamed the rundown conditions on the tenants. Ms. Kinchen swore they tore up the apartments as fast as she could repair them. He had no choice but to back off since she could show him work orders and invoices." Earl paused dramatically. "Until now."

"Why now?"

"None of the tenants had been willing to talk to him, a guy in a suit with a Midwestern accent. But I told him about your series and he's very interested."

"Did you tell him about the DA investigating, too?" Michelle stared ahead deep in thought.

"Yes."

"Will you give me your friend's phone number? Tell him I'll be calling him in the next day or so. I've got an idea." Michelle began to write in a notepad.

"What do you have in mind?" Earl searched in his wallet, finally pulling out a business card. He handed it to her. "Here. You can keep it. I have another one."

"Be interesting to see if he can remember which apartments he reviewed and compare it to the requests for repairs I get from my source."

"Kinchen could still say the tenants just tore it up afterward."

"Maybe . . ." Michelle said in a reflective tone. Suddenly a light seemed to pop on behind her eyes. "Gotta go." She grabbed her large bag and the notepad.

"See ya." Earl watched her retreating back. He reached down to her keyboard.

"Almost forgot to log out." Michelle spoke over his shoulder causing him to jump back from the computer.

"I was, uh, just trying to clear that for you."

"Sure you were, Mr. Snoop." Michelle saved the file under her password. Patting him indulgently on the head, she left.

"LaWanda, open up." Michelle knocked on the door.

"Hey, girl. What you doin' here so late? Get your butt in here. You crazy? I don't hardly look out my window this time of night." LaWanda pulled her inside. "It's after eight o'clock."

"Hello, sugarplums." Michelle smiled at the children as they spoke to her shyly.

"Go on now, it's time for y'all to be in bed." LaWanda shooed her oldest two into a back bedroom. After pouring them both a glass of cola, she sat down on the couch next to Michelle. "What's up?"

"I've got a source in the Authority giving me information.

And I may get a connection in the HUD office," Michelle said, keeping her voice low.

"So?"

"Turns out they've been keeping an eye on Charlotte Kinchen for a while now. They aren't at all satisfied with the way things are going."

"Well, they sure ain't done a whole lot about it." LaWanda snorted in disgust. "What makes you think they gone do somethin' now?"

"For one thing, they couldn't get the goods on them. Charlotte Kinchen has the paperwork to cover her butt. For another, the last time a HUD official came to investigate, none of the tenants complained to him." Michelle took a drink of her cola.

"What did he expect? Miz Kinchen took him to the Evergreen Street complex. They keep them up so anytime they get somebody important wantin' a tour, that's where they take 'em. Then they went to Weston Place. Them old people wasn't gonna complain with her standin' there lookin' down their throats. If they had, she'd have chucked 'em out on the sidewalk soon as he left town." LaWanda shook her head.

"Damn, LaWanda, why didn't y'all tell the man?"

"When we knew anything 'bout it, he was long gone. Baby, they don't advertise them visits. But you better believe if we had talked to him, he woulda got an earful."

"Well, that same man is a friend of a friend of mine." Michelle leaned toward her and placed a hand on LaWanda's arm.

"Get outta here!" LaWanda's mouth flew open.

"And I've got a plan to turn the heat up." Michelle dropped her voice even lower.

"Things are going pretty smooth right now." Charlotte Kinchen straightened the designer silk scarf draped across one shoulder. With her short-cropped black hair and meticulous makeup, she was the consummate successful working woman. Her teal skirt was short enough to reveal shapely legs yet long enough to be businesslike.

"You've chilled out lately. Glad to see it." Lonnie Mason lounged in the chair facing her desk.

"Things have been very hectic. But certain concerns have been taken care of." Charlotte shuffled papers on her desk.

"The DA took you off his list or something? You must have some good connections to make that happen."

Charlotte eyed him distastefully. "The DA has no evidence to prove any improprieties have occurred."

"You mean your sugar daddy gone take care of any evidence. Ain't that so, sweet thing?" Lonnie leered at her.

Charlotte tilted her chin higher. "I mean there is no evidence because there has been no wrongdoing."

"What about how you been jugglin' records around? If you ask me, I'd say you was gettin' set to shred 'em anytime you got a phone call." Lonnie watched her face closely.

"Records have not been 'juggled around' as you put it. And I didn't ask you. You just be head janitor, that's what you're being paid to do." Charlotte sniffed.

Lonnie grinned despite her jab. "Calm down, brown sugar. I'm on your side. I wanna help. All you gotta do is say the word." He sat on the desk and leaned down. With his face inches from hers, he ran his tongue over his lips. "What you need is a man, a real man."

"Is that right?" Charlotte's breath came in short gasps. "You, I suppose?"

"Don't be so quick to turn up your nose. I got a lot to give." Lonnie's hand rubbed her thigh, pushing the skirt up.

"An ex-con with nothing. You must be kidding." Charlotte's voice broke as she watched his hand in fascination. "You couldn't supply half of what I need." Despite her words, she did not move away or stop his hand from lifting her shirt.

"Money is no problem. As for lovin', I can damn sure do better than either one of those fools you been leadin' around by the nose." With a sly smile, he gave her inner thigh a sharp squeeze then pulled his hand away. He chuckled softly when he saw her shiver slightly. Casually, as if nothing had happened, he went back to sit across from her.

"I don't know what you're talking about." Charlotte closed her eyes for a few seconds and cleared her throat.

"I mean Bridges and Batiste. Don't tell me they know about each other 'cause you'd be lyin'."

"How dare you!"

"Hey, you gotta use what you got to get what you want. Something I totally understand, brown sugar. What I'm sayin', you don't need them. Look out the window."

"What?" Charlotte's arched eyebrows came together giving her a look of puzzled caution.

"Go look out the window." Examining his hand, Lonnie twisted a gold ring on his finger. "It's yours."

"Oh, my." The sight of a white Infiniti Q46 made Charlotte bite her lower lip.

Lonnie stood behind her. "It's the right color, ain't it?" He put his hands on her hips, pulling her back against his chest.

"Yes, but—"

"I've got the keys."

"Mine," Charlotte said. She already accepted the car as rightfully hers.

"See that's what a real man does for his woman. I heard you talkin' 'bout what kinda car you'd like to have, so I got it." Lonnie's hands moved over her hips to her buttocks.

"I can't let you do this. What would James say?" Charlotte leaned against him matching his gentle rocking motion.

"He ain't gone say nuthin'. Now that you got Batiste in your corner, you can dump the punk. Batiste got the real power you need. Course you figured that out by yourself, didn't ya, baby?"

"Umm." Charlotte gripped his thighs.

"We gone keep usin' him for a while until we have everything in the palm of our hands. He'll get a little of what he wants, we get all we want." Whispering in her ear, he yanked her away from the window. He raised her skirt with one hand and dangled the car keys temptingly with the other.

"You mean—"

"Yeah, baby. You and me gonna get it all." Lonnie shook the keys causing them to jingle.

A slow smile spread across Charlotte's face as she reached out to grasp the keys to her new car.

"Now remember, you gotta keep all these rent records in chronological order for me. Last assistant I had got 'em all messed up," Buster said.

"Okay." Dominic looked around at the shelves of folders.

"And on the third Monday of every month, I want you to do a property inspection and look for any damage." Buster waved a ledger book then opened it to the page to show him. "The ones I got marked, see?"

"I see." Dominic scanned the list of addresses with a check mark next to them in red ink.

"Them ain't no government units, they mine. If they don't keep it up, I throw 'em out."

"What about the ones not marked? How often do I inspect those?"

Buster shrugged. "About every three months, if we have time. Don't worry about them."

"But how do you know when they need repairs and stuff?"

"Look, them people don't know how to take care of nothin' nohow. I ain't wastin' time or money on 'em." Buster puffed on a large cigar.

"What do I do when a unit needs repairs?"

"Fill out one of these work order forms. Give it to me. Then if I tell you, send one of the guys out to take care of it. Understand?"

"Yeah, I got it." Dominic still stared at the list of houses and apartments, a frown on his face.

"What's wrong?"

"I noticed a lot of the public housing units needed some repairs when Johnny took me around in the last three days. Shouldn't I fill out work orders?"

"Hell, no. Listen, first thing you gotta learn is you don't rush to fix those places 'cause they tear it up by the time you get off the parking lot." Buster stood up to leave.

"But the damage just gets worse if you let it go." Dominic looked up at him.

"Son, I decide what gets fixed and when. Remember that. Learn the ropes before you start tryin' to be the boss." Buster gave him a slap on the back, but there was a definite edge to his voice. He looked up to see his secretary standing in the doorway. "What is it Deniecia?"

"You got a phone call on line two." Her jaws worked on a big wad of chewing gum. "It's Mr. Batiste."

"Here, get started on straightening these out. Just record 'em as completed and put 'em on my desk." Opening a folder, Buster pushed a stack of work orders in front of him.

Dominic began placing a check mark on a blank line indicating repairs done on housing units. He set aside each one in a second neat file. Buster went into his office and closed the door.

"Hey, Ike. What's goin, on. Yeah, he doin' okay. Nah, far as I can tell it don't bother him one bit that we business partners. His daddy told him, but he says he took the job and he's gonna keep it. Yeah, I bet his old man is pissed off." Buster cackled. "But the kid's gonna come in real handy. Uh-huh. You gonna do what? Damn, man! You always schemin'."

"Knock, knock." Marcus strolled in.

"What you doin' still here?" Lonnie gave him a stony stare. "It's after six o'clock." He checked the Rolex watch on his wrist.

"I noticed you were burning the midnight oil and thought you might need a little help."

"You thought wrong. Go home." Lonnie closed a file as Marcus came closer.

"I'm just trying to be helpful. Looks to me like you got your hands full." Marcus took a seat in the chair opposite him.

"Say, man, who asked you to sit down?" Lonnie's lip curled. Standing, he leaned forward, his massive fists planted on the desktop. "Get out."

"If you say so." Marcus lifted his hands as if surrendering. "Just thought you'd like to know a couple of competitors are giving three of your boys a cut to steer customers to them." He continued to sit completely relaxed in the chair. "You're losing a big chunk of profits."

"How you found all this out so fast? You only been workin' here a coupla weeks. You supposed to be one of the office boys."

"I didn't stay in the office. I notice things. One of them offered me a deal." Marcus crossed an ankle on his knee.

"So why didn't you take it?" Lonnie eyed him with suspicion. In his world, taking advantage of someone else for personal gain was the norm.

"That's pocket change. I want real money."

After several seconds of examining Marcus, Lonnie stood straight. "What you got in mind?"

"I think we can come to a reasonable agreement. One that will be profitable to us both," Marcus said. The corners of his mouth lifted slightly as Lonnie sat down again.

Eight

Michelle stood on the balcony and took a deep breath. Pulling the sash of her velour robe tighter, she gazed around at the vista spread before her. The morning had dawned crisp and clear with a cloudless sky. Rolling hills still thick with foliage surrounded the bed and breakfast. In the distance a lake sparkled with reflected sunlight. A plume of smoke rose from the chimney of one of the lovely old homes tucked away somewhere in the woods of West Feliciana Parish. The air was fragrant with the smell of burning oak. Lilting bird-song provided the perfect background music to such a lovely day.

"It's all yours, baby." Anthony came out of the bathroom wearing pajama pants only. His broad chest was covered with the same curly, dark hair on his head.

"In a minute. I'm enjoying the scenery."

Wrapping his arms around her from behind, he rested his chin on her shoulder to stare down the front of her robe. "Umm-hmm, what a view."

"I'm talking about the hills." Michelle gave him a playful slap.

"So am I." Anthony brushed her neck with his lips.

"Cut it out or we'll be late for breakfast." Michelle began to breathe faster as his hands roamed over her body.

"They serve breakfast until ten thirty. It's only a quarter to eight."

"Somebody might see us out here." Michelle let out a tiny gasp as one of his hands found the soft inside of her thighs.

"Then let's go back inside," Anthony whispered.

Anthony tugged her away from the balcony toward the large canopy bed. With one quick motion, he pushed the robe down on her shoulders in thick folds as he kissed the cleft between her breasts. Michelle sank to the bed pulling him with her. They teased each other, relishing the erotic sensation of touching without consummation until both quivered in a delirium of passion. In concert they moaned at the fiery contact of flesh on flesh. For what seemed an eternity they moved as one with lingering strokes. But these soon gave way to the frenzied motions of lovers lost in ecstasy. And then they shared the wonderful moments of merely holding each other, savoring a dreamy state of love made complete.

"Now what time is it?" Michelle snuggled against his chest with a sigh of satiation.

"Umm, who cares." Anthony made no move to look at his watch.

"I do. I've worked up a big appetite."

"So have I." Anthony slipped a hand beneath the covers to cup a full breast.

"For breakfast, you rascal," Michelle giggled.

"Oh, right. I guess we have to get out of bed sometime." Anthony gave a mock frown.

In a happy playful mood, they dressed in warm sweaters, jeans, and comfortable boots. After a hardy breakfast of grits and eggs, they ventured onto the walking paths that wound through the forest. The cool snap of weather in the first weeks of November had resulted in a wonderful pallet of colors. Strolling hand in hand, they admired the leaves of deep reds, gold, and light green swaying in the breeze. They spoke in hushed tones as if doing otherwise would be disrespectful to the peaceful setting. After more than two hours they returned to the inn and their room.

"Chelle, you keep outdoing yourself. This was a great idea."

Anthony hugged her tighter as they sat in front of the fire in the small sitting room of their suite. Pale fall sun rays slanted through the window. Their bags were packed, yet they dawdled not wanting to leave the magic of three glorious days alone.

"Thank you, sir. We aim to please."

Anthony looked around with a wistful look. "Now we have to get back to the real world."

"Unfortunately." Michelle took a deep breath before dragging herself from his arms to pack the last of her things.

The thirty-minute drive back to Baton Rouge was spent in cozy silence. Arriving at his apartment complex, Anthony maneuvered his car next to Michelle's. He put her bag in her trunk before they went upstairs.

"Too bad the weekend has to end." Michelle stretched out on the sofa, her head in his lap.

"Yeah, but we can plan more great times. And not just on the weekend." Anthony curled a thick tendril of her hair around one of his fingers.

"I'm going to be tied up for a while on this big assignment. That's why it was so important to me that we have this weekend. I really appreciate you making time for it." Michelle touched his cheek with her fingertips.

"Don't thank me. I was being very selfish when I said yes."

"Still, I know you have pretty big projects of your own." Michelle smiled up at him.

"Cedric is the perfect partner. Having him allows me time off. So what's the grand story you're working on?"

"Uh, it's on public housing." Michelle sat up, her relaxed mood vanished.

"Really? Say, I caught the end of your profile on that family trying to improve conditions at the project where they live. It was great."

"Yeah. I've got an idea, let's go out for Chinese."

"Sounds good. You know my uncle has done some work on a couple of the housing projects."

"I know." Michelle looked away. The last subject she wanted to discuss was Ike or public housing. Not today, not with Anthony.

"In fact, he's had a hand in making more than a few livable, though there's little profit in it for him."

"Humph, not hardly," Michelle muttered.

"What?"

"Let's not get into this, Anthony." Michelle tried to ignore the bile rising in her throat. To think Ike had the nerve to act as though he performed noble work for the poor! She started to stand but Anthony placed a hand on her shoulder.

Anthony's brows drew together. "You got a funny look on your face when I mentioned Uncle Ike doing work on those housing projects."

"The units could be in better shape." Michelle clenched her teeth suppressing the urge to say what she really thought.

"What's that supposed to mean?"

"Nothing." She wanted to close this discussion. "Let's go to that new restaurant on Chimes Street. House of Hong Kong." Michelle reached for her jacket.

"No, wait a minute. I want to know what you're implying." Anthony caught her arm.

"One of the big problems the tenants have is getting repairs done right or at all for that matter. From what I've seen, they have a right to be angry."

"My uncle didn't invent the problems with public housing projects, you know."

"And he's not doing much to make it any better, either." Seeing the stiff set of his jaw, Michelle regretted her words instantly.

"That's not fair. Uncle Ike has done a lot of good work. I've seen what he's done to a few of them." He stared at her hard.

"Okay, forget it." Michelle looked away. "Let's go."

"No, I want to hear these accusations being thrown around without proof."

"The problems are very real, Anthony. The tenants have legitimate complaints." Michelle turned to him.

"A lot of the damage is their fault. I've been to some of those apartments."

Michelle bristled. "So have I. Most of the tenants are people who just want to be treated with respect. The Housing Authority could do more to deal with the few troublemakers, but they won't. Any property needs constant maintenance to keep looking decent. There's a lot of normal wear and tear. But some of our esteemed Black entrepreneurs are taking advantage of poor people."

"Is that so?" Anthony's face became a rigid mask.

"They get contracts that could help our community. What do they do instead? Stuff their pockets at the expense of people who don't have the power to stop them." Michelle's voice had risen.

"You can't miss any opportunity to dump on my uncle. Talk about using poor people for personal gain. You just want revenge. You don't give a damn about the tenants." Anthony glared at her.

"I'm a reporter. It's my job to inform the public. Information empowers people so they can't be pushed around. That story came to me. I didn't even know your uncle was in any way involved," Michelle yelled at him.

"Bull! You did the same thing when you were on the radio. Oh, yes, I heard those reports you did for KSAL on construction industry ripoffs." Anthony stabbed an accusing finger at her.

"I can't help it if your uncle and his scumball friends keep crawling out from under every rock that gets turned over in this town." Michelle jerked on her jacket.

"I can't believe this. No matter how I try, just mentioning Uncle Ike gets you started all over again. You've got a real problem, sweetheart."

"You're right. My problem is I give you too much credit for having the sense to someday see him for what he truly is."

"So much for not trying to make me choose between you two. It's obvious you haven't grown up as much as you think."

"I don't need this." Michelle snatched her purse from the coffee table.

"Neither do I." Anthony leaped up from the sofa.

"You insisted on talking about Ike," Michelle said angrily.

"After you made it a point to let me know you had something to say about my uncle."

"I'm outta here. It's obvious this isn't going to work."

"At least that's one thing you've got right." Anthony shouted.

Michelle stormed out slamming the door behind her.

"You insulted the man's uncle and you're surprised he took offense?" Shantae cocked one eyebrow at Laree over Michelle's head.

"I saw that," Michelle snapped.

It was three days later and all three were at a popular soul food restaurant and bar near downtown. A stereo system tuned to the local R and B radio station blared as waiters maneuvered between tables with loaded platters. The smell of fried chicken, fried catfish, and meat loaf filled the dining room. It was separated from the bar by a thin sheet of painted plywood that cut the large room in half. Raucous laughter filtered through the clink of dishes. The bar was jumping. A man dressed in a gray wool jacket stared at them, trying to make eye contact. They had been studiously ignoring him and his two friends for the past half hour.

"Shantae is right, Chelle. You can't talk the man's kinfolk down and expect everything to be fine between you. You gotta learn to curb that mouth of yours," Laree said.

"What you're saying is I have to grin and pretend. Even when I know his uncle is up to the same old crooked tricks." Michelle lowered her voice.

"Who appointed you district attorney? If the man is up to no good, he'll eventually pay for it." Shantae wiped her mouth daintily with a paper napkin.

"The bottom line is we're poison for each other. Far as I'm concerned, it's good riddance to him and his crooked uncle." Michelle stuffed her mouth with corn bread.

"So you can live happily ever after without Anthony? Girl, pu-leeze." Laree shook her head.

"That's right. I've been doing it." Michelle swallowed only to load her mouth with cabbage.

"Yeah, sure. For the past six years you didn't find any man good enough. Don't even tell me about Dosu." Shantae held up a hand when Michelle began to protest. "You treat him more like a brother than anything else."

"Oh, no. We're about to have company." Laree grimaced watching the three men approach.

"You ladies doin' all right this evening?" The man in the gray jacket smiled. He made a show of adjusting his sleeves, revealing a gold watch and diamond ring.

"Okay," Shantae mumbled. She didn't look up from her plate.

"We'd like to pick up the check for you. Why don't you join us over in the lounge area. Such lovely ladies should be pampered and complimented." Gray jacket gave Laree an exaggerated wink.

"That's nice of you." Laree gave him a fleeting smile that faded as Michelle scowled at her.

"We have to be somewhere soon. We can't stay." Michelle spoke quickly.

"I'm Fred Dorsey. You can call me Freddy D., the D is for dynamite lover." He leaned close to Shantae. His friends hovered at his shoulder leering at them. "What do you say, glorious Nubian queen? Why don't I give you a call so we can get to know each other better."

"Sure, baby." Shantae scoured him with a contemptuous glance. "Just dial 1-800-GET-LOST."

His cocky grin evaporated. "Be like that. It's your loss." He and his pals sauntered back to the bar with wounded dignity.

"Men," Michelle snarled watching them. "See what I mean?"

"You can't compare Anthony to . . . that." Laree looked at the men with a sour expression. They were trying to pick up other ladies with no more success.

"For sure. And you know damn well you miss the man." Shantae shook a finger at Michelle.

"Why did you have to say anything about his uncle? You could have let it pass and not hurt Anthony's feelings," Laree said.

"It came out before I knew it. But it's still how I feel," Michelle grumbled.

"Because you couldn't keep quiet, you've both been miserable for the last three days." Shantae took a bite of fried catfish. "That's a cryin' shame."

"Yeah, I can see how upset you are." Michelle watched her take a long drink of cola.

Shantae ignored her dig. "Cedric says Anthony has been walking around with his chin on his chest. You were wrong on this one. Call the man and apologize."

"She's right, Chelle." Laree folded her arms.

"You her echo or something?" Michelle put down her fork. "I guess I did say more than I should have under the circumstances," she grudgingly admitted.

"Call him." Shantae stared at her and pointed to a pay phone at the same time.

"I don't have any change." Michelle halfheartedly peered into her purse.

"Here you go." Laree placed three quarters in Michelle's palm. "In case you lose one, you got two backups. Now go."

Michelle started to back out of calling, but her friends shook their heads slowly and pointed at the phone. She stood holding the receiver for several seconds before dialing.

Anthony eagerly accepted Michelle's invitation to her apartment when she called him. After an awkward fifteen minutes, they were in each other's arms.

"It was my fault. I don't like how your uncle operates but I shouldn't put him down to you." Michelle rested her head on Anthony's shoulder. "I didn't stick to our agreement."

"And I should know better than to get so defensive any time you criticize Uncle Ike." Anthony took a deep breath. "I know he's no angel."

"Anthony, he really hasn't kept up repairs the way he should. It's not something I'm inventing to get back at him." Michelle peered up at him. She was nervous at the effect her words would have on him.

"Look, report what you see, babe. Just don't be so quick to assume Uncle Ike has malicious intent. He cuts corners to make a buck, but he's not a crook."

"Maybe so," Michelle said in a weak voice. She felt torn.

There was no question of her duty to get the facts. Yet she wanted to protect Anthony from the pain of learning his uncle's true nature. Though communicating was her job, Michelle could not find the words to tell him she suspected Ike of much more than skimping on repairs.

"I'm just glad we got through this."

"So am I." Michelle rested her head against his broad chest. She fought to silence the troubling voice that told her worse would come.

"I want you back in my life to stay," Anthony said, his voice soft yet fervent.

"At least this time we talked it out," Michelle said.

"Yeah, and we cut the time lapse down from six years to four days." Anthony laughed softly. "But the best part of breaking up is making up." Lifting her face, he covered it with tiny kisses.

Michelle pulled away only to take his hand and lead him to her bedroom. Somehow she would hold onto him, Michelle swore to herself. She must find a way.

"Congratulations! Weekend co-anchor." Gracie hugged her. "I knew it could happen."

"It hasn't happened yet. I'm just filling in until they decide on Nancy's permanent replacement." Michelle wore a happy smile despite her words.

"You've got the inside track. Don't worry, it'll become permanent soon." Gracie placed a cup of coffee in front of her.

"It would be the best of all possible worlds. I'm not ready to give up reporting. This way I can do both." Michelle leaned back and took a sip of coffee.

"Still going after that Housing Authority story?"

"It's going to be good, Gracie." Michelle's eyes gleamed with the excitement. "The best work I've done yet. I've got invoices on repairs that were never done but paid for and great interviews with tenants. The big finish will be an exclusive interview with Earl's friend from HUD."

"When will you start?"

"Not until the first of next month at least."

"That won't give them a very Merry Christmas. What about Anthony?" Gracie peered at her over the rim of her coffee mug.

"He'll understand." Michelle felt little confidence in her words.

"Sure about that? You didn't speak to each other for years because of his uncle."

"Anthony loves his uncle, but he doesn't approve of how he operates. He told me so."

"Saying it is one thing. But watching you trash his uncle on the news for the whole city to see could put a serious strain on your relationship."

"What do you suggest I do? Back off? I can't do that, Gracie. Not even for Anthony." Michelle sighed.

"I'm not saying you should. Maybe you could give the story to someone else." Gracie looked down.

"Forget it! I've put in long hours on this story. I'm not handing it to anybody on a silver platter." Michelle put her mug down with a loud thud.

"I thought you'd say that." Gracie nodded at her and leaned forward. "Look, hon, I've lost friends and lovers when I refused to back off from stories. For a while I seriously considered giving up this career and selling real estate. But you know what? I found out that true friends stick by you no matter what. As for the lovers—well, let's just say I didn't lose much."

"But what if Hal could get hurt? What if your marriage was on the line?" Michelle looked at her closely.

"I don't know. I'd like to think I wouldn't compromise my principles or ethics and that Hal wouldn't ask me to. But I just don't know." She turned and began writing.

Michelle stared morosely at the computer monitor filled with words. This should be the best time of her life. Not only was she working on the story that could establish her as one of the best investigative reporters in this region, but she had a shot at landing her dream job. Once she had been so sure of her goal. For years thoughts of making Ike Batiste pay for what he had done to her family had consumed her. Michelle had watched as her father battled to restore his reputation and business while Ike Batiste flourished. Her parents grew further apart until the contempt and bitterness became a thick wall between them.

The reason journalism had attracted her was the possibility

of exposing men like Batiste. Though she worked briefly at a small public access station in Dallas, Michelle had every intention of finding her way back to Baton Rouge. And when she got a chance at a job, even at a radio station, she did not hesitate to come home. Until now Michelle had done only a couple of stories that were mere nuisances to Batiste. But in this report she had the means to tear him down. Revenge. She had always imagined how thrilling it would be. Now she felt as though the story was a grenade she held in her hand. The damage from the explosion could take her and Anthony down, too.

A word on the screen caught her eye. Hope. That's what Batiste, Charlotte Kinchen, and all those milking the system were denying LaWanda and her children. No matter what her original motives, backing away now would betray them. The image of little Relondo playing near a broken electrical outlet jarred her into action. Michelle began to edit the text of her first report.

Dominic climbed into the passenger seat of Buster's fancy black pickup truck. He sank into the plush upholstery and gazed around the large well-appointed cab in admiration.

"Like it? Yeah, top of the line." Buster paused before getting in to stamp dirt from his boots. "We gonna make a stop over to the Housing Authority. We do a little business with them, too. Fact, since you been doin' so good, I may just let you start handling it."

"I appreciate what you've done for me, Mr. Wilson."

"Call me Buster, son. Look here, for the past three weeks you been the best employee I had since I started this business. Keep this up and you gonna get yourself promoted." Buster clapped Dominic's knee.

"Thanks." Dominic beamed proudly. "What exactly do we do for the Housing Authority?"

"We got a contract to do some plumbing repairs for three

projects. You know I was a master plumber myself for years.
I got two crews, four men, that I use. Here we go."

Buster parked along a crowded downtown street and led
the way to a four-story brick building near the complex that
housed city government offices. He was greeted warmly by
several men dressed in city parish work uniforms as they
entered the large lobby of the building.

"Hey, T'aneka. How's it goin', sweet thing?" Buster
perched on the secretary's desk.

"Fine, Mr. Wilson." T'aneka did not return his smile.

"Now what I told you 'bout that Mr. Wilson stuff? You
call me Buster, baby." Dropping his voice he leaned over her
typewriter.

"Miz Kinchen stepped out for a minute." T'aneka pushed
her chair back from the desk.

"I'm gone look up old Lonnie then if he's here." Buster
stood.

"He just went back to his office." T'aneka began to type
a letter.

"Wait for me, Dominic. I'll be back in a minute." He
winked at the young woman before swaggering down the
hall.

"You work for him?" T'aneka jabbed a thumb in the direction Buster had gone.

"Almost a month now. How long have you worked here?"

"Well, I started when I was still in high school. One of
them programs to give kids summer jobs, you know. Then
when I graduated, Miz Conrad—she was here before Miz
Kinchen—offered me a permanent job. It's okay." T'aneka's
tone lacked enthusiasm.

"It's obvious you don't like it that much." Dominic sat in
the metal chair closest to her desk.

"What I'm sayin' is, it's a paycheck. See this?" T'aneka
held up a lottery ticket. "When I win, look out."

"That's a long shot," Dominic laughed.

"Hey now, I won fifty dollars one time." T'aneka smiled

at him, then lowered her eyes shyly. "You gone be comin' over here a lot, I guess."

"Buster is thinking about letting me handle this contract, yeah." Dominic sat in awkward silence for several minutes listening to the soft clicking of the keys. "Say, you wanna go out? I mean, if not, I understand." Dominic shrugged, looking down the hall as if seeing Buster.

"What?" T'aneka's eyes went wide with shock. "No way! He's old enough to be my daddy. Here." T'aneka gave him a pink business card with her name on it.

"You're a hairdresser? When do you find time?"

"On Friday nights and Saturdays. I plan to have my own business someday." T'aneka looked at him steadily. "Give me a call."

Dominic's eyes lit up. "I will."

Buster came back. "What's this, soon as my back is turned he gets next to my baby. Oh, well, that's the breaks. Besides I don't think she ready for the big leagues anyway." He gave Dominic a playful punch on the shoulder.

"Here comes Miz Kinchen," T'aneka said. She made a face behind his back when Buster turned to look.

"Hey, Charlotte. Got a minute to talk? I wanna introduce you to my new man here. Dominic Toussaint, this is Miss Kinchen. Dominic just may be handling this here contract. After some trainin' of course. He's a fast worker. He's already started gettin' friendly with the staff." Buster gave a coarse guffaw at Dominic's embarrassed expression.

"Nice to meet you. Come on in." Charlotte gave them a crisp nod and led them into her office.

"Talk to you later," Dominic whispered to T'aneka before closing the door to Charlotte's office.

T'aneka smiled for several moments before continuing to type.

Lonnie passed her on his way to the stairs. "I'm gonna be out making rounds for the rest of the afternoon. Beep me if Calvin calls."

"Okay." T'aneka watched him leave, then picked up her phone. "Joanne, catch the phone for me. I gotta go get something out of the file room. Thanks."

Because it was after two o'clock, the office was quiet. T'aneka went into the storeroom first instead of going to the file room. She pulled out a drawer in one of the old metal cabinets and stuffed papers from it into an expanding folder. Moments later, she came out again and shut the door quietly. Glancing around to make sure she had not been observed, she entered the file room. T'aneka fed papers through the automatic feeder of the photocopy machine.

Nine

Lizabeth eyed her only child affectionately as he closed his eyes. Anthony chewed the chocolate cake slowly. "Like it, huh?"

Anthony smacked loudly. "Ahh. Mama, nobody does it better."

"I've got some here for you to take home." Lizabeth pointed to a plate wrapped in aluminum foil.

"You're too good to me. Save some for Thanksgiving though. I want Michelle to taste this."

"No, I thought I'd make a pineapple upside-down cake." Lizabeth smoothed a tiny wrinkle in the tablecloth.

"Have mercy. You're going to knock her socks off with that one." Anthony's eyes were wide with delight.

"Well, it's not every day my new daughter-in-law comes to dinner."

"Now don't start. Michelle and I are taking things one step at a time." Anthony held up one hand.

"Judging by the way you're acting, this is serious business. You've made up for lost time obviously." Lizabeth's eyebrows went up.

"We're doing okay, yeah." Anthony blushed.

"More than okay—much time as you've been spending with her."

"We've been getting reacquainted so to speak. Working out a few differences."

"Your uncle Ike, you mean." Lizabeth nodded when he looked at her. "Oh, I remember how hurt you were when all that happened."

"Michelle still hasn't gotten over it, either. She's convinced Uncle Ike deliberately tried to ruin her father to save himself. I said some things, she said some things and bam! We didn't talk or see each other for almost seven years." Anthony rapped his fork against the saucer.

"You know how I feel about your uncle Ike, Anthony. He's been good to us and he's a kind man in his way. But he's like your father in a lot of ways." Lizabeth picked up the dishes and started for the kitchen.

"No way, Mama. Uncle Ike doesn't run out on family. They may be brothers, but Uncle Ike can be counted on when things get tough." Anthony spoke angrily as he followed her.

"Anthony, listen to me. I've known that family for over thirty years. They may not have the same daddy, but they been close all their lives. Neither one likes playing by the rules. The difference is Ike takes joy in beating the system by getting to know important people. Your daddy never wanted to be tied down. Sonny liked to come and go as he pleased, hated being on somebody else's schedule. Even his brother's." Lizabeth began washing plates in the kitchen sink.

"No, he couldn't bother to be tied down by a little thing like supporting his family. Or pay child support so you wouldn't have to work two jobs to keep us from being thrown out on the street. I don't understand how you can say Uncle Ike has anything in common with that man." Anthony still refused to call Sonny his father or say his name. "You sound almost like you're defending him."

"It's been so many years now, Anthony, that I'm not angry anymore. I was very bitter when you were young and I was struggling to keep us off welfare. But I learned to let go of it, son. Truth is, I knew Sonny wasn't the most responsible man around. That's part of what made me so crazy about him. How he could make me laugh." Lizabeth paused to gaze out of the kitchen window above the sink. It was as if she could see the handsome man standing in the backyard.

"Great sense of humor. Only the joke was on us." Anthony remembered the smiling face that took him to fun places when he was a small boy. But the memories were tainted by Sonny's abandonment of his family.

"All I'm trying to say is you have to learn to see people for who they really are, son. The whole person, good and bad." Lizabeth dried her hands on a red-and-white dishcloth.

"I know Uncle Ike has his faults. But he's not the devil, either." Anthony began drying the dishes and stacking them on the counter.

"You think Michelle can put aside how she feels about Ike? Can you make it with him between you?" Lizabeth put a hand on his arm.

"We are going to make it, Mama. Chelle is beginning to understand that Uncle Ike isn't so bad. In fact, we even talked about this a couple of times. I'm telling you when she gets to know him, things will be all right. Maybe we can even get this misunderstanding between him and Mr. Toussaint cleared up." Anthony began putting the dishes away.

"For both your sakes, I hope you're right, baby." Lizabeth patted him on the back.

"Dominic, even I won't defend you on this one. Why in the world would you take a job working for Ike Batiste!" Michelle folded her arms and glowered at him.

They were in the garage apartment their parents had fixed up for him. With two bedrooms, a bath, full kitchen, and large living room, it was spacious and well furnished.

"I don't work for him. I work for Buster Wilson. I've told you that fifty times already." Dominic placed a can of diet cola on a coaster in front of her. He plopped down into the chair next to the sofa and swung a leg over its arm.

"It's the same thing and you know it. Everyone knows Ike

really owns Quality Building Contractors. The man tried to destroy Daddy. Our family has never been the same since."

"Get over it, Chelle. Even Dad didn't make this big a deal about it." Dominic took a swig from his can of soft drink.

"Are you trying to tell me Daddy isn't angry that you're working for that crook? Oh, come on! I saw the look on his face when you dropped your little bombshell."

"He's not crazy about the idea, no. But after the first month, he said he was pleasantly surprised with the change in me."

"Quit lying."

"I go to work every day. I don't stay out late on work nights, and I've been paying my own bills." Dominic held up a forefinger. "Including the utility bill on my apartment for the first time."

"So what are you doing at this dream job that's made you into a new man?" Michelle wore an amazed expression.

Dominic sat up straight. "I manage Buster's rental property. See to repairs, handle complaints, and I've started collecting the rents."

"He's got some Section Eight Program houses—you know where the government pays him part of the rent. You manage those, too?" Michelle frowned slightly.

"Sure. Not many though." Dominic shrugged. "Most of the property is pretty nice, even those. They were a bit rundown, but I've been able to get them repaired for very little. Buster was impressed." His chest stuck out a little.

"He let you get them fixed up?" Michelle began to relax.

"Sure. He's giving me more and more responsibility."

"Maybe he's not as bad as Batiste, then. I sure hope not." Michelle bit her bottom lip.

"Huh?"

"I mean, maybe he just sticks to running his business and doesn't get involved in shady schemes." Michelle tensed again hoping Dominic would not press her.

"Will you stop it? It must be the reporter in you, always looking for the worst in people." Dominic grinned.

Relieved, Michelle grinned back. "Maybe so."

"I'm learning a lot, Chelle." Dominic propped his legs on the coffee table. "I actually enjoy going to work. I get to help tenants solve their problems. I helped this one lady get a rail for her porch steps. She said I was the best thing ever happened to Buster's tenants."

"That's fantastic, Dom. You know, I haven't seen you this at ease and happy for a long time. It's got to be more than the job." Michelle examined him as his grin spread. "That dopey smile on your face means a woman is in the picture somehow."

"Ahh, you know." With a shrug, Dominic brushed invisible lint from his pants.

"What are you being so shamefaced about? She's not married I hope."

"No, indeed."

"Then who is she? Let's see, you broke up with Chandra. Did you get back together with Kenice? No, she just got married. Pam?"

"None of them." Dominic pressed his lips together, enjoying her attempts to guess.

"Wipe that superior look off your face and tell me." Michelle reached over to slap his knee.

"Her name's T'aneka Johnson. I met her at work."

"Go, boy. How long have y'all been dating?"

"We've been out only a couple of times. She's so different from the other women I've run around with. T'aneka has had it tough, but she still has dreams. Those other ladies had Mama and Daddy giving them everything they wanted. They're interested in status symbols. The kind of car you drive, designer labels on clothes, stuff like that. Spoiled, you know?"

"Oh, really?" Michelle's eyes went wide in mock surprise.

"Yeah, well, you don't have to say it. That goes for me,

too. Just like the crowd I was running with, I didn't think about anybody much but myself. T'aneka has been giving money from her paycheck to her mama since she was fifteen to help with her younger brothers and sisters."

"She sounds like quite a young woman."

"She is. Makes me look at my life, you know? I mean Dad's been right, I was going nowhere and thinking I was all that." Dominic shook his head.

With a gasp, Michelle leaned toward him. "Dom, is that you in there?" She peered into his eyes.

"Cut it out." Dominic threw back his head in laughter.

"But do you understand you just said Daddy was right about something? You agreed with him, about you no less! Lord have mercy."

"Gotta admit, I was dizzy from shock for a few days myself."

"You told Daddy all this, I hope."

"Hey, we still have our differences. He's not the easiest person to talk to, either. So don't make too big a deal out of this."

"Yeah, but it's a start. At least you called a cease-fire for a while. This Thanksgiving may actually be nice." Michelle smiled at the prospect.

"Don't count on it." Dominic eyed her mischievously. "Now I'm going to get in your business. You and Anthony are back together, I hear."

"We've been seeing each other again," Michelle said.

"Uh-huh. Like spending a weekend together. Thought I didn't know about it, didn't you?"

"You've turned into a gossip, too?" Michelle chided him.

"Never mind about me. Does Dad know?"

"We haven't talked about it. I don't know. But he never had anything against Anthony." Michelle shook her head.

"Still, don't get your hopes up about a warm family holiday season." Dominic's face became grim. "No cease-fire has been called over there." He pointed toward their parents' home.

Michelle's smile faded. "He and Mama lead separate lives in that house. I swear, I hate to be around when they're in the same room."

"I wish I knew what's up with them." Dominic sighed.

"Whatever it is, it's gotten worse over the years." Michelle stared, remembering the happy family outings of her early childhood. Then she turned six, Dominic was born three months later and things changed. Smiles and hugs between their parents turned to sullen silences. Muffled, angry voices came from behind closed doors. "And Ike Batiste and his rotten trick seemed to set them at each other's throats even more."

"But that was a long time ago. Dad's back on his feet and doing better than ever in business. You'd think they would have worked it out by now." Dominic threw the empty soda cans in the large kitchen trash can.

"Maybe if Daddy wasn't so cold." Michelle spoke to him over her shoulder.

"All I know is, it's not getting any better."

"Every year it seems to get worse. I don't know what to do."

"Chelle, I don't think it has anything to do with us."

"Now you sound like Brian. This is getting spooky, man." Michelle grinned at him. "I'll be believing in alien abductions if you keep this up." She ducked a balled-up paper towel aimed at her head.

"Very funny." Dominic sat next to her. "Seriously, don't get your hopes up that things will change between them. Like I said don't expect—"

"A warm family holiday," Michelle finished for him. "I know." Michelle took a deep breath. "At this point, I'd be satisfied with room temperature."

* * *

"So tell me about Thanksgiving dinner with your sweetie." Shantae sat down and immediately stood again. "I'm so sick of finding these things all over the place. She picked up a toy superhero action figure from the love seat cushion and threw it across the room. It landed in a big toy box set against the wall.

They were in Shantae's small living room. Sounds of mortal combat came from the bedroom where her little boy played an electronic game with Laree. Laree gave a whoop of surprise. Then there was a childish snigger of triumph.

Laree came into the living room. "That kid is brutal. He whipped my butt without breaking a sweat. I used to change your diapers young man," she yelled over her shoulder.

"I told you so." Shantae waved at her to sit down. "Now hush. Michelle's going to give us the scoop on the holiday with her honey."

"There's not much to tell. His mother cooked a delicious dinner, we talked, and that was it." Michelle lifted a shoulder.

"And you got along with his uncle? Will wonders never cease," Laree said.

"His uncle wasn't there."

"He didn't invite y'all to come over?" Shantae chimed in.

"No. Anthony decided we should spend the Thanksgiving with his mom."

"Uh-huh." Shantae gave Laree a look.

"What?" Michelle glanced at them.

"Nothing." Shantae picked at her blouse.

"Nah, you've got something to say, so say it."

"You can't avoid the man forever. He's not just his uncle, he practically raised Anthony," Shantae blurted.

"You're putting off the inevitable," Laree added.

"Yeah, you might as well get used to seeing a lot of Uncle Ike and learning to deal with him," Shantae said.

"Listen, we're working through our differences. Remember we haven't been back together for very long. We need to take things a little slow. It's way too soon for us to be spending time with his uncle."

"That's a good point." Laree nodded.

"Typical, Laree. You switch sides at the speed of light." Shantae snorted in exasperation.

"Hey, I have the ability to see all sides of an issue," Laree said in a huffy voice.

"Anthony and I agreed to wait a while before we visit Ike." Michelle continued ignoring their bickering.

"But your feelings about the man haven't changed. Might as well get it over with." Shantae shook a finger at her.

"Anthony doesn't expect me to hug Ike to my bosom and start calling him uncle. I'll make occasional brief duty visits, be polite during said visits, and that will be that." Michelle lounged on the couch.

"*You* are going to bite your tongue around Ike Batiste? Videotape those visits for me, please, because that's the only way I'll believe it." Shantae tittered.

"She's right, Chelle. Steam comes out of your ears at the mention of his name," Laree said.

"Don't worry, honey. I've got it under control. When we go over there Christmas Eve . . ." Michelle smiled at the shocked expressions.

"Get outta here!" Shantae shouted.

"You're joking!" Laree's mouth hung open.

"His uncle called while we were at Anthony's the other night. He asked to speak to me and that's when he invited us over."

"You said yes?" Shantae sputtered.

"Sure did." Michelle examined her fingernails nonchalantly.

"I think that's wonderful, Chelle. Anthony must be happy about you two getting together." Laree gave her an approving pat on the shoulder.

"Wait a minute, we're not going to be kissin' and huggin' getting together. I'm doing this for Anthony."

"But I'm sure Anthony hopes this is the beginning of you and Ike being on good terms. And it just could be." Laree, ever the peacemaker, beamed at Michelle.

"Not hardly. Like I said, I'm only doing this to avoid tension. Anthony doesn't expect me to be friends with his uncle. He knows better. We have an understanding."

"Um-hum. I can't wait to hear about your Christmas." Shantae rubbed her hands in anticipation.

"I'm sure your visit is going to be very nice, Chelle," Laree chirped.

"It will be brief hopefully." Michelle sighed.

"Have mercy. Talk about walking into the lion's den." Shantae stared at Michelle in wonder.

"Don't worry I can take care of myself. Ike Batiste doesn't scare me." Michelle lifted her chin.

"I meant him, sugar," Shantae said with a devilish snicker.

"What do you think?" Michelle watched their faces for any sign.

Jason, Nathan, and Lockport still stared at the small screen even though the taped segment had ended. The technician continued to turn dials and adjust the elaborate equipment in the viewing room. No one spoke for several minutes, causing Michelle to squirm with nervous energy, yet she kept quiet. Nathan sat scratching the stubble on his chin. He tipped the swivel chair back. Jason stood with his arms folded, alternately glancing at Lockport then back at the monitor. Lockport seemed to be somewhere else mentally. His eyes were focused on some distant point on the ceiling.

"You've got the work orders you referred to, right?" Nathan began to rock in the chair.

"Yes. Copies actually." Michelle bit her lip.

"Wonder if that's considered public record?" Lockport asked no one in particular.

"I checked with legal. It is," Michelle said.

"Starting kind of slow, I think. I mean, so a few repairs haven't been done." Jason shrugged.

"But contractors are getting paid a great deal of money for those repairs." Michelle tried to keep the irritation from her voice.

"They could say the residents did the damage after the repairs were made," Nathan said.

"The tenants have been reporting the repairs in writing. I randomly chose six sites months ago. The work orders are kept in the maintenance supervisor's file until they're marked completed and the invoice has been paid. I have copies of the tenants' requests and the work orders showing the contractors were paid. And those are the sites I went back to videotape after my source gave me copies of the work orders." Michelle tapped the table with each point.

"Okay, fine. Some small-time operators are ripping off the system. I figure this is good for one, two segments tops. I thought you had evidence linking people at the top to all this," Jason said.

"I do. Batiste is very cozy with Charlotte Kinchen. His company is the main contractor. I'm betting those two are getting kickbacks." Michelle looked at Nathan and Lockport.

"Proof?" Nathan turned to her.

"No, just adding two and two."

"I still think it's not the big exposé she said it would be. Stick with the repairs and do two stories is my vote." Jason leaned toward Lockport.

She leaned toward him, too. "That's the tip of the iceberg, Mr. Lockport. It's all connected with widespread scams. If we drop it, one of our competitors will take the ball and run with it." Michelle could see Nathan's lip twitch with amusement at her use of Lockport's favorite sports analogy. "After working on this thing for months, I can tell you the big story is just beneath the surface. It won't take them long to hit pay dirt."

"Strong indications of other wrongdoing?" Lockport faced her.

"Drug dealing and extortion by Housing Authority employees. Every time I follow up on one thing, something else comes out." Michelle knew she had him interested.

"Tenants are willing to speak out?" Nathan said.

"Not on camera, they're too afraid. But they don't have to be. I found out a lot of the employees in the maintenance department are ex-cons. Most were convicted of drug offenses and assault. Some while employed with the Authority."

"What do you think?" Lockport turned to Nathan.

"Michelle has done a helluva job here, gentlemen. With what I'm hearing from my friend in the DA's office, she's on target."

"You should share any information about possible crimes with the district attorney. Certainly we have a duty to notify the proper authorities." Lockport looked back at the monitor.

"Of course, Mr. Lockport." Michelle nodded in agreement. She smiled at Jason.

"It would be a real coup for us if your report leads to action by the district attorney." Lockport was already seeing the ratings jump in his head. His eyes gleamed at the prospect.

Twenty minutes later Michelle worked furiously to organize her notes and thoughts. The newsroom was decorated with fake holly. Plastic garlands were strung around doors and along the top of the walls. A small Christmas tree stood in a corner with blinking lights of different colors. Its pine fragrance filled the room. Even amidst the hustle to get ready for the next news broadcast, there was a holiday mood in the air. Christmas music came from a portable cassette on top of a bookcase.

"You can't be stopped, tiger. I hear you got it goin' on." Earl grinned at Michelle.

"Yeah, truth and justice will triumph." Michelle grinned

back. Her desk was covered with papers. The laser printer was spitting out the results of her recent labor.

"Hey, Earl. Like that piece you did on Christmas savings clubs." Gracie sat with her feet up on a desk drawer pulled out.

" 'Tis the season. Next will be a piece on toys. Got some rug rats lined up to test which toys are favorites."

"Little Earl Junior included, I'm sure." Gracie laughed.

"Nah, these are four- to ten-year-olds. Little Earl's only nine months. Give him a spoon and a sauce pan to beat on, he's in heaven." Earl turned to Michelle. "So tell me, Toussaint."

"It's going to be hot." Michelle sifted through the chaos of her desk. Finally she found a tattered sheet of notepaper.

"When do you start?"

"After Christmas. Mr. Lockport and I decided we would start off the new year with a real bang. Between your Christmas pieces and Jennifer's fluff stuff, it just makes sense."

"My oh my. No wonder Jason is having such a hard time getting into the Christmas spirit. You know how jealous he is." Earl wagged a finger at her.

"What if the DA moves and Channel Eight or Six pounces on it?" Gracie chewed on a chocolate snowman.

"Nathan checked with his pal over there. They're going slow. Making sure they do everything right. A month at the most before they make any more big announcements. Meantime, all the other guys can do is a tired rehash of the same old same old." Michelle pulled her copy from the laser printer.

"Sounds reasonable." Earl began munching on candy from the wreath-shaped dish on Gracie's desk.

"And nobody else is working on anything to do with public housing, not even the newspapers. I've been keeping my ear to the ground." Michelle scanned the pages. With a red pencil, she made revisions.

"That gives you some breathing space, too. You can concentrate on a cozy Christmas with your new love." Gracie made kissing sounds.

"Grow up." Michelle continued to read.

"Don't forget my friend at HUD." Earl spoke around a mouthful of cinnamon reindeer.

"I've already got an interview lined up with him to get his reaction to my reports. That's going to be the fourth segment in my series." Michelle grimaced at a paragraph then went to work on it.

"Taught her everything she knows." Earl rose from the chair.

"In your dreams." Michelle gave a short laugh.

"Well, ladies, if I don't see you again, Merry Christmas. I'm off to another round of festive shopping with the frantic missus." Earl pulled on his overcoat. He waved good-bye.

"How close are you to Ike Batiste?" Gracie peered over her shoulder.

"We barely speak." Michelle sat back in her chair, rubbing her eyes.

"That's not what I mean and you know it." Gracie pointed her pencil at her.

"The repair scam has got his fingerprints all over it. Of course there are ways he can wiggle out of it. He's distant enough from the day-to-day business that he can let his foreman take the fall. But his connection to the drug dealing and extortion is even more shadowy. I don't know. Maybe he isn't part of the bad stuff." Michelle stared at her narrative. She shuffled the pages around as though they were pieces of a puzzle.

"He can't know everything his employees and associates do, right?" Gracie said.

"Right. Those ex-cons could be taking advantage of his generosity. Maybe Charlotte Kinchen and Bridges got greedy. Maybe they decided to build themselves a nest egg. Maybe they've all got Ike fooled."

"Maybe." Gracie returned her gaze for a time.

"Are you buying any of this?" Michelle said finally.

"Hell, no."

"Me neither." Michelle raked fingers through the thick tangle of her hair.

Marcus stood in the cold night air outside the apartment. The loud booming that came from his fist hitting the metal door reverberated through the dilapidated cinder block complex. He waited patiently, knowing he was being scrutinized through the camera mounted above his head.

"Whaddya want?" a gravelly voice called out.

"Lonnie sent me." Marcus lifted his head slightly to make sure they got a good look.

"Come on in." The door swung open. The owner of the voice was at least six five. His face a mask of watchful caution as he closed the door. Not once did he turn his back to Marcus. With a tilt of his massive head, he directed him down a hallway.

Voices came from a back room. Boisterous laughter broke out as Marcus came to what should have been a large bedroom. Instead there were two card tables. Seated around one on battered chairs, were four men playing poker. At the other sat three other men. One counted money, a pile of twenty- and fifty-dollar bills. The other two bundled them into stacks. In the few minutes Marcus stood taking in the scene, loud knocking came twice. Both times, one of the three left with small bags of white rocks. He returned after only seconds to add bills to the pile of money yet to be counted.

"I'm Marcus."

"What's up, man? I'm J.J., these my boys. Andre," J. J. said. He pointed to the man counting. Andre didn't stop or look up. "That's Barrone takin' care of business. That's Bobby, Derrick, Leo, and T-Bone." A chorus of grunts greeted Marcus. Five pairs of eyes sized him up rapidly.

"Got your business straight. Nice." Marcus nodded toward the money.

"We doin' all right. Lonnie say you the one put him on to them boys stealin' our money." J. J. took a drag on his cigarette.

"Yeah."

"You a smart businessman s'posed to tell us some big plan." J. J. squinted at him through smoke.

"You got something against making more money?" Marcus spread his hands wide. The room got quiet as they stared at each other.

"Nah, not a damn thing." J. J. pulled out an empty chair as an invitation for Marcus to sit down.

For the next hour they sat talking with their heads close together. As Marcus spoke, he gained the attention of the other six men. They mapped out a strategy to sell a higher volume of drugs by moving their operation to a house just off Government Street near downtown. Marcus told them how to attract more upper-middle-class customers.

"But the real money is in moving large quantities through Texas from Colombia, El Salvador, and other Latin American countries. We process the product. Then sell to big-time dealers with their own network of boys on the street. It won't be overnight. We've got to make connections with people I know. Once they see we got the serious cash to do business, no problem. We start small at first. Hook up with some dudes I know in Easy Town, on the Lakes, like that. Pretty soon we'll be making money."

"So how you know all this?" a female voice cut in. "I ain't never heard of you."

Marcus peered over his shoulder. A woman the color of caramel walked over to stand next to J. J. Her hair was in long braids to her waist, with small gold beads woven in near the scalp, circling her face. Each earlobe sparkled with four diamond studs. She wore high-heel black leather boots and a black leather miniskirt. Underneath a multicolored suede bomber jacket she wore a black cashmere turtleneck sweater. For all that, Marcus thought she did not look cheap or gaudy.

"Like I said, I know people."

"Why you ain't in business for yourself then? Why you need us?" She popped her gum loudly.

"Tia, this here is Marcus," J. J. said.

Marcus did not question her right to demand an explanation. Clearly she held a position of power with this group. "You've got manpower. I've got connections. By merging our respective assets, we can realize substantial profits."

"How substantial?" Tia's slight smile revealed a set of even pearly teeth between lips painted a dark copper color.

"Millions. There's no reason we can't make millions. As long as everybody understands we're moving to a new level."

"Talkin' big. Hope you can back it up." Tia gave him an appraising glance from head to toe.

"I can deliver the goods." Marcus regarded her curvy body encased in leather and suede.

"Come into my office." Tia led him down another hall to a room furnished very differently from the rest of the apartment.

An expensive sofa in a dark brown, green, and peach floral pattern was set against one wall. Chairs, some leather, were scattered around the spacious room. Opposite the sofa was a bar with red velvet trim and three matching bar stools. A compact disc played a thumping, slow rap melody as background music. On the heavy mahogany coffee table were spread various drug paraphernalia, including a pipe. A white powdery mound sat on a large rectangular mirror.

"This place is really big." Marcus glanced around him.

"Yeah, enough space for business and pleasure." Tia walked away from him with swaying hips. She turned slowly. "Drink, coke, or both?"

"Crown Royal if you got it."

"Sure." She waved a hand at the table. "That's top-quality product. Help yourself." Tia brought him a glass.

"Maybe later. Business first." Marcus gulped some of the amber liquid. He licked his lips with a tiny flick of his tongue.

"Tell me 'bout this master plan." Tia sat next to him and crossed her legs.

"Friend of mine got his own private plane. We can move some of the product like that. But we got to have different routes in case we lose a shipment. Some by truck. Eighteen-wheeler. Some by boat. If we get it all through, great—we make more money. If we lose one, we still make a profit. I've got some other ideas." Marcus stared at her legs, then let his gaze travel up her body to her face.

Tia lifted an eyebrow at him. "I see you do. How we gone finance all this?"

"You got enough in that room alone. At least to start." Marcus jerked a thumb in the direction of where J. J. and the others still carried on their transactions.

"You been thinkin' this up a long time. Gone mean a big change for my organization." Tia let her jacket fall open to reveal full breasts stretching tight against her sweater.

"I think you're ready," Marcus said huskily. He placed a hand on her waist.

"Is that what you think?"

"Sure you are. You wanna be a big player, too. Don't you, baby?" Marcus nibbled her earlobe. "I'm gonna take you there."

Wearing a sly smile, Tia guided his hands over her body. "Then let's do it."

Ten

"Ready?" Anthony gave her a nervous half smile. He fumbled with the car keys trying to get them out of the ignition.

"Sure." Michelle smiled back though she felt anything but sure.

The huge house was brightly lit. Tiny white lights surrounded the carved double doors, while green lights were strung around two large windows on either side of it. A large heavily decorated tree dominated one of the windows.

"This is one gorgeous home." Michelle was dazzled despite herself.

"One of Uncle Ike's friends is an architect. Uncle Ike built it for his first wife. It was her dream home."

"Marcus's mother?"

"No. Aunt Delores was his second wife."

"How many—" Michelle snapped her lips together quickly. Michelle knew of Ike's reputation with women. But she had sworn to avoid any subject that could lead to an argument.

"How many what?" Anthony tugged at his already straight shirt collar.

"Wonder how many lights it took to decorate so beautifully." Michelle was grateful that Anthony was too preoccupied to detect her response as improvised.

"I don't know." Anthony vigorously brushed his jacket

sleeve. Looking at her red jacket with black velveteen lapels, he began brushing them, too.

Michelle lightly slapped his hand. "Will you stop it. We're not paying a call on Queen Elizabeth. He's your uncle. I'm the one who's supposed to be jittery."

"Okay, okay." Anthony drew his hand back with a laugh. "You're right. I just want everything to go well."

"Don't give me that look. You want me to cross my heart and hope to die I won't say something offensive?" Michelle held up one palm.

"Of course not." Anthony turned to ring the doorbell then faced her again. "Would you?" He dodged another slap. "Whoa now! I'm joking, I'm joking."

Ike opened the door with a drink in his hand. "Hey, you two. Come on in."

"Merry Christmas." Anthony shook Ike's hand.

"Same to you. Well, young lady, don't you look beautiful this Christmas Eve. The lady in red." Ike bent forward as if expecting to kiss her.

"Happy holidays." Michelle moved her head away and stuck out a hand instead.

Ike wore a tolerant grin. "Come on in. Let me introduce you to these old buddies of mine. That old goat is Buster Wilson and his wife, Macie. This is James Bridges, and his lovely wife, Sheila. And that's my son, Marcus. And this is Caroline." He put an arm around the waist of the short busty woman who was obviously his date. "I'm expecting a few more people."

The next two hours were spent in small talk, eating, and drinking. Ike played the role of gracious host to the hilt. He made sure everyone's glasses stayed full. A wide range of foods were spread out on a large table buffet style. There was a large pot of seafood gumbo sitting on a burner in the large den, chilled jumbo shrimp, fried chicken, salads and desserts of all kinds. The voices of Otis Redding, Charles Brown, and Luther Vandross singing Christmas songs came from the speakers of his compact disc system. Michelle was surprised how at ease she felt after only a few minutes. It certainly was not what she had expected. These were interesting, even engaging, people. She had been fully prepared to spend the evening pretending not to be bored. Instead she found she was enjoying herself, with Caroline especially. With a down-to-earth sense of humor, she kept them all in stitches with stories of her family. It was clear Ike was genuinely fond of her.

"How long have you known Mr. Batiste?" The reporter in Michelle came out. She was intrigued by this intelligent, witty woman and wanted to gain insight as to what she could possibly see in Ike.

"For over twenty years. And yes, I know all about his other women." Caroline had a naughty glint in her eyes.

"I didn't mean— That is I was just wondering—"

"You were wondering if I'm an old standby or something. No. He is." Caroline winked at her over the rim of her wineglass.

"You go, girl." Michelle laughed out loud.

"Me and Ike go a long way back. We understand each other."

"What about all those wives?" Michelle's hand flew to cover her mouth. She tensed waiting for an explosion.

"Only four, sugar. He had plenty of time for me," Caroline said with a saucy lilt. They both laughed long and loud.

Michelle finally caught her breath. "You're something else, Caroline."

"Seriously though, Ike's first wife was the sweetest person you'd ever want to meet. She died of breast cancer. You met Ike's daughter? She looks just like her. Portia was the love of his life. If you don't believe it, look at this house." Caroline waved a hand around the room.

"I never thought of Ike Batiste as being in love." Michelle gazed at him across the room. He sat on a bar stool gesturing wildly as he told a tall tale.

"He's got faults, plenty of 'em. But he's got his good points, too." Caroline gave her a knowing look. "You must be crazy about Anthony."

"What?" Michelle blinked at the sudden twist the conversation took.

"You've got guts to come here and not cuss the rascal out after what happened between him and your daddy. That means you care a whole lot about Anthony."

"Well, yes." Michelle blushed under her scrutiny.

"Y'all make a nice couple. I care about Ike, too. But he got his ways. When I get my fill of his crap, I just ease on down the road. What I'm sayin' is, don't let him come between you." Caroline patted her hand.

"These women over here plottin' on us, Anthony." Ike strolled over to where they sat.

"When I got something for you, I'm gonna do it to your face, not behind your back," Caroline said.

"You can believe that." Macie Wilson barked a gruff laugh.

Sheila Bridges alone did not seem amused. In fact, she remained tight-lipped, defying all attempts to lighten her mood. She looked every bit the part of a proper society dame in a teal-blue tunic with tiny poinsettias in silver thread, black satin pants, and black satin pumps. "James, that's your third drink."

"Loosen up, Sheila. Me and Buster will give y'all a ride home if James gets too boozed up." Macie slapped James on the back so heartily he grabbed the arm of his chair to keep from toppling over.

"Thanks, Macie. But I'm just fine. Two of those glasses were only ginger ale, Sheila." Bridges spoke to his wife in a tight voice.

"That's a change." Sheila lifted her nose in the air.

"I haven't seen you in a while, Sheila. I saw James at the Black and White Ball, but I didn't see you." Macie sipped her beer.

"Macie, you want another drink?" Caroline made faces at her behind Sheila's back, gesturing furiously for Macie to be quiet.

"I ain't finished this one yet. That was a time, wasn't it?" Macie was having a good time and missed her signals.

"I wouldn't know. I was out of town that weekend. Tell me about the ball, James. The one you said you weren't interested in attending." Sheila stared at him with cold, angry eyes.

"Uh-oh. Think I will have that beer." Macie sprang from her seat between them, heading for the refrigerator behind the bar on the other side of the room.

"I changed my mind," Bridges muttered into his glass, his eyes down.

"Really. I have a fascinating party game. Let's guess who changed his mind and what his date wore to the ball." Sheila wore a smile devoid of humor.

"Things are getting a little tense," Michelle murmured to Caroline.

"Come on, pretty lady, you owe me a dance." Buster tugged Sheila onto the floor. He guided her around to the sound of Nat King Cole.

"Damn, that Buster knows how to respond in a pinch." Ike chuckled watching his friend charm the frosty Mrs. Bridges. "He'll flirt with her enough until she's gotten her revenge on James. At least that's what she'll think."

"Macie won't like that very much," Michelle said.

"Macie's a sensible woman. She knows exactly what Buster's doing, heading off trouble." Ike laughed as Buster dipped Sheila, causing her to smile in spite of herself.

Caroline left to greet a couple who were at the door. Michelle was dismayed to find herself standing alone with Ike. Anthony was deep in conversation with another man across the room.

"Been watching those stories on the projects. Very good.

Some of those people are really trying to pull themselves up. What you working on now?" Ike smiled at her.

"Mostly following the new school board members." Michelle thought his question was not so casual as his tone suggested.

"I thought maybe you were going to do some more on public housing. You know about the repairs. I contract for some of that work. So does Buster. Those people tear up as fast as you can fix stuff. If you supposed to tell the whole story then you oughta tell that, too."

"Yes, there are a few tenants causing problems for the rest." Michelle glanced around the room hoping to find a graceful way out. Anthony, still nodding at something his companion was saying, smiled at her obviously pleased to see she and Ike together.

Ike's expression relaxed into a genial grin. "But all in all, you did a fine job. Can't wait to see what you do next."

The smug sound of his voice scraped a nerve. Michelle smiled at him. "Thank you. I hope you find my future work as interesting."

Michelle left him abruptly to join Anthony. Laughing and talking, they moved from one group to the next. Anthony proudly introduced her to those of his acquaintances she did not know. Michelle caught Ike eyeing her curiously several times.

"Thank you for a very entertaining evening." Michelle was quite sincere. This was the closest she had been to Ike and the people of his world. She had much to think about.

"Thank you, darlin'. I'm glad you decided to come. Say, I give a New Year's Eve blowout to beat any party in town. We'll have it at the Century Club this year," Ike said proudly. "You be sure and bring her, Anthony."

The Century Club was a combination restaurant and private social club. Part of it was rented out for special occasions. Over two dozen prominent black business and professional men had founded it five years before. Ike took

Anthony's coat, allowing him free hands to help Michelle into hers.

"Hey, that would be nice. You'd love that, babe." Anthony took her hand after putting on his coat.

"Yes." Michelle fought the urge to sigh deeply. The thought of having to spend another evening resisting the temptation to wipe that arrogant smirk from Ike's face was unappealing to say the least.

Later, at Michelle's apartment, they listened to Christmas music. They sang "Please Come Home for Christmas" with gusto right along with Charles Brown and danced to Otis Redding's "Merry Christmas, Baby" until they were breathless. Turning the volume way down on the compact disc, the mood turned mellow.

"Thanks, babe. I know tonight wasn't easy for you," Anthony called out to her. Michelle stood stirring eggnog in a small saucepan on the stove.

"Actually I had a pretty good time." Michelle carried a tray with mugs of the hot, creamy liquid into her living room.

"You don't have to say that. I know Uncle Ike's friends can be a little hard to take. But they're nice when you get to know them."

"I love Caroline and Macie." Michelle giggled, remembering some of their sassy talk. "And except for that little scene Mrs. Bridges made, it was very nice."

"They can get a little earthy sometimes. Not like your usual crowd of society folks. Mrs. Bridges barely hides her contempt." Anthony sniffed the aroma that rose from his mug before taking a cautious sip.

"Mrs. Bridges certainly has no reason to look down on anybody. I've seen her at some of the balls. Trust me, those 'society folk' can be just as earthy."

"All the same, what you did tonight was greatly appreciated." Drawing her close, he kissed her deeply.

Michelle shivered deliciously at the sweet sensation of his

full lips on hers. She cupped his face with both hands, eager for more. With a simultaneous sigh, they parted.

"Merry Christmas, baby," Anthony sang in a melodious voice, his eyes shining. He turned off the lamp on the end table next to the sofa.

Sitting in front of her Christmas tree in the dark, they held each other and watched the lights blink on and off. Michelle lifted her face to his. The warm happiness glowing in his mahogany eyes worked its own special magic. Michelle forgot Ike and the rest of the world.

The Grand Oaks Hall was decked out in finery for the New Year's Eve Gala. The women of the Omega chapter of Alpha Kappa Alpha had seen to its professionally decorated splendor with an attention to detail that would put an army of interior designers to shame. The room swam in a metallic Technicolor splashing the formally dressed dancers with enchanted sparks of light. As if in a dream, they swayed beneath the large ball suspended from the ceiling.

Michelle clung to Anthony relishing the feel of his muscular arm draped around her waist. The bass rhythm pulsated up through the floor beneath their feet. Its power flowed into her, causing her body to move as if a part of it. Burying her face in his neck, Michelle breathed deep. She found the spice and heat of his skin intoxicating. Anthony let go of her hand and wrapped her in a tight embrace with both arms. Their bodies melded together deliciously.

"For the hundredth time, you look absolutely ravishing tonight." Anthony spoke in a throaty voice close to her ear.

"Thanks. And you can say it as many times as you like, sugar." Michelle smiled up at him.

"I thought you said these sorority dances were boring. This is great."

"Usually. Depends on who you're with, I guess." Michelle brushed her lips on his chin lightly.

Anthony kissed her forehead. His chest rose and fell rapidly as he moved his hips with hers to the beat of the music. The song ended, and they walked back to their seats unsteadily. Michelle tugged at the gold blouse, afraid any sign of disarrayed clothing would tempt her friends to make bawdy comments.

"Excuse me, ladies, there are some business associates I want to say hello to." Anthony was swallowed up in the crowd that gathered on the dance floor again to another song.

"Girlfriend, that gold blouse is something else. Sheer sleeves, low cut. And with that black miniskirt, too. Flaunt your stuff!" Laree had crossed the room from her table to visit.

"Well, look at you. Lady in red," Michelle said. She gestured at the dress cut deep in the back with a saucy bow at the waist.

Laree giggled. "Yeah, we both got it. Whoa, but looka here!"

"Hello, dears. Kiss, kiss." Shantae strolled up with one hand on Cedric's arm. She wore a strapless royal-blue gown. Cedric was handsome in his black tux.

"My oh my." Michelle gave a low whistle. "Don't you both just put us to shame."

"Don't hate us because we're beautiful." Shantae waved her fingers in the air regally.

"Y'all slum for a while. Sit with us." Laree got up to curtsy.

"Well, I suppose the mayor can wait a little longer." Shantae let out a cackle as Cedric pulled out a chair for her.

"What took y'all so long to get here?" Michelle munched on an hors d'oeuvre.

"We got sidetracked," Shantae said casually.

"Um-humph. I'll go get us some drinks." Blushing furiously, Cedric beat a hasty retreat.

"Shantae, you devil!" Laree winked at her.

"Why did you bother to come? Wait, don't even go there!"

Michelle held up a hand quickly seeing the mischievous grin on Shantae's face.

They screamed with laughter, teasing each other with bawdy puns and comments the way they had since high school. When their men joined them, they exchanged conversations loaded with double meanings. At Michelle's insistence, the two couples abandoned plans to sit separately. They all crowded around the tiny table, having a jolly time. Michelle was leading them in a chorus of "Heard it Through the Grapevine" when her smile faded. Keisha came toward them with hips swinging seductively. She turned heads with the form-fitting jade dress she wore.

"Hello, Anthony. My, but you look handsome as ever." Keisha batted eyelashes thick with mascara.

Anthony stood to greet her. "H-Hi," he stuttered.

Keisha put both hands on his face and kissed him full on the mouth. "Anthony, you promised to call me about that subject we discussed." She turned back to Anthony, clearly dismissing everyone else.

"What? Oh, you mean the building renovations for New Jerusalem Baptist Church. Yes, Rhonda will call you to set up a meeting with the building committee." Anthony spoke in a loud voice, putting emphasis on each word. He turned to place a hand on Michelle's shoulder. "Keisha, you remember Michelle. And these are our friends—"

"Yes, hello. We should meet before your plans are presented to the committee. Lunch on Friday?" Keisha placed a hand on his arm.

"Well—"

"Good. See you then." Keisha strutted off with a wave.

"Let's dance." D'Andre grabbed Laree, tugging her up from her seat.

"But, wait—" Laree tried to resist.

"Now, Laree." D'Andre pulled her away.

"Let's go." Cedric jerked a thumb in the direction of the dance floor.

"My feet hurt." Shantae ignored his hint. "Girl, who does she think she is?"

"That's your aunt over there, Shantae. Let's go say hello. Now come on." Cedric lifted her up, and with a hand firmly planted in the small of her back, guided her across the room.

"What was that about?" Michelle folded her arms and glared at Anthony.

"Like you heard, it's strictly business," Anthony said.

"Does she always start off her business conversations by sticking her tongue down a business associate's throat?" Michelle snapped.

"Keisha is the building committee coordinator for her church. It's a project I got the bid on months ago. Straight-up business, baby." Anthony held up his hand as if taking the oath.

"She's got taking care of business on her mind all right. Swinging her butt in your face. And you ate it up." Michelle jabbed a finger in the air near his nose.

"Stop being silly," Anthony said with a laugh he cut short when she scowled at him.

"Oh, I'm silly." Michelle spoke through clenched teeth.

"No, I said you're being silly." Anthony frowned at her in irritation. "I thought you were more mature than this."

"Childish and silly. Unlike Ms. Keisha, I suppose." Michelle turned away from him angrily.

"Hold up. Let's not go there. Take time to reason this through before you go off on me."

"You let her kiss you, then tell me I'm being silly for getting upset. She makes a date to have lunch with you. Hmm, have I left anything out?" Michelle fixed him with a withering stare.

"You're so lovely when you're irate." Anthony tried to joke her out of being angry. It backfired.

"Don't patronize me." Michelle stood up, pushing her chair back so hard it made a screeching noise.

"Chelle, come back here." Anthony tried calling out over

the rising clamor of the band starting a new song. He sighed in frustration at her retreating back.

"I'm going to the restroom if you don't mind!" Michelle yelled over her shoulder.

Michelle weaved through the tables set up around the dance floor. Her progress was slowed by friends and acquaintances she met along the way. Finally she reached the exit leading outside to a long dim hallway. The sounds of merriment became muted with the closing of the doors behind her. Michelle sat in a velveteen-covered chair near the large glass windows that made up the front of the building. The sounds of distant laughter and the strains of the band's lead singer wailing a love song made her feel lonely. Michelle winced as an instant replay of the scene played out in her head. She did indeed feel silly.

"I let that hussy play me. She's probably planting her rump next to Anthony while I'm out here," Michelle muttered.

Footsteps approached and she turned, hoping it was Anthony. Instead Marcus loomed over her.

"Hello, sweet thing. Got too stuffy in there for you, too?" He sat in the chair next to her.

"A little." Michelle grew uneasy with the way his eyes lingered on her legs. "How have you been?"

"Not bad. And you?" Marcus draped an arm around the back of her chair.

"Okay. Anthony is here." Michelle inched away from him.

"Really? Damn, you look tasty." Marcus smacked his lips crudely.

"Thanks." Michelle recoiled at the strong smell of alcohol on his breath. His eyes were glassy. She glanced around. For the first time she noticed how isolated they were from everyone.

"I mean it." Marcus began to rub her shoulder. "Wanna hook up sometime?"

"I don't think so. Excuse me." Michelle rose and walked away.

WE INVITE YOU TO JOIN THE ONLY BOOK CLUB THAT DELIVERS HEARTFELT ROMANCE FEATURING AFRICAN AMERICAN HEROES AND HEROINES IN STORIES THAT ARE RICH IN PASSION AND CULTURAL SPICE...

And Your First 3 Books Are FREE!

Arabesque is the newest contemporary romance line offered by Pinnacle Books. Arabesque has been so successful that our readers have asked us about direct home delivery. We responded to your requests. You can start receiving three bestselling Arabesque novels a month delivered right to your door. Subscribe now and you'll get:

- ⟡ 3 FREE Arabesque romances as our introductory gift—a value of almost $15! (pay only $1 to help cover postage & handling)
- ⟡ 3 BRAND-NEW Arabesque romances delivered to your doorstep each month thereafter (usually arriving before they're available in bookstores!)
- ⟡ 20% off each title—a savings of almost $3.00 each month
- ⟡ FREE home delivery
- ⟡ A FREE monthly newsletter, Zebra/Pinnacle Romance News that features author profiles, contests, special member benefits, book previews and more
- ⟡ No risks or obligations...in other words, you can cancel whenever you wish with no questions asked

So subscribe to Arabesque today and see why these books are winning awards and readers' hearts.

After you've enjoyed our FREE gift of 3 Arabesques, you'll begin to receive monthly shipments of the newest Arabesque titles. Each shipment will be yours to examine for 10 days. If you decide to keep the books, you'll pay the preferred subscriber's price of just $4.00 per title. That's $12 for all 3 books with FREE home delivery! And if you want us to stop sending books, just say the word...it's that simple.

See why reviewers are raving about ARABESQUE and order your FREE books today!

WE HAVE 3 FREE BOOKS FOR YOU!

FREE BOOK CERTIFICATE

Yes! Please send me 3 *Arabesque* Contemporary Romances without cost or obligation, billing me just $1 to help cover postage and handling. I understand that each month, I will be able to preview 3 brand-new *Arabesque* Contemporary Romances FREE for 10 days. Then, if I decide to keep them, I will pay the money-saving preferred subscriber's price of just $12.00 for all 3...that's a savings of almost $3 off the publisher's price with no additional charge for shipping and handling. I may return any shipment within 10 days and owe nothing, and I may cancel this subscription at any time. My 3 FREE books will be mine to keep in any case.

Name _____

Address _____ Apt. _____

City _____ State_____ Zip _____

Telephone ( ) _____

Signature _____ AR0696
(If under 18, parent or guardian must sign.)

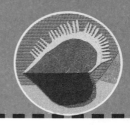

3 FREE
ARABESQUE
Contemporary
Romances
are reserved
for you!

(worth almost
$15.00)

see details
inside...

ZEBRA HOME SUBSCRIPTION SERVICE, INC.

120 BRIGHTON ROAD

P.O. BOX 5214

CLIFTON, NEW JERSEY 07015-5214

"Nah, now. Don't be like that." Marcus pushed up on unsteady legs to follow her. "Where you runnin' off to?"

Michelle tried to stay one step ahead of him. Walking faster, she realized they were moving farther away from the crowded banquet room. They were alone in the shadowy hallway. Marcus clutched her upper arm and pulled her around a corner. He held her against a wall with his face inches from hers.

"Wait a minute. Listen, we oughta slip on outta here. You and me." He fingered the sheer material of her sleeve.

"No, Anthony is looking for me. I have to go." Michelle attempted to leave, but he crushed his body to hers, pinning her back.

"You smell so good. Oh, baby, lemme—" Marcus began to nuzzle her neck.

"Stop it, Marcus. Stop!" Michelle shoved him with all her might, trying to escape.

"Come on, baby." Marcus breathed heavily in her ear as he made a grinding motion with his hips against hers. His hands began pulling her skirt up.

"No, get back!" Michelle punched the side of his face, causing his head to jerk back.

"I'm gonna give you a lesson you won't forget. When I get through, you'll be begging for more." He shoved her into a small room with brooms and mops. "Get in there. Think you too good for me? Let's see what Anthony been getting."

Michelle stumbled over a wash pail as he pushed her into the dark. She kept herself from falling only by grabbing a shelf. She spun around to face him.

"Listen, you got messed up and a little carried away. Let me out of here and we'll forget this ever happened." Michelle tried reasoning with him.

"I ain't too messed up to give you something good." Marcus fumbled with his pants zipper.

"I said no!" Michelle slapped him. Frantic to find a way out, she clawed her way back against a wall.

Suddenly a rush of air was followed by loud clattering. Mops and brooms fell across her as Marcus seemed to take flight before her eyes. Michelle swung out, thinking he had intensified his attack only to find nothing in front of her.

"You're dead, you bastard." Anthony shouted. He shook Marcus like a rag doll, then slammed him into the opposite wall.

"Git your hands off me, man. She was beggin' me to—"

The rest of his words ended sharply, his voice muffled by Anthony's fist pounding his face in two rapid blows. Marcus went down hard but immediately began to struggle back upright. He launched himself at Anthony by pressing both palms against the wall. Marcus swung wildly. Anthony's head snapped as several glancing blows fell on his head and chest.

Michelle staggered out of the closet. "Anthony, be careful!" she screamed. "Help! Somebody, please!"

The two men hammered away at each other oblivious to the growing crowd around them. Marcus snarled as he tore at Anthony's clothes. He kicked Anthony in the knee. Anthony bent double but not before delivering a crushing jab to his left jaw. Marcus responded with another jab to Anthony's stomach.

"Come on, man. Y'all gonna wind up in jail." Cedric broke through the crowd with D'Andre at his heels.

"Get back." D'Andre blocked Marcus from another attack on Anthony.

"It's over, man!" Cedric shouted. He grabbed both of Anthony's arms, pinning them to his sides. "Let's go. All right? Let's go."

Marcus struggled to free himself from several men holding him. "This ain't over! You hear me? This ain't over! Get offa me. Man, I'll kill you!"

A security guard appeared and cleared the area after making sure no one needed medical attention. The men with Marcus assured him he would be leaving with them.

"I'm not through with you . . . or her," Marcus said, his eyes full of malevolence.

"Maybe y'all should leave, too." The security guard turned to Anthony. He nodded in the opposite direction Marcus and his friends had taken. Checking to make sure Michelle had her purse, they headed for the exit.

Cedric slammed a fist into his palm on hearing what led up to the fight. "I wish I'd known, man. I woulda helped you kick his butt."

"How you feeling, honey?" Shantae and Laree hovered around Michelle protectively.

"I'm fine." Michelle tried to sound brave. The slight tremor in her voice betrayed her.

"You should press charges," Laree said.

"I just want to go home." Michelle sighed deeply.

They said their good-byes and Michelle insisted Anthony let her drive them back to his apartment. Once there, she placed a towel wrapped around ice cubes on his head.

"Are you hurt?" Michelle stared at him with eyes large with fright. "You should see a doctor, Anthony. He hit you really hard." She put her arm around him but drew back quickly when he flinched with pain.

"Just bruised up. Are you okay? Did I get there in time?" Anthony stared into her eyes.

"Right on time." Michelle kissed him tenderly.

"Messed up my plans for the evening. But maybe—ouch!" Anthony recoiled from an attempt to move toward her.

"I've got an idea." Michelle disappeared down the hall to his bathroom.

"What are you doing in there?" Anthony gingerly got up from the sofa.

"Come on in. I have a reward for my gallant rescuer."

The large sunken tub was filling up with steaming water. Michelle wore nothing but one of his pajama tops with the sleeves rolled up. She beckoned him forward and pointed to the tub. A wonderful scent came from the bubbling water.

She held up a bronze bottle. "I found this bath foam in the cabinet. Now let me handle everything."

Michelle helped him undress. Angry blue bruises had already appeared on his shoulders. Yet the sight of his muscled thighs, narrow waist, and broad shoulders stirred her. She helped him into the tub carefully. Michelle massaged him gently with long, slow strokes.

"There's room in here for two, you know." Anthony reached under the pajama top to brush his fingers along the underside of her breast.

"None of that now. Not after the way you got knocked around tonight," Michelle admonished him.

"Hmm, I'm feeling better by the minute." Anthony rose and pulled her to him.

"You're getting me soaking wet." Michelle made no attempt to pull away.

"Good," Anthony whispered.

"Now look what you've done." Michelle pointed to the suds sliding down the front of her top.

Anthony reached behind her for a large fluffy towel. With a grin, he unbuttoned the top and began wiping her skin with slow, deliberate motions. "How's that?"

"Thanks," she said in a tiny voice. Michelle's breathing accelerated as he propelled her from the tub and toward the bedroom. "Are you sure you feel up to this?"

"Uh-hmm." Anthony buried his face in her hair.

"Guess so." Before sinking to the bed, Michelle let the top fall around her feet.

They lay facing each other. Michelle continued her delicate massage of his arms, back, and chest. Anthony nuzzled her neck, letting his tongue trace a fiery path down to her breast.

"I can't stand the thought of him pawing you." Anthony hugged her to him.

"Nothing happened. I'm all right," Michelle whispered.

"If he comes near you again—" Anthony spoke with his lips pressed to her skin.

"Shh . . . let's concentrate on us. You seem to have bounced back. Dancing all night and then getting into a fight. You're something else. Anthony? Honey?"

Soft, steady breathing was the only reply. Michelle looked down to find Anthony sound asleep. Nestling his head between her breasts, he moaned softly. She felt a fierce stab of love gazing at the dark lashes against his brown skin. Michelle stroked his hair until she too dozed off.

"Say man, what the hell happened to you?" Lonnie laughed. He gulped the last drop from a bottle of malt liquor.

Loud, profane rap music blared away. A horde filled Lonnie's house. Writhing, bumping bodies jumped in time to the heavy bass beat. A couple groped each other in a darkened corner. A steady procession of couples left the dance floor to find greater privacy.

"Nuthin'. What ya got good?" Marcus glanced at the throng not interested in anyone or anything he saw.

"In there." Lonnie nodded toward the kitchen.

Marcus staggered into the room. He took a turn snorting a line of cocaine. Wiping his nose and sniffing, Marcus shook his head. Lonnie sat in a tattered chair, inhaling deeply from a cigarette. The party continued without them.

"I want to bring Anthony down," Marcus snarled. He slapped the table so hard it moved.

"Man, we in business. Business comes first. We got our first shipment comin' in day after tomorrow. We ain't got no time for this right now." Lonnie took another deep drag on his cigarette.

"I don't care, man. He's gonna pay. His bitch, too."

"I don't care what you do on your own time, but you better not mess up this deal. You hear me? You hear me?" Lonnie's voice was low but deadly. He and Marcus stared each other in the eye.

"I hear ya." Marcus looked away.

"Good. Maybe we can take care of them and boost business later on. That reporter been stickin' her nose in the projects too much lately."

"What you mean?" Marcus perked up.

"Them stories on the projects. She gettin' on my damn nerves. Yeah, we can talk about it later."

"I wanna get Anthony, too," Marcus said eagerly.

"Man, he's family. You oughta be nice to him. Cut him in on some business." Lonnie grinned at the look of shock on his face.

"What're you talkin' about, Lonnie?"

"Fact is, he's already in the business. He don't know it though. One of my boys works for him."

"So what? They work for you and work for him part-time." Marcus opened his second bottle of malt liquor.

"Hey, one of his trucks makin' some of my deliveries. His warehouse is storin' some of my inventory."

"You mean . . . ?" Marcus blinked at him.

Lonnie nodded. Suddenly his grin melted and his lips curled with hatred. "But he been stealin' from me. I been plannin' to deal with Troy. Maybe we can solve my problem and yours, too."

"Oh, yeah?" Marcus wore a smile that held no humor.

Lonnie watched Marcus steadily. "Take care of several problems at the same time. Got possibilities to turn this to our advantage."

"Lots of possibilities." Marcus laughed harshly along with Lonnie. "I got some ideas on that for sure."

Eleven

"Millions of tax dollars are spent each year on public housing programs in this country. But are we getting our money's worth? And are the residents who live in government-subsidized housing really being given a safe, clean place to live as well as an affordable one? In the first of a series of exclusive reports, Michelle Toussaint reveals some disturbing answers to those questions." Chad Brunson intoned in his best lead anchor voice.

Michelle came on the screen. "This is Kent Plaza, a two-hundred-unit public housing development in north Baton Rouge. This is home for the families, mostly single mothers, whose income qualifies them for these low-rent apartments. They are a lucky few of the thousands who are still in need of public housing. Yet many don't feel so lucky. Just take a look at why."

"Damn it, I knew that first story wasn't going to be the end of it." Charlotte Kinchen struck the arm of her chair.

"I don't see what you gettin' so worked up about." Ike barely paid attention as they watched the television in her office.

"First the DA starts asking questions, now this. Ike, this is serious." James Bridges twisted the end of his silk tie through his fingers.

"That's Anthony's girl, you know. Cute little thing, ain't

she." Ike, the picture of a man without worry, leaned back in the captain's chair with his feet on Charlotte's desk.

"I'd like to get my hands on her cute little neck," Charlotte spat.

LaWanda spoke directly into the camera as she led Michelle on a tour of the project. She pointed to broken toilets, holes in walls, and chunks of broken concrete. "This ain't unusual, either. If it gets fixed, it ain't done right."

"Who is that, Charlotte?" Ike lit up a cigar.

"Ringleader of a tenants group. All they do is complain. Just typical welfare mothers wanting something for nothing. She's going to get more than she bargained for, I promise you." Charlotte's top lip twisted with malice.

"You shoulda taken care of her long time ago if she's been causin' trouble. Evict her butt." Lonnie leaned against the wall near the window.

"Don't worry. Miss Sibley and her snotty-nose kids will be sitting on the sidewalk. She can find somewhere else to live since she dislikes the projects so much." Charlotte glowered as she watched LaWanda describe the formation of the tenants association.

"We want our kids to have a safe and decent place to live just like other people." LaWanda stood tall as she spoke. A small group of tenants murmured assent.

"We've spoken to officials with the Housing Authority, who say in effect the tenants cause more damage as fast as they fix things." Michelle aimed the microphone at LaWanda though a chorus of protest came from the group behind her.

"Most folks here take care of their apartments. But nothin' lasts forever." LaWanda's voice rose with indignation. "The Tenants Action League wanted to work with the Authority, to clean up, fix up, and clear out the folks causin' problems. They won't even talk to us."

"Thank you, Miss Sibley. Chad, in my next report we'll examine closely charges of favoritism in apartment assignments and awarding repair contracts. This is Michelle Toussaint for Channel Twelve."

"Don't you have friends at that station, Ike? We ought to do something about her." Charlotte turned down the volume as a noisy car dealer shouted about great deals.

"Michelle's all right. Besides, what she's reportin' ain't nothin' new." He rocked back in the chair.

"How can you be so calm about this? Didn't you hear her say there are going to be more reports? Charges of wrongdoing she said." Bridges got up and began pacing. "I've got a business to protect. With the DA sniffing around, this is the last thing we need."

"Man, you need to chill." Lonnie spoke with contempt. His eyes narrowed as he watched Charlotte hand Bridges a drink and pat his arm.

"James is right. First thing we should do is deal with those tenants." Charlotte let her hand rest on James's arm. Glancing aside, she smiled at Lonnie's reaction.

"Don't worry, I'll handle the tenants." Lonnie wore a menacing grin.

"What does that mean?" Bridges stopped pacing and sat down.

"Means I'll handle it. That's all you need to know," Lonnie snarled at him.

"Okay." Ike dismissed the subject, his attention already on the papers in front of him. "Now when we gone hear 'bout the new housing developments, Charlotte?"

"Anytime now. It's gone through all the approval stages."

"Good. I wanna be able to finish renovatin' by early May at least. They gonna be a gold mine." Ike sat back wearing a satisfied expression.

"Sure will, Ike. You won't have a problem getting a good price whether you rent or sell them." Charlotte lowered her voice and leaned close to him.

Lonnie stood abruptly. "I'm goin'. Charlotte, come on," he barked.

"James will bring me back to the office." Charlotte did not look at him.

Lonnie slapped a fist against his thigh as he stared at her for several seconds before stalking out. The door banged shut behind him. Ike glanced at Charlotte.

"Lonnie acts like he's your boss instead of the other way 'round." Ike wore a veiled expression.

"I can take care of him." Charlotte cleared her throat.

"He's an accident waiting to happen, Charlotte. Fire him." James gripped her hand.

"We need him. Besides, Lonnie isn't the type to go away quietly. It's under control, hon. Let's go." Charlotte pulled him to his feet with her.

"Goin' straight back to the office, I'm sure." Ike grinned at them.

"Of course." Charlotte looked at him with an expression of mild amusement.

"Such a dedicated public servant. Don't work too hard. You might hurt yourself." Ike let his gaze wander down the length of her body. His eyes held a warning.

She wore an imperious smile. "I never take on more than I can handle."

"I hope not, baby," Ike murmured as he watched them leave. "I sure hope not."

"Did you see your sister on TV last night?" T'aneka leaned against Dominic as they cuddled on his sofa.

"Yeah."

"What did you think about it?"

"I dunno." Dominic pulled back to look at her. "What do you think?"

"It was right on. Don't tell me you never noticed how nothin' seems to ever get fixed even though we've got all them work orders."

"With all those apartments and houses, there is bound to

be some places that get missed. Besides, I know certain repairs are being done," Dominic said.

"You're doin' what you supposed to, but you're probably the only one."

"Buster hasn't asked me to do anything wrong. He's been straight up with me." Dominic's voice had a defensive edge to it.

"Just keep your head up is all I'm sayin'."

"Hey, the man flirts with you and you got him doing all kinds of crimes." Dominic pinched her chin.

"It ain't just that, Dominic. Mr. Buster got some heavy friends, Lonnie for one. Don't let him lead you into nothin' shady."

"Buster is no angel, but he's a good man in his own way." Dominic moved farther from her.

T'aneka reached out to touch his hand tentatively. "Just be careful."

"You know something you're not telling me, T'aneka?" Dominic gazed at her steadily.

"No, uh-huh. It's just . . . with this stuff on the news and rumors 'bout Buster and Mr. Batiste. I was only worried you might get in trouble." T'aneka spoke in a rush. She did not meet his eyes.

"Then stop worrying. Ike Batiste has nothing to do with my job. And you know what they say, believe half of what you see and none of what you hear." Dominic smiled as he put his arms back around her.

Michelle glowed from the praise of her colleagues. Her next segment had taken up a good portion of the story meeting. For the next two days, her reports would be the centerpiece of the evening newscast.

"Fabulous work, Michelle." Gracie winked at her.

"Great reporting, Toussaint." Earl slapped her on the back.

"Okay, we've got our assignments. Let's move it," Jason

said with a sour expression. He gathered up loose papers rattling them loudly.

"My goodness, she hasn't won the Pulitzer prize yet." Jennifer snorted.

"Green is a lovely color on you, Jennifer, dear." Gracie flashed a grin at her.

"I'm not wearing gr—, very funny." Jennifer shot her a venomous look before leaving.

Weston Lockport startled them all when he walked in. Seldom did he attend these meeting. "Michelle, stay awhile. You too, Nathan."

Jason moved back into the room quickly. "Yes, Mr. Lockport." He wore a puzzled frown.

"The public housing series." Lockport looked from her to Nathan. "With allegations of drug dealing, possible fraud, it seems doing three short reports isn't enough."

"I agree." Michelle held her breath.

"What about two additional reports with more air time?"

"Have mercy!" Michelle yelled jumping up. She sat back down immediately. "I mean, the magnitude of what I've uncovered so far certainly warrants it."

"Good. Do the last three next week. Jason will give you any extra help you need." Lockport left the room not bothering to glance at his assistant.

"Way to go, Toussaint." Nathan winked before leaving.

Jason seemed unable to make his mouth work. He liked being in charge and letting everyone know he was in charge. Michelle in particular did not respond well to his posturing. Now he was made to seem her assistant. Noticing Michelle beaming at him and that Lockport was gone, he scurried after him.

Back at her desk, Michelle began outlining the contents of the two additional segments. She whistled a cheery tune as she organized her notes.

"So what's next?" Gracie chewed on a jelly donut.

"Follow up on the drug dealing. I've got an interview with

a confidential source. Then I'll interview Charlotte Kinchen to get her side in the last segment."

"And Uncle Ike?" Gracie's eyebrows arched.

"I, uh, haven't decided."

"I understand."

"What's that mean?" Michelle glanced up sharply.

"Well, not wanting to upset Anthony. You two are getting along good, and if you don't have to mention Uncle Ike specifically, why should you?"

"I haven't decided if it will add anything to the feature, Gracie. It has nothing to do with being afraid of how Anthony will react."

"If you say so." Gracie lifted a shoulder and started tapping out a story on her computer.

"I say so."

Michelle labored for another thirty minutes. Her sunny mood had evaporated as she sat confronted with the obvious. Not only did Ike have lucrative contracts, but so did most of his friends. And several of them subcontracted portions of the work to Ike. Michelle cursed softly at the paper trail leading to Anthony's uncle. There was no way around it. The connection between Ike, Bridges, and Charlotte Kinchen was pivotal to the story. With a sigh, she began putting the pieces together.

"How is everything?" Anthony gave her a tight smile.

"Fine." Michelle answered his smile with one of her own. They sat across from each other in a booth at the China Gardens restaurant. The dim lighting and small candle on the table combined to give the booth an air of private intimacy even though they were surrounded by diners in the small room.

"How are your folks doing?"

"They're fine. Your mother okay?"

"Fine."

The waitress took their orders and left. Michelle carefully unwrapped her silverware from the cloth napkin. She sipped the hot tea. Anthony glanced around the room.

"How is the new project coming?" Michelle broke the awkward silence.

"Pretty good actually. We're ahead of schedule. We could earn a substantial bonus for every day we finish before the deadline," Anthony said.

"Wow, that's some incentive." Michelle poured another cup of tea for herself.

"Sure is." Anthony stared down into his cup. He had not touched his tea.

"I wish the station gave me a bonus for beating a deadline. All we ever get is another assignment."

"Really?"

"Yeah." Michelle clamped her lips together. She cursed silently realizing her mistake in bringing up work at all, especially hers. The waitress setting out the platters of food brought a welcome interruption. But before she made an attempt at changing the subject, he spoke up.

"Your present assignment seems pretty deep. I don't expect you'll be working on anything else for a while." Anthony busied himself pouring soy sauce on his food.

"Oh, we work several stories at a time. I've got two others I'm working on right now. Mustard?"

"No, thanks. Seems like you've spent a great deal of time tracking down facts about the Housing Authority. Don't see how you found time for much else."

"Yeah, well. Say these egg rolls are great. Try one." Michelle held up the saucer.

"Not right now. So are you about finished with it?" Anthony wiped his mouth with the large red napkin.

"The egg roll?" Michelle mugged at him, wiggling an egg roll.

"The story, Michelle. I'm talking about the story." Anthony stared at her with an irritated expression.

She stopped smiling and inhaled deeply. "I've got two more segments to do."

"Is my uncle going to be mentioned?" Anthony stabbed at the food on his plate without taking one bite.

"Look, let's not—"

"You're planning to imply that he's done something illegal, aren't you?" Anthony put his fork down.

"I didn't go into this to make your uncle look bad, Anthony. That's just the way it turned out," Michelle blurted. "Listen, I'm sorry."

"You expect me to believe that?"

Michelle's temper flared. Maybe a healthy dose of the truth was what he needed. "Ike is making big money on these contracts, but he's not delivering the services."

"A few disgruntled tenants, some dilapidated apartments and presto, you get lots of air time. Revenge on my uncle and a career boost. A neat package." Anthony pushed the plate from him.

"Are you suggesting that I manufactured this story?" Michelle's mouth flew open.

"I'm suggesting there probably wouldn't be an investigative series if you hadn't found out Uncle Ike was involved."

"Wrong, the district attorney is investigating, too." Michelle lowered her voice.

"At your instigation, no doubt."

"With Ike's track record, they sure didn't need me to tell them anything." Michelle threw her napkin on the table.

"Uncle Ike is a shrewd businessman. Has it ever occurred to you that the DA might be targeting him because he's a successful African-American man?"

"Oh, come on, Anthony. Whenever Ike gets into hot water, it's usually well deserved." Michelle forgot her best intentions not to insult Ike. It galled her the way Anthony assumed she had twisted the facts. His loyalty to Ike was automatic, unlike his trust in her.

"Everything you've reported so far is speculation and innuendo. There is no proof to any of the accusations you've made." Anthony pointed a finger at her.

"Wrong! I've got invoices showing payment for work no' done. There's drug dealing going on, intimidation. Your uncle is in it up to his neck, Anthony. It's time you see him for who he really is." Michelle fought to keep from shouting.

"Why can't you give up this vendetta? Uncle Ike is no gangster. And I don't need you to tell me what kind of man he is. Uncle Ike is a good man." Anthony's voice trembled with fury.

"Ike doesn't care who he steps on. My father was just one in a long line of his victims. Eventually he's going to go down."

"And you plan to be the one to see he does, is that it? Whether it's right or not. So much for journalistic integrity."

"You have the nerve to question my character with Ike Batiste for your uncle? You find excuses for every despicable stunt he pulls. Just like before." Michelle grabbed her purse and coat.

"There are at least five other contractors, but his name is the only one you've mentioned in your reports. Why is that, Michelle?" Anthony stood to face her.

"Is that what you think?" Michelle said through clenched teeth. "That I want revenge bad enough to go to any lengths?"

Anthony lowered his voice and leaned across the table. "Just what do you expect me to think, Michelle? You're acting on rumors."

Michelle scrambled to get out of the booth. "This is pointless. You can't handle the truth about him."

"Sit down and be reasonable." Anthony grabbed her arm and tried to pull her back.

"Oh, I'm being very reasonable. Considering what you've accused me of, I should have crammed my napkin up your nose. Let go of me." Michelle jerked away from him.

"You don't have any more proof now than you had six

years ago when you claimed Uncle Ike deliberately tried to ruin your father."

Michelle raked him with a withering gaze. "And like six years ago you find it easier to excuse his behavior because you benefit from it."

"What are you talking about?"

"Back then Uncle Ike paid for your car, put you through school. These days . . . Well, good old Uncle Ike set you up in business and used his connections to get you some pretty juicy contracts." Michelle's mouth turned down at the corners in an expression of disgust. "You always said you wanted to be like him. Guess you've made it."

"Are you saying—" Anthony spluttered, so angry he could not finish.

"What I'm saying is good-bye!" Michelle shot back before heading for the door.

Anthony strode after her, fuming. "If that's what you believe then you only used me to get to my uncle. You played your part very well."

Michelle turned on him. "You and your uncle can go straight to hell, Anthony Hilliard." She got into her car and slammed the door.

"Mister, you forgot to pay. Mister—" The waitress stood in the doorway waving their bill.

"Damn!" Anthony stood watching the taillights of Michelle's car disappear. Finally he went back into the restaurant.

A chill of fear went down her spine as Michelle read the profanity spray painted on the outside wall of LaWanda's apartment. "Maybe you shouldn't do another interview. I can use shots of the apartments to tie up. I've gotten plenty from you already."

Michelle did a quick review of the material she had for this last segment. With the invoices and the video, her final report could still pack quite a punch without putting LaWanda in more jeopardy.

"I told you, let's do it." LaWanda wore a grim determined expression. "They ain't gonna push us around."

"I don't know. . . ." Michelle chewed her lower lip.

"Ready, Michelle," Bob said after talking into his headset.

"I've gotta do this, okay?" LaWanda took her hand.

Michelle gave her hand a quick squeeze then nodded for Bob to begin taping. "For the past few weeks, we have shown you some of the serious problems residents of public housing face. Ms. Sibley, you've heard Ms. Charlotte Kinchen's response to our report. What are your thoughts?"

LaWanda stared at the camera. "We've tried to keep our homes nice, but there's just so much we can do. Charlotte Kinchen don't have to live here. If she did, we wouldn't need to be on television."

"We understand that there have been attempts to intimidate you and other members of the tenants association," Michelle said.

"Yeah, but we won't stop. That's what they want. New Orleans is sending us some help, too."

"The regional Housing and Urban Development, I take it."

"Yeah, that's right. We called 'em, and they gonna help us pilot tenant management in this complex. We gone turn things around one project at a time."

The camera zoomed on a close-up of Michelle. "Sources tell Channel Twelve that District Attorney Hanson Connely has been conducting a probe of the East Baton Rouge Parish Housing Authority." Michelle stepped close to LaWanda so she could be back on camera with her. "And as you've heard, the Tenants Action League is determined to make a better life for themselves and their children. This is Michelle Toussaint reporting for Channel Twelve News."

"That's a wrap. Let's get out of here while it's still light," Bob whispered to Michelle as he passed her.

"LaWanda, please be careful. Maybe you could stay with friends for a few days. Some of these guys have got bad records. Especially Lonnie Mason."

"Don't worry. We got police patrolling more frequently, and a local security firm donated a patrol for the next two weeks." LaWanda smiled, her face full of hope. "For the first time, we feel like things are gonna get better 'round here."

"You've got guts, LaWanda. I know you can do it." Michelle hugged her.

"Humph, not so much guts as hardheaded." LaWanda laughed loudly.

"Let's pray you don't have any more problems." Michelle glanced around her with a frown. She knew with terrifying certainty that the gang would not give up so easily.

Back at the station, Michelle worked hard at being in a gay mood as Gracie, Kate, and Earl insisted on toasting her. They drank sparkling cider in a bottle that made it look like champagne. Before long, they were joined by a crowd of staffers more than willing to party. Yet amidst the lively chatter and jokes, Michelle's smile hid her true feelings. The story that everyone assumed she considered a triumph left a metallic taste in her mouth. Anthony's stinging accusations still echoed in her ears. Nagging doubts made her feel morose instead of triumphant. Doubts that left her wondering if she truly had a reason to rejoice. Had her personal feelings skewed her view of the facts so much that the story fell short of being balanced or credible?

"Mr. Lockport," Kate spluttered. Wide eyed, she seemed unable to say more.

"Carry on. Oh, thank you." Lockport accepted a glass with dignified good humor. "Congratulations on the series, Toussaint. Caused quite a stir in some circles."

"No kidding? Details, give us details." Gracie waved her hands to quiet the others.

"I hear James Bridges has complained to his friends with the mayor's office, who complained to members of the Red Stick Business Association, who complained to Gerald Mansur, II." Lockport sipped at the cider and dabbed his lips with a paper napkin. He paused for dramatic effect, seeming not to notice the expectant hush his words had caused. "The old man told them to go suck an egg, though not in those exact words."

Shouts of glee and applause broke out. The party resumed. Michelle felt nothing, no apprehension about the waves her story had caused nor relief at the expression of support from the powerful Mansur patriarch. At what should have been a high point in her career, all she could think of was the empty apartment she faced after the party. The story that would lead to greater success in her professional life was devastating for an important part of her personal life. Michelle looked around at the merry faces. *What was that old saying? Be careful going after what you want; you just might get it.*

"Try to restrain yourself, honey. With all this jumping for joy you'll hurt something." Gracie perched next to her on the end of her desk.

"Guess I'm just exhausted now that it's over." Michelle sighed.

"You and Anthony must have one good time planned for later, huh?"

"Not really." Michelle traced an invisible line on the tile floor with the toe of her boot.

"Just a quiet celebration. That's even better." Gracie hunched her with an elbow.

"Very quiet. He won't even be there. But who needs him, right? If he can't understand my work or wants to defend that slimy uncle of his, to hell with him."

"Right." Gracie nodded and pounded the desk with a fist. "It's not like you will miss the guy."

"Who needs him questioning my professional judgment, my motives? The man is inflexible and basically dishonest. He knows what Ike is and expects me to play that game. I'll be damned if that's so." Michelle threw the empty plastic cup into the trash can.

"Besides, you told him that there was evidence Ike wasn't on the up and up. He shouldn't blame you. It's not like he was blindsided, taken totally off guard about the seriousness of the allegations. Right?" Gracie clapped a hand on her shoulder.

"I told him about the series," Michelle blurted out in defense, noticing the penetrating look Gracie gave her.

"Exactly what did you say?"

"Really, Gracie. I couldn't risk telling him too much."

"But I thought you were going to sit down with him right before the first segment. Did you at least give him a sort of broad outline of what you'd be saying about Ike? You already had the evidence. Anything he told Ike at that point would not have made a difference."

"I told him I would be doing a few more stories on the housing thing. Or something to that effect."

"I see." Gracie continued to stare at her.

"What? I hope you're not going to tell me this is my fault. No way." Michelle's hair bounced as she shook her head vigorously.

"A bit more detail would have been better," Gracie said in a cautious tone.

"Hey, you were the one who said someone you loved would understand your attempts to do the right thing. Anthony isn't even looking at the content of my story, not thinking about how the tenants are suffering."

"You could be right. But you were the one who said how much Ike meant to him. How Ike filled a void for a young boy hurt at being abandoned by his father. Pretty heavy stuff."

"I gave him warnings, Gracie. This isn't the first time

Anthony has heard of Ike's antics. I won't become part of the fantasy that Ike is a lovable roughneck with a heart of gold."

"So what now?" Gracie put an arm around Michelle's shoulders.

"Life goes on, that's what. In fact, let's go out and have ourselves a blast. What do say? Hey, Earl, you want to?" Michelle yelled to him over the noise.

"I'm game." Earl lifted his cup to her.

"Me, too," Kate called out along with several others.

"Then let's kick it." Michelle grabbed her coat and headed for the door.

Three hours later the inevitable happened. Michelle sat at home alone. She scrolled through stations hoping to find a movie, sitcom, or some other mindless entertainment. Images flashed by as she watched each for a few seconds before moving on dissatisfied. A snatch of harmony caught her attention, causing her to pause at a music video. With a sinking fascination, she watched a couple embrace to the strains of a popular love song. The story of anguish when a promising love goes wrong tore at Michelle's heart. Tears streamed down her face as the male vocalist crooned: "Why," a mournful voice wailed, "Why did we have to say good-bye? If only I could see you again." The words could have been her own. Michelle hugged herself tightly, rocking slowly in time with the melancholy tune.

Long shadows stretched across the apartment complex. Voices calling children into supper bounced from the concrete block walls. Tired workers straggled in from low-paying jobs. One by one windows lit up as the tenants settled in for the night.

LaWanda stood at the stove stirring a large pot of black-eyed peas. Occasionally she checked on the corn bread baking in the tiny oven. The television blared away as her three children played on the floor in front of it. Her eldest seemed oblivious to the clamor as she concentrated on homework. The *tat-tat* did not immediately attract LaWanda's attention. But soon the high-pierced screams of her babies made her drop the large spoon. Turning, she prepared to settle yet another fight. Instead her screams blended with theirs at the sight of her youngest on his back, covered with blood. She stumbled across the room, falling on her knees beside Relondo. LaWanda cradled the child with one arm and punched the phone buttons with her free hand. Pounding on her door went unanswered as she shrieked her address at the 911 operator.

"The bullet went right through the little guy. Missed all his vital organs. Miracle." The tired resident rubbed his reddened eyes.

"But he's going to be okay?" Michelle wanted to shake him for not getting to the point.

"Yes. Might even go home in a few days." He wandered off at the call of his name from a nurse.

"Thank you, Lord." Michelle slumped into the hard plastic chair of the waiting room. Her whole body shook with relief.

"You oughta go on home, sugar. LaWanda's family is here." Candy, LaWanda's friend from the tenants group, sat next to her and patted her arm. "I'll tell her you were here."

"In a while maybe." Michelle pulled the fleece jacket closer around her. "I'd like to see them before I leave."

The glare of harsh fluorescent lights made the charity hospital lobby appear even more bleak than usual at four thirty in the morning. Michelle brushed her hair wondering for the first time how she must look. She glanced down to notice she was wearing one blue and one green sock, a result of having dressed at top speed. The ringing of the phone had shaken her from sleep at one o'clock. A male voice, one of the tenants active in the association with LaWanda, told her of the shooting. The drive to the hospital was a blur. As the tension drained away, her mind began to spin. What if she were to blame?

Earl walked in still speaking into his compact cellular phone. "Right. Got it. I'll fax it to you from home."

"Thanks for stepping in for me, Earl. Sorry I fell apart." Michelle got up to hug him.

"Don't apologize for being human," Earl said.

"Yeah, but I'm a professional. Instead of getting hysterical, I should have been getting the facts." Michelle wiped her eyes.

"The best advice I ever got was from my journalism professor at Howard. He said good reporters sometimes do get involved. Otherwise, you're like some cold-blooded scientist staring at specimens under a glass. Once you lose all ability to feel a story, it's time to start selling used cars."

"Maybe I should sell used cars or real estate or cosmetics." Michelle bit her lip.

"What do you mean?" Earl took a seat.

"I let ambition and hatred of Ike Batiste cloud my judgment. I was so hot to nail him, I couldn't see where to draw the line. I let LaWanda take a dangerous chance when she didn't have to," Michelle said, her voice quivered as she fought to keep from crying.

"Child, that ain't so. We knew better than you some of them men workin' for Miz Kinchen come straight outta jail," Candy broke in. She placed one arm around Michelle. "You helped get us the attention from the big folks in New Orleans so we could make some changes."

"LaWanda went as far as she did because of me, Candy. I kept pushing for more information."

"You did your job, Toussaint. You reported a story about people who wanted a way out of a bad situation." Earl spoke in a firm voice.

"Earl, I have to be honest with myself. Getting this story, especially exposing Ike Batiste, was important to me. Maybe so important that I went too far." Staring down at her hands, Michelle frowned as if in pain at the words she forced out.

"Don't beat yourself up like this, Michelle." Earl spoke softly.

"A little kid is lying in a hospital bed with a bullet hole in his chest. I can't help feeling I helped put him there." Michelle's voice broke. She covered her face with her hands.

"Listen to me, slugger." Earl pulled her to him. "You're not to blame. Nothing you said or did was enough to put a gun in some bastard's hand and make him point it at babies."

"He's right, sugar. Don't get all tore up now." Candy brushed her hair with soothing strokes.

"Let me drive you home, all right? Come on, you won't be any use to anybody in this state." Earl stood up and reached for her hand.

"But LaWanda—" Michelle wiped her eyes with a damp tissue.

"LaWanda got me and a lot of other folks here to help. Go on, baby. Get some rest." Candy took out several dry tissues and wiped Michelle's face with maternal tenderness. "Besides, we countin' on you to do some more stories and help the police find them no-good punks what done this." She squeezed Michelle's hand.

"Okay, but call me." Michelle wrote down her home and work phone number for Candy. After extracting promises from her and Earl that they would call her if anything changed, she let Earl lead her out of the hospital.

Seated in Earl's car, Michelle leaned her head back and closed her eyes. The tension and fear of the past few hours had held her in a viselike grip. Now released from that grip, she felt weak with exhaustion. Sensing her need for quiet, Earl said nothing during the ride home. Michelle stared out of the window but saw little of the passing scenery.

"You okay, kid?" Earl walked her to the door of her apartment. He lifted her chin to search her face.

"Yeah, okay." Michelle tried and failed to smile back at him.

"Get some sleep. And call me if you need anything. Anything at all. Okay?"

"Okay." Michelle blinked at him in the early morning sun. "You're a friend indeed, Earl Gaines."

Once inside she found herself too wound up to sleep. She went in for a quick revitalizing warm shower. Later, wrapped up in her favorite terry cloth robe, she wandered into the living room with a cup of herbal tea in hand. Two hours had passed, two hours of trying to untie the knot in her gut. Michelle settled in front of the television as the Channel Twelve morning show came on at seven. The smiling host turned serious as he reported the news. Film of Earl reporting from the hospital appeared. Once again she felt a chill of dread as she listened to the horrible details. Michelle could still hear LaWanda's hysterical sobbing.

Earl sat at the news desk next to the early morning news show hosts. "Doctors are calling little Relondo Sibley a miracle baby. The bullet passed through his tiny body, missing all vital organs. He's listed in stable condition and considered out of danger."

Michelle closed her eyes, sinking further into the sofa as if attempting to escape a frightening world. "Is he? Oh, God, is he out of danger?"

"Tell me, Uncle Ike. Repairs paid for that were never done, kickbacks, even drug dealing. Could any of it be true?" Anthony measured Ike's every movement and expression. *It can't be true.*

The wounding of Relondo finally spurred him to face Ike head on. He could no longer ignore the gnawing feeling that maybe there was a grain of truth to the accusations against Ike. Anthony despised himself for being suspicious. Yet

Michelle's scathing words still burned in his mind. Was he running from the truth?

"I was wonderin' when you was gone come and ask me outright. Been worryin' you, son?" Ike poured coffee into a large mug and sat back behind his desk.

"How much do you know about it?"

"Anthony, I cut corners sometimes to make a little cash. Hell, what businessman doesn't? But I ain't no crook. Soon as I got wind of what them tenants was sayin', I checked on it personally. Some of the work coulda been done better or faster, that's no lie. But them damn tenants been tearing up them projects as fast as we fix 'em. I'll take you with me if you don't believe it." Ike spread his hands wide.

"You don't have to do that, Uncle Ike. But are you sure some of this isn't happening without you knowing it?"

"Hey, no matter what your lady friend says, I ain't runnin' the Authority. I'm just another businessman with a contract. Do you think I'd go along with drug dealin' and such?" Ike's brows drew together in an expression of pained dismay. "I hope you know me better than that."

"Of course not," Anthony said. He felt a stab of unease at the unpleasant questions in his mind. "But—"

Ike put a hand on his shoulder. "I'm tellin' you, they just tryin' to make out I'm responsible for stuff that's been happenin' for years."

"A three-year-old was shot, Uncle Ike. In his own home." Anthony's voice held a plea for some answer that would make sense of such a thing.

"Son, it happens all the time in them projects. All you gotta do is look at the evenin' news or read the papers. When them drug dealers get to fightin' they don't care who gets hurt." Ike shook his head, a look of regret on his face.

"So this was just another drive-by shooting that takes an unintended victim, you think?" Anthony looked to him with hope.

"What else? Look, drugs and poor people been a problem

in these neighborhoods for years. Anthony, that's the way of the world. But Michelle didn't tell the whole story."

"I don't understand," Anthony said.

"Well, that interview with Charlotte was doctored up to make her look bad. Didn't talk about all we've done to help them people. Like that community recreation room we built in one of them apartments. Another thing, me and some of my buddies sponsored trips to the zoo for a group of kids. All she wanted was to spread dirt on us. After I saw what she did to Charlotte, no way I was gonna talk on camera."

"Really?" Anthony stared ahead, frowning.

"Damn straight. Listen, I know how you feel about the girl, but she's been out to get me for a long time. On one hand it's understandable, with her thinkin' I tried to ruin Tommy. But then again . . ." Ike lifted his shoulders.

"She is still pretty emotional about what a tough time her father had back then." Anthony glanced at Ike.

"Yeah, never mind, Tommy brought it on himself. He begged me to help get that contract. Then blamed me when he couldn't come through. Truth is, I lost a bundle on that deal myself. Even so, I tried to help him get a line of credit."

"You never told me that." Anthony looked up in surprise.

"I tried to help. But what thanks did I get? None. Michelle's got a problem with me. Right or wrong, I accept that. But what she's sayin' in those reports is only patched-together truth. She's out to get me, son. Always has been." Ike sat forward to stare at Anthony.

"Guess you're right, Uncle Ike." Anthony sighed deeply.

"Let's go over to Stella's café for some of that down home cookin' like we did back when you was workin' for me after school. Remember that? Not long after your daddy took off, we started goin'." Ike gazed out of the window with a solemn expression. He shook himself out of his reverie and beamed at Anthony. "Whenever things got tough, we headed over to Stella's Snack Shack for some of that good sweet potato pie." He gave Anthony an affectionate slap on the back.

"Sure, Uncle Ike. Whatever you say." Anthony smiled at him.

Though he kept up with Uncle Ike's steady stream of chatter, nodding and answering in the right places, Anthony's mind was far away. Across town to be exact. The deep pang of loss stayed with him. His mind argued that the end to their relationship was for the best. He tried to hold on to the image of an angry, vengeful Michelle slinging unfounded accusations to reassure himself. Yet his heart kept substituting her smiling face with those lovely brown eyes lit with desire. Anthony came to the bleak realization that learning to live without her would be much harder this time.

Twelve

Charlotte pulled the belt of her satin robe tight before sinking next to Lonnie on his sofa. She accepted the glass of her favorite expensive wine from him with a smile.

"Sure you know what you're doing?" Charlotte lay back against the cushions, purposely ignoring the way her robe fell open to reveal one breast.

"Damn right." Lonnie's eyes were glued to the exposed copper flesh. He licked his lips.

"Ike thinks you went too far with that shooting." Charlotte traced an invisible line down his shoulder to his arm with a long lacquered nail.

"Yeah, but ain't nobody lining up to be on TV now. Sure the police been pokin' around, but they got nothin'. And don't think them tenants ain't figured out the cops can't baby-sit them. Nah, once this here dies down, it's gonna be business as usual."

"How did you like my second television appearance? 'Naturally we deplore the senseless violence that is an unfortunate fact of life in public housing. We have planned a meeting with the tenants to address security issues.' " Arranging her face to show just the right mixture of dismay and outrage, Charlotte repeated the performance she had given when reporters showed up at her office. "I loved it. Ms. Toussaint couldn't do a thing." She chuckled.

"Like I said, business as usual. Come here, sweet brown

thing." Lonnie spoke in a husky voice. His hand stroked her thigh roughly.

Charlotte put her hand over his. "Ike says we ought to be careful for a while. Make some major repairs and ease off any other . . . activity."

"The old man's crazy if he thinks I'm losin' money." Lonnie clenched a fold of her skin. His lips twitched up with glee at the tiny gasp this caused.

"He all but came out and told me he knows about us."

"So?" Lonnie's hands grew still. His gaze flickered to her face.

"He doesn't care." Charlotte squirmed closer to him and began touching his face with the tip of her tongue. "But we'd better be careful James doesn't find out."

"You don't need that fool. Dump him." Lonnie grimaced.

"Not yet, sugar. James has political influence in Louisiana and D.C. I—, we still need him." Charlotte drew back and studied his face. "Don't tell me you're jealous?"

"You seem to enjoy runnin' off to nursemaid him," Lonnie snarled. His fingers dug into her flesh.

Charlotte stroked his hands until his fingers relaxed. "There's a big job appointment coming up soon to be a district administrator. I want it and he can get it for me. We will both make a lot of money if that happens. Loads of lovely cash."

"I'm making lots of cash now. Yours, baby, all yours," Lonnie groaned. He yanked her to him, forcing her to straddle his lap.

"Be patient and we can have it all. Now let me show you who I really enjoy taking care of." Charlotte slipped the robe down over her shoulders and smiled with satisfaction at the glazed, lustful expression he wore.

Anthony set a furious pace. He bid on two large projects, three smaller ones, and ordered Cedric to hire more men.

Anthony seemed to be everywhere at once, attending as many meetings as possible. He only went home to shower and fall into bed. Then he was up early the next morning to start all over again. Time alone to think was not something he wanted.

"I have those figures on the Carlston job. Came out pretty good." Anthony strode into Cedric's office.

"Hmm. Yeah." Cedric wiped his mouth with a paper napkin. His jaws worked as he tried to down a large chunk of his oyster po-boy.

"Look here, Talley is willing to work with us on the materials. I figure we'll come in well below Fredricks and the other bidders."

"Sounds fine." Cedric choked on a piece of food. He downed some of the large cola in an effort to stop coughing.

"Some of the new crew could get started marking off the layout for the slab first." Anthony pulled up a chair, ignoring Cedric's distress and lunch.

"Since we don't have the job yet, you think maybe I could finish my lunch?" Cedric swiped his soft drink cup from Anthony, who was moving to toss it into the garbage.

"Oh, you're eating." Anthony frowned with mild annoyance.

"Yeah, funny thing is I been doing it every day for, oh, twenty-six years now." Cedric sat back to study his friend. "What's up with you, man? You're rushing around like you plan to prove Rome can be built in a day. Take it easy. For everybody else's sake at least."

"You sound as though you don't want the business."

"Sure I do, but what happened to pacing ourselves. What's the big hurry all of a sudden?"

"These days staying one step ahead of the competition is what means the difference between just doing okay and being a big player. And I didn't start my own company to do okay." Anthony continued to scrutinize the plans.

Cedric tried to take the plans from him, but Anthony pushed his hands away. "Have you had lunch?"

"Not hungry."

"Did you have breakfast?"

"Coffee and a donut."

"Half a donut." Cedric began folding up the plans.

"Hey, cut it out." Anthony tried to spread them out again.

"You're going to have a sandwich." Cedric jerked the plans quickly from the desk.

"I'm not hungry, I don't have a sandwich, and I'd rather be working anyway. Now give me—" Anthony glared at him.

As if on cue, Rhonda came in and set a bag on the desk in front of him. "Here you go, Anthony. A catfish po-boy, strawberry shake, and a small order of curly-cues. Your favorites."

"Rhonda, I didn't order this." Anthony folded his arms.

"We did. You need something in your stomach. Now eat." Rhonda marched out. She stuck her head back in the door to wag a finger at him. "Every bit."

"Take the easy way out—do what she says or you'll get no peace for a week." Cedric placed the plans on his bookshelf.

"This is crazy. I have a zillion details needing my attention. And you two are treating me like a child." Anthony tore open the wrapper of the sandwich as he grumbled.

"When are you planning to call Michelle?" Cedric propped his elbows on the papers. The clutter of his desk was in sharp contrast to his partner's.

"I don't know what you're talking about." Anthony stabbed the straw into the cup as though it were a spear.

"This drive to succeed has more to do with trying to keep busy so you won't miss her."

"Ridiculous. And I'm not going to call Michelle, okay?"

"She reported the facts." Cedric fiddled with the cup of soft drink, not looking at Anthony.

Anthony glanced up with eyes flashing fury. "Michelle slanted that story because of what she thinks Uncle Ike did to her father. And she left out information that would have presented a more balanced view."

"I suppose Ike told you that."

"That's right." Anthony's jaw muscles tightened. "So?"

"What did you expect him to say? Anthony, Michelle wouldn't lie and you know it. Maybe Ike isn't telling you everything." Cedric still did not look at Anthony.

"You got something to say, say it." Anthony stiffened.

"Look, I know Ike's been like a father to you. But he likes to make up his own rules."

"Wait a minute—" Anthony placed both fists on the desktop and stood up.

Cedric held a restraining hand and cut him off. "Before you lose somebody that means a lot to you because of him, think real hard. Michelle is definitely not the first to bring up serious questions about his way of operating."

"Ike saved my life, man. He kept me and Mama off welfare." Anthony's voice pleaded for empathy.

"So you'll defend him, right or wrong? Shantae says Michelle is as miserable as you are. Make the first move." Cedric nodded toward the phone.

"I don't know, Cedric."

"It's the right thing, man."

Anthony placed his hand on the receiver but didn't pick it up. He sat staring at the phone. Cedric left the room, shutting the door quietly.

"Hi." Anthony stood in the doorway. He hesitated to make a move before she did.

"Hi." Michelle gripped the doorknob so tightly her fingers hurt.

"Can I come in?"

"Yeah, sure." Michelle stepped back motioning him inside. "Want a soft drink? Or I have coffee if you prefer."

Michelle wanted to find some reason to move around and be busy, at least for a few minutes.

"Coffee sounds good."

"Okay."

When she turned to go into the kitchen, Anthony pulled a handkerchief from his pocket and wiped his moist palms. He was still standing there when she came back with the cups.

Michelle paused in front of him. "Sit down."

"Right." Anthony stuffed the handkerchief out of sight. He cleared his throat nervously. "Thanks for agreeing to see me."

They sat on opposite ends of the sofa. Both drank in silence, careful to look everywhere but at each other. Anthony cleared his throat again, causing Michelle to start. But he did not speak, only took another sip of coffee. Michelle stole a glance at him. Seeing the tense posture and light sheen of perspiration on his top lip melted her cool resolve.

"Anthony, I—"

"No, Michelle. Let me start." Anthony put down the cup and took a deep breath. "Uncle Ike may be in over his head with this Housing Authority business."

"Oh, Anthony." Michelle struggled to put into words the extent of Ike's involvement.

"Let me finish. Sometimes his methods are unorthodox. You had to do your job. I understand that. I shouldn't have said such nasty things the other night."

"But let me—"

"No, listen. I'll never believe that Uncle Ike is involved in drug dealing or extortion, but it's possible that he's gotten mixed up with some unsavory characters. He wouldn't approve of those things, for sure. But if he's making money, he would definitely say whatever else they do is none of his business." Anthony forced the words out. He wrung his hands together. "What I'm trying to say is, I'm sorry."

"Anthony, I'm sorry, too. I should have given you more details about the story." Michelle turned to him.

"You did try to warn me." Anthony put down the cup.

"In a very vague way. Too vague to prepare you for that bombshell. I took the easy way out."

"I hated being apart from you, Chelle," Anthony whispered.

"I know." Michelle blinked back tears. The truth tore at her. They could never have a future. Her reports had destroyed even the outside chance they could make it work. There could be no happy ending for them.

"Chelle," Anthony said reaching for her.

"No." Michelle pushed his hands away and moved farther from him.

"But I thought—"

"We can't make it this way, Anthony. You can't turn your back on Ike, and I can't tell you that there won't be another story about him." Michelle looked at him. Her eyes were filled with sadness. "It'll be the same thing all over again."

"No, it won't, baby. I swear." Anthony ignored her attempt to resist him and put his arms around her.

"Anthony, my report is just the beginning. You won't be able to forgive some of the things I'll have to say about him." Michelle wrenched from his embrace and stood up.

"Don't do this, Michelle. Uncle Ike means too much to me. Don't let the past blind you to the truth," Anthony implored her.

"Are you sure I'm the one blinded by the past?" Michelle went to the door and opened it. "Good-bye, Anthony."

Anthony walked with heavy steps. Michelle held her breath when he paused and turned back to her. Her mind and heart still battled each other; one hoping for a way to keep him, the other arguing the impossibility of it.

"Good-bye," he said in a strained voice and walked out the door.

Michelle nodded mutely, not trusting herself to speak.

Fighting the urge to call him back took all the strength she had. At the sound of his car engine starting, she closed the door. She pulled aside the curtain of her front window slightly to watch his taillights melt into the night. As the lights grew smaller, she felt more alone than ever before.

"T'aneka, what are you doing in here?" Charlotte glanced at the files on the table with a slight frown.

"Oh, making some copies for, uh . . . The files needed straightening up." T'aneka shuffled the papers and turned them facedown. "A lot of these pages are all torn so you can't hardly read 'em."

"We worked on these files over a month ago."

"Not these, Miz Kinchen. These are from two years ago. Remember, we only worked on the ones from six months back." T'aneka stacked the files she had been copying under others.

Charlotte puckered her lips in annoyance. "Yes, but I told you we decided not to do those."

"Yes, ma'am. But I was caught up so I was workin' on them now." T'aneka had her back to Charlotte. She began putting the folders in a file cabinet.

"Let me see those." Charlotte strode toward her, holding out her hand.

"It's just the files of late rent notices and stuff." T'aneka handed her several of the brown folders.

"T'aneka, look at these." Charlotte spoke sharply, pointing to them.

"Ma'am?" T'aneka went rigid with dread.

"These are from this year. You've been pulling the wrong year, silly." Charlotte shook her head.

"Oh, yeah. Stupid me." T'aneka let out a shrill laugh. "I never noticed. But most of 'em was this year though. I need to get me some eyeglasses." She shifted from one foot to the other.

"Well, be careful. We can't afford to waste paper on dozens of files that shouldn't be copied. Besides, I want you to concentrate on putting old files on microfilm. We're running out of space," Charlotte said.

"Yes, ma'am, you are so right. Lord, these files all crammed in here so tight they all fly out when you try to pull one out." T'aneka began to move around busily. "I'm gonna sure do that."

"See that you do." Charlotte eyed her steadily for a few seconds before leaving. She passed Lonnie on the way to her office. "Lonnie, come in here a minute."

"What's up?" Lonnie shut the door behind him.

"T'aneka was in there copying a bunch of files she didn't need to copy. And she was acting very nervous when I walked in on her." Charlotte rubbed her chin.

"So?" Lonnie shrugged.

"So how did Michelle Toussaint get all those details of work orders, dates of invoices and such? I wondered who was talking. I thought maybe it was one of the ex-employees. Somebody we fired in the last six or seven months. Now I don't know." Charlotte stared past him at the closed door.

"That reporter did know a lot. Matter of fact some of the stuff she reported on was kinda recent." Lonnie's eyes narrowed to slits.

"What should we do? With T'aneka having access to those files, she could cause us big problems. If she's the one." Charlotte paced the office wringing her hands.

"Take it easy. I got an idea. Gimme a file folder with some invoices from Buster or Ike."

"What for?"

"We gonna bait a hook and see if she takes it."

Lonnie opened the door to Charlotte's office a little. Seeing T'aneka back at her desk, he signaled to Charlotte to play along.

"Look here, we got some big invoices got to be paid to

Buster for the Wesley Park complex." Lonnie spoke in a conversational tone. His back was to the open door.

"Yes, but as usual they only did a little of the work. With that reporter sniffing around maybe we shouldn't . . . well, you know what I mean." Charlotte rustled papers loudly.

"Yeah, but we told him he'd get his money. We don't wanna get him mad with all he knows." Lonnie shut the door and crossed to Charlotte. "Keep talkin'," he mouthed.

Charlotte raised her voice. "Sure he may want his money, but he doesn't want to risk answering questions from the district attorney, either."

"If the DA had anything, we'd be on trial." Lonnie eased the door shut.

Charlotte lowered her voice. "I ought to fire her right now. She's going to keep feeding that reporter ammunition," she hissed.

"No, she won't." Lonnie's nostrils flared. He looked at the closed door again with a feral expression.

"You'd better be careful. The uproar over that last incident hasn't died down yet." Charlotte's face showed anxiety and excitement.

"Let me handle it."

"Just don't do anything to make the situation worse for us." Charlotte's face twisted with malice. "But take care of that back-stabbing little wench."

He nodded to her then opened the door again. "Well, I'm going to file this then. You say you gonna go on and pay it?"

"Yes, T'aneka can copy it and I'll cut the check."

"Say, T'aneka, give Charlotte a copy of this for me." Lonnie smiled at her.

"Sure, Lonnie. And I'll put it in the files for you." T'aneka took the papers from him.

"Thanks, babe. Got yourself a real efficient worker, Charlotte," Lonnie called out, winking at T'aneka.

"I'm going to take care of it." T'aneka eyed the form for a few seconds, then smiled up at him.

"I know you will." Lonnie's smile curled into a grimace as she walked away. "I'm counting on it."

Michelle delivered the news flawlessly. She was somber when reporting crimes and smiled when reporting upbeat news items. No one would have guessed that she felt disconnected from the calm, articulate woman viewers saw. It was as if the voice was not hers. This night was far from being her shining hour. Being weekend anchor had the dull finish of tarnished silver. For weeks she had planned her celebration. A celebration that had included a glorious night with Anthony. Grief stabbed deep as a needle into her heart at the thought of him. She could not deny how much she missed Anthony's kiss. Night after night, she struggled to fall asleep. But images of his smile, his hard body, and his hands gently touching her played across her mind as clear as a videotape. Michelle closed her eyes and willed herself to stop thinking of him.

"Hey, I know it feels good to sit in the anchor's chair, but you gotta get up now," Kate said grinning at her.

"Oh, yeah." Michelle started as her eyes flew open.

She stood and gathered up the papers in front of her, trying to conceal her confusion. With one last look, she left the set. Her heart sank at the sight of jolly faces filling the newsroom. With a deep breath, she steadied herself to pretend.

"For she's a jolly good fellow!" Earl lifted a cup of punch.

"Great work, Toussaint." Nathan nodded at her.

Forcing a smile, Michelle accepted the shower of congratulations on her performance. Seeing the banner of congratulations, the punch bowl, and the nuts and cookies brought tears to her eyes. Michelle opened her mouth but words would not come out.

"You worked hard to get there, Michelle. We're happy for you." Earl gave her a peck on the cheek.

"Thanks, everybody. Really." Michelle grabbed tissues from Kate's outstretched hand and dabbed her eyes.

After a few minutes the crowd shifted, leaving her standing apart with Gracie.

Gracie studied her face before speaking. "So this is a big night, huh?"

"I've looked forward to this for a long time." Michelle's voice was subdued. She stared down at the full glass of now-lukewarm punch she still held.

"If you don't mind my saying, you look less than overjoyed. Want to talk about it?" Grace gave Michelle's arm a pat.

"No. Not now. Let's join the party." Michelle left without looking back at her. She plunged into a lively conversation with Earl and Bob pretending a heartiness she did not feel.

Later that night, Michelle sat with Laree and Shantae at the Shake, Rattle, and Roll Lounge, a nightclub featuring live bands playing the blues. Her friends saw right through her act despite her attempts to be merry. They had tried to lift her spirits for over an hour.

"This is more like a wake than a celebration," Shantae finally blurted out.

"Hush, Shantae," Laree admonished her. "Michelle is trying to have a good time even though she's heartbroken. I'm sorry," she stammered and fidgeted.

"Will you two stop it. I'm fine." Michelle avoided looking at them and took a sip of her strawberry daiquiri.

"We've been doing most of the talking, 'Chelle. And the dancing. Every time a guy asks you to get on the floor, you look at him as if he had horns sticking out of his head. You're miserable." Shantae shook a finger at her.

"I'm not miserable," Michelle snapped. "I'm not interested in any men right now. Being uninvolved has its advantages." She sat up straight, squaring her shoulders.

"Is that right?" Shantae arched an eyebrow at her.

"Yes, that's right," Michelle said defensively. "I can concentrate on my career for one thing."

"Sure, you'll have plenty of free time now. No long weekends with Anthony. No reason to rush home for a date with him . . ." Laree's voice trailed off as she saw the gloomy look on Michelle's face. "I mean, think of all the things you can get done. Not being distracted and—"

"Don't try to help, Laree." Shantae cut Laree off as she floundered to repair the damage. "Have you tried talking to Anthony, Chelle?"

"What's to talk about? Our relationship was doomed from the start. He can't accept that Ike is a crook, and I won't pretend he isn't." Michelle's face hardened from one of sadness to determination.

"It's a shame, though. Y'all are crazy about each other." Shantae sighed.

"Well, it's time to move on. I've accepted that ending our relationship was for the best." Michelle scanned the room. She smiled at a man approaching. "You're right. I'm going to stop moping around. Dancing isn't a bad idea at all." Ignoring their looks of disbelief, she sprang up to follow him.

Michelle got home at two in the morning. She undressed quickly and took a warm shower. All night she had done her best to be the life of the party. Yet her laughter sounded hollow. The dancing and loud music had shut out painful memories for only a short while. Now she lay in bed curled up with the comforter pulled around her. The quiet closed in on her. Her battle to blot out the ache of wanting Anthony began again. Michelle cried softly into the pillow as she drifted into a fitful slumber.

"What's wrong, Anthony?" Lizabeth put down her fork. "You've been picking at your food for ten minutes. Those candied yams are mashed up fine enough to pass through cheesecloth." She pointed to his still full plate.

"Guess I'm tired from all the hours I've been putting in at work." Anthony squirmed under her gaze.

"Try again." Lizabeth folded her arms and continued to watch him.

"Aw, Mama. Cut it out. I'm fine." Anthony wiped his mouth. He still would not meet her gaze.

"You had it out with Michelle about that story on Ike. Yes, I saw all of them." Lizabeth nodded at him as he looked up sharply.

"Then you know how one sided it was. Nothing is more important to her than getting revenge on Uncle Ike. Except maybe being a big-time television news celebrity," Anthony said in a bitter voice.

"I know how much she means to you, child. I also know Ike."

"She is not right, Mama! Uncle Ike would never put people in danger so he can stuff his pockets." Anthony spoke vehemently.

"Michelle may have had no choice but to report what others are saying," Lizabeth said in a calm, level voice. Reaching out, she placed a hand on his arm. "She can't be just making all this up to get revenge on Ike. They wouldn't let her say those things on television if that were so."

"Mama, the name of the game is ratings. They'll report lies, rumors, innuendo—anything to grab a big share of the viewing audience." Anthony wore an angry frown. He pushed his plate away.

"I've known Michelle since she was a child. I can't believe she'd do anything like what you're saying. And from the way you talked about her, I don't think you believe it deep down, either." Lizabeth touched his hand.

"Mama, I've got to accept that Michelle and I can't make it. It's over between us." Anthony got up and began clearing the dishes from the table. "Let's talk about something else."

Lizabeth did not press the issue. As they had at least once a week since his return home, they spent the rest of the evening talking about his work, church projects, and playing a trivia game. Yet beneath his light chatter, Anthony felt a heaviness in his chest. To have Michelle back in his life only to lose her again pained him more than he could put into words. He had foolishly convinced himself that they could work out differences about his uncle. Anthony could not deny the strong passion she kindled with only a smile. But he felt used and betrayed. Maybe she had even used him to get information for her reports. Anthony closed his eyes and immediately the sweet memory of her fiery kisses, the smooth satin brown skin beneath his fingers, and the tiny gasps in his ear as they made love came to him. Doubts assailed him. Could he be wrong? He could almost hear her musical laugh. With a start, he realized he was hearing her laugh. It came from his mother's television. Anthony opened his eyes to see Michelle joking with the weatherman. His anger returned as he watched her flash a lovely smile at the camera before signing off. What did she care for the truth? At last she was an anchorwoman. Michelle was on top of the world. And she had stepped on him to get there. Anthony clenched his teeth. Punching the buttons of the remote, he changed the station.

"I don't understand what this is all about." James Bridges mopped his forehead with an expensive linen handkerchief. "You know how those reporters operate. They'll do anything for a story that'll make a big splash." His eyelids twitched as his eyes darted an anxious glance at the faces around him.

"Let's talk about some of your dealings with the East Baton Rouge Housing Authority, Mr. Bridges. The Mayfair construction project for example." The young man in the dark gray business suit did most of the talking while the district attorney sat quietly.

"Mayfair?" Bridges squeaked in a strained voice. He

shifted in his seat. "Why that was, uh-hum, straightforward. I mean . . . well, Ike Batiste got that work. Why are you asking me this?"

"You played a role, we understand, with Ms. Kinchen?"

"Look, Mr. Connely, just what is your assistant implying? I have my rights." Bridges mustered up an indignant tone.

"Wheelwright isn't my assistant, Mr. Bridges. He's with the U.S. Attorney's office."

Bridges stared with wide eyes, his mouth slack. "Th-thh—the U.S. Attorney?" he croaked.

"Because federal funds could be involved, U.S. Attorney Lewis has asked that his staff be brought in on our interviews to review what we have so far." Connely spoke crisply.

Bridges twisted the damp handkerchief between his fingers. "I want my lawyer."

"Dominic, if anything happens to me, you talk to the police, all right?" T'aneka glanced over her shoulder nervously.

"T'aneka, what is going on with you? Calling me at eleven at night to meet you here." Dominic waved a hand at the mostly empty table of the all-night diner.

"They know. Something should have told me what was up when Lonnie kept letting me handle a lot of paperwork he used to do himself." T'aneka chewed on a fingernail.

"Know what? What paperwork? T'aneka, you're not making any sense. Calm down and tell me what's wrong." Dominic pulled her hand away from her mouth and held it tightly.

T'aneka took a deep breath after looking over her shoulder for the third time. She spoke in a low voice with her head close to his. "You know Michelle had those stories on the news about crooked stuff going on at the Authority, right?"

"Right." Dominic nodded.

"She's been getting information from a source inside the Authority." T'aneka gripped his hand and whispered, "Me."

"What?" Dominic yelled then immediately lowered his

voice when startled restaurant employees stared at them. "Are you crazy? You shouldn't be taking a chance like that with somebody like Lonnie. Wait until I get my hands on Michelle!" His face hardened. "Letting you take that kind of risk so she can get a story."

"She doesn't know it's me, Dominic," T'aneka said quickly. "A friend of mine gave her the stuff I copied. He didn't tell her who was giving it to him."

"But why, T'aneka? I thought you were so loyal to Charlotte."

"I grew up in the projects, Dom. It's never been the best place to live, but it was home. For years people in charge of the projects have stuffed their pockets while we live in run-down apartments. I got sick of it," T'aneka said in a voice heavy with resentment. "Things are getting worse. We figure it's time the tenants get active in cleaning the place up."

"But a few repairs not getting done isn't a reason—" Dominic loosened his hold on her hand and began to draw away.

"Dominic, come on. You saw some of those apartments. A lot of them are unsafe. Not to mention unfit to live in. Lonnie and his gang control drugs in the projects and take money from folks for protection; not making repairs ain't the half of it." T'aneka held on to his hand. "And Buster is in it, too."

"It's hard for me to believe Buster would go for that, T'aneka." Dominic frowned.

"I've seen the work invoices. He knows about Lonnie cause his buddy Ike Batiste helped him get out of jail." T'aneka's eyes narrowed with anger. "I'm not lying about all this, Dom."

"No, no. I didn't say you were, it's just . . ." Dominic drew his palm over his face as though trying to clear his head.

"Buster Wilson is up to his neck in it, Dom."

Dominic spoke in a low voice. "I didn't want to admit it, but some of the conditions did shock me. Now I understand why invoices were date-stamped paid before I did the repairs.

And why he got so mad when he found out I'd done them. Man!"

"He's as much a crook as Lonnie." T'aneka hammered home the unpleasant truth.

Dominic's face was grim as he accepted it. He glanced uneasily at two men who entered the restaurant. They sat at a table across the room. "What makes you think Lonnie's on to what you've been doing?"

"Little things. Like going out of his way to give me work orders. He made a comment about how much I know about what goes on around there. The other day I was in the storeroom moving some boxes to make room for more records. I turned around and he was standing right behind me. 'Be careful with them files. You could get hurt,' he said." T'aneka shivered. "And he had a nasty grin on his face."

"You better quit that job tomorrow, T'aneka. Go stay with your auntie in North Carolina. Get far away from here, baby." Dominic held both her hands. Seeing the two men glance at them, he lowered his voice even more. "Let's get out of here. We'll go to my place."

T'aneka grabbed his arm, restraining him. "I don't want to leave Baton Rouge, Dom. Besides, what if they take it out on my family?"

Dominic pulled her to her feet. "T'aneka, let's not argue about it now. We'd better leave."

He made an effort not to look at the two men as they passed them on the way out. He walked behind T'aneka to the glass double doors leading to the parking lot.

"Hurry up, babe." Dominic hustled her toward his car.

"But what about my car?"

"We'll get it later."

"Say, man," a gruff voice just over their shoulders barked. "You got a light?"

"No." Dominic did not look back but put his key in the car door.

"Say, man, hold up a minute. You know how to get to

Terrace Street from over here?" The second man spoke. He grinned revealing several gold teeth.

"No, sorry." Dominic fumbled with the lock.

"What's your hurry? Help a brother out, man." The first man hunched his shoulders.

"Yeah." The second man spread his hands wide. "Hey, pretty woman. What's up with you?" He stood to their left while his partner stood on their right leering at T'aneka.

T'aneka said nothing. Dominic finally got the door open, but one of the men pushed it shut again.

"Say, look—we wanna ask you somethin'. We tryin' to talk and y'all actin' uppity. That ain't right."

"Naw, that ain't right," the second man echoed.

"Get out of my way." Dominic faced them. He stood with his feet apart. His arms hung down loosely with clenched fists.

"Who you talkin' to, man? Huh?" The first man shoved Dominic against the car. "You want some of this?" He held up a fist.

The second man jerked T'aneka hard. "Come here. I got somethin' for you."

"Let go of me!" T'aneka aimed a kick at his knee but missed. She screamed in terror to see Dominic fending off the blows of the other man. "Dom! Oh, no!"

When she started toward him, she was thrown down to the pavement. She went limp when her head hit the concrete of the parking lot. The man left her lying unconscious to join his partner.

"We gonna help you and your bitch learn to stay outta business that don't concern you. You hear me, punk?" The first man pounded Dominic's head against the hood of the car while the second man held him.

"Yeah, and we got a treat for the pretty woman. Too bad she won't be awake to enjoy it," the second man said in a vicious voice.

Thirteen

Red, green, and gold leaves rustled in the wind. Typical for late January in south Louisiana, a chill breeze made heavy coats and hats a necessity in spite of the bright sunshine. Men in heavy work boots and wool jackets moved around the construction site full of purpose. Most of the outside work was completed, making it less of a hardship on such a cold day. Anthony and Cedric were bundled up for warmth in heavy coats as they toured the site.

"Looks good. We're right on schedule, Cedric." Anthony examined the room they stood in. He turned full circle to take in everything.

"Yeah, though I had to knock some heads a couple of times." Cedric stood looking around with his gloved hands on his hips.

"You have to expect that, you know? But we got a good group of men." Anthony walked over to run his hand along a wall of Sheetrock.

"Yeah, they do pretty well, I have to say," Cedric said. "Except for that new guy, Troy Quarles. One more screwup and he's outta here."

"Why?" Anthony's dark eyebrows drew together.

"He's lazy. Plus, a couple of times he's gone to pick up supplies and disappeared for over four hours. He's always got some lame excuse for messing up. Matter of fact, he didn't even show up for work today." Cedric gave a grunt of disgust.

"Well, all right then. If he's not doing his job, get rid of him," Anthony said in a gruff voice. He turned away.

"Sure, I mean he's more trouble than he's worth," Cedric continued.

"Go on, say it." Anthony whirled around to face him.

Cedric looked at him sharply, a puzzled frown on his face. "Say what?"

"I told you so. You weren't too thrilled about hiring him. I convinced you because Uncle Ike is on the board of that program. You might as well jump right in with the rest of the Ike Batiste critics."

"I'm only telling you about a problem employee like I've done before, Anthony," Cedric said calmly. "I wasn't even thinking of Ike."

Anthony's chest rose as he took a deep breath. He exhaled slowly and closed his eyes for a few seconds. "I'm sorry, man. You're right. I didn't mean anything. . . ." He walked to another part of the building to inspect window facings.

Cedric watched him for several minutes before speaking again. "How you doin'? I haven't been seeing much of you lately except at the sites."

"Fine." Anthony pointed to a maze of red wires sticking from a hole. "Have Kendricks double check this wiring for me."

"Sure thing." Cedric cleared his throat. "You been goin' out much?"

"No. I forgot to tell you that the border paper came in yesterday. It's going to look great with this paint." Anthony compared the labels on several cans with a color chart in his portfolio.

"Yeah. Me and Shantae went to Diggy-Do's last Saturday. They had their first big Mardi Gras party. I was surprised you didn't show up, much as you love his Mardi Gras parties." Cedric spoke casually as he appeared to scrutinize exposed beams. "Didn't see Michelle, either."

"Hmm." Anthony continued checking the paint.

"Man, we had a ball. Shame y'all missed it." Cedric strolled around looking at nothing in particular.

"Let me save you the trouble of stumbling toward the obvious question—no, I haven't seen or talked to Michelle and it's unlikely that I will." Anthony closed his portfolio with a sharp snap.

"What are you talking about? I wasn't going to ask anything. I was just saying—" Cedric was the picture of innocence.

"Don't even try it, Cedric." Anthony fixed him with a hard stare.

"I uh, I mean . . . What I'm saying is— Okay, so maybe I might of kinda been leading up to it." Cedric gave up his attempt at denial.

"This is why we couldn't get away with anything when we were kids. All an adult had to do was look at you and you'd spill your guts." Anthony wore a slight smile.

"I never could lie. But don't try to change the subject. You and Michelle haven't even tried to get back together?" Cedric walked over to him.

"It's over." Anthony's lips turned down, erasing all signs of humor.

Cedric put a hand on Anthony's shoulder. "Finding that special woman is maybe a once in a lifetime thing. Be very sure before you let it go so easy."

"Easy? You think it was easy?" Anthony's voice was coarse as though the words themselves hurt.

He thought of all those lonely nights spent in agony, going over their dilemma, trying to convince himself that maybe through some miracle they could be together. But Michelle's biting accusations against his uncle were too hard to take. Not once did she try to see him in a different light.

"I know it's tough," Cedric said.

"Michelle is out of my life." Anthony leaned against the window, staring outside. The chill that went through him did not come from the weather.

Cedric took a deep breath. "I'm really sorry, Anthony." He approached Anthony and put a supportive arm around his shoulder.

"Hey, I'm going to be okay." Anthony lifted his head. He wore a resolute expression. "Now let's go to the library site. There are a couple of things I want to check on before we give the word it's complete."

Anthony and Cedric went over details with the thoroughness that made them a successful and sought-after team. They settled for nothing less than having it done right. As they came out of the nearly completed library building, they turned to admire the large circular cut glass window set above the wide entrance.

"Beautiful. We did a fantastic job, if I do say so myself." Cedric nodded with satisfaction.

"Better believe it. Partner, we're on our way. With this one under our belt we can go after the big projects. This is proof we can handle it." Anthony clapped his friend on the back.

"Excuse me, Mr. Hilliard?"

They glanced around to find two uniformed police officers standing behind them.

"Yes, that's me." Anthony faced them.

"I'm Detective Majors and this is Detective Oubre." Officer Majors nodded toward his partner. "We'd like to ask you some questions. Could you come with us down to the station? You could follow us in your vehicle, sir." The muscular Black policeman spoke while his partner gazed around at the building and landscaping.

"Questions about what?" Anthony glanced at Cedric then back at Majors.

"It seems there are some . . . problems with one of your employees. Probably won't take long." Officer Majors regarded them with calm stoicism.

"What kind of problems? I hired most of these men," Cedric replied in a guarded voice.

"Really? Then we need a statement from both of you."
Majors looked from Anthony to Cedric.

"Why can't we talk here if it won't take long?" Cedric
raised an eyebrow.

"We'll explain it all downtown." Detective Majors half
turned as if ready to leave, then paused when he saw neither
man moved.

"Now hold on—" Cedric protested hotly.

Anthony placed a hand on his friend's chest. "Stay cool,
Cedric," he said in a quiet voice. Then in a conversational
tone, "Fine, officer. We'll be right behind you."

Anthony and Cedric talked about every man in the three
work crews during the fifteen-minute ride to the police station. They searched for a clue that might explain what kind
of trouble could be so serious to involve the police. They
arrived at police headquarters just as baffled.

"This way, gentlemen."

Detective Majors ushered them through the squad room,
a maze of desks with uniformed and plainclothes officers
milling around, into a small spartan interview room. Detective Oubre disappeared for several moments. He returned
with a tall, lean man dressed in a crisp white shirt, charcoal-
gray suit, and dark green tie.

"I'm Chief Detective Robin of the Homicide Division."
He spoke curtly. "Mr. Eames, Detective Oubre will take your
statement." He pointed to Oubre standing in the still open
door.

"This way, sir." Detective Oubre gave a sharp nod of his
head. The close-trimmed crown of black hair gave him the
look of a drill sergeant directing an errant recruit to the bar-
racks.

"Why?" Cedric began looking around at them.

"Procedure, sir. It will save time if we get your statements
simultaneously," Detective Robin said.

Cedric followed Detective Oubre with one last worried
glance at Anthony.

Detective Robin opened a slim folder with several sheets of paper in it. "Now, Mr. Hilliard. Do you know a Troy Quarles?"

"Yes, he works for me. But you already know that." Anthony looked at the papers, trying to read them upside down.

"How long has he worked for you?"

"About five months, I think."

"Any trouble with him?"

"Minor things like goofing off. What's going on?" Anthony looked around at Detective Majors, who stood against the wall with his hands folded in front of him.

"Were you aware of his criminal record?" Detective Robin continued without acknowledging his question.

"Yes. But he'd served his time and came with a good recommendation from his probation officer. So I gave him a shot."

"As part of an ongoing investigation, one of our undercover officers reported that Mr. Quarles had resumed his illegal activities. Specifically, involvement in the drug trade. Were you aware of that?" Detective Robin leaned both elbows on the file and stared at Anthony hard.

"Of course not. If I had known—"

"In fact, he's been using one of your trucks to transport illegal drugs."

"If you have solid evidence of that, then he won't have the chance to do it after today!" Anthony said angrily.

"Mr. Quarles won't be doing anything. He's dead. We found him in his car at three o'clock this morning with a single bullet wound to the head," Detective Robin said evenly.

"My God." Anthony shook his head slowly.

"And you say you were unaware of his activity?"

"No, I— You think I'm involved in drug dealing?" Anthony's head snapped up. "This is incredible!" He fell back in his chair, stunned.

"We had some indications before his death that you did know about the movement of the drugs."

"Wait a minute, what indications?" Anthony leaned forward.

"Mr. Eames usually handles hiring. Isn't it true you hired Quarles in spite of his objections?"

"Sure, Cedric was skeptical. But my uncle said that he'd done well working on some temporary jobs for him. Knowing how hard it is for men with a prison record to get work, I didn't want to hold his past against him."

"That would be Ike Batiste. Mr. Batiste has hired quite a few ex-cons over the years." Detective Robin glanced down briefly at the papers before him.

"He's worked closely with an ex-offender rehab program for a long time, yes. Because we try to help these guys doesn't mean we're crooks." Anthony spoke with intensity.

"According to several monitored conversations, Quarles said his boss had a 'piece of the action.' "

"That's a damn lie!" Anthony sprang from the hardwood chair.

"Do you know Dominic Toussaint?"

"What?" Anthony, thrown off balance by the abrupt change in the questioning, blinked in confusion. "Sure I know him, or at least his sister. I don't understand what that's got—"

"Two days ago he was beaten severely. So severely that he's in intensive care. What do you know about that?" Detective Robin shot the words at him like bullets from an automatic weapon.

"Dominic in intensive care?" Anthony sat down again heavily.

"You know what we think, Mr. Hilliard? We think it's related to the Quarles killing. The common thread seems to be the business dealings of Ike Batiste. Quarles first worked for him and then Buster Wilson on contracts with the Housing Authority. We've long suspected that some of the men Batiste hired helped establish a lucrative drug trade in the projects around town."

"I don't know anything about any of this." Anthony's fist crashed down on the table between them.

"Seems Quarles started skimming a few ounces of cocaine each time he picked up a kilo. He went into business for himself. Our undercover officer met with him several times." Robin hammered at him in a cold voice like granite.

"I don't have anything to do with drugs, and I damn sure don't know anything about a murder. This is insane! The only contact I've had with the police is a couple of parking tickets." Anthony glared at the detective defiantly.

"Yet you knew Quarles."

"I gave him a job, that's all." Anthony made a sharp chopping motion in the air with his hand.

"Dominic Toussaint worked for Buster Wilson. His sister is Michelle Toussaint, the news reporter. Sources tell us he was beaten because of his sister's stories—stories damaging to your uncle's business."

"I didn't even know Dominic was attacked." Anthony imagined the torment Michelle and her family must be going through. If only he could comfort her.

"We've spoken to the Toussaint family. There seems to be some history between Thomas Toussaint and Mr. Batiste." Robin crossed his arms. He regarded Anthony steadily.

"That was years ago and had nothing to do with Dominic." Anthony shook his head.

"Ms. Toussaint seems to think her brother stumbled onto something. She thinks Batiste gave the orders for the attack on her brother." Robin squinted at him under the harsh fluorescent light.

"Michelle still has a grudge against my uncle for what she thinks he did to her father. They were in business, it went sour, and her father suffered heavy financial losses. My uncle tried to help him. And he doesn't order hits on people." Anthony sighed deeply. Those were words he wanted desperately to say to Michelle.

"She said you'd defend him. You're very close to Mr. Batiste, I understand. You might go to great lengths to protect him."

"Did you tell her about these ridiculous allegations against me?" Anthony felt a tightness in his throat. The thought that Michelle suspected he was a party to the savage attack on her brother filled him with a horror no accusation made by the police could possibly inspire. Surely she must know him better than that?

"Mr. Hilliard?" Majors leaned forward, speaking in an emphatic tone to get his attention.

"Am I being charged with anything?" Anthony looked from Detective Robin to Majors.

Several seconds passed before Detective Robin spoke. "No." His dour expression seemed to say he wished the answer was different.

"Then if that's all, I'll be going." Anthony pushed his chair back roughly and started for the door.

"Not yet. We need a written statement before you leave, sir." Detective Robin still sat at the battered table.

"How long will that take?" Anthony noticed Detective Majors stand straight as though on alert. Majors seemed poised to stop any attempt to leave by force. Anthony felt trapped in a bad dream from which he could not wake up.

"A clerk will be in shortly. Take a seat, please." Detective Robin rose slowly. He started to leave the room, then paused in front of Anthony. "Would you like to call your attorney?"

"No. Let's get this over with," Anthony said in a crisp tone.

Anthony wanted to pound the walls with frustration. Instead, he forced himself to focus on getting through this obstacle to finding Michelle. He answered the same questions and gave the same answers for another maddening hour. Then he had to review the printed statement before signing it. At last he emerged from the small interview room to find Cedric waiting for him on a hard wooden bench in the hallway. It was almost nine o'clock, four hours since they had left the library site.

"Man, what the hell's been going on? I've been out here for two hours." Cedric matched Anthony's long strides as they left the building.

"They think I've got something to do with Troy's murder. Detective Robin says they have information that I was involved in drug dealing with Troy." Anthony yanked open the door to his car.

"Damn!" Cedric got into the passenger side. They sat in bleak silence for several moments.

"What did they ask you?" Anthony leaned his head back against the seat.

"A bunch of questions about how we hired Troy and why. Officer Oubre asked if I ever noticed you spending time talking to Troy or sending him on errands. If you worked late a lot; how well I knew Troy. Stuff like that. I gotta tell you, this is blowing my mind." Cedric rubbed tired eyes.

"It gets worse. Michelle's little brother, Dominic, was beaten up. Not only do the police suspect Uncle Ike is involved, but Michelle thinks I'm covering for him. God, Cedric. What is happening?" Anthony spoke in a strangled voice.

"I wish I could tell you."

"I've got to go see Michelle." Anthony gunned the engine.

Cedric placed a hand on the steering wheel. "Hold on, Anthony. That's a bad idea. The cops may think you're trying to intimidate her. They're probably watching you."

"I don't care what the police think! Michelle has got to listen to reason. She's got to." Anthony gripped the wheel tightly.

"Listen to me." Cedric spoke with urgency in his voice. "Her brother is in intensive care. If she really believes your uncle is responsible, what chance do you have of making her see reason? Besides, she's probably at the hospital and that's not the place to hash this out."

"I can't take it, Cedric. Knowing she thinks I'd hurt Dom is tearing me up inside." Anthony squeezed his eyes shut as if in pain.

"I know. But rushing into anything isn't the answer." Cedric watched his expression anxiously. "Give it a day at least. For your sake and hers."

"Maybe you're right." Anthony's shoulders sagged. "I feel like I'm standing in a dark tunnel with a huge train heading straight for me." He loosened his hold on the steering wheel.

"I hear you, man." Cedric put a hand on his shoulder. "Let's get my truck and head over to my place for a beer. Come on, it's been months since we just hung out. What do you say?"

"Thanks, Cedric. Going home to an empty apartment right now would be rough——" Anthony broke off. He stared straight ahead. With a deep sigh, he put the car in gear and nosed out into traffic.

"The police think Anthony is connected to that murder and . . ." Michelle said. Her voice quavered before she could go on. "And to the attack on Dominic." Michelle held on to the edge of her desk. For one brief moment the room seemed to dip and sway around her. She swallowed hard in response to a surge of nausea that hit her.

"It's only a suspicion, Chelle. They can't prove a thing." Shantae placed steadying hands on Michelle's shoulders. "Maybe you should sit down." She eyed the pasty look on Michelle's face with concern.

"Then why did they question him?" Pushing Shantae's hands away, Michelle ignored her attempts to guide her into a chair.

"They think Anthony was in on this guy's drug dealing. Ike got Anthony to hire him when he got out on parole. And

there's some kind of connection to the Housing Authority."
Seeing the growing horror on Michelle's face, Shantae
rushed on. "It's circumstantial, Chelle. They have no proof."

"Anthony has been defending Ike for years. Maybe he has
more of a motive than family loyalty." Michelle closed her
eyes, trying to blot out the ugliness of the picture forming
in her head.

Shantae's voice became a distant hum as her mind raced
replaying scenes of she and Anthony together. Could she
have misjudged him that much? Had she been so blinded by
desire she saw Anthony as the man she wanted him to be,
completely missing the real man? Yet he had never denied
that Ike was his role model, especially when it came to the
business world. And she had been foolish enough to trust
him again. Only this time Dominic may have been hurt because of her.

"Anthony would never deal drugs." Shantae shook
Michelle's arm to get her attention. "Chelle, are you listening
to me?"

Michelle gazed around her as though trying to find her
way. Shantae's voice broke through her thoughts as if waking
her from a hypnotic state. Michelle's grief-stricken expression became venomous. "Anthony can rot in jail with his
precious uncle for all I care. Don't ever defend him to me
again."

"Now just a minute, Michelle Toussaint," Shantae
snapped, wagging a finger under her nose. "If Cedric says
Anthony is being framed, then you can count on it." Her
chin jutted out pugnaciously.

"Then maybe he's fooled Cedric, too."

"Oh, Chelle," Shantae wailed in exasperation.

"Shantae, Dominic almost died. He still could for all we
know." Michelle's eyes welled with tears.

"And whoever did it ought to get sent away for a long
time," Shantae said in a gentle voice, putting an arm around

her. "But nobody can tell me Anthony would murder somebody and sell drugs to children."

"Lord, Shantae. I just don't know what to think anymore." Michelle covered her face with both hands. Her shoulders trembled.

Shantae embraced her. "You've worked two hours past quitting time. Let's get out of here. You're spending the night with me."

Michelle pulled away, wiping her face with a wad of tissues. "I'll be okay."

"Don't argue," Shantae said firmly. She handed Michelle a handful of dry tissues. "I'll drop Devonne off at Mama's. Me, you, and Laree are going to have one of our sister-to-sister group healing sessions."

"That sounds good," Michelle said, her voice weak with emotion.

"We're going to survive this together," Shantae whispered. She held Michelle tightly for a second before stepping back. "Now, first thing we'll do is call Laree. Then we'll stop by your apartment to pick up a few things."

With Michelle in tow, Shantae and Laree rounded up a wide selection of comfort foods at the grocery store. They cajoled her into their game of finding things to lift their spirits. Microwave popcorn, hot chocolate, marshmallows, and tabloids with outrageous headlines were thrown into the shopping cart. When they got to Shantae's house, they put on fuzzy slippers and oversized T-shirts. But the playful chatter quickly changed as the evening progressed. Hours of talking out anger, fears, and frustration left the three women drained. Michelle did most of the talking. She grappled with her conflicting feelings about Anthony.

"Chelle, I've got to agree with Shantae for once." Laree wrapped both arms around her knees. They sat around Shantae's living room on big fluffy pillows. "Anthony couldn't have done what they're accusing him of."

"He's just not like that," Shantae put in, looking at Michelle. "Deep down, you don't think so, either."

"Deep down I don't want to believe it. But what I want and the truth could be two very different things." Michelle bit her bottom lip.

"The truth is Anthony isn't the kind of person who would hurt anyone, Chelle," Shantae insisted.

"Maybe not. But he still stands up for Ike," Michelle said with a grimace.

"Now wait—" Shantae began.

"No, Shantae. He defends Ike no matter what. That makes Anthony an accessory to every horrible thing Ike's ever done as far as I'm concerned. Now I don't want to discuss it anymore. What's important to me now is that Dominic gets better." Michelle breathed deeply. "That's all I care about."

The women fell silent for several minutes, lost in their own thoughts. Bundling themselves in blankets, they remained curled up on the pillows, watching television and talking until they fell asleep sometime after three in the morning. Michelle was the first to wake up. She smiled at the sight of her friends sprawled on the floor. Their support and caring helped to blunt the pain but not remove it. A now-familiar grip of sorrow took hold as thoughts of Anthony pushed through. Somehow she must find a way to banish him from her mind. To forget the sensation of his warm lips on hers or the sweet, tangy smell of his skin. Despite her bitter pledge, Michelle knew forgetting Anthony was her biggest challenge. One that would test her beyond anything else she had to face. The picture of Dominic lying unconscious in intensive care came to her and she felt ashamed. How could she sit here longing for Anthony? How could she feel anything but loathing for a man who may well have taken part in the brutal beating of her brother? She would do well to remember that Anthony was, first and foremost, Ike's devoted nephew. That alone should help destroy any feelings she had for him. Michelle could almost laugh at the bitter irony that she at last could agree with Anthony on one thing: family should come first. Never again would she let emotion rule. Michelle stood and began preparing for a new day.

"Anthony was down talking to the police yesterday." Buster chewed on the stump of a cigar. He took it out of his mouth and dropped it into a large ceramic ashtray on the bar.

"Yeah, I know. So what? The boy don't know nothin'." Ike swallowed the last drop of whiskey in the glass he held. He sat on the sofa in his den.

"I told you that Lonnie is too dangerous to mess with. Didn't I tell you that when you put him over all them other ex-cons?" Buster pointed a finger in the air between them.

"They ain't gonna be able to trace anything back to him." Ike stared into the empty glass. "He knows how to cover himself."

"I ain't goin' to prison, Ike. We been through a lot together, but this is too much. Things done got way outta hand. You know what I'm talkin' 'bout." Buster scanned the room nervously.

"What's wrong with you, Buster? Think we bein' bugged? You been watchin' too many of them cop shows." Ike barked a harsh laugh devoid of humor. He tapped his fingers rapidly on the arm of the sofa.

"This ain't no joke, Ike. We talkin' 'bout a killin'," Buster said in a hoarse whisper.

"Stop actin' like a scared old woman," Ike bellowed. "Look here, not a damn thing Lonnie does can be connected to me. I made sure of that. He ain't never told me details of what he's been up to; thinks he's slick. But that's suited me just fine. He's on his own if the police ever catch up to him. And if you had any sense, you been stayin' away from him as much as possible, too." Ike glanced sharply at Buster, who squirmed in his chair.

"I-I only talked to him a few times," Buster exclaimed.

"We just talked about maintenance on some apartments, that's all." He rubbed his chin with a shaky hand.

"You better practice that story so you can sound more convincing when some sharp detective is questioning you." Ike snorted in disdain. He poured himself another drink.

"What about that Toussaint boy? Lonnie must a been clean crazy pickin' on him." Buster began pacing the floor.

"Go home, Buster. You startin' to get on my nerves." Ike had his back to him.

"But what we gonna do, Ike? We can't sit around waitin'—"

"I said go home!" Ike's voice boomed menacingly. He threw his head back and closed his eyes. He spoke in a more composed voice. "I'll call you later."

Buster started to speak but stopped, seeing the look on Ike's face. Buster left without saying good-bye. Ike sat alone staring at nothing in particular. A deep frown creased his features.

"Has the doctor said anything lately? Is he the same?" Michelle rushed through the doors. The sight of Brian coming through the hospital lobby with heavy steps sent a spike of dread through her stomach.

"No change. They still don't know if he'll come out of it. At least he's survived the first twenty-four hours." Brian's face was haggard. His usually unruffled look gone.

"What about T'aneka?"

"She's bruised up, but okay. They let her Mama take her home a few hours ago."

Michelle let out a long breath. "Thank God for that at least."

"Let's sit over here. I couldn't take Mama and Dad another minute. I needed some fresh air."

"What do you mean?" Michelle sat on the edge of a bright blue vinyl bench next to her brother.

"For a while they barely spoke to each other. That was bad enough. Now they're sniping at each other over the least little thing." Brian kneaded his temples with both hands.

"God, they could at least put aside their differences at a time like this. I'm sure Daddy is doing his best to blame Mama somehow," Michelle said in a weary tone. "This is especially hard on her. She and Dom are so close."

"Michelle, Dad is suffering just as much. He shows it differently. Mama isn't exactly the victim you seem to think she is," Brian said in a cutting voice.

"What are you talking about, Brian?" Michelle leaned toward him. She studied his face intently.

"Nothing."

"No, there's something else," Michelle persisted.

"All I'm saying is Mama can take equal blame when it comes to how bad things have gotten between them. She does her share of taking potshots at him, too." Brian avoided meeting her gaze.

"You're not telling the truth, at least not all of it." Michelle grasped his wrist. "What do you know?"

"Nothing, really." Brian shook her hand loose. He glanced at his wristwatch. "I better get to the office for my meeting. I'll be back tonight."

The anxiety in his face made Michelle back away from forcing the issue. "Okay."

"Dom is going to make it, Chelle. He is." He hugged her fiercely before striding away.

Michelle rode the elevator to the fifth floor. Stepping into the hall, she started toward the intensive care unit when familiar voices raised in fury stopped her. She whirled around and headed in the direction of the sound.

"If you hadn't alienated him all these years, he wouldn't have needed to go somewhere else for a job. You pushed him to this!" Annette's voice was full of resentment. She and Thomas were alone in the family waiting room down the hall, away from the rooms and nurses' station. A television played softly in the background.

"Stop it, Annette. One of these days—" Thomas stood with his back to her.

"Dominic is dying because you wouldn't do one simple thing for him. You've been punishing him for what you think I did."

"I don't think, I know what you did!" Thomas spun around. "So did all our friends. Sneaking around with Ike."

"Gossip made it more than what it was, but you could never believe that." Annette spoke with resignation. "I don't care anymore. I'm sick of begging you to forgive me. Think what you like. Just stop taking your anger out on my son."

"Your son, eh?" Thomas towered over her.

"You never treated him like he was yours. Having you was worse than having no father at all. At least Ike gave him a job," Annette said in a level voice, her eyes bright with animosity.

"If you think Ike would have been a better father, why didn't you leave me? I'll tell you why: because Ike was through using you. He wouldn't have you, would he?" Thomas snarled in a brutal tone.

"He made me feel wanted, something you don't seem capable of anymore." Annette did not back down under his attack.

"Then go to him. You deserve each other!" Thomas snatched up his overcoat and stormed past Michelle in the hallway. In his anger and pain, he did not even see her.

Annette's eyes were round with alarm when she saw Michelle standing in the doorway as though paralyzed. "My Lord, Michelle! It's not what you think." Her hand flew to her mouth.

"What should I think about you and Ike Batiste, Mama?" Michelle said. She desperately wanted to hear another explanation that would wipe away the ugly thoughts racing through her mind. Yet the look of guilt and fear in her mother's eyes said no such assurance would come.

"Michelle, baby." Annette went to her, wringing her hands.

Michelle walked into the room slowly to stand before Annette. "What did Daddy mean when he said you deserved each other?"

"Your father is a cold unfeeling man. He says the most horrible things to me." Annette reverted to her familiar whining tone.

"Tell me about you and Ike Batiste, Mama. Tell me what that has to do with Dominic being in this hospital." Michelle brushed aside her attempts to blame Thomas.

"Dominic is in the hospital because some thug beat him up, baby. It doesn't have anything to do with—"

"Stop lying, Mama. All these years I blamed Daddy for treating you so badly. You taught me that. But he had a reason, didn't he?" Michelle's eyes bored into her. "Didn't he, Mama?"

Annette collapsed into a chair. "It's not what you think. Thomas poisoned Brian against me. And now you."

"You said Ike wanted you. Your words, not Daddy's. It won't work, Mama. You can't make Daddy the villain this time."

Annette straightened her shoulders and glared at Michelle. "This is between your father and me. How dare you interrogate me! It's none of your business, young lady." She tried to rally and assert her parental authority.

"You made it my business when you deliberately tried to turn me against Daddy. So don't say it doesn't involve me. You owe me more than an explanation, you owe me the truth."

"What does it matter?" Annette pleaded with her. "It won't help any of us now. Leave it alone."

"If you want any chance at saving our relationship, you'll tell me," Michelle said softly.

Annette hung her head and shuddered. "How can I? You'll

despise me as much as I despise myself." She covered her mouth to muffle a moan of despair.

"Hiding from it won't help. I can't pretend nothing happened, Mama." Michelle sat next to Annette. She stared ahead with a face of stone, not wanting to look at her mother. "I'm listening."

Fourteen

Michelle moved woodenly around the newsroom, going through the motions of preparing her reports for the six o'clock broadcast. Outwardly, she was the same: a competent professional editing copy, contacting sources, and making notes. Inside, she felt disoriented. The world now seemed a strange combination of foreign and familiar. Even the most common objects seemed to have changed just enough to make her wonder if she was in the right place. Layered onto the pain of losing Anthony was the new awful knowledge of her mother's deceit.

"How're you doing, babe?" Gracie's brow furrowed.

"I'll live," Michelle said in a voice empty of emotion.

Jason approached them. "Toussaint, come into my office."

"Can it wait? I've got to finish this by four at least, and I'll need to visit the library again." Michelle continued tapping her keyboard.

"Mr. Lockport and Nathan are waiting for us." Jason's voice held an ominous, self-satisfied edge.

Michelle got up to follow him after exchanging a glance with Gracie.

Gracie caught her hand, stopping her for a moment. "Watch yourself. That little snake is up to something," she whispered.

Lockport sat at Jason's desk with his elbows propped on the blotter as he doodled on notepaper. "Have a seat,

Michelle. Terrible thing about your brother. How is he?" He put the pen down and arranged his face into an expression of concern.

"No change. Thanks for asking." Michelle nodded back at Nathan as she sat next to him.

"The public housing story." Lockport rocked back in the chair to gaze at the ceiling. "Tell me about the information that came from Housing Authority records."

Michelle threw a questioning look at Nathan before answering. He shook his head slightly.

"There were invoices paid for work that wasn't done. You saw that in the reports aired," she said.

"And they were authentic?" Lockport's gaze traveled around the room before resting on her.

"Definitely." Michelle's eyes narrowed. "What are you getting at?"

"It seems that an employee of the Housing Authority claims those invoices were faked. That you manufactured them when she told you they had been sent to archives at the district office. You—"

"We understand if you were faced with a difficult decision, Michelle," Lockport cut him off. "Ike Batiste almost ruined your father's business."

Michelle sat forward, eyes blazing. "How dare you suggest I'd fake a story for revenge." She glowered at all three men. "I based my report on solid information. Those invoices are real. They were given to me by a reliable source."

"Then you won't mind showing them to us." Jason's eyebrows lifted up to his hairline.

"No problem." Michelle marched to the large row of cabinets along the back wall of the newsroom with them close behind. When she turned her key to unlock it, the lock turned around without making the familiar clicking sound. The mechanism was broken.

"Well? Let's have it," Jason said.

"Something is wrong. . . ." Michelle examined the cabinet. Deep scratches on the gray paint revealed the metal beneath. She yanked the drawer out and searched frantically through file folders. "It's missing. The invoices and work orders are gone!"

"Very convenient." Jason's voice dripped with sarcasm.

"Is something wrong?" Jennifer joined them.

"I don't understand this. All of those photocopies were here with my notes." Michelle dumped stacks of papers on the desk.

"Are you sure that's where you left them?" Nathan sorted through several sheets in an attempt to help her.

"Of course I'm sure. I had them, Nathan." Michelle turned to him.

"Let's discuss this in Jason's office." Lockport lowered his voice and took her arm.

"They were here! It's obvious someone, probably paid by Ike Batiste, stole those documents." Michelle pointed to the broken lock.

Jason grunted. "A stranger got past the security guard and, unobserved by all the staff that are constantly in here day and night, broke into one file drawer. In one of the busiest rooms in the station? Oh, come on."

"Sounds farfetched to me, too." Jennifer cocked her head at Lockport.

"Michelle, if we could just go—" Lockport tried again to guide them away from dozens of staring eyes.

"Nathan, you believe me?" Michelle pleaded with him.

"I . . ." Nathan rubbed his cheek as he looked at the file cabinet.

"This isn't the place for such a discussion. My office, Ms. Toussaint," Lockport commanded. Through playing the role of the empathetic boss, he stalked off down the hall.

"Mr. Lockport, I had those photocopies," Michelle burst out the minute his door closed behind them.

"Then where are they? And how do you explain the employee's story?" Jason pounced before Lockport could speak.

"A man has been murdered, my brother and his girlfriend attacked. Obviously, he or she is scared stiff." Michelle ignored him, speaking directly to Lockport.

"Under the circumstances, I'm afraid you have to be suspended. Without proof that you had unaltered documentation that supported your story, I have no choice. You've put this station in a precarious legal position." Lockport spoke firmly.

"Nathan, you know I would never do such a thing." Michelle's voice trembled.

"Give us a chance to straighten this out, Toussaint. Until then, you can take time to be with your family." Nathan put out his hand to her.

Michelle drew back. "Thanks for nothing." She left, slamming the door behind her. Michelle walked back to her desk on shaky legs, trying to ignore the speculative stares and whispers as she passed others. Clearly word had spread.

Gracie sprang up to meet her before she got to her desk. "That little troll, Jason, makes me want to puke," Gracie fumed. "You fight back, honey. With your high profile and us backing you up, we could—"

"I'm so tired, Gracie." Michelle threw items from within and on top of her desk into a large book bag. "Truth is, part of me is relieved."

"What?" Gracie's mouth flew open.

Michelle sat down and massaged her neck. "Performing for Channel Twelve is one less thing to worry about. I haven't been doing it very well anyway."

"Michelle, listen to me." Gracie kneeled down and placed a hand on her arm. "You've taken a couple of hard hits, sure. But don't just lie down. What about your career? I don't believe for one minute you don't care about that anymore. Or about LaWanda and the people who live in the projects. If you go down, so do they."

"What good am I to them now? My credibility is on the line." Pulling the bag to her, Michelle started throwing things inside it again.

"Then defend it," Gracie said fiercely squeezing her hand.

"I know you're right. But I can't think about anything else right now except Dom and—" Michelle choked off. Turning away, she drew on her coat.

"Maybe a short rest would help. Go on home and think about what I said." Gracie placed both hands on her shoulders, forcing her to look up. "Call me if you need anything, okay?"

"Sure." Michelle's eyes filled with tears. "You're a good egg, Gracie O'Hannon." She gave her a hug then left.

Despite Gracie's advice, Michelle went straight to the hospital. She walked into the fifth-floor family waiting room to find her father seated alone. His face was tired and drawn.

"Hello, Daddy. How long have you been here?" Michelle perched on the edge of a chair across from him. She looked at him with new eyes. The man she had thought of as hard and judgmental seemed to have been her own misguided invention. What she saw was a man who had suffered a great hurt by someone he had loved and cherished. Something she now understood only too well. Michelle felt a twinge of guilt remembering her sharp criticisms of him.

"A little over an hour," Thomas said in a low voice raspy with fatigue. "Your mother is in with him now."

"You haven't had much rest. How long did you sleep?"

"I didn't. I've been at the office working. Anything to keep busy."

Michelle sat next to him and put a protective arm around his shoulders. "You'll collapse if you don't get some sleep. Try, all right? Go on home for a few hours at least."

Thomas shook his head. "Annette was right. I've pushed Dom since he was a little kid. He's never been like you or Brian." He smiled to himself. "A real scamp. Always pulling pranks and figuring out ways not to work. He could come up with more wild schemes to make a fast buck. Even when I was angry at him, I had to laugh." He hung his head. "I only wanted him to grow up and make something of himself. Maybe if I'd accepted him for who he is . . ."

"Don't, Daddy. Don't blame yourself." Michelle held him tightly.

"Your mother seems to have understood him better than I did." Thomas swallowed hard.

"You understood that he needed firm direction. And you were right. When he got into trouble, Mama let you be the bad guy. I didn't help by always criticizing you," Michelle confessed.

"Annette has never handled tough situations well."

"You mean she's weak." Michelle's voice was harsh.

Thomas frowned at her. "I've never heard you say a word against your mother. Has something happened between you two?"

"I guess I'm still a little angry about the way she jumped on you the other day," Michelle offered weakly.

Thomas cupped her chin with one large hand and turned her face to his. "How much did you hear?"

"Enough. Daddy, I'm so sorry."

"Mr. Toussaint." A tall man dressed in a blue scrub suit stood in the door. He still wore a stethoscope around his neck.

"Yes." Thomas stood up, his eyes wide with alarm. "Doctor Frazier, is anything wrong?"

"No, in fact we think there's reason to believe he'll be okay. And we don't think another blood transfusion is necessary. But he has a long road ahead to full recovery. Dominic will need extensive rehabilitation therapy. He's growing more responsive each day, though he hasn't spoken yet. Good thing you were able to give blood. With the AIDS scare, our plasma supply is low. Especially on rare types like his and yours. The other donor was completely incompatible." The doctor scratched his head, looking at Thomas quizzically. "Why did you think—"

"My wife panicked," Thomas put in quickly. "How much longer will he be in intensive care?"

"Another two days at least. But we'll want to get him started in rehab therapy soon after. Come by my office on the sixth floor later and we'll go over the details." Dr. Frazier shook his hand before leaving.

"You heard that? Dom is going to make it." Thomas's eyes shone bright with joy.

Michelle could manage to only nod she was so overwhelmed by the good news. Tears coursed down her face as they embraced. After a time, they sat together again.

"It's past time Dom and I really got to know each other. I had to almost lose him to realize that," Thomas said. He stared down at his hands. "I've got my son back, and I don't intend to lose him."

Michelle pressed her cheek to his, closing her eyes. "Things are going to be just fine, Daddy."

Thomas drew in a deep breath composing himself again. "Toussaint and Son, Electrical Contractors. How does that sound?"

"Beautiful." Michelle sat silent for a few minutes puzzling over something the doctor had said, or tried to, before her father stopped him. "Daddy, what other donor?"

"Hmm?"

"The doctor mentioned another donor. Who was he talking about?"

After several moments, Thomas said, "Ike Batiste. Your mother called him thinking he could give blood to Dom."

"Because Dom has a rare blood type. But the doctor said . . ." Michelle drew a sharp breath as the significance hit her. "That means Ike can't be Dom's father. Did you know?"

"I never needed a blood test to tell me Dom is my son, Michelle. I love all of my children." Thomas brushed her hair with gentle strokes. "Fathering a child is more than biology."

Michelle took his hand and kissed it softly. "I love you, Daddy."

Annette had come in so silently, her voice took them both by surprise. "Thomas, you can go in now."

Thomas gave Michelle a little kiss on the forehead before leaving the waiting room. He walked down the hall with a new spring in his step.

"Doctor Frazier says Dominic is coming along well, considering." Annette spoke in a faltering voice.

"Yes, he stopped in here on his way out." Michelle turned away from her mother to gaze out of the window.

"This has been a terrible ordeal for us all," Annette ventured.

"True."

"But now everything will be better."

"You think so?" Michelle's tone was cold and unyielding.

"Dominic is our son. Now that Thomas knows that—" Annette began.

"Daddy has always known Dominic is his son, Mama," Michelle said sharply. "He was hard on Dominic because he wanted him to be a better person, not because he thought Dom was Ike's son."

"So you've decided to be on his side," Annette whined. "You're more like your father than I thought. One mistake and I'm branded for life as a cheat."

"I could forgive you easily for one bad judgment, Mama. But you've lied to me for years." Michelle turned to her mother. "You portrayed Daddy as an insensitive brute who enjoyed trampling on your self-esteem. How could you use me like that?"

"Thomas threw himself into work and put everything else ahead of me. I was so lonely. Instead of understanding how he'd contributed to what happened, he placed all the blame on me!" Annette twisted her hands in her lap.

Michelle's eyes were hard as rock, causing Annette to shrink from her. "At least Daddy never tried to turn me against you, Mama." She moved to the other side of the room as Annette began to cry softly.

Brian rushed into the room followed by a frightened T'aneka. "What's wrong? Has something happened?"

"Oh, no," T'aneka cried.

"Dom's going to be okay." Michelle hurried to reassure them. "Doctor Frazier says he's getting better all the time."

"Then why are you so upset?" Brian went to Annette. She only shook her head and looked away. "Dad, what's going on?" He looked up as Thomas came back in.

"T'aneka, Dominic is actually moving his hands now. You can go in to visit him. The nurse won't mind." Thomas smiled at the young woman. He led her down the hall then returned. "I'll take your mother home. She's overwrought." He gently guided Annette out toward the elevator.

"Michelle, what is going on? If Dom is going to be okay, why is Mama crying?" Brian watched his mother move away with slumped shoulders.

Michelle took his hand and led him to a seat. "Brian, this is going to be a big blow, but, well—"

"What?"

"Mama had an affair with Ike Batiste, and Dom was born nine months later. All this time Daddy thought Dom was Ike's son, but now it turns out he's not." Michelle rubbed his shoulder to ease the blow of such terrible news. "I know what a shock this must be."

Brian eyed her for a few moments. "So you finally found out."

Michelle wore a stunned expression. "You knew? Why didn't you tell me?"

"I only heard it as ugly gossip about fifteen years ago. It's not the kind of thing you tell your eleven-year-old sister, you know. Dom was my little brother regardless. Besides, Dad never treated him differently than he treated me. He was tough on both of us." Brian shook his head.

"But I haven't been eleven for the last fifteen years. You should have told me," Michelle scolded him.

"And make things worse? No way."

"Well, Mama certainly fooled me all this time. The way she manipulated everyone. To think I used to get so mad at him for the way he behaved toward her. Under the circumstances, he was a saint." Michelle snorted.

"There you go again. Passing judgment." Brian threw up his hands in exasperation.

"But—"

"But nothing. Dad shut Mama out in his drive to succeed. He tried too hard to prove to her family and friends that she didn't marry beneath her. He forgot how much Mama needed him. And Mama? She's spoiled and used to being the center of attention. Even her mother said so more than once, remember?" Brian stared ahead with a sad expression. "They both made mistakes that led to this fix they're in, Chelle."

Michelle shook her head as if to clear it. "Maybe you're right. It's just a lot to take in at once. I feel as though I'm seeing our parents for the first time."

T'aneka came in, her face beaming. "Dom looks better. He opened his eyes a little, but I don't think he saw me. That's still a good sign, isn't it?"

"Sure is. Look what the kids made him." Brian held up a colorful crayon drawing with "Get Well, Uncle Dom" scrawled in childish handwriting. It was signed by Brian's two children. "I'm going to stick it on the wall when the nurse turns her back." He grinned at them before leaving.

"Michelle, I'm sorry about what's happened." T'aneka sat three chairs from her, staring at the floor.

"Honey, you don't have anything to be sorry for." Michelle got up and went to her. "You're just as much a victim here."

"No, Dominic wouldn't have gotten hurt if he hadn't been protecting me," T'aneka said in a wavering voice. She wiped her eyes with an already damp tissue.

"Of course he protected you. Dom wouldn't stand by and let someone he cares about get hurt—"

"No, you don't understand. Those guys were really after me." T'aneka turned teary, swollen eyes on her. "He was

lmost killed because of me." She buried her face in her
ands. "I've hurt you, too. I wouldn't blame him if he never
wanted to see me again."

"T'aneka, tell me what you're talking about." Michelle
pulled T'aneka's hands down and patted them.

"Lonnie and Miz Kinchen found out I was the one copying
hem invoices. Somebody had been following me for days
before me and Dom got attacked. So then I denied there was
nvoices like you talked about. And I'm sorry for getting
Dominic hurt and making it look like you made everything
up in your reports," T'aneka finished with a sniff and hiccup.

"You were the secret source passing information to Greg?
Why didn't you tell me?" Michelle exclaimed.

T'aneka nodded. "I got so scared after they beat Dom up.
Lonnie likes hurting people, and when he's mad . . ."
T'aneka shuddered. "Please don't hate me," she pleaded.

"Of course I don't hate you. It took a lot of guts to do
what you did." Michelle squeezed her hand.

Tears rolled down T'aneka's cheeks. "But if it wasn't for
me, Dom wouldn't be in the hospital and you wouldn't be
in trouble. I heard 'em say on Channel Six that you got suspended. I messed up everything."

"Stop that right now," Michelle said firmly. "It's not your
fault at all that Dom got hurt. And as for denying you gave
me those work orders, you were terrified for your life. Don't
blame yourself for that, either."

"Lonnie's got a big gang. I just hope they don't try to hurt
Dominic again." T'aneka dabbed her eyes.

"I doubt they'd be that stupid. Not with the police still
investigating." Michelle gave the young woman what she
hoped was a convincing smile of encouragement. She certainly hoped those thugs were not so desperate or bold to try
again. But for T'aneka's peace of mind, she dared not share
her own fears. "And what about you? Are you okay?"
Michelle asked gently.

"Sure, a coupla men drove up before they could— you

know. No, I'm fine." T'aneka squared her slight shoulders "I'm gonna take care of Dom. We'll come out of this okay Someday those men are gonna pay for what they've done."

"Men like that seem to get away with . . ." Michelle bi her lip.

"Murder," T'aneka said in a low voice, completing the horrible word in both their minds.

Michelle thought of Ike Batiste and all the evidence implicating him in the growing scandal surrounding the Housing Authority. Truthfully, she had always known him to be a man given to questionable business deals. Yet even she was shocked at the evidence of crimes being committed—if not with his consent, at least with his knowledge. No doubt he or his partners were responsible for the assault on Dominic and T'aneka. And maybe murder. She cringed at the thought that Anthony was somehow involved. Michelle felt a rush of warmth at the memory of his gentle hands stroking her. The hours spent holding each other, sharing intimate thoughts and feelings; those had been some of the most fulfilling hours of her life. The sharp pang of loss pierced her once more. *With all that's happened, he should be the last person on my mind. What's the matter with me?* Yet, she had to know.

"Did you ever hear Anthony Hilliard's name come up?" Michelle spoke in a steady voice. She tried to make the question sound neutral even though her heart was pounding in the few seconds it took T'aneka to respond.

T'aneka frowned in concentration. "No-oo, never heard of him. Least his name wasn't on none of them invoices or bills. Who's he?"

"Ike Batiste's nephew." Michelle watched her face carefully.

"Nah, his name never came up. And I'm sure he never did any work for them, either. Miz Kinchen's secretary is a lazy heifer. She always left all the filing for me. Walks around with her butt on her shoulder callin' herself an 'executive assistant.' " T'aneka lifted her top lip in scorn. "Anyway, that's how I was able to see all the invoices."

"You're sure?" Michelle's heart leaped with hope as she gripped T'aneka's arm without realizing it.

"Positive. Hey, Dominic told me 'bout you and him. Tough luck he gotta have Ike Batiste for a relative." T'aneka clucked sympathetically.

"Oh, that's over. I was just wondering—, I mean for purposes of the story," Michelle finished lamely. She let go of T'aneka's arm and stared at the floor.

"Uh-huh." T'aneka eyed her skeptically.

Thankfully, Brian came back at that moment. Michelle wasted no time escaping T'aneka's scrutiny. It was mortifying to realize her feelings for Anthony were so transparent. Michelle left T'aneka with Brian for her turn visiting Dom.

Entering the intensive care unit, she suppressed an involuntary gasp at the sight of her little brother so pale and lifeless. Michelle shivered at the thought of how close he came to dying. She took his hand and massaged it tenderly as she gazed at him. After a time his eyelids fluttered and he opened them.

"Oh, Dom. You're going to be just fine. Can you hear me, honey?" Michelle was thrilled to see a slow smile spread across his face briefly before his eyes closed again. She kissed his hand. "If you can fight against the odds then so can I," she promised.

Michelle left the hospital with a new determination. Not only would she help find the men who had attacked Dom, but she would prove her report was valid. She would do it for LaWanda, her baby, Dom, and all the others Ike had hurt.

For the next two days Michelle spent every hour putting together more evidence of the dirty deals going on at the Housing Authority. T'aneka helped her reconstruct from memory a list of repairs paid for but never done. T'aneka felt sure the regional HUD office had audit records showing expenditures. They organized dozens of photographs of apartments needing substantial work. Michelle converted her dining-room table into a desk. Stacks of papers piled up on it in short order. She sat sifting through the maze of federal housing regulations when the doorbell rang.

"Mrs. Hilliard." Michelle was flustered to find Anthony's mother at her door.

"Hi, Michelle. I apologize for showing up like this, but I was shopping nearby. Can I talk to you for a little bit? Of course if you're too busy—" Lizabeth scanned Michelle's face nervously as she knotted the strap of her purse.

"No, ma'am. Come on in. I don't know what I'm thinking letting you stand out there so long." Michelle patted her hair and looked around the living room. She began to pick up stray magazines and straighten the pillows on her couch. "Have a seat. Can I offer you something? A cup of coffee maybe?"

"Baby. Don't go to any trouble." Mrs. Hilliard sat down.

"No problem. Actually I'm making a pot now." Michelle smiled at her before going into the kitchen. She returned a few minutes later with a tray. "Here you go. Hope it's not too strong; I've been drinking it to keep going."

"Working hard, I see." Lizabeth nodded at the piles of books and papers on the table.

"Yes, ma'am." Michelle tensed up, hoping Lizabeth would not go over there. She remembered leaving a rough draft of another damning report on Ike's activities. When Lizabeth glanced away from the dining table to look at the rest of the room, Michelle exhaled slowly in relief.

"Lovely apartment." Lizabeth smiled tentatively at her.

"Thank you." Michelle shifted in her seat.

After several seconds of silence, Lizabeth put down her cup. "Anthony would throw a fit if he knew I was here, but I had to come. You can tell me this is none of my business. I'll understand if you do—"

"No, ma'am, I wouldn't do that," Michelle broke in.

"Now let me finish. You and Anthony belong together. There, I said it," Lizabeth said in a resolute tone.

"Mrs. Hilliard, I'm not sure what to say. But . . ." Michelle's voice trailed off.

"But it's none of my business." Lizabeth studied her face.

"Oh, I didn't mean that." Michelle wondered how to explain without insulting Ike. Surely Lizabeth must be as loyal to him as Anthony

"Ike," Lizabeth said as if having read her thoughts. "I know all about it. Let me tell you something. Ike has been wonderful to us. There were months he paid my electric bill, water bill, and house note because I couldn't. He treated Anthony like he was his son. If I tried to tell you everything he did for us during the first two years after Anthony's daddy left, I'd be here all night."

"Anthony told me how much Ike helped you both." Michelle looked down at her hands in her lap. She braced herself for a tongue-lashing about the news stories.

"Oh, he has. And I love him for it. But he's got some low-down dirty ways, too." Lizabeth chuckled at the look of astonishment on Michelle's face. "Baby, you think I had no idea what kind of shenanigans that rascal has been up to all these years? In fact, I could tell you things that would keep you writing for months."

"But Anthony worships Ike."

"Anthony still looks at Ike with the eyes of a little boy. He was young, impressionable, and in pain. I did the best I could trying to make up for the loss of his daddy. But there are times when a boy needs a caring man in his life. Ike was there when he needed him most. I can see both sides of Ike. Anthony hasn't gotten to that point yet." Lizabeth leaned forward, a worried frown creasing her face. "I'm afraid he'll be devastated. That's why it's important that he have you."

"Not me, Mrs. Hilliard. Anthony will never forgive me

for those reports I did." Michelle could still feel the sting of angry words they had exchanged.

"You love him. I can see it in your eyes when you talk about him. He'll need that love when he has to face up to what Ike is." Seeing Michelle open her mouth to speak, Lizabeth held up a restraining hand, cutting off her protest. "And to lean on while he fights to clear his name. Unless you believe he's guilty." She held Michelle's gaze for a long moment.

"No," Michelle said in a small voice.

"I thought not." Lizabeth smiled at her warmly.

"At least not directly."

"What does that mean?" Lizabeth asked. The smile vanished.

"There are a lot of ways to be an accessory to wrongdoing. Anthony has helped shield Ike from the consequences of his actions for a long time. Ike has gone way past 'shenanigans' as you call them."

"Anthony cares for the man who has been a father and friend. His only fault is loving Ike too much to see his faults." Lizabeth's hands trembled as she gripped her purse. "Anthony could go to jail."

Michelle looked away. She felt a chill of fear at the idea of Anthony being sent to prison. Yet how could she be sure of how much he knew of the attack on Dom. "Mrs. Hilliard, I'm sorry. I hope that doesn't happen. I really do. But Anthony and I don't have a future together."

"I see." Lizabeth stood up. "Giving up on a good man has been the sorrow of many a woman, Michelle. Trust me, I'm a living witness. Before I married Anthony's father, I was dating a man named Fred. I thought he was so boring. He didn't have one ounce of romance in him. Then along came handsome, charming Sonny Hilliard. Sonny said all the right words and did all the right things. I fell for him hard. Fred is still his same old plain self. But he's stuck by his wife for thirty years now and has been a wonderful father." She paused before going out. "Take my advice, Michelle. Don't be too quick to judge because of one mistake. Keep the whole man in mind."

Michelle locked the door and leaned her forehead against it. Brian's voice came back to her. He, too, had admonished her against making harsh judgments quickly. Michelle wanted to believe in Anthony. Part of her yearned for his touch even while a sharp inner voice warned her he could never be trusted.

Her mind reeled with the effort of sorting through the tangle of thoughts and feelings assailing her. But Michelle did not want to think anymore. Work seemed the only constant left in her life. Everything else seemed to shift and change shape. Writing always helped to center her no matter what else was going on. But she could not look at anything to do with Ike just now. Instead she sat down and plunged into finishing an article on Black tourist attractions in Louisiana for a magazine.

Fifteen

"You got yourself in a mess of trouble, I hear." Marcus sprawled across the large leather chair in his father's den. He regarded Anthony with a sardonic smile. "Tsk, tsk, cousin. Getting involved in drug trafficking."

"Very funny." Anthony fought the urge to knock the smirk from his face.

He had come over to have a private talk with his uncle only to find Marcus waiting with Ike. Marcus made it plain he would not voluntarily leave them alone. Ike sat nursing a drink.

"I think so, cuz." Marcus guffawed.

"Shut up, Marcus," Ike muttered into his glass.

"Come on, Pop. Lecture him on the evils of hanging with the wrong crowd. If you ain't up to it, let me. I remember all the ones you gave me word for word. They're classics." Marcus winked at him.

"Ignore him, Anthony. He's acting like a fool, as usual." Ike shot Marcus a cutting glance. "The cops won't charge you with nothin'. No evidence."

"But where did they get the idea I was involved with Troy's drugs deals? They mentioned a connection to the Housing Authority and some of the guys you helped get jobs, Uncle Ike." Anthony took a seat across from Ike.

"I dunno. Maybe some punk is tryin' to throw them off by fingerin' you." Ike avoided returning Anthony's gaze.

"But why me?" Anthony rubbed his chin.

"I said I don't know." Ike rose abruptly and strode to the bar. "Look, quit worryin' about it, all right? I'll fix it."

Anthony stiffened at his words. "Fix it? What are you talking about?"

"Please, Father dear, please let me tell him." Marcus leaned forward, sneering at Anthony.

"I told you to shut up!" Ike whirled on Marcus, his eyes blazing with rage.

"No, I want Uncle Ike to tell me." Anthony spoke in a tight, grim voice.

"I have contacts. They can get the police to see this was a set-up job," Ike said evasively.

"How can they prove it when I can't?" Anthony pressed.

"Because— Look, I said don't worry about it, all right?" Ike yelled. "I got business to see to." Without a backward glance, he stalked out. A quiet descended in the room as though his departure created a vacuum that sucked out all sound.

"He didn't answer your question, did he?" Marcus jeered.

"Since you're so eager to, you tell me." Anthony was not sure he wanted to hear. Ike's reluctance to explain planted a seed of fear that grew with each passing minute.

"Pop doesn't know details because he's made a point not to know them. Code words like 'take care of it' come in handy. Personally, I don't think Dad can save your butt. He's got his own problems." Marcus smiled with satisfaction.

"So Michelle was right about Uncle Ike all along." Anthony sat down as the full meaning of his words hit home.

"Don't be naive. Pop couldn't care less what Lonnie and his gang does as long as what they do don't hurt his pocket." Marcus shrugged. "It's his version of employee benefits, you know? Sort of like profit-sharing."

"And the contracts to repair or renovate low-rent housing?" Anthony said in a strangled voice.

"What can I say? Pop has his own way of handling overhead, too. Getting paid for work you don't do makes for a nice profit margin." Marcus watched the effect of his words on Anthony with relish. "So your girlfriend had his number all along. Unfortunately she can't prove it now."

"But her reports—"

"Word is she can't back them up with evidence. I hear she may have forged all those invoices. Too bad her little purple notebook has vanished," Marcus snickered. "Our lovebirds are both in hot water. You can't prove you're not a drug dealer and murderer. And little Lois Lane can't prove she's not a liar."

"No, it can't be," Anthony mumbled, staring ahead. "Uncle Ike connected to drug dealers and looking the other way?"

"Get off it, man! You knew," Marcus barked viciously. "You've been hearing it like I have for years. So don't come on with that innocent act. Hell, he's made me what I am today. I don't intend to scrounge around in the dirt with a lot of other guys for scraps. I want to be a big-time player. Just like dear old Dad."

Anthony jumped up and marched down the hall after Ike. He found him in his library punching the buttons of a large black phone on his desk. Ike took no notice of him but spoke into the phone.

"Tell him I want to talk to him. I don't give a damn if he is, get him on the phone now! Lonnie, this situation with my nephew." Ike's face grew rigid with rage as he listened. His fist came down on the desktop with a tremendous bang. "You listen to me, I know about a certain incident that happened on St. Claude Street two years ago. There are a couple of men still very pissed off. They'd be very interested to know who was responsible. I thought you'd see it my way." He slammed down the receiver.

"I need to talk to you, Uncle Ike." Anthony stood in front of him.

"It's going to be handled, okay? Quit worryin'." Ike downed the rest of his whiskey with one gulp.

"Thank you. Is that what you expect me to say? I should be happy you've got the criminal connections to help clear me of something I didn't do anyway? What the hell do you think you're doing?" Anthony placed his palms flat on the fancy blotter and leaned forward.

"Business, boy! Takin' care of business," Ike shouted.

"Drugs and murder have become regular business for you?" Anthony shouted back.

"You oughta know me better than that! Some of them guys I helped get out of prison been up to their old tricks, but I can't help what they do. Sure, I cut a few deals here and there. But that's as far as it goes."

"You can't just turn your head and say it has nothing to do with you." Anthony stood erect and grunted with disgust. "It seems Marcus is right. As long as it's good for your wallet, you don't care about anything else," he said. A sick feeling took hold in his chest. He could only feel repulsion as he saw the unrepentant look on Ike's face.

"Goddamn it, boy! I've been fightin' to make it in this world a long time. Diggin' my way out of the dirt with nothing but brains and guts. There's white guys doin' things a helluva lot worse than me. Know what they're called? Sharp businessmen, that's what. Tycoons, yeah. They makin' millions suckerin' the rest of these fools into thinkin' they been done a favor." Ike got up and paced as he spoke. "I built what I got from nothin'. Used to be a Black businessman couldn't get the time of day at Louisiana Premier Bank downtown. Now I got a five-hundred-thousand dollar line of credit. I didn't get nothin' without takin' risks." He whirled to face Anthony.

"That's your excuse? Because everybody else does it?" Anthony shook his head, his face a mixture of disbelief and dismay.

Ike drew himself to his full height. "Excuses are for men who feel guilty 'bout what they've done. That ain't me."

"Then we don't have anything else to talk about." Anthony turned to go.

"Wait, son." Ike caught his arm. "Maybe you think there was a better way; maybe you're right. But this is a hard world with a lotta folks waitin' to kick you down. Survival takes bein' ready to kick back. One thing you gotta believe, anything I've ever done was to make a better way for my family."

Anthony looked at Ike's hand on his arm then up into his uncle's eyes. "But not like this. You've built the family estate on a garbage dump. You can dress it up all you want. But the stench is still there." Anthony pulled away from him.

Outside, Anthony paused to look at the house one last time. He felt a lump in the pit of his stomach as he realized once more he was saying a final good-bye to someone he loved dearly.

"Hey, Gracie. Come on in." Michelle smiled broadly at the sight of her friend. "It sure is good to see somebody from the old salt mines."

"How are you holding up, kiddo?" Gracie gave her a peck on the cheek.

"Fair to partly cloudy. I miss it though. Damn, I feel cut off. I never realized how little we really say in those reports."

Gracie laughed. "Oh, yeah. Between unconfirmed rumors, material that would hurt somebody without adding to the story, grounds for a lawsuit, or somebody whipping our butts, a whole lot gets left out." Gracie nodded rapidly, her curls bobbing. "So you're doing good, huh?"

"Not bad. Park it anywhere, red." Michelle made a sweeping gesture toward the sofa and two large comfortable matching chairs.

Gracie sat down and cleared her throat. "Place still looks great." She gazed around.

"You were here only last month, Grace. What'll ya have? I got your favorite, Dr Pepper."

"So you're doing pretty good? Well, heck—you just said so, right? So you must be doing okay." Gracie's voice was shrill with forced cheer. She fidgeted with the stuffed pillows.

Michelle came back into the room with two glasses and a large bottle of the soft drink. She studied Gracie for several moments. "What's up? Come on, spill it."

"Nothing," Gracie screeched then pressed her lips together. "Nothing . . . really." She forced her voice unnaturally low.

"Gracie, your voice just went from soprano to bass in five seconds, which means you're lying." Michelle slid the bottle out of Gracie's reach. "No truth, no Dr Pepper. And don't forget, I know how bad you need Dr Pepper when you're stressed out."

"Grand jury," Gracie blurted then grabbed the soft drink, taking a deep swig. She wiped tiny beads of sweat from her forehead.

"Speak in complete sentences, please." Michelle inched to the edge of her seat.

"God, I thought you knew. But you don't, do you? I mean, you would have said something, called me at work if you had. Maybe it's not as bad as it looks. I mean the grand jury is only investigating." Gracie gulped down some of the soft drink. "I'm so sorry."

The doorbell rang, forestalling Michelle from further questioning Gracie. She went to the door and opened it. Shantae rushed in wearing a look of concern and sympathy.

"Girl, how are you holding up? Now don't jump to conclusions just because the grand jury is going to question him." Shantae patted her shoulder rapidly.

"What are you talking about?" Michelle stood between them. She looked at one then the other.

"You mean she doesn't know?" Noticing her for the first time, Shantae crossed to sit beside Gracie.

"Must not have watched the noon news show," Gracie said in a solemn voice.

"No!" Michelle shouted. "I don't know. So somebody tell me what's going on.

"The DA has called a grand jury to examine the evidence they have on the Troy Quarles murder so far. Anthony has been subpoenaed. They say he's the prime suspect." Gracie looked down at the floor.

"Prime suspect." Michelle sank onto the sofa slowly. She shook her head as if to clear it.

"An accusation isn't proof of guilt, Chelle," Shantae said with fervor.

"She's right, Michelle," Gracie said.

"First Dom is beaten up, and then this man is found dead. Could this be my fault? Maybe those reports put so much pressure on Lonnie Mason and Ike that they got desperate." Michelle raked her fingers through her hair. "Or Anthony could have repeated something I said to his uncle or Marcus, making them panic." She rubbed her forehead trying to remember their conversations. "What did we talk about?"

Shantae sat forward and took her hand. "Don't do this. You're not to blame for what happened to Dominic or that other guy."

"My Lord, what a mess." Michelle closed her eyes.

Gracie tried to soothe her. "I know, sugar. It seems to get worse by the hour." She started at the sound of her cellular phone. Taking it out, she spoke into it softly. "Okay. On my way." Gracie shoved the phone back into her satchel and stood up. "Listen, I've got to go. The DA has called a press conference. Since Earl's down in Plaquemine covering that big refinery accident, I'm on this story for now. Take care. I'll call you later." She raced off.

Michelle locked the front door and fell back onto the sofa with a low sigh. "I don't want to think what I'm thinking,

Shantae. Anthony meant the world to me." A tear slid down her face. She quickly wiped it away.

"Cedric says it's got to be a setup. He swears Anthony has never been in on any of Ike's crooked deals." Shantae handed her a tissue.

"But Ike wouldn't set Anthony up. He may be a sleazy character, but he really cares about Anthony. No, that doesn't make sense." Michelle turned to her. "And aside from what Cedric thinks, T'aneka says Anthony hasn't been in on the those contracts with the Housing Authority."

"So you do believe in him." Shantae grinned at her. "He hasn't done anything, Chelle."

"Then why is Anthony a suspect?"

"Stereotype. He's a well-dressed, successful Black man. One of his employees was involved in drugs and turned up dead. You figure it out," Shantae said hotly.

"Uh-uh, too many coincidences. First, this Quarles guy starts working for Anthony, deals drugs, claims the boss is in on it, then turns up dead. With the connection to Ike, and everything else that's coming out . . . it's logical to suspect him. No, there's another angle to this." Michelle stared ahead thoughtfully. Her mind whirled trying to sort through the contradictions. She rubbed her eyes making them even redder.

Shantae tapped Michelle's knee. "Come over to my house for dinner. Don't sit here alone agonizing over this."

"No, thanks. You and Laree have done a very good job baby-sitting me." Michelle smiled at her. "But I'm all right."

"You sure?" Shantae rose, picking up her purse.

"Positive. You go on and give that handsome son of yours a big kiss for me." Michelle walked with her to the front door.

Shantae gave her a worried look. "I'll check on you later."

"Fine. Now go on home." Michelle waved her out.

Closing the door, Michelle sat on the sofa with her feet

tucked under her. Using the remote, she switched on the television and found Channel Twelve. She reviewed her experiences with grand jury investigations. Being questioned might not lead to an indictment, but it could certainly leave an ugly stain on a man's reputation. Especially a businessman. Michelle tried to examine the facts objectively. Her anger at Anthony for defending Ike could be clouding her judgment. Surely the man she knew could not have deceived her so completely for so long. Anthony had never given her cause to suspect him of aiding Ike in his schemes. Yet didn't Anthony admit that he was headed down a path to prison until Ike stepped in? Could those tendencies be hidden under a veneer of respectability?

"I have to find out one way or another," Michelle said.

Seeing the five o'clock edition of the news starting, she turned up the sound of the television. Gracie appeared shortly with her report as the lead story after a short introduction by the anchor. Michelle flinched when Anthony's face came on the screen. Yet she steeled herself to watch. She pushed aside her reaction to the terrible accusations and made detailed notes.

"Missing? How long?" Michelle exclaimed, staring at him with amazement.

Earl draped himself over her living room sofa while Gracie sat in the chair with her feet propped on the matching ottoman. Her friends had joined Michelle for lunch at her apartment. They were stuffed on shrimp po-boys, curly-Qs, and giant-sized soft drinks.

"Two weeks. His sister reported it when she couldn't get him at his office or home. Mrs. Bridges dumped him before that. Seems adultery was one thing, but putting up with him *without* the money isn't a sacrifice she's willing to make." Earl wore a lopsided grin.

"You think he's been . . ." Michelle hesitated.

"Killed? Could be. James Bridges was the weakest link in their chain. And from what I hear, he'd been spending a lot of time with the DA. Maybe somebody decided to shut him up." Earl drew a finger across his throat.

Gracie shivered. "This is getting too scary."

"Tell me about it. These dudes play for keeps. Anyway, Connely doesn't seem to be acting real panicky. Maybe he's got enough already to drop the hammer on Ike and Co." Earl shrugged.

"Then why hasn't he moved to get a grand jury indictment? No, something else is going on. I just wish I could figure it out." Michelle chewed on a fingernail.

"Don't be surprised if they find poor old James floating facedown in Bayou Manchac." Getting up, Earl wiped his mouth and tossed his empty cup into the large kitchen garbage can. "Gotta move, good people. There's a meeting of the state senate's judiciary committee in twenty minutes. Keep keepin' on, babe." He kissed Michelle on the forehead. "And I'll see you back at the sweatshop." He waved goodbye to Gracie.

"How are things in the wonderful world of Channel Twelve?" Michelle poked Gracie's foot with hers.

"SOS. Same old stuff." Gracie giggled. "Jason swaggers around giving orders. Most of us nod and do what we want anyway."

"And the lovely Jennifer?" Michelle grimaced.

"Still obnoxious."

"At least she's consistent." Michelle joined Gracie in laughter. A knock on the front door made them both start. "Wonder who that could be?" Michelle peered through the peephole then stepped back, staring at the closed door.

"Well? Who is it?" Gracie whispered. She wore a frightened expression seeing Michelle move away from the door. A louder knock made her jump behind the sofa. Michelle opened the door slowly. "Hi."

"Hi." Anthony stood uncertainly in the door without moving forward. "Can I come in?"

"Uh, yeah." Michelle swung the door wider, her heart beating double-time. She watched his handsome profile, breathed in the sweet aroma of him, as he passed within inches of her. "You remember my friend Gra—" Michelle turned around to find only the top of Gracie's head and eyes visible from behind the couch. "What are you doing?" Michelle placed both hands on her hips.

"Oh, I was looking for, I mean . . . , I dropped . . . something." Gracie popped up with a sheepish grin. "Hello again." She waved at Anthony.

"My friend Gracie. A good, though slightly strange, friend." Michelle gave her a baffled sideways glance.

"Nice seeing you again, too." Anthony smiled briefly at her then looked at Michelle intently for a few seconds. "I came by to tell you I'm sorry about Dominic. How is he?"

"Dom is doing better than expected. Every day he's more responsive. Thanks for asking." Michelle fidgeted with the drawstring on her sweatpants. She wondered what to do or say next.

Gracie tugged on her shoes and grabbed her purse. "Umhmm. Well, I gotta be going. Lots of . . . stuff to do."

"Stay right there," Michelle barked at her. "Uh, I mean we haven't finished that story you were helping me with." She fixed her with a pointed stare.

"Oo-kaay. If you say so." Gracie sat down as if she had been pushed hard.

Michelle squirmed at the silence that stretched between them. Looking up into Anthony's troubled brown eyes sent a tremor through her body. Her arms ached with the desire to hold him. She set her jaw firmly, bent on resisting this powerful attraction he exercised on her even now. *Stop thinking of him like that!* Michelle struggled to compose herself.

"Is that all?" Michelle regarded him in what she hoped was a cold manner.

Anthony's face was drawn with disappointment. "I guess. I'm really glad Dominic is going to recover."

"No thanks to those thugs who tried to kill him," Michelle said angrily.

"Do the police have any leads?" Anthony shifted from one foot to another.

"A few," Michelle lied. The police had no clues as to the identity of the attackers. "Hopefully they'll make an arrest soon." She studied his face for signs of guilt.

"I hope so, too." Anthony started to move toward her then stopped. "If I can help you at all—"

"We're fine. Thank you." Michelle went to the door and opened it.

Anthony's shoulders drooped seeing her implacable expression. "Good-bye." Anthony nodded to Gracie before leaving.

"Bye." Michelle closed the door hard behind him. She kept her back to Gracie for a few seconds before turning around. "That's that."

"Want to talk about it?" Gracie asked in a soft voice.

"No," Michelle said in a curt tone. "Subject closed."

"If you say so. Well, what's next?"

"Work. Thankfully my career in radio isn't dead. WDUP-102 lost their reporter to a rival station. Steve Peters is the station manager now, and he offered me a job. And I still haven't given up on the Housing Authority story."

"Will work be enough?" Gracie raised an eyebrow at her.

Michelle went to the table and picked up a stack of papers. "I'll make it be enough."

"That's the third one this week, Anthony." Cedric sat down heavily in the chair across from Anthony's desk. "I thought we had that job sewn up. Man, sure do find out who your real friends are when you're down."

"Um-hmm." Anthony continued to gaze out of the large window to his left that gave him a lovely view of the early spring day. The courtyard was bright with sunshine and the light green burst of new vegetation coming forth. But his melancholy expression was in stark contrast to the scene before him.

Cedric got up and poured a cup of coffee. "Old man Taylor was stuttering and stumbling about some kind of delay. He's trying to back out because of those damn rumors. We oughta sue his behind. We signed a preliminary agreement with him."

"If you think we should," Anthony said in a flat voice. He sat as still as before.

"Damn straight. We got a letter from his assistant saying we should prepare the specs, too. Who does he think he is anyway? He's been in caught up in so many scandals, the reporters in this town have him on speed dial."

"Maybe so."

"Say, you're not listening to me." Cedric frowned at him. "Oh, forget about those jerks. We'll get more and better jobs. Wait and see." He tried to lighten his tone.

"I guess." Anthony could muster no strong emotion. No anger and certainly no hope.

"Say, man. It's going to get better."

"How? Projects that we spent weeks working to get are drying up. It's only a matter of time before we have to lay off some of the men." Anthony massaged his temple. "Maybe it's a sign that coming home wasn't such a hot idea after all. Atlanta is looking real good to me right now. And without me holding you back, it's a cinch the phone would start ringing again."

"No indeed, brother man. We went into this business as partners and we're going to fight to save it together." Cedric jabbed a finger at him.

"Cedric, I don't have the heart for it. Things are crashing down on me." Anthony squeezed his eyes shut.

"You've taken some hard knocks here lately, but hang tough." Cedric leaned toward him to put a hand on his shoulder. "I'm with you all the way."

"I appreciate it, Cedric. I really do. But finding out about Uncle Ike . . . I feel like such a fool." The despondency Anthony felt was etched on his face.

"Ike did a number on you and a lot of other people."

"It's as though he's two different men. The Uncle Ike that reached out to help me and Mama doesn't look anything like the man I saw three days ago. Did he change or have I been that blind all these years?" Anthony held out both hands to Cedric, begging for understanding.

"He was two men, Anthony. That's the thing. Nobody is all good or all bad. With Ike, he just swung between both extremes. He'll go the extra mile to help his family and friends. Problem is, he goes about it the wrong way." Cedric lifted a shoulder.

"Wrong is an understatement. Try criminal," Anthony said, his voice laced with bitterness. "And the worst thing is I've lost the woman who means the world to me. All because I was too stupid to see the truth."

"No chance?"

Anthony shook his head, his eyes full of misery. "I went by her place yesterday. To talk to her." He fell silent, unable to go on.

"Didn't go too well, huh?" Cedric gave him a sympathetic pat on the forearm. "Listen, it's still kind of soon. It may take a few days or weeks, maybe longer, but Michelle will come around. Shantae says she's crazy about you, man."

Anthony attempted a smile but his mouth turned down instead. "Thanks for trying, buddy. But with the attack on Dominic, I doubt she can ever feel the same about me."

"Michelle can't believe you had anything to do with that!"

"Yeah, but my uncle, the one I've been defending so long,

probably did." Anthony's voice rose in anger. "I can't say I blame her, either."

Cedric placed both hands on Anthony's shoulders and stared at him hard. "Don't give up, Anthony. Maybe you can talk to her."

Anthony moved Cedric's hands firmly. "It's no use, Cedric. You didn't see the coldness in her eyes when she looked at me."

"I've got to get out of here. Listen, you do whatever you think best. I don't really care anymore." Anthony's eyes were dulled by pain as he gazed at his friend. "I'm no good for you, Cedric. With all you put into this place, you deserve better than me."

"Anthony, don't give up everything you have," Cedric pleaded.

"Trouble is, I probably did that months ago. I just didn't know it." Anthony walked out.

Anthony drove aimlessly for over two hours. Thoughts of Michelle filled his mind, blocking out his sense of time or place. The knowledge that her smile would never welcome him again or her voice soften with affection saying his name created a blunt ache no medicine could cure. He headed toward False River. Without realizing it, he traced a favorite route of theirs for long Sunday drives in the country. The parking lot of Sonnier's boat landing in downtown New Roads had only a few cars with empty boat trailers. Anthony got out of his car and sat on a bench. He watched the water gently lap against the bank. The reality of learning to live without Michelle settled on him like a gloomy fog that dimmed the bright sunlight.

"We can't find him nowhere, Lonnie." J. J. eyed him with an uneasy feeling.

Lonnie had been striding back and forth for ten minutes alternating between shouting obscenities and ominous si-

lence. The news of James Bridges disappearance disturbed
them because they were not the cause of it. Tia sat next to
Marcus on the battered couch of their headquarters. Of the
men spread around the living room, she alone seemed unaf-
fected by Lonnie's blasts of rage. She watched him with a
calm expression.

"Maybe somebody beat us to it, man. What I'm sayin',
could be he's dead already." T-Bone grinned foolishly, flashing gold teeth. "Saves us trouble and bullets, yeah."

Lonnie whirled around. His eyes filled with wrath. Clearly
he was eager for a target. "This some kinda damn joke to
you, huh?" Both of his arms were down at his sides with his
hands balled tightly into huge fists.

"Nah, man. I'm sayin' . . ." T-bone let his voice trail off
seeing the savageness in Lonnie's face.

"T-Bone's right though," Tia said in a controlled voice.
She allowed her gaze to flicker across them all. "Bridges
could only make things a little hot for us. After all, how
much does he know?"

"He knows me! He's been over to Charlotte's office with
me and Ike," Lonnie shot back, striking his chest with a thud.

"And you talked in front of him?" Tia's eyes closed until
her eyes were almost hidden. It gave her the appearance of
a tigress about to strike.

"Nothin'," Lonnie blurted, looking away. "I didn't say
nothin' outright he can testify to in court."

"But you said somethin'. Humph." Tia's voice dripped
with scorn. "Real smart. What you're sayin' is you gave him
enough to put the DA on the right trail."

"Look b—" Lonnie started toward her. All five men
blocked his path with menacing stances. Lonnie staggered
back in shock at the protective ring they formed around her.

"Back off," J. J. growled, no trace of fear on his coarse
features.

Her position established, Tia sought to smooth over the
tense moment of friction. "Listen up, we got to get our heads

together. This ain't no time for fightin' between us. Let's consider all the options. Bridges know about a lotta skeletons that could get some powerful folks jail time. Maybe one of them decided to take him out."

Lonnie let his shoulders relax. "It's possible. But we gotta make sure somehow," he muttered, still eyeing the other men with hostility.

Tia turned. "J. J. and Leo, I want everybody we own, everybody that owes us, to get the message out. Five hundred for whoever can tell us where Bridges is. Concentrate on the crack heads for sure. The bourgeois ones especially. They got friends of friends in his social circle. Tap the most desperate, offer 'em merchandise. But find him. Alive or dead."

Marcus placed a hand on her thigh. "One way or the other, Bridges won't be a problem much longer. We'll get him."

"You think so?" Lonnie snarled. "How do you know he's not somewhere spillin' his guts to the DA or some cop? They could have him stashed in any of a hundred places."

"I doubt that, man," Marcus said with confidence. "My old man has a source down there. If they had him, Pop would be meeting nonstop with his attorney."

"Then where the hell is he?" Lonnie shouted.

"Why don't you ask Miss Charlotte?" Marcus smirked at him. "They're pretty close, I understand."

"Be real careful," Lonnie said. His chest rose and fell rapidly. "He ain't nothin' to her, you hear me? Nothin'." He stood very still in front of Marcus.

After several taut seconds, Marcus lifted his hands palms out as if surrendering. "Okay, no problem."

"He's got a point, Lonnie." Tia stood between them. "Everybody knows they were goin' together before she met you. Could be she'd be able to give us an idea where he is."

Lonnie inhaled sharply then let the air out noisily from flared nostrils. "I already asked her. She don't know," he admitted grudgingly.

"Well, we need to get to him fast, no matter where he is or who's hidin' him." Tia tilted her head up to look Lonnie straight in the eye. "Meantime, let's all just hang loose."

Lonnie lifted both arms in a casual gesture. "Hey, I'm cool." He cracked a humorless smile at everyone in the room." He moved back. "Let's take care of business."

For another ten minutes, Tia issued instructions to J. J. and the others. Plans to use every gang member and all of their contacts were put into action. J. J. began muttering into the small cellular phone he carried. The other four gang members left hurriedly.

Lonnie rubbed his jaw while eyeing Marcus with eyes clouded with suspicion. "Bridges been hangin' with your old man a long time."

"Yeah. So?" Marcus raised an eyebrow.

"So he could be hidin' Bridges." Lonnie shot a sideways glance at Tia, who continued to examine her long, acrylic fingernails studded with rhinestones.

"No way. I would definitely know."

"Maybe not. Your daddy don't exactly think all that much of you," Lonnie retorted. He spoke to Tia directly, ignoring Marcus. "They could be cuttin' their own deal. Givin' us, you and me, up to the DA right now."

"Interestin' theory. What about it, Marcus?" Tia said without looking up from her hands.

"That's crazy! I'd know if my old man was up to something like that." Marcus glared at Lonnie. "Don't try it, man," he warned. Turning to Tia, he rushed to close any beginning distance Lonnie may have caused with his suggestion of treachery. "Besides, he's got as much to lose. My old man wouldn't cut no deal. He'd rather go down fighting."

"A man gonna do whatever it takes to save his ass when push comes to shove. Know what I'm sayin'?" Lonnie's lip curled in contempt.

"Let's find Bridges first," Tia cut in to head off another confrontation between them. "Then we'll do whatever is necessary to get rid of any threat to our business interests." Her cold, probing gaze flickered between the two men as they both grasped the deadly meaning behind her words.

Sixteen

The hallway outside the grand jury room was crowded with reporters from as far away as Shreveport. Michelle stepped over light cables and dodged cameramen as she made her way closer to the crew from Channel Twelve.

Bob swung the minicam around, checking the settings and pointed it directly at her. He smiled broadly. "Hey, now. You still looking good."

"Hello, Bob. How's the news game these days?" Michelle looked around recognizing most of the reporters. "Lord, what a zoo."

"Yeah, they smell blood all right." Bob frowned at her. "Sorry, champ. I forgot he's a friend of yours."

"Don't sweat it." Michelle gave him a reassuring pat on the arm. "Gracie with you on this one?"

Jennifer strode up to them, pointedly ignoring Michelle. "Bob, one of the law clerks just told me Connely is coming out that door. If we position ourselves here, he'll have to pass right by us."

"Don't you think it would be better for me to wait outside? I could get footage of the witnesses coming into the court-house. More dramatic." Bob shot Michelle an exasperated look. "You could always interview Connely on his way out or later today."

"Just do what I tell you," Jennifer said, a peeved note in

her voice. "I decide how we're going to lead this off, okay? We'll film the witnesses leaving."

"But you probably won't get a quote then. Most of the time they're too tired or cranky after being grilled for hours." Michelle gave Bob a mischievous wink. They both knew there were pros and cons to both ways, but she enjoyed irritating Jennifer.

Jennifer's lip curled with disdain. "Advice from you isn't worth much these days. If you were so smart, you'd be covering the story instead of reading headlines on a dinky radio station."

"Yes, but I do it with style." Michelle lifted her nose in the air.

"I guess you have to tell yourself something. Well, excuse me. I have a real job to do." Jennifer walked off to another group of television reporters. Glancing over her shoulder, she made it clear that Michelle was the topic of conversation.

"Real sweet lady, huh?" Bob snorted.

"Charming," Michelle said. She looked at her watch. "They're five minutes late."

"There was some kind of delay until the DA's top investigator could bring over more documents before the first witness." Bob turned sharply, hearing the hum of voices behind them rise. "I better move it." He rushed off to stand beside Jennifer.

Michelle started forward then froze. The sight of Anthony, his lawyer beside him, surrounded by the reporters, made her tremble. His handsome features were blank as he pushed his way forward without speaking. Michelle knew only too well how he must be suffering under the pressure of constant media attention. Anthony and his attorney swung abruptly to face the pack shooting questions at them. Several microphones were thrust forward abruptly. Both men blinked in the glare of a large light pointed by a news crewman.

"Mr. Hilliard has every intention of cooperating with the

investigation fully. That's all we have to say at this point."
The attorney spoke in a gruff voice.

Anthony stared ahead at no one. He seemed to be far away
from the madness that swirled around him. Michelle knew
the reporters had a job to do, yet she cringed to see him
assailed so. Suddenly Anthony's gaze found her. Michelle
looked away unable to bear the sadness and disappointment
in his eyes. When she dared glance up again, he was disap-
pearing through the doors of the grand jury room.

Moments later, Connely strode down the hall and went
through the double doors, leaving one of his assistants, a
smartly dressed young woman, behind.

Adjusting wire-frame eyeglasses, she gave a chilly professional smile. "We have no comment at this time." She turned
disregarding questions being yelled at her.

Jennifer turned a sober face to the camera. "Sources tell
Channel Twelve that Mr. Hilliard is being questioned in connection to the murder of Troy Quarles. As we've reported
earlier, Mr. Quarles was a known drug dealer with a long
arrest record. He was also an employee of Mr. Hilliard at
the time of his murder. There is speculation that his death is
somehow related to drug trafficking and that Mr. Hilliard
was involved. We'll update this story at ten. This is Jennifer
Lang reporting." She lowered the microphone once the camera was off and looked at Michelle. "Seems your boyfriend
is in a tight spot."

"Being questioned isn't a conviction or even an indictment." Michelle wanted to convince herself more than Jennifer.

"I hear Troy Quarles got the job with your boyfriend on
a recommendation from Ike Batiste. You dug up the dirt on
his uncle that led the police straight to him. Seems Mr. Hilliard has you to thank." Jennifer smiled maliciously.

Michelle took a step toward her. "I'm sure you have some-
place you need to be, right?" Her voice was raw with anger.
Jennifer backed away and scuttled off.

"Don't let her get to you, champ." Bob shook his head watching Jennifer strut down the hall.

"Not to worry, she won't. See you later." Michelle waved good-bye to him and several others as she left.

Michelle had all she needed for the short news spot on WDUP. She headed back to the radio station. Once there she wrote her copy and collected other stories from the on-line news service. She finished up at six that evening, the last newscast of the day. Too keyed up to go home, she turned her car toward the hospital. Dominic had been moved to a regular room when his condition was upgraded to serious.

"Hello, sport." Michelle kissed the top of Dominic's bandaged head gently. "How're you feeling today?" She took his hand in hers.

"Can't complain." Dominic smiled. He still spoke in a slow, raspy tone. "You just missed T'aneka. I finally got her to go home." He shifted. He pressed a button to raise the head of his hospital bed.

Michelle pulled the smaller of two chairs next to him. "She's a real sweet person."

"Very special. For the first time in my life, I'm thinking about somebody other than me." Dominic grinned at her. "Those lectures Dad gave must have been planted subliminally. Me going to work every day, sticking to one woman at a time—and all *before* I got hit on the head."

"All a part of Daddy's master plan. You've been programmed, little brother," Michelle teased.

Dominic's expression became serious. "One day when I was still in intensive care, I woke up and saw Dad sitting in the corner with his head in his hands. He looked worn down. Man, when I think of all the stupid stuff I did just to piss him off. And there he was, right by my side." His eyes grew bright with tears.

"Daddy may be a bit . . . hard-nosed, shall we say? But he truly wants the best for us all," Michelle said softly.

Wiping his eyes, Dominic chuckled. "Yeah. For the first time in my life, we agreed I should quit my job."

"Have you heard from Buster Wilson by the way?"

"He called yesterday. That's when I quit. I could hear the relief in his voice on the phone." Dominic reached for her hand. "T'aneka told me you left the station. I'm sorry, sis."

"I've already bounced back." Michelle gave his hand a reassuring squeeze.

"I saw the news story about Anthony. T'aneka is positive Anthony had nothing to do with Lonnie and his gang. Now Marcus, sure. In fact, Marcus got in tight with the Park Boulevard Posse within a few weeks of working at the Authority."

"Who are they?"

"A group of gang-bangers in the project on Park Boulevard. T'aneka knows more about it than I do." Dominic looked at her with worried eyes. "You and T'aneka be careful. Those guys are running scared. They're capable of anything on a normal day, but now . . ." He grimaced.

"Take it easy." Michelle tried to calm his fears. "With this murder and the police bearing down on the flow of cocaine, they've got other worries now. We'll be all right."

"Anthony didn't do anything. Lonnie sent his punks after T'aneka because she gave you those invoices. Shantae says you broke up with him." Dominic studied her face.

"You just concentrate on getting well and forget this other garbage. Shantae talks too much." Michelle drummed her fingers, annoyed at her friend.

"Don't fuss at her. I nagged until she told me the whole story. Chelle, just the look on your face when his name is mentioned tells me you still love him like crazy. Don't you put him on trial, too."

"I promise to think about it." Michelle was touched by the concern in his eyes. She gently pushed him back against the pillows. "Now get your rest."

Later at home in bed, Michelle tossed about for an hour

before deciding to give up trying to sleep. Thoughts of Anthony, Ike, and Marcus chased around her head keeping her alert and edgy. She decided to review her notes and research. Michelle spent the night piecing together all she knew about Charlotte Kinchen, Ike, Buster, and James Bridges. None of it led to Anthony. Michelle fingered the sheets of paper in front of her. At least she knew with certainty that Anthony was not a criminal. That was something. But the gulf between them was still too great. How could he ever forgive her for doubting him? Michelle pushed the mound of newspaper clippings aside to uncover her cordless phone. Though they would never be together, she could at least help get at the truth.

"You sure you don't know anything 'bout where he is?" Lonnie spoke in an even tone. He sat in the chair across from her desk, watching her face carefully.

"How many times are you going to ask me that?" Charlotte snapped.

"Seems strange he ain't tried to call or see you. He was hot for you."

"James may not be the brightest man in the world, but he's not a complete idiot. I think he suspected I was seeing someone else." Charlotte chewed the eraser of the pencil she held. "He acted kind of distracted the last time we . . . saw each other." Gripping the pencil tightly, she shot a guarded look at Lonnie.

"Humph, took the sucker long enough." Lonnie shrugged.

Charlotte's shoulders relaxed. "Ike could be hiding him. He's certainly has a lot to lose if James talks."

"Ike does seem to be playin' it mighty cool now that you mentioned it. Maybe I oughta pay him a visit," Lonnie grumbled.

"I'll save you the trip." Ike pushed the door to Charlotte's office shut with a bang. "You got somethin' you wanna ask me?"

"Yeah. Matter of fact I do." Lonnie rose from the chair to face him. "Got any ideas where to find your pal, Bridges?"

"No. What else?" Ike stood with his legs apart and both hands on his hips.

"Now why do I find that kinda hard to believe?" Lonnie's nostrils flared. His gaze raked Ike from head to toe aggressively.

"Because you're an ignorant fool who ain't got sense enough to conduct business without lettin' the police know your every move," Ike said with a growl. "Course I was stupid for not seein' that. After all you been in and out of prison so many times, they got a uniform embroidered with a permanent number just for you."

Lonnie snarled like an enraged pit bull. He launched across the room clutching for Ike's throat. Ike jabbed his fist into Lonnie's midsection with one quick motion, then drove it into his chin knocking him against the far wall. Ike kicked him twice in the side when he tried to stand.

"Oh, my God!" Charlotte cowered in a corner trying to get as far from them as she could.

"Get up!" Ike bellowed at Lonnie. "Get up, I said!" A group of large men rushed into the room.

Lonnie struggled to his feet coughing painfully. He panted with the effort. Charlotte stood close to Ike looking at Lonnie with dispassionate eyes.

"I kept telling him we don't know where James is, Ike." Charlotte placed a hand on Ike's forearm.

"You back-stabbing bitch," Lonnie growled through swelling lips.

"You're fired. Charlotte, take care of the paperwork. Of course, your parole officer will have to be notified." Ike nodded to the men. Two of them moved forward and grabbed Lonnie's arms.

"This ain't over," Lonnie yelled at them as he was dragged from of the room.

"You better hope it is, fool," Ike said in a rough, dangerous voice.

"Thanks for coming." Michelle gave LaWanda a hug after closing her front door.

Lawanda strolled in and took a seat. "Girl, you know I'm gonna help you. Besides, you just crazy enough to bring your silly butt back over to the project."

"The tenants group members had any more problems? I've been out of touch what with spending time with my brother and not being at Channel Twelve anymore." Michelle handed her a diet soda.

"Nah, child. We got security patrols now. The big boys from HUD in New Orleans showed up a few weeks ago. They hired a group of men who was unemployed as security guards. It's workin' out nice. They get a salary for it and doin' simple repairs, too. Besides, the cops put some heat on them gangsters." LaWanda chuckled. "They got more than us to worry 'bout these days."

"And how's little Relondo?"

"Honey, that little rascal actin' almost like nothin' happened, praise the Lord." LaWanda waved a hand in the air.

"Amen." Michelle smiled thinking of the brown bundle of energy darting around the apartment.

"Speakin' of you not bein' at Channel Twelve, that really sucks. We all know you didn't make none of that up. And we told it to that Gerald Mansur, too." She nodded at Michelle before taking a sip.

"Say what?" Michelle's eyes went wide.

"Sure did. Candy and me went to see the man the day after we found out. Told him in no uncertain terms what we thought about his jive station not standing behind you."

LaWanda shrugged in apology. "Sorry they didn't listen and give you your job back."

"Hey, I appreciate the show of support. You folks are something else." Michelle felt good knowing how much others were behind her. She sat forward eager to begin the real work of tracking down clues that would lead them to the men responsible for the attacks on Dominic and Relondo. "Tell me what you know about the Park Boulevard Posse."

"You mean Tia and her boys? They deal outta the projects over there. They run drugs, guns, do burglaries, you name it."

"Ever hear of Marcus Batiste?"

"Yeah, Ike Batiste's son. Word is he's goin' with Tia. Little criminal started workin' at the Authority and fell right in with them. Lonnie Mason got his gang, too. But I hear him and Tia's gangs on the verge of a showdown. See . . . Lonnie thought he was in charge. Now he's findin' out Tia's been pullin' the strings all along. She just let him think he was top dog. Fit her plans, see what I'm sayin'?" LaWanda sat back and crossed her legs.

"How do you know all this?" Michelle shook her head in amazement.

LaWanda laughed. "Honey, the grapevine in the projects is better than any twenty-four-hour news channel."

"Then tune me in. I want to know everything." Michelle got a notepad from the dining-room table. For over two hours, she made notes furiously while LaWanda talked of the intricate pecking order of the gangs, beginning with how they got started.

For the next three days, Michelle divided her time between the radio station and chasing down facts surrounding the Park Boulevard Posse, Lonnie Mason, and the sinister connections both had with the parish Housing Authority. What she found was alarming. Not even LaWanda and her friends knew the extent the gangs controlled life in the projects. Lonnie had a group of ex-cons loyal to him. They organized a crime syndicate of petty thieves and drug dealers into a wide network with branches in all of the large projects. Tia's gang was mostly young people who had grown up in public housing. A battle for control seemed inevitable. The Park Boulevard Posse was showing signs of resentment at being ordered around by Lonnie's gang.

Michelle was ready to begin using this material for a series of reports on crime. The station manager at WDUP had given her the green light. She spent hours writing and rewriting the first report. Once it was finished, she asked Earl and Gracie to critique it. They sat in a nearly deserted sandwich shop late one afternoon. The three met regularly for lunch to share opinions and insider tips and good old-fashioned gossip. They took turns choosing where to meet. Poor Boy Pete's was always Earl's pick. Earl scanned the pages spread in front of him while Michelle tapped one foot nervously.

"Well?" Michelle could hardly sit still as she watched his brows draw together in concentration.

Earl swallowed a portion of his sandwich. "Needs something else." He gazed up at the ceiling.

"What?" Michelle leaned over to peer at the report.

"Tabasco sauce." Earl reached for the bottle.

Michelle groaned in frustration. "Can you please think about something other than your bottomless belly?"

"He's obsessed with food. That means Cheryl has them on another diet." Gracie tittered.

"My wife is now on an organic vegetarian kick. We can only shop at this health food store." Earl swallowed. "I feel like Bugs Bunny with all the leaves I've been gnawing on lately."

"Well, she's just trying to keep you healthy. That greasy meal certainly isn't good for you." Gracie pointed to the mound of curly fried potatoes on his plate.

"Excuse me, but could we get back to this?" Michelle waved her notes in the air.

Gracie pushed her empty salad plate aside. "You should

get a police interview and some crime stats on the projects for the past two or three years."

"Yeah. Maybe start out with that instead of the tenants' viewpoint?" Michelle took a sip of seafood gumbo from the small cup in front of her.

"No," Earl broke in. "You had the right idea starting out with that. It's the human interest angle that hits home with the audience. But put them together for a stronger effect."

Michelle snapped her fingers. "I've got it. I could say something like the tenants' concerns are borne out by the crime figures in the projects." Michelle scribbled in the margins of the page. She finished a sentence with a flourish. "Perfect."

Gracie cleared her throat. "Michelle, did you find out anything about Anthony?"

"No. So far nothing connects him to the drug deals or the rest of it." Michelle stared down into her gumbo, stirring it slowly.

"So the guy is innocent? Good deal, right? No reason you can't get back together." Earl looked at her.

"It's not so simple." Michelle did not look up.

"Remember the story she did on his uncle?" Gracie jabbed him in the side with her elbow. "Don't bring that up," she whispered close to his ear.

Earl flinched. "Ouch! I mean . . . oh, yeah. But anyway this is good work you've done tracking down the scoop on those crooks." He kicked Gracie's foot with his in retaliation, causing her to jump.

"Oww! I mean, great work, Michelle. Every bit as good, better even, than the series at Channel Twelve." Gracie nodded.

"Thanks. Now quit beating up on each other." Michelle squinted at them through her bangs. "Do I have 'Fragile— Handle with Care' stamped on my face?"

"Don't blame me." Earl shot Gracie a cutting look.

"It's just that you've been through the ringer lately. What

with your brother getting assaulted and you being suspended from work," Gracie said.

Michelle squeezed her hand. "Thanks, but things are looking up. Dominic is on the mend and I'm not suspended anymore."

"When did Lockport tell you?" Earl sat back with a surprised expression.

"For real? Fabulous. When are you coming back?" Gracie stared at her wide-eyed.

"Lockport didn't tell me anything," Michelle said to Earl. "And I'm not going back." Smiling, she looked at them both. "I quit. Turned in my resignation letter yesterday and left it with his secretary."

Gracie gasped. Earl let out a long whistle.

"I've sold three freelance articles already. And WDUP is going to do an early morning talk show. Steve wants me to be the host." Michelle beamed with pride.

"You've got guts. Go on with your bad self." Earl winked at her.

"I'm thrilled for you," Gracie said. "I can't wait to see the look on Jennifer's face when I tell her you've got your own show." She rubbed her hands together in anticipation.

"Okay, but I get to spoil Jason's day." Earl grinned impishly.

"You two are worse than teenagers planning a practical joke." Michelle laughed.

Michelle worked at the radio station reading news briefs and lining up guests for the talk show for the rest of the day. She was happy at least with her career. Being in control was frightening and exhilarating. Frightening because she did not have the security of a regular paycheck. Yet the challenge of setting her own course gave her a charge she had never experienced before. With a much smaller income now, Michelle learned to adjust her spending habits down. But she did not mind at all. The future looked bright. More opportunities were opening up all the time with help from friends. Michelle sat in her office totally oblivious to everything as she sorted through stacks of articles looking for ideas to develop for the talk show.

"Hello, Michelle." Dosu stood in the open door, smiling. The dark gray suit was impeccably tailored. "How have you been?"

Michelle gave him a welcoming hug. "Fine. It's so good to see you. What have you been up to lately? How did you know I was here?" She grabbed a chair and pulled it next to her own.

"Steve is a good friend of mine. As for what I've been doing—a great deal of travel really. I've just come back from St. Thomas. You would have loved it." Dosu smiled revealing ivory teeth set against dark chocolate skin. "I would have invited you if not for . . ." His voiced trailed off.

"I've been very busy working," Michelle said a little too sharply. She squirmed under his amused gaze.

"Michelle, who do you think you're deceiving?"

"Anthony and I are no longer seeing each other." Michelle tried to keep her voice matter-of-fact. She rearranged items on an already neat desk.

"You may be apart physically but not in your hearts." Dosu waved a hand in the air. "An old African proverb says—"

"Dosu, please," Michelle cut him off. "Can we talk about something else?"

Dosu smiled benignly. "Fine. So how is the news game? You do not miss being before the camera?"

Michelle sighed. She could not deny the excitement of a live news broadcast was a big part of why she loved television reporting. "It was an adjustment. The hard part is all the pitying looks I get from colleagues. They see it as a big comedown."

"What about you?"

"I'm too busy working to feel sorry for myself. Besides, all I have to do is quote the demographics for WDUP. I get a kick out of seeing their faces. The audience of young, working African-Americans listening to our blend of rap and urban contemporary music equals the size of the audience tuning in to the five o' clock news on Channel Twelve every day," Michelle bragged.

"Yet as you say, it is a big change." Dosu inclined his head. "If you need help financially you have only to ask."

"No, thanks," Michelle said quickly. "I'm doing okay. I'm in no danger of being homeless and hungry." She smiled at him with fondness. "You're sweet to offer though."

"Where do you go from here?"

"Things are looking up. I've gotten stories printed in a couple of magazines and my own show here."

Dosu studied her for a moment as if reading her innermost thoughts. "Then why is there a hint of sadness in your voice?"

"Well, I don't like the way I left Channel Twelve for one thing. I didn't falsify those reports." Michelle felt the same outrage as the day Lockport suspended her.

"Anyone who knows you does not believe you did," Dosu reassured her.

"And I intend to clear my name." Michelle's eyes narrowed at the thought of how she had been set up.

"No doubt you will." Dosu favored her with a confident nod. His expression became grave. "I understand your Anthony is also under a cloud of suspicion. A most deadly suspicion of murder."

"Yes. There's a grand jury looking into it." Michelle bit her bottom lip.

"He may be indicted for the death of an employee and trafficking in cocaine." Dosu rubbed his chin. "A very bad business." He glanced at Michelle from the corner of his eye.

"Yes." Michelle's face became pinched with gloom. "It looks very bad."

"You believe these accusations?"

"No," Michelle blurted. She blushed under his questioning gaze. "And not because of our . . . history. The whole deal smells of a setup, too."

"But the proceedings are secret. Maybe they have strong evidence against him." Dosu nodded. "Why else would he be a target?"

"That doesn't mean a thing! An accusation is not proof of guilt," Michelle said, her voice hot with indignation.

"Such fervor in your words. You still care for this man deeply." Dosu held up a hand to forestall her denial. "It is all over your face, Michelle."

Michelle exhaled slowly. Her jaws muscles tightened with irritation. "Dosu, you have a most annoying way of—"

"Hitting the nail on the head?" Dosu gazed at her with affection. "Do not be angry with me. I won't point out the truth anymore."

The phone on her desk rang before she could retort. "Hi, Earl." Michelle listened for a few moments. "I'm on my way." She grabbed her large bag, throwing an extra notepad into it. "The grand jury's findings are going to be announced at a press conference in fifteen minutes."

"Good-bye then." Dosu stood to one side. "And Michelle"—he touched her arm lightly, causing her to pause before rushing past him—"I wish the best, for both of you."

Michelle could only nod in response.

A mob of reporters from around the state filled the hallway outside of the DA's office. Michelle pushed her way through, trying to get close to Earl. He was interviewing one of Connely's assistants about the investigation of the Housing Authority.

The stocky man seemed nervous in front of the camera.

He kept tugging at his necktie. "Yes, that is correct. The U.S. Attorney is handling the Housing Authority case now since it involves the possible misuse of federal funds by federal employees. Our office will continue to pursue the Troy Quarles murder investigation."

"Do you have any other leads or suspects at this time?" Earl stuck the small microphone under his nose, causing him to jump back.

"Uh, all we can say now is that our investigations are continuing."

"Thank you. That was Lyle Kramer, assistant district attorney. As we've been reporting, the East Baton Rouge Parish Housing Authority has been under close scrutiny based on allegations that we first reported in an exclusive series. Numerous allegations of fraud, mismanagement, and even criminal activities surfaced over the last five months. We will continue to follow this situation closely. We'll be back to report on the findings of the grand jury the moment they are ready. Earl Gaines reporting for Channel Twelve. Back to you, Chad." Earl visibly relaxed once the camera went off. "Hey, Michelle." He loosened his necktie.

"So even though Lockport and Jason accused me of making up a story, they've got you still on it." Michelle's smile was more of a bitter grimace.

"Exactly. Lockport asked me about your missing notepad and the work orders. I think he realizes he moved too fast. Even Nathan jumped his case about not standing behind you." Earl clapped her on the back. "Reliable sources say he's planning to give you a call real soon."

Michelle shook her head. "Too little, too late."

"Now don't let emotion cloud your judgment. Look at it this way, you can come back on your own terms."

"I'm on my own terms now," Michelle broke in.

"Full- or part-time, the money is good." Earl pressed on undaunted.

"It's not worth it if I can't depend on them to back me up," Michelle countered.

"Getting a call from Lockport is a vindication of sorts."

"He hasn't called me yet. And if he does, look how long it's taken him to do it."

"And . . ."—Earl gave her a wink—"even more important, you can rub Jason's face in it."

Michelle chuckled imagining the look on Jason's face seeing her walk into the newsroom. "Hmm. Maybe I shouldn't hold a grudge."

They waited for another tense five minutes before a flurry of activity signaled the press conference was about to begin.

"Here he comes." Earl spotted the district attorney coming from his office. He hustled forward, motioning the minicam operator into position. "Yeah, we're ready." He spoke into headphones, alerting the station to switch back for a live report.

Connely's face was stern as he stood just outside the double glass doors to his office. At least five microphones from various television and radio news departments were perched on the podium in front of him. Michelle held her breath waiting for him to speak. A low murmuring began whose focus seemed to be to her left. Glancing over her shoulder, she saw Anthony, Cedric, and Anthony's attorney striding from an elevator on their way out of the government building. Three reporters broke from the crowd to race after them. Their exit blocked, Anthony's attorney shot out terse answers to their questions. Connely's voice boomed out, drawing her attention back to him. Michelle's heart raced in anticipation of calamity.

"The grand jury has declined to return an indictment." Connely stared straight ahead. He did not react to the clamor of shouted questions. When it was clear he would not respond, the voices died away and he went on. "It is their determination that at this point there is insufficient evidence to warrant an indictment. The investigation into the murder of Troy Quarles will continue. We hope to reconvene the grand jury at a later date. Thank you." He tucked his notes into an inside jacket pocket.

"Mr. Connely, does this mean that Anthony Hilliard is no longer a suspect?" This was shouted by a female reporter from a local newspaper.

"Mr. Hilliard is one of the individuals who knew Mr. Quarles that we have questioned and will continue to question in an effort to resolve this case," Connely intoned in an impassive voice.

"So you have other suspects?" Earl yelled over other voices.

"We are pursuing other avenues based on recent information given to us. Thank you." Connely turned and disappeared into the large office.

Michelle gasped with relief. She leaned against the wall for support. Like a tide going out to sea, the gaggle of newshounds moved toward the three men still caught between the elevators and the doors leading outside. Drawing in a shaky breath, she turned to find Anthony staring at her. He seemed impervious to the crush of people around him. Michelle walked toward him glancing neither left nor right, unable to break from the steady gaze that seemed to draw her closer step by step.

His attorney stood erect. "We felt certain that Mr. Hilliard would be cleared of any involvement in this crime."

A tall reporter addressed Anthony directly. "Mr. Hilliard, do you have a statement?" He held a small microphone out toward Anthony.

Anthony's gaze never left Michelle's face as he spoke. "I'm glad this is over. I only want to get back to my life . . . and those I love."

Gradually the reporters dispersed having no more questions to ask. Michelle took a deep breath before meeting Anthony halfway across the lobby.

"Hi, Michelle." Cedric smiled at her. "I'll meet you outside, Anthony."

He only nodded at him as Cedric headed out of the doors. "How have you been?" His eyes were bright with expectation.

Michelle hesitated. She wanted to blurt out how happy she was for him. Yet guilt restrained her. Had she not played a part in throwing his life into turmoil? "Okay. Congratulations. I'm glad things turned out the way they did."

Anthony's face was drawn. He rubbed his forehead with a weary gesture. "There's still a cloud of suspicion hanging over me. I wanted to be cleared completely."

"Come on," Michelle said. She started to reach out and touch his arm then drew back. "Don't look at it that way. No indictment means there is no evidence linking you to the murder. That lack of evidence points to your innocence."

Anthony stepped closer to her. "It's enough to know that you don't think I'm guilty."

Michelle looked up into his deep brown eyes. The curve of his lips sent a charge of excitement that began in her chest and ended with a tingle in her toes. Before she could speak her beeper went off. Rattled by her strong reaction, Michelle fumbled with it for several embarrassing moments. She pressed the button to retrieve the message.

"Station calling. Guess I better get back." Michelle smiled self-consciously. There was so much she wanted to say. But where to begin? Thoughts and feelings crowded her so, she could not find the right words.

Anthony's attorney joined them. "Excuse me, Anthony. Hello." He gave Michelle a polite nod. "I wanted to talk to you. Don't go, miss. This will take only a few minutes."

"Yeah, wait, Michelle. We won't be long." Anthony moved toward her when she began backing away from them.

Michelle felt the distance growing between them again. Sounds around her became muffled as she struggled to reach out somehow. But a sense of being powerless held her. "I have to leave anyway. Congratulations again. See you around."

Anthony watched her walk away. "I hope so," he called out. His voice echoed plaintively in the large hallway.

Seventeen

Lonnie paced the length of Charlotte's large living room like a restless panther. He had smoked four cigarettes in the last thirty minutes. Charlotte watched with wary eyes, afraid to complain about the haze that filled her luxury apartment.

"Damn it, somebody's got to know where he is!" Lonnie inhaled deeply. "Either he got scared and ran or somebody lyin'." He stopped short in the middle of the room to stand directly in front of where Charlotte sat stiffly on the edge of the large ivory sectional sofa.

"Wouldn't we know by now?" Charlotte was careful to keep her voice calm and steady.

"That's just it. If the DA got him, what they waitin' on? It don't add up. I'm bettin' Ike Batiste got him tucked away somewheres and his punk son knows about it." Lonnie's voice held a deep, ominous timbre. His heavy black eyebrows pulled together.

"Ike wouldn't be acting so nervous if he knew James was no threat to him," Charlotte said. Her facial expression was all openness.

"Don't be fooled by that." Lonnie sat next to her. "It's an act, like you said. Think about it. Ike keeps us all in the dark until he and Bridges can cut a deal with the DA."

"Oh, no. I can't believe they would do such a thing. Especially not James."

"Get smart, babe. We talkin' some heavy stuff goin' down.

We talkin' the U.S. Attorney. Long federal sentences." Lonnie snorted. "If you think old James is gonna do hard time just 'cause you gave him some, you outta your mind."

Charlotte grew very still. "And then there's a murder. But James didn't have anything to do with that. You did."

"Yeah, but he can help the damn cops come straight to me." Lonnie blew out a long stream of smoke.

"You were careful, weren't you? I mean getting rid of the gun." Charlotte swallowed hard. "Nobody saw you, right?"

Lonnie turned on her with bared teeth. "Never mind that! Ain't nothin' gone lead the cops to me unless somebody talked too much."

Charlotte drew back from him and became silent for a few moments. "Tia and Marcus have gotten very . . . close. You don't think Marcus and she would try to set you up? Maybe they know something, too." Charlotte watched the effect of her words on him. "Having you arrested would take the heat off them." She bit her lip and stared at him with wide, guileless eyes. "I mean, isn't that the way people like that think? Maybe James has been threatened and is too frightened to let anyone know where he is. You know how paranoid he was the last month or so."

Lonnie stood up and resumed pacing. "Could be Tia has decided she can kill two birds with one stone. Get all the action for herself and give the police a neat package. I been thinkin' somethin' like that myself." He seemed oblivious to her presence. He rubbed his hands together as he walked. "I ain't never trusted them two since they got together."

"Baby, come try to relax. Tomorrow you could ask around—"

"Hell, no! I'd be a damn fool sittin' around waitin' for them to make the next move." Lonnie grabbed his jacket draped over a portion of the sectional sofa. "I'm gonna get my boys out again. Ain't nobody sleepin' until we find somethin' out one way or another." He was out of the door in three strides.

Charlotte did not move for several minutes. Hearing the roar of his car starting, she jumped up and went to the window. She was careful to move the draperies only a little to watch him leave. Charlotte watched the red taillights of his black Ford Bronco disappear completely before she went to the phone.

Tia unwrapped herself from Marcus and sat on the side of the bed. She lit a cigarette. When the phone rang she paused to push back her long braids before picking up the receiver. "Yeah. Uh-uh, we'll deal with it soon. Yeah, I'll tell you about it." She hung up without saying good-bye.

"Who was that, baby?" Marcus ran his fingers along the smooth nut-brown skin of her back.

"J. J." Tia stood up and stretched in front of the mirror. A small smile tugged the corners of her mouth at the effect this had on Marcus.

"What's up? He found James?" Marcus sat up in the bed.

"Nah, just some minor business." Tia put on a green-and-gold silk robe.

"Like what?" Marcus held a shiny silver lighter to the end of a long cigarette.

"Routine stuff. Listen, you sure your old man don't know where this Bridges guy is?" Tia went to the large closet. She sorted through several outfits before pulling out a form-fitting pair of red leather pants and matching cropped sweater.

"He wouldn't have any reason to hide it from me." Marcus blew out a circle of smoke.

"Y'all don't get along too good. Maybe he ain't hidin', just ain't mentioned it." Tia walked back to stand in front of him.

"I know him," Marcus said with a trace of irritation. "He would have told me by now. Why you keep asking me that anyway?"

Tia looked at him for a moment before speaking. "Lonnie's right. Seems strange Bridges wouldn't call your old man since they've been buddies all this time."

"Yeah, well he hasn't. James could be somewhere in Argentina for all we know." Marcus frowned. "It's Lonnie we need to worry about. He's crazy. That night we picked up Troy was wild. Hell, I didn't think he was gonna kill the dude."

Tia shrugged. "That's business, too. But puttin' his body on your cousin's property was a bad idea."

"It got them a suspect." A baleful grin spread across his face. "I bet Anthony's been sweating bullets for weeks."

"It also made the cops keep lookin' at the connection to the Housin' Authority." Tia regarded him steadily.

"Hey, baby, don't worry about that. It'll blow over. Hell, they probably got Anthony staked out thinking he's the head of a drug ring." He chuckled.

"With Lonnie gettin' some fool to shoot into that apartment hittin' that kid, we been havin' to lay low for a while. Business is down, which means profits is down. We ain't been able to move a big shipment in two months. Now the DA pissed off 'cause he didn't get to indict your cousin." Tia took a long pull on her cigarette.

"I told you not to worry about it, didn't I? I'm the one made the connections we needed to get into the big money. Me and the boys can take care of things. You just relax." Marcus got out of bed. He pulled open her robe. "Don't bother 'bout the details. I'm gonna make sure you get everything you need," he whispered in her ear and buried his face in the smooth skin of her neck.

Tia's lips curled into a menacing sneer as she watched him in the mirror. "I'm gonna take care of you, too, sugar."

"Are you crazy? Anthony wants you so bad he can taste it. And you feel the same way," Shantae cried out loudly. Other patrons at the restaurant stared at them.

"Don't tell us you're over him." Laree folded her arms. "It won't fly. No man could replace him when y'all broke before. He's the only man for you."

"Speak up. I think there may be ten people in Baton Rouge who didn't hear you," Michelle hissed, keeping her voice low. She nodded toward all of the eyes turned in their direction.

Shantae plowed ahead. "You call him right now." She dug a coin out of her purse and pointed to the pay phone in a far corner.

"That's right. There is no reason for you to be apart. You need each other, especially now." Laree placed a hand on Michelle's. "This is a time for coming together. For holding each other tight in a warm embrace against the bitter cold of adversity," she said dreamily.

"Lord have mercy, Laree. You've been watching those old low-budget movies on the 'Late, Late Show,' again, haven't you?" Shantae wisecracked.

"Be Still My Heart starring Lenore L'amour is a classic for your information." Laree sniffed.

"Lenore who? Be real, girl," Shantae turned her attention back to Michelle. "Look, Chelle, you want him, he wants you. The chemistry is smoking and the math adds up. Jump on it." She held up the quarter.

"How many times do I have to go over this? It won't work," Michelle said. She pulled at her hair in frustration.

"Yes, it can, Chelle. Sure the road to love and happiness can be rocky, but—" Laree's face was soft with sentimentality.

"Laree, do you mind?" Shantae cut in. "You don't have an excuse anymore because Anthony has washed his hands of Ike." She smiled with satisfaction at the startled look on Michelle's face.

"Really?" A look of hope spread across Michelle's features then immediately died. "No, that's impossible. The way he talked about how much Ike meant to him and his mother? Anthony would stand by Ike through anything."

"Come on! You really think Anthony would keep defending Ike after everything that's happened?"

"Anthony has never believed all the accusations made against Ike." Michelle raised an eyebrow at her, obviously skeptical at such a change. "Why now?"

"Ike all but admitted he was involved in the mess when Anthony confronted him about it. Cedric says Anthony hasn't spoken to Ike since then and won't return his phone calls."

"Poor Anthony. He worshiped Ike. If what you're saying is true, it must have hit him hard." Michelle could certainly empathize. Learning about her mother's affair with Ike had left her deeply shaken.

"He's heartbroken. And even more miserable since y'all broke up because of Ike."

"Oh, Chelle, he's crying out to you. Go to him. Run to his outstretched arms." Laree's eyes were misty.

"Pu-leeze, Laree! You're making me nauseous." Shantae squinted at her in annoyance. "She's right about one thing, though. You should call him. No, go on." Shantae pushed Michelle out of her chair.

Michelle gathered her courage as she dialed. After four rings, she started to hang up with a mixture of relief and disappointment. Then she heard the fifth ring cut short by a "Hello?" The sound of his deep, mellow voice melted all her misgivings.

"Thanks for seeing me on such short notice." Michelle stood just inside the door to his apartment self-consciously. Her rehearsed speeches fled at the sight of him, tall and alluring, so close. The rise and fall of his broad chest brought back only too well how fabulous it felt to lie against him. Looking up to into his eyes, she blushed, sure her face mirrored her passionate thoughts. Michelle shifted around so as not to face him. She needed time to think and a clear head.

"No problem." Anthony touched her elbow to lead her farther into his living room. He bustled into the kitchen after getting her settled on the sofa. "I made some apple-and-cinnamon herbal tea. Your favorite."

"And dark-roast coffee for you, I bet." Michelle laughed. "I know you haven't given up your strong coffee, have you?"

"Well . . . no. But I've cut back. And what's more, I'm having a cup of tea with you." Anthony grinned at her. He placed a cup and saucer in her hands and sat next to her.

"Wow, you'd do that for me?" Michelle said in a playful tone.

Becoming serious, he placed his cup on the coffee table in front of them. "Chelle, that's the least of what I'd do for you."

"Anthony, I feel awful about the way I've behaved."

"No, wait. I was as wrong. I know that now. Uncle Ike is everything you've always said he was and worse." Anthony's eyes glittered with anger. "He's lied, cheated, and stole all his life. His excuse is that he did it for his family. He crossed the line from shady business practices to being an accessory to crime." Anthony breathed deeply. "I didn't want to believe those things about him. And instead of facing the truth, I blamed you for telling it. Can you forgive me?"

"Anthony . . ." Michelle started, but her voice failed her. Setting the cup aside, she wrapped her arms around him. "Of course I can," she whispered, caressing his cheek with her lips. "Can you forgive me for all the dreadful things I said to you?"

Anthony cupped her chin and stared into her eyes. His answer was a deep, long kiss. Michelle clung to him for several sweet moments before she pulled back.

"Wait. Some things need to be said while I can still think clearly." She heaved a deep sigh. "I've been wearing blinders, too."

"What are you talking about?" Anthony touched her face tenderly.

This would be harder than she thought. "I've always felt sorry for my mother and blamed my father because their marriage went sour. It never occurred to me that she might be just as much to blame. Ike and Mama dated while they were all in high school, but Mama married Daddy. Several years later, she had an affair with Ike. Ruining their marriage and Daddy's business was the perfect revenge for Ike. Suddenly here was this woman I'd never seen before. Weak and selfish. I still haven't forgiven her." Michelle turned to him. "Now I truly understand how you couldn't see Ike for anything but the loving uncle who cared what happened to you. And how you must feel now."

"Uncle Ike seems to spoil everything he touches." Anthony's face creased in a morose frown.

"Not everything. In his own way, Ike does care about you. I was so intent on pointing out his faults, I didn't see how good he's been to you and your mother."

"That doesn't justify what he's done," Anthony insisted.

"No. But people are rarely all good or all bad, Anthony." With loving fingers, she lightly touched his forehead smoothing away the sullen ridge above his eyes. "I guess we have to see them as human beings with the same failings as everyone else."

"How did you get so smart?" Anthony held her tightly.

"Getting hit over the head a few times will either kill you or teach you something." Michelle smiled with a shrug. She nestled into his arms and looked up at him. "You think you can put up with an opinionated reporter always poking into things folks would rather keep quiet?"

Anthony lowered his face to hers. "Definitely," he murmured.

Anthony took her mouth completely while his hands stroked her face and neck. His tongue parted her lips in a loving quest to taste her. From far away Michelle heard her own voice, a soft moan from the base of her throat. She clung to him, straining to press her body ever closer to his. With the urgency of passion too long denied, they tore loose from their clothes as if breaking free of chains.

"Right here, right now," Anthony said in a voice hoarse with desire.

They sank onto the sofa, pushing the pillows from around them. Their lovemaking had all the heat and potency of a flash fire. Between eager kisses, Anthony whispered assurances he would never let her go. Michelle molded her body to his in blissful surrender and answered with vows of love.

Michelle retrieved a pillow. She rested against him as he reclined on the arm of the sofa. The warm, spicy scent of his cologne sent a thrill through her. "I like the way you apologize." She closed her eyes, savoring the wonderful sensation of having him in her arms again.

"You've got a real gift for saying 'I accept.' " Anthony stroked her thick, dark hair.

"Anthony, we've got some unfinished business." Michelle gazed ahead. The real work of their reconciliation must begin. "I mean, maybe we need to talk about what happened between us."

"Uncle Ike." Anthony grunted with displeasure. Getting up, he went into the bedroom. He returned wearing pajama pants and handed her the matching top.

Michelle put it on. "No, about trusting each other. I should have trusted you would never condone getting paid for nothing or criminal activity—not even for your uncle."

Anthony put his arms around her again. "And I should have trusted that you wouldn't lie or misuse your position as a reporter just to get revenge. I see what you're saying. So where do we begin?"

"First, why don't we get some more hot tea?" Michelle smiled. "And then . . ."

"I know, we need to talk." Anthony eyes twinkled with mischief. "For once those words don't send a chill down my spine." He dodged a playful swat Michelle aimed at his arm and headed for the kitchen.

Warmed by the tea and each other, they lay curled together on the sofa for hours. They shared their dreams, fears, disappointments, and hopes as never before.

Michelle felt light as air moving around the radio station the next day. Everything seemed shiny and new. It took effort to keep a cheerful lilt from her voice as she read even the most solemn news items from the wire service. She finished up with a weather update and began gathering her notes to leave. The disc jockey went back on to introduce the next tune.

"Next up, an oldie but goodie," Danny, a short, muscular man with a sonorous voice, crooned into the microphone. " 'Reunited' by Peaches and Herb."

Michelle had turned to leave but hesitated when she heard the opening strains of the ballad. "Reunited and it feels so good," Michelle sang. She swayed to the music.

"Somebody is feeling mellow today." Danny raised an eyebrow.

"I just really like that song." Michelle gazed off, a serene expression on her face.

"Hey, if I'd known that I would have played it before now." Danny snapped his fingers in time to the music. "I'm off at seven tonight. You and me down at the Blue Room—how about it?"

"Sorry, I'm involved." Michelle smiled at him. Those words had a fabulous sound. The happiness on her face proved she was anything but sorry. She went back to her office still humming.

Shantae and Laree were waiting for her. Both wore knowing smiles as they watched her approach.

"What's up, girl?" Shantae gave her an appraising look from head to toe. "You're in a very good mood."

"Yeah, she sure is," Laree agreed.

Michelle meticulously straightened her desk and filed away old news copy. "What are you two doing here?"

"We were just out this way," Laree blurted.

"Yeah. We decided to go out for dinner after work and figured you might want to go." Shantae gave Laree a conspiratorial wink.

"Oh, I can't tonight." Michelle pressed her lips together.

"Really? Working late, huh?" Shantae raised an eyebrow at her and nudged Laree with an elbow at the same time.

"Not exactly." Michelle said keeping her voice cool.

"How can you 'not exactly' work?" Laree followed Michelle closely around the room. "You're either working late or not. Which is it?"

"I'm not working, but I can't go out to eat with y'all." Michelle had her back to them, putting folders into a large cabinet.

"Why not?" Shantae stepped closer to Michelle.

"Yeah, what's the big secret?" Laree moved in, too. She fixed Michelle with a sardonic gaze.

"No secret—" Michelle turned to find herself almost nose to nose with both of them.

"Then what's the deal?" Laree smirked at her.

"None of your business." Michelle giggled pushing between them to pass.

"Let's guess, Laree." Shantae blocked her attempt. "Now, judging from the grin on her face I'd say a man is involved."

"Yeah, she's got that look all right," Laree chimed in.

"Not just any man, either. I'd say this was *the* man. Know what I'm saying?" Shantae glanced at Laree sideways.

"I hear you. This is Dr. Feelgood, honey. She's got that afterglow." Laree snickered.

"Shut up, you two." Michelle tried to sound aggravated as she pursed her lips to prevent a smile.

Laree laughed. "Sugar, don't even try it. We knew what the deal was when we didn't hear from you last night."

"For real. As soon as we walked in I said to myself, uh-huh. They're rockin' steady again." Shantae nodded.

"Come on, girlfriend. Enquiring minds want to know." Laree took a seat and crossed her legs. "Give up the details."

"It was incredible," Michelle breathed. She dropped all pretense of being cool and collected. "We talked for hours."

"Just talked?" Shantae's lips curved in a knowing smile.

"Like I said, incredible," Michelle said. Her face was radiant with joy.

"That's great, Chelle. You and Anthony belong together." Laree hugged her.

"Cedric says Anthony has been grinning all day even with business being down since—" Shantae's hand flew to her mouth. "Sorry, Chelle. I had to spout out bad news just when you're feeling good for the first time in over two months."

"That's okay. Don't think it hasn't been on my mind. Things would be perfect except for this suspicion hanging over Anthony." Michelle's brows drew together. The subject tempered the buoyant mood.

"But he wasn't indicted," Laree said in a bid to cheer them.

Michelle sat down with a thump. "It doesn't matter. Some people apparently feel an accusation is the same as a guilty verdict."

"What he needs is for them to catch whoever killed that guy." Shantae perched on the arm of the chair Laree sat in.

"And soon." Michelle nodded. Her stomach tightened with fear at the possibility Anthony could be sent to prison.

"The cops must be searching for another suspect since they didn't have enough evidence against Anthony." Laree looked from Michelle to Shantae. "I mean, it makes sense."

"I hope so. But who knows. They're not saying a whole lot these days," Shantae replied. "You'd think Ike would lift a finger to do something. After all, he got Anthony into all this. He should get him out of it."

"What could he do without getting himself in trouble?" Laree asked.

Michelle stood up and grabbed her purse. "Laree is right, Shantae. Even if he had the conscience, Ike would have to admit to some knowledge of drug dealing and who knows what else. No, he probably wouldn't do it even if he wanted to."

"I guess so. It just seems a shame that Marcus is the little criminal, but Anthony is getting all the heat." Shantae followed Michelle and Laree down the hall.

Michelle turned sharply causing them both to jump back. "That's it!" She snapped her fingers.

"What?" Laree gave her a baffled look.

"My Lord! You scared the life out of me." Shantae put a hand to her chest.

"That little scumball, Marcus." Michelle looked at them both. *"He's* working at the Housing Authority. Marcus is jealous of Anthony, always has been since they were kids. He'd do anything to get back at him."

"Set his own cousin up for murder? Not even he could be that low," Laree gasped.

"You obviously don't know him," Shantae retorted.

Michelle glanced at her watch. "Four thirty, two hours before Anthony picks me up. I've got time if I hustle."

"For what?" Laree quickened her pace to keep up.

"Michelle, this isn't the fifty-yard dash. Slow down." Shantae began to trot behind them both.

Michelle dug inside her purse for her car keys. "Earl should still be at work. He'll be able to check it out. See y'all later." She strode to her car.

"Earl? I don't understand what she's talking about," Laree panted.

"Gotta go. I'll call you later," Michelle yelled. She drove off. Her friends stood on the parking lot completely astonished.

"What the—?" Shantae stared after her.

Laree shrugged. "Love scrambles the brain, honey."

* * *

Michelle parked next to Anthony in front of her apartment. Anthony leaned against the fender, waiting patiently. Michelle felt a surge of excitement seeing his easy grace. He stood straight as she came closer. As handsome as ever, he was dressed in a dark brown sweater with a brown, olive, and gold striped shirt underneath. Matching olive cotton pants were just close fitting enough to hint at the muscular thighs beneath the narrow waist.

"Hi, baby." Michelle brushed her lips across his. "Sorry I'm late."

Anthony clutched her to him and covered her mouth with his. His warm tongue traced a fiery route on the soft inside of her mouth. "Umm, that's better." He buried his face in her hair. "I haven't seen you for over eight hours. I needed more than a peck on the lips, woman."

Michelle leaned against him. "I missed you, too."

"Then why did you keep me waiting ten agonizing minutes?" Anthony pretended to admonish her. "Now you're going to have to make it up to me."

"Oh, no!" Michelle's eyes widened in mock horror. "What terrible price must I pay?"

Anthony ogled her. "Ten extra minutes in my arms tonight, young lady."

"Don't be so easy on me. Better make it a couple of hours."

"You're right." Anthony shook a finger at her. "You need to be taught a lesson. Never put work before romance."

"Work." Michelle drew back remembering why she arrived late. "We might find out something to prove you didn't murder Troy Quarles."

"We who? I hope you haven't been taking any risks." Anthony tensed, a worried look replacing the mirth in his brown eyes.

"No, I haven't—scout's honor." Michelle grabbed his hand. "Let's go up so I can tell you about it."

Anthony followed her up the stairs. Though he tried to question her, Michelle made him wait until she poured them both a glass of soda.

"Whew, that hit the spot." Michelle smacked with satisfaction.

Anthony drummed his fingers on his knee. "Okay, tell me exactly what you've been up to."

"You know my friend Earl, right?" Michelle continued when he nodded. "He has a contact in the state police records section. We call her whenever we need information on someone's arrest or prison history. It's all public record. But if you don't have a contact, you wait forever."

"How interesting." Anthony crossed his arms. "Like you're making me wait right now."

"I'm getting there." Michelle settled back into her tale. "As I was saying, Earl is going to get a prison record on Troy Quarles and Lonnie Mason."

"But we already know they've been in prison."

"Yes, but when and where is the question," Michelle said, pleased with herself.

Anthony scratched his chin, deep in thought for several moments. "Help me out. Why is that important?"

"Maybe they knew each other in prison. The police might find it very interesting. Drug dealing in the larger public housing projects took a sharp increase in the past few years. About the time a lot of folks with prison records started getting jobs there."

"I see what you're saying now." Anthony leaned forward with a look of interest.

"And Marcus has been working there for a while, too." Michelle watched his face. "And he's been hanging with Lonnie Mason and Tia Sanders. It's too much of a coincidence."

Anthony shook his head in disbelief. "Sure Marcus has always resented me, but frame me for murder?"

"Anthony, Marcus feels something much stronger than resentment toward you," Michelle said gently, knowing this was one more terrible truth he must face. "Remember, he threatened you after you fought that night."

"I know but—"

Michelle put a hand on his arm. "I bet Marcus saw an opportunity to implicate you in a drug ring."

Anthony still resisted her suggestion. The whole world seemed to tip at a crazy angle at the thought that those he'd known all his life were people he really did not know. A few days had changed a lifetime of relationships.

"But I can't believe Marcus hates me that much." He shook his head as if to clear it.

Michelle reached to comfort him. "I know how you feel, honey. But everything I've dug up so far seems to lead to it. I'm sure it'll be important in clearing you of suspicion," she said, her voice intense.

Anthony's expression softened. "Thank you, babe. I keep forgetting how much time you've put into tracking all this down." He kissed the top of her head.

"Listen, nobody messes with my man." Michelle snuggled closer to him. "Anybody that does is going to have to answer to me."

Anthony grinned. "I feel safer already. Now let's forget about everything and everyone else. Stay right there."

He went over to the stereo system and popped a compact disc into it. The smooth strains of Al Green singing "Love and Happiness" filled the room.

"Solid-gold soul." Anthony moved sensuously to the beat and held out his hand. "May I have this dance?"

Michelle watched the rhythmic motions of his body as though hypnotized. She placed her hands on both his hips and matched her movements to his. They lost themselves in the music. Long passionate kisses left them breathless.

Michelle lovingly guided Anthony's hands over her breast, thrilled at the tantalizing sensation of being caressed through the soft fabric of her blouse.

"Come on." Michelle danced him into the bedroom.

Michelle still wondered at the hunger he roused in her. Anthony seemed to be reading her mind. His tender touch at just the right moment made her cry out for more. Through song after song, they made love. They held each other trembling and unable to speak after each fantastic wave of ecstasy. They drifted off to sleep with arms and legs entwined.

Morning dawned bright with a clear blue sky. Michelle and Anthony lingered over coffee and toast.

"So what's on the agenda for you today?" Anthony began clearing the breakfast dishes. He filled the sink with soapy water.

"I'm going by the hospital to see Dom. Then over to the radio station." Michelle stretched lazily. Gazing out at the beautiful weather she thought how it perfectly mirrored her mood. "You don't have to do that."

"I might as well get in the habit. I plan to be a fifty-fifty husband." Anthony spoke with his back to her as he dried his hands on a dishtowel.

"What?" Michelle's mouth dropped open.

Getting down on one knee, he took both her hands in his. "I said, will you marry me?"

Michelle traced the line of his strong jaw with a forefinger. "Yes, yes, and yes!" she said, her eyes shining. A beautiful dream, one that seemed impossible only a few days ago, came true.

Anthony ran his fingers through the soft curls of her hair. "I love you so much," he whispered.

Michelle could not stop the tears that flowed. "I love you, too."

Drawing back, Anthony held both her shoulders. "Now all you need is an engagement ring."

Michelle sniffed. "Baby, I don't need anything fancy. Something simple will do."

Anthony reached into his pocket. He sighed in a loud, exaggerated fashion. "Then I guess I should return this."

Michelle shrieked when she saw the two-carat diamond solitaire set in white gold. She lunged forward to clasp him around the neck, causing them to topple onto the floor as she covered his face with kisses.

Anthony lay on his back laughing. "Hey, lady. I know you want me bad, but try to control yourself."

Michelle leered at him. "This is only the beginning, darlin'." She smiled down at him. Then her face grew solemn. "But can you afford a ring like this?"

Anthony placed a finger on her lips. "Don't worry. I've gotten a vote of confidence from three of my biggest clients. They assured me the building projects they hired me to complete are still mine. Now give me back that beautiful smile."

"Oh, Anthony," was all she managed before he smothered her attempt to speak with his kiss.

Driving to the hospital, Michelle waved gaily at everyone she met. She wanted to shout her happiness to the whole world.

Michelle breezed into Dominic's room. "Hello, brother. How are you this fine day? I must say, you look marvelous."

Dominic sat next to the window in the recliner. "Wow, try to cheer up." He grinned at her. "Spill it. What have you been up to?"

Michelle assumed a nonchalant pose. "I have no idea what you're talking about. I happen to be in a good mood, that's all."

"Don't give me that. You've got that goofy, dazed look in your eyes that could mean only one thing: true love."

"What makes you the expert?" Michelle sat on the side of his hospital bed swinging her legs back and forth.

"Hey, I had my share of love-struck ladies before I settled down." Dominic studied her with amusement. "You've got all the signs. And I don't have to be psychic to know Anthony put that smile on your face."

"Okay, so we're back together, Mr. Know-it-all." Michelle giggled.

"It wasn't hard to figure out. I'm really happy for you." Dominic patted her knee.

"This time we won't let anything keep us apart." Michelle gazed down at the ring on her finger. This symbol of love still awed her.

Dominic did a double take when the stone sparkled in the sunlight. "Whoa, look at that rock. You go, girl. When's the big day?"

"We haven't set a date yet. He only gave it to me this morning. I'm still recovering from the proposal." Michelle's eyes went wide. "I hadn't even thought about the wedding." Her head swam at the prospect of all the arrangements needed. "So many details." There was no question she wanted it to be a special day.

Dominic struggled to his feet to shuffle forward with small careful steps. He sat next to her on the bed. "Well, there's no need to panic. If I know Mama, she's been planning the wedding of her only daughter for the last twenty years at least. She'll know which caterer to use, the best flower shop, and everything else down to the last detail."

Michelle lost the contented look. "Mama won't have to bother. A big circus with a lot of snobby, pretentious people is the last thing I want."

"What did she say when you told her you didn't want a big wedding?"

"Nothing." Michelle did not turn around.

"For real? She didn't beg, threaten, or lay a guilt trip on you?"

Michelle cleared her throat. "Like I said, nothing."

"Amazing." Dominic was silent for a few moments. "Wait

a minute, when was the last time you talked to Mama, Michelle?"

"A while." Michelle folded her arms and stared out at the traffic below. No matter how she had tried, she had been unable to do more than engage in mechanical chatter with her mother for brief moments. She could not blot out the ugly image of her mother sneaking around with Ike Batiste.

"Michelle, come over here." Dominic slapped the bed sharply. "Right now or I'll come over there."

Michelle sat beside him with her arms still folded. "Dom, you don't understand."

"Mama had an affair with Ike and Pop knew about it. Mama's been milking our sympathy all along and letting us think Pop was the bad guy. Does that sum it up?" Dominic held up a hand. "Wait, I left out the part about Pop not knowing for sure if I was his kid."

"My Lord, who told you all this?" Michelle sputtered. "Brian? I'm going to wring his neck."

"Chelle—"

"The last thing you needed was to have a bombshell like that dropped on you. He's going to be sorry."

Dominic clamped a hand over her mouth. "Shut up, will you? I overheard Pop and Mama talking one night when they thought I was too drugged to hear them." He took his hand away. "Now if he can find a way to forgive her, so can you."

Michelle looked away. "I've tried."

"Talk to her about it. I'm sure Mama is in a lot of pain that this has come between you."

"I'm so angry with her. . . . I'm afraid of what I might say." Michelle bit her trembling lower lip.

Dominic took her hand. "You miss her as much as she misses you, Chelle. Tell her how you feel. Scream at her if it'll help. But don't treat her like a stranger. We're close to really being a family again."

"Dom, I just don't know."

"Please, Chelle." Dominic's voice broke. "Please try for me."

Michelle enclosed him in a gentle embrace. "Shh, don't get upset. I swear I'll talk to Mama." Despite the ease with which she made her promise, her stomach churned at the thought of confronting Annette.

Eighteen

Michelle stood near her old desk in the newsroom of Channel Twelve. In spite of the unpleasant circumstances surrounding her exit, she felt surprisingly at ease. She gazed about her as though it had been years instead of a few months since her departure. Michelle searched for lingering anger or resentment but found none. Several staff greeted her warmly, as though she were returning from exile. Michelle was secretly amused at the underlying tone of sympathy in their voices. Far from languishing in self-pity, she had cultivated her skills and seen her career blossom in a promising new direction. Weston Lockport, with Jason in tow, strode forward wearing a broad smile. Jason hovered at his shoulder.

Lockport stuck out his hand. "Michelle, wonderful of you to come." They walked toward his office. "I've been following your work on that little radio station. You've certainly made a name for yourself."

Michelle gave a short indulgent laugh. "Why, thank you. Being featured in *USA Today* is also pretty good."

Lockport's face registered shock, but he quickly recovered. "Really? Congratulations, my dear." He ushered her to one of the leather chairs around a glass table set in front of a large window with a view of the Mississippi River. "Jason, get us some coffee please. How do you take yours, Michelle?"

Michelle did not bother to look at Jason. "Cream, no sugar." The corner of her mouth lifted just a bit.

A chagrined Jason pursed his lips. He fought to keep his expression blank. "Yes, sir."

Weston leaned back and beamed at her. "Well, well. You wasted no time getting established in both radio and print media. Fine article in *Parade Magazine* on self-help groups in the African-American community. Very fine indeed. Of course, we at Channel Twelve recognized your talent long ago."

Michelle inclined her head in gracious acceptance. "Yes, and *most* of my time spent here was rewarding."

Weston cleared his throat. "You're referring to that incident with your notes. I did what seemed prudent at the time. After all, Charlotte Kinchen and James Bridges had high-powered attorneys sitting on my doorstep. When your notes couldn't be found . . ."

Michelle's eyes narrowed. "You leaped to the conclusion that I faked the story. Even though Nathan said he saw some of the invoices."

Weston shifted in his seat. "He couldn't swear the two or three he saw were genuine. And then an employee at the Housing Authority denied the invoices existed."

"Didn't it occur to you that T'aneka was scared witless by those thugs?" Michelle's eyes bored into him.

"Well, Nathan said that was a possible motivation. Sure she tried to change her story later, but frankly we felt her credibility had been compromised." Lockport lifted a shoulder.

"T'aneka came to talk to you for me?" Michelle's eyes misted. "Such a sweet kid." Her soft expression hardened when she turned her attention back to Lockport. "So what did you want to discuss with me, Mr. Lockport?" she said in a crisp, businesslike tone.

Jason came back in bearing two large mugs with the Channel Twelve logo on them. After setting them down on the glass table, he started to pull up another chair.

"Take that report on my desk with you on your way out. I made notes in the margins. Rework some of the verbiage." Lockport dismissed him with a short wave of his hand. "Thank you, Jason."

"I, uh, wanted to—" Jason stammered, searching for a reason to stay.

"Thank you, Jason." Lockport stared at him hard. When the door closed behind him, he faced Michelle again. "As I was saying, let's put that unfortunate incident behind us. Channel Twelve is on the cutting edge of news reporting in this state, and you fit right in with where we're going. With your talent and our resources, we can do great things in this city."

"What about the 'unfortunate incident'? I never found my notes or proved I ever had them." Michelle had no intention of letting him off easy.

"Maybe we acted in haste. In any event, it has been a learning experience for us all." Lockport wore a paternal smile. "We have the exposure and ratings that can launch you nationally, my dear. We need you and you need us." Lockport smiled at her.

Michelle arched an eyebrow at him without returning his smile. "I don't think so."

Lockport's smile stretched tight. "Excuse me? I don't understand."

Michelle leaned on the table, crossed her arms, and cocked her head to one side. "While I agree with you about my talent, this invitation didn't come for that reason alone." She gazed at him, waiting for the real explanation. "Well?"

"As I said, you have the talent and resources to do great things. The Housing Authority story is one example. We had such a hold on the ratings."

"Which I hear have really slipped," Michelle said with ice in her voice.

Lockport fingered his designer silk tie. "And the stories about community groups working to help themselves."

"Which you took from me after *I* came up with the idea. Jennifer not doing so well, eh?" Michelle pressed on. She enjoyed watching him squirm.

Lockport lifted his nose. "I wouldn't say that exactly."

"Mr. Lockport, let's cut to the bottom line." Michelle held up one finger. "One, Channel Six has been beating the pants off this station since they picked up on the Housing Authority scandal. They even wanted to interview me."

"Now, Michelle," Lockport said in a flustered voice. "Why take second billing on a story you made?" His face turned bright pink. "You deserve better."

Michelle ignored his remark. She held up a second finger. "Two, the sources that helped me break the story will talk only to me—you know it and I know you know it." She grinned at him and held up a third finger. "And three, Jennifer's handling of the series on community groups making a difference in this city has hit a dead end. From what I've seen, it's become a video society page with low ratings."

Lockport rubbed his chin and stared out of the large window at a tugboat slowly pushing four barges along the river. He turned back to her wearing a resigned expression. "What can I say? I let Jason and that jittery lawyer convince me when I should have listened to my gut instinct. But listen, young lady, this is a tremendous opportunity for you. You'll get exposure, a regular feature, and the chance to fill in as anchor at least one weekend a month. How about it?"

Michelle formed a steeple with her fingers. "Let me think it over. Of course, I may only work part-time since I have my radio show twice a week now." She expected him to balk at the idea.

Lockport nodded slowly with a large satisfied smile. "We can certainly work with you on that. You'll get in touch with me, let's say by Thursday?"

Michelle stood up. "Definitely." She gave him a firm

handshake before leaving. Once the door closed behind her, she did a little victory dance in the hallway.

Michelle sat with Anthony in her apartment listening to music and having a glass of wine. She told him every detail of her meeting with Lockport over dinner, relishing the feeling of triumph once again.

Anthony put his arms around Michelle's waist. "That's fantastic, honey. I'm just sorry you had to suffer such a humiliating experience because of me."

Michelle drew away and looked at him in surprise. "You didn't have anything to do with my being suspended."

"But either Uncle Ike or Marcus did. Probably both." Anthony glowered.

Michelle placed her hands on his shoulders. "Now look, don't start accepting blame for everything they do. You of all people shouldn't feel guilty."

Anthony sighed. "I do though. Chances are one of them picked up on something I said and used it. I was so dumb to keep defending Uncle Ike all those years. It's like I had a part in every dirty trick he's pulled."

Michelle rubbed his cheek. "Loving and supporting your family isn't a crime. It's hard when someone you love dearly lets you down. But, honey, Ike made his own choices."

Anthony touched the smooth flesh of her lips with the tip of his tongue. "Have I told you how marvelous you are?" he murmured.

"Yes, but you get bonus points for repeating yourself." Warmth spread through her at the sensation of his rising passion. She lifted her mouth to receive him once more. The annoying sound of the doorbell somehow filtered through the velvet haze of sensuality that enveloped them.

"Better get that," Anthony mumbled without taking his lips from hers.

Michelle whimpered softly. "Hmm, they'll go away if we

keep quiet." Her hands traveled the length of his muscular body.

"Say, Toussaint! Open up!" Earl pounded on the door. "We know you're in there."

Michelle groaned. "I forgot. Earl and Gracie called this afternoon to say they were coming over." She wore an apologetic smile.

"It's okay." Anthony leered at her. "When they leave, you're mine."

"I'm going to hold you to that, mister." Michelle was still giggling when she opened the door. "Quit all that racket and get in here." She swung the door wide to let them in.

Gracie came in first. Her eyebrows shot up when she saw Anthony sitting on the couch. "Hello again."

Earl strolled in with a knowing smirk. "Hey y'all, what's up?" He slapped hands with Anthony in greeting. "Uh, we're not interrupting anything, I hope?"

Anthony's even white teeth flashed. "It's cool, man."

Earl winked at him. "All right, all right."

Michelle reached out to box his ears but missed when Earl ducked. "All right—nothing. Sit down and hush."

Michelle got them all tall glasses of iced tea. After setting a tray of nuts and corn chips out for everyone to munch on, she sat next to Anthony on the sofa.

"Congrats are in order on the professional front, I hear. Way to go, Michelle." Earl gave her a thumbs-up sign.

"Yeah. We know things went well because Jason has been in a foul mood. Success is the best revenge." Gracie slapped palms with her. "Even better, he had to fetch your coffee," Gracie crowed.

Michelle laughed. "Not even making Lockport admit he screwed up topped that."

"So are you coming back?" Earl asked.

"Part-time. I don't want to give up the talk show at WDUP or freelance writing. Being on television isn't the big thrill it used to be," Michelle said. "Lockport is right about one thing, though—I want the exposure. But more for what it can do for our community than my own career."

"Good for you," Gracie said. "Besides, don't rule out being a big wheel in the television business. You got the right stuff."

Anthony placed a hand on her knee. "Look at what you were able to do for the public housing tenants."

"I'd still like to get my hands on whoever stole my notes," Michelle said. "That was my favorite purple folder," she pouted.

Anthony glanced at her sharply. "Did you say purple?"

"Yeah, it had deep pockets that held plenty of papers. And it was easy to spot in that landfill I called a desk." Michelle grinned. "Why?"

"Nothing." Anthony grew quiet and thoughtful.

"Well, that little plan backfired. Channel Six jumped on the trail you uncovered and dug up as much dirt as you did." Gracie took a healthy swig from her glass.

"Yeah, that beehive is still buzzing from the lick you landed on it. Word is things are very uncomfortable for Lonnie Mason right about now." Earl grabbed a handful of peanuts.

"Speaking of which, what did you find out?" Michelle sat forward.

Earl wiped his hands on a napkin and swallowed hard. He reached into his inside jacket pocket and pulled out a worn notepad. "Lemme see . . . here it is. Lonnie's old classmate from Angola State Penitentiary, Jeron 'Sweet' Glasper, is serving twenty years for armed robbery. He was a member of the Park Boulevard Posse before he got sent away. Lonnie was released on good time and got a job with the Authority through that prison outreach program."

"Ike is on the board of this nonprofit agency to help 're-integrate ex-offenders back into the community.' Marcus met Lonnie when he started working there. Lonnie hooked him up with Tia Sanders," Michelle explained to Gracie.

Earl nodded. "Right. Now guess who Troy Quarles used to hang with when he was a young drug dealer in training?"

Michelle snapped her fingers. "Jeron Glasper."

"Right again." Earl pointed an index finger at her. "There's the connection to Lonnie. Troy was probably ripping off some of the product for his own business on the side. But Troy also had a coke habit. Seems he started sampling the product within the last year, and as we all know, a coke habit is very expensive."

"Great work, Earl." Michelle clapped his shoulder. "What else? You said something on the phone about how we can connect with the police to be sure they take us seriously."

Earl hesitated, tapping one foot, then cleared his throat. "Um-humph, I took the liberty of inviting Detective Majors over here."

Michelle jumped up. "You did what? Earl has lost his mind! Have you lost your mind?" She planted her feet apart, standing in front of him.

Earl flinched back into the cushion of the love seat. "Hey, he went to school with my older brother. He's an okay dude."

Michelle huffed for a few moments. "That 'okay dude' tried to charge Anthony with murder."

"Calm down. The man is just doing his job." Earl held up both hands to ward off her wrath.

Anthony stood up to put a hand on her arm. "He's right, Michelle. Majors only questioned me based on what he had to go on. With the link to me and a tip that I was doing business with Troy, he had to talk to Cedric and me."

The doorbell caused them all to start. Michelle eyed Earl. "You better be right, Earl Elvis Gaines." She stomped to the door.

"Elvis? No wonder you refused to tell anybody your middle name! Wait until I get back to the station." Gracie hooted.

Earl blew air through flaring nostrils. "Thanks a lot, Toussaint. Mouth of the south here is going to tell the whole world."

Michelle threw him a look without sympathy. "Serves you right." She jerked the door open.

"Good evening, ma'am. Is Earl Gaines here?" The burly detective dipped his head a little at Michelle.

Earl went around her and stuck out his hand. "Detective, come on in."

Michelle raked the detective with a critical gaze as he passed. He entered without appearing to notice her hostility.

Majors appeared vigilant yet at ease at the same time. He stood just outside the enclosure created by the living-room sofa, chair, and love seat. "Evening, Mr. Hilliard. Ma'am." He acknowledged Gracie.

Earl bounced on the balls of his feet. "You want something, Detective Majors?" He approached the counter where Michelle had left large bottles of cola.

Michelle glanced at Earl sideways. "I'll get it."

"No, thanks," Majors said in a clipped tone. "You have information regarding the Troy Quarles murder?" He looked at each of them in turn.

Earl fumbled for his notepad again. "Lonnie Mason was in prison with a guy named Jeron 'Sweet' Glasper, a member of the Park Boulevard Posse."

Detective Majors crossed his arms over his immense chest. "Who got him in the outreach program. He got a job with the Housing Authority, which is where he met Tia Sanders and Troy Quarles. We know all that. Contrary to what you see on TV, we aren't dumbbells who can't see a clue unless some clever amateur detective points to it."

Michelle faced him with a grimace. "Then why haven't you dragged them in for questioning?" she exclaimed.

Majors turned to her. "Because it isn't enough. Quarles knew lots of people with criminal records."

"But you have to admit, it's a connection to known drug dealers," Michelle broke in. "Anthony has no criminal record and no other connection to drug trafficking."

Majors studied Anthony for a long moment. "True

enough. All I can tell you is that we're keeping all avenues open. We're following up a couple of interesting leads."

"What does that mean? Anthony is walking around under a cloud of suspicion. You should make it known if he isn't the main suspect anymore." Michelle stabbed a finger at him.

Anthony gazed at Majors with a thoughtful expression. "Chelle, be cool."

"But, Anthony, he—"

Earl picked up Anthony's cue. "Yeah, Michelle. The man's got a job to do. Thanks for everything, brother. Take it slow." He tapped fists with Majors.

Anthony did the same. "See you, Detective."

Michelle and Gracie watched their exchange with puzzled faces. They looked at each other and then at the three men.

Majors turned around before leaving. His granite face transformed when he gave Earl a small smile. "Tell that brother of yours he owes me a rematch on the court. And I'm going to whip his butt next time." He waved good-bye.

Michelle stood with both hands on her hips. "What was that all about?"

Earl looked at Anthony, who lifted a shoulder.

"Don't tell me it's some kind of 'man thing' us women wouldn't understand," Michelle retorted.

Anthony shook his head slowly. "No, baby. The man can't tell us certain things. He's looking to nail Lonnie and his pals, including the Park Boulevard Posse."

"He's on their trail, all right. The police want to keep them guessing. You know, psych them out," Earl added. "It's a mind game. They're going to be on edge. Criminals are naturally suspicious. Pretty soon, they're going to be wondering about each other."

"Which means turning on each other." Anthony sat down on the sofa again.

"Which means somebody is either going to talk or make a stupid mistake." Earl slapped hands with Anthony before sitting on the love seat. "Somebody is going down real soon, man."

"Sounds like it." Anthony crossed one ankle on his knee.

"Unbelievable." Gracie fell into the chair next to the sofa.

Michelle threw up both hands. "You mean to tell me you got all that from 'We're keeping all avenues open'?" She imitated the detective's basso voice.

Gracie blinked in confusion. "Where was I when all this information came out?"

Earl laughed. "Ladies, the man already knows about the connection between Troy, Lonnie, and the gang. He told us that."

Anthony nodded in agreement. "They've got the resources to track down those bums no matter where they hide."

"Anthony, you realize this might be bad for your uncle Ike," Michelle said in a somber voice.

Anthony took a deep breath. "I know."

Michelle sat next to Anthony. "I'm sorry, honey. Now I wish I'd been wrong about Ike." She worked her fingers through the tight fist of his right hand. The tension dissolved at her touch.

"Thanks, babe." Anthony kissed her hand.

"I hope all this is over soon." Michelle gazed at him. She wanted him out of danger more than anything in the world.

"I'm afraid there will be more fireworks before that happens," Anthony said. He wore a dark, dismal frown.

Earl's face became grim. "You're right, my brother. Don't count on those guys going out quietly."

Michelle felt a chill of fear at the thought of more violence.

Michelle bit her lower lip when her mother appeared to answer the door. "Hello, Mama."

Annette embraced her but let go quickly to lead her inside. "Come on in, sweetie."

Michelle stood in her parents' large den for the first time

in weeks. Her father, Brian, and Dominic had taken turns urging her to see Annette. Now she was here and had no idea what to do or say. Her stomach churned with anxiety, guilt, and a tinge of anger still.

Annette fussed about getting coffee. "I fixed café au lait for you, baby. And voila." She presented a dessert plate with a flourish. "Beignets, made from Monmon Chenevert's famous recipe."

Michelle managed a thin smile. "That's nice." She took off her light jacket and hung it in the small closet.

"Your show on the radio is the talk of the town, honey. I've listened to it every week since it started." Annette handed her a cup. She placed two beignets on a saucer, putting them on the coffee table in front of Michelle.

"I'm glad you like it." Michelle took a small sip of the hot, smooth liquid. "So how are you?"

"Oh, fine. And you?" Annette wore an eager-to-please expression. "I love that color on you. You always look so pretty in that shade of green." She patted the deep emerald silk shirt Michelle wore.

"Thanks." Michelle looked around the room to avoid meeting her mother's anxious gaze. "You've changed the furniture around. I like it."

"Thank you, dear."

"Gives the room a more open look."

Annette put down her cup. "The only harmless small talk left is the weather, but then we'd be right back where we started. You have a right to be angry with me, Michelle. I've been a selfish, silly fool. Right?"

"Mama . . ." Michelle started but could not go on.

Annette wore a sad smile. "I know, you're too respectful to agree. Can I at least try to explain?" At Michelle's nod, she continued. "Thomas was always the serious type when we were in high school. I guess it was because he had to work to help his father support the family. I didn't have to do anything like that, you know. Even back then Ike was a fast-talking go-getter. While Thomas put his money in the bank, Ike bought flashy clothes and a car. Ike ran with the 'in crowd,' and I found that exciting. To make a long story short, Ike and I had an affair. When I caught him with another girl, we broke up. I started dating Tommy mostly to rub Ike's nose in the fact that I could get someone else. But Tommy was so good to me, better than any boy had ever been, that I really began to admire him. We got married. After a few years Tommy seemed more interested in working than spending time with me. We argued a lot and, well, you know the rest."

Michelle's jaw tightened. "But why did you do it, Mama?"

Annette gazed at her with moist eyes full of misery. "Loneliness, vanity, I don't know. When Tommy found out, it was horrible. He looked at me with such disgust," she said, her voice choked with grief. "I swear, it never happened again. But Tommy couldn't forgive or forget what I'd done. We stayed together for a lot of reasons, none of them good. He never forgave me for the affair. I struck back by telling him it was his fault."

Michelle looked at her mother in a whole new light. What she saw was a vulnerable, sensitive woman who had made a terrible mistake. Annette was no saint, but neither did she deserve to be treated with contempt. Michelle put a hand on her shoulder. "Have you ever tried talking about it without accusing each other?"

"No," Annette said in a quiet voice full of anguish.

"Then maybe that's where you should start. Daddy may want to hear you say how much you love him before he trusts opening his heart to you again."

Annette wiped her eyes dry. "After the affair, I realized Tommy is twice the man Ike could ever hope to be. But by then, I'd lost him."

"I don't think you lost him, Mama." Michelle embraced her mother.

"Maybe we'll find a way back to each other after all this

time." Annette clutched Michelle's hand. "But can you forgive me? I can't stand the thought of losing you, baby. I love you so much."

Michelle tasted salty tears flowing down her cheeks. "I love you too, Mama. I love you, too." She went into her mother's open arms.

They talked for hours. For the first time, they spoke openly of their true feelings. Annette shared the pain of her mistakes with Michelle. Michelle confessed her childhood fears of losing both her parents and the agony of watching them hurt each other. Both felt strengthened knowing they could lean on each other as they sought to mend old wounds.

The shabby hotel formed a square U-shape with faded orange doors facing inside around the parking lot. The office sat at the end of one arm, with four parking spaces in front of a dirty plateglass window. Charlotte wrinkled her nose in distaste as she eased her car past it to park in front of room 313.

As she walked to the room, the heel of her expensive alligator pump twisted in the cracked cement. "Dammit!" Charlotte examined the torn leather with a scowl.

She knocked twice then three times spaced apart. The curtains twitched slightly. The rattle of locks being released followed several seconds later.

"Hurry up and come in." Bridges stayed out of sight behind the door. He snapped the door shut, almost catching the hem of her skirt.

Charlotte sucked air through her teeth. "Will you get a hold of yourself? I told you nobody knows you're here. And you certainly could have found a better place to stay. Lafayette has several decent hotels." She glanced around at the dingy carpet and tacky furniture.

Bridges sat in a faded brown chair next to the bed. "That

would be the first place they'd look. Or do you want them to find me?" His eyes narrowed.

Charlotte dropped the irritation from her voice. "Of course not, honey. You know how I feel about you. I guess my nerves are raw with everything happening." She sat on the bed as close to him as she could. When she reached out to stroke his arm, he moved away.

"Did you bring it?" Bridges got up and began pacing.

Charlotte pulled out a fat envelope and handed it to him. "All of the files showing how Ike cut deals with contractors, invoices that even that reporter didn't get her hands on, the works. There is some pretty damaging evidence against me, too. Are you sure the DA won't come after me?"

Bridges turned his back to pour whiskey into a plastic cup. He downed some of it before facing her again. "Baby, I told you I'd take all the blame. Just stick to the story like we agreed. You trusted me because we had an affair. You had no idea Ike and I were cutting corners." He walked closer to her. "It won't do your career any good."

Charlotte leaned back on her arms and kicked off her pumps. "Humph, better to be seen as a gullible, infatuated woman than go to jail."

Bridges stood over her. "Of course, you were smart enough to help us find ways to beat the system. We could never have done it without having someone on the inside."

"What can I say? I'm a very enterprising woman. Too bad that smart-aleck reporter had to stick her nose in. We were doing very well." Charlotte rubbed a sapphire-and-diamond ring on one hand.

"That deal with those renovated houses was especially profitable. We got paid twice. Big tax breaks and renting them at a good price to middle-class tenants. You were right about the rules being so loose. Nobody ever verified we rented to poor families."

Charlotte's mouth twisted into a sneer. "Sure. Those dumb bureaucrats didn't even question us about it. That was the best moneymaker." Her face softened to a devoted smile. "I helped you then, and I'll help you now, sugar. You can count on me no matter what happens."

Bridges sat down in the chair again. His face hardened. "What about Lonnie? Don't bother to lie, Charlotte. I know about him and your affair with Ike."

Charlotte massaged his thigh with long fingers. She sat forward to let the neckline of her blouse reveal more cleavage. "Baby, Ike was long before you. And Lonnie means nothing. I just used him to find out what he was up to. He's been out to get you from the beginning. You know that. It's always been you that I wanted."

"You did it for me then?" Bridges stared at her.

"All for you and me, sweetheart." Charlotte's voice became husky.

Bridges sat forward just a little. "But weren't you scared? I mean, Lonnie's a very dangerous man. After all, he murdered that Quarles kid."

Charlotte got up to get a cigarette from a pack on the dresser. "That's the kind of animal he is, James. What else can you expect from somebody like him? Look how he grew up. In a ratty shotgun shack over on Forty-eighth Street."

"So you knew Lonnie Mason was going to kill Quarles?"

"Are you kidding? You know how Lonnie is. All mouth. He told me that and more." Charlotte blew a plume of smoke at the ceiling. "I could tell you plenty that should help you get an even better plea bargain. You'll probably only get a few months." She switched on the radio and found a station playing jazzy music. Wetting her plum-colored lips, she began to undulate to the beat while undressing. Soon she was down to her bra and panties. "Then it's going to be you and me. Just give me the location of the accounts. With what I've put away and what you have, we should be living in style for years."

Bridges began breathing heavily as his eyes traveled down her soft curves. "Sure, babe. You and me. Just let me freshen up." He looked down at his shirt in embarrassment. "I've been sweating like a pig for three hours, afraid you wouldn't come."

"Okay, but don't make me wait for my man too long. I've missed the way you touch me." Charlotte puckered her lips at him. At the sound of the shower behind the closed bathroom door, she turned to smile at her reflection in the mirror. "Girl, you've got it going on." Her lips curved up in satisfaction.

Anthony let himself into Ike's two-story house with his key. The only vehicle in the driveway was Ike's fancy pickup truck. Even so, Anthony called out. When there was no answer, he went upstairs. He opened the door to a large bedroom dominated by a queen-sized black lacquer bed. Moving quickly, he searched through drawers then started going through the large walk-in closet. A top shelf was piled with miscellaneous junk including a collection of adult magazines. Anthony pushed it aside and noticed an old gym bag stuffed way back into a corner. Using a small step stool, he was just able to reach it. The bag contained a small handgun, a plastic sandwich bag of marijuana, and a purple folder.

"Well, well." Marcus leaned against the doorframe of the closet. "Nice of you to drop by, cuz. You lost something in my bedroom?"

Anthony held up the folder. "Is this what I think it is?"

Marcus eyed the folder uneasily, yet still put on a face of false bravado. "Gee, if you think it's a folder then you win a prize."

"Oh, it's more than just 'a folder.' It's the folder you stole from Michelle's desk at Channel Twelve." Anthony opened it and flipped through several pages.

"Who, me? Get serious. I've never been near that station."

"You or one of your scuzzy little friends. Same species of rodent." Anthony grunted with disgust.

"You've been asking for an ass whipping a long time," Marcus said through clenched teeth.

"I knew you'd be too arrogant or scheming to destroy it." Anthony scanned the papers. "Planning a little blackmail, I'd bet."

Marcus pulled a small gun from his belt. "Drop it right back in the bag. Now," he growled. "This may be your last time getting in my damn way."

Anthony did as he was told. "The cops are closing in, Marcus. Those invoices are the least of your worries."

"Don't count on it. Move." Marcus waved him out of the closet with the gun. "Go on, down the stairs."

"You're going to kill me like you killed Troy Quarles?" Anthony walked ahead of him into Ike's office.

"Oh, I didn't kill Troy. You did, remember?" Marcus jeered.

"Pretty pleased with yourself for setting me up, huh?" Anthony heard the click of the back door. Marcus's expression didn't change, and Anthony realized he had not heard the sound. "Who helped you do it?"

Ike walked through the door. "Marcus, put that thing down," he bellowed. "Somebody tell me what the hell is going on in here."

Marcus lowered the gun. "I caught him burglarizing the place. Probably looking for evidence to rat you out or plant a bug for the cops." His eyes were hostile slits.

Ike turned on Anthony. "What is he talking about?"

Anthony stared at Marcus. "I found Michelle's notes on the Housing Authority story in his room. Marcus talked about her missing purple notebook when I was here three weeks ago. I figured there was only one way he could know exactly what it looked like."

"Fool! What did you keep the damn thing for?" Ike snarled at Marcus.

Anthony gazed at his uncle with distaste. "You knew he had it?"

"Hell, no. If I had, it would be a pile of ashes." Ike shot his son a venomous look. "Get rid of it today." He turned to Anthony. "And you . . . go on home. Go on," he said in a voice heavy with regret.

Michelle and Earl stood amidst the pack of reporters surrounding Ike and his attorney. Questions were being thrown at them from all sides.

A reporter from the New Orleans *Times-Picayune* called out. "Mr. Batiste, was it a shock to learn that your longtime friend and business associate, James Bridges, agreed to testify against you and Charlotte Kinchen for the U.S. Attorney?"

"My client is confident that he will be cleared of all charges. Mr. Bridges is lying to save his own skin." The attorney spoke in a monotone.

"So you plan to enter a not-guilty plea?" Earl yelled.

"My client emphatically denies all charges made against him."

Michelle stepped forward. "Does that include involvement in alleged drug dealing and murder? What about your son's connection to Lonnie Mason and the Park Avenue Posse? Sources say a gang member will testify that your son arranged major drug shipments; that he helped Mason murder Troy Quarles when they suspected him of stealing some of the cocaine."

Ike's face twisted with rage when he turned to look at her. He opened his mouth but was cut off by his lawyer.

"Mr. Batiste has never been involved in any criminal activity. He has been a hard-working member of this community for over thirty years. There is not one shred of evidence to prove otherwise. That's all." The lawyer spoke curtly. He grabbed Ike's arm and led him away, walking at a fast pace.

A steel-gray Mercedes Benz pulled up to the curb just as they went through the double glass doors of the court building. Ike shoved several reporters as they plowed through them to reach it.

"Here come the others," a voice called out.

The reporters turned as one, like a pack of wolves scenting fresh meat. Charlotte Kinchen stared around her with reddened glazed eyes. Her attorney guided her gently with a hand on her back. James Bridges emerged from another hallway surrounded by federal marshals. Charlotte's eyes burned with fury at the sight of him. She lunged forward, knocking her attorney aside. Somehow she managed to claw her way past the marshals, who were taken by surprise at her attack. Bridges howled when her long nails raked his face.

"You filthy no-good bastard!" She struggled to get at him, but three marshals pinned her arms behind her.

Bridges was hustled to a waiting elevator while reporters clamored to get footage of a screaming, cursing Charlotte being dragged away.

"Oo-wee, is she mad." Earl let out a long whistle. "That lady came close to taking him out."

"Yeah, Bridges did a job on everybody. He pointed the feds to all the skeletons in Ike's closet and got the goods on Charlotte." Michelle shook her head in wonder at the turn of events.

"Miss Cutie-Pie thought she had the old boy wrapped around her little finger. And all the time he's wearing a wire. Those tapes are kinda hard to explain away." Earl let out a sharp laugh.

"Can you believe she tried to sell that tale about conducting her own secret investigation? And that her affair with Lonnie Mason and Ike was part of it?" Michelle tucked her notepad into her purse and followed Earl outside.

"Gotta give her credit for coming up with a creative story." Earl glanced at his watch. "Wow, I better get moving. This is going to be the lead story on the five and six o'clock shows. See ya, kiddo." He dashed for the Channel Twelve car where Bob was already waiting.

Michelle waved good-bye to them then turned to gaze back at the courthouse. For years she had hoped for the day when Ike Batiste would be held accountable for his actions. Now she felt sadness instead at the lives destroyed. She walked away thinking of how she could comfort Anthony.

A warm breeze rippled through the leaves, causing a soft rustle that seemed to be nature's way of murmuring contentment. Anthony and Michelle strolled the paved path through the gardens on Avery Island. White-and-pink azaleas bloomed. The delicate lavender petals of wisteria swept the ground. Michelle breathed in deeply as they passed fragrant gardenias in full bloom. They both savored the pastoral peace after the uproar of the past few weeks. Finding a stone bench, they sat down.

Michelle rested her head on Anthony's shoulder as they gazed at the little bayou that snaked through the island. The water made a soothing sound as it lapped against the embankment. "It's been a wonderful three days. I hate to go home."

Anthony kissed her forehead. "I know what you mean. But the real honeymoon is only a couple of months away."

"Wasn't it wonderful of Mama and Daddy to give us a Caribbean cruise as a wedding present? They've been great these past few weeks."

"Both of them are special people. She and Mama did a fantastic job on the wedding and the reception. And your dad had a ball showing off his dancing skills. They really seem to care about each other."

"Yes, I think they do." Michelle thought of the subtle change in her parents. Gone was the brooding tension between them that often exploded into animosity. It was touching to watch them treat each other with tender consideration.

Michelle no longer doubted that marriage could be a beautiful part of life. She gazed down at her wedding ring and the matching band of gold on Anthony's finger. They seemed to glow with a magical sparkle.

"Aruba, Barbados, and St. Maarten. Especially the French side of St. Maarten with those nude beaches." He winked at her.

Michelle giggled. "No, thanks. I plan to keep my clothes on, sir. At least in public," she breathed, stroking his chest.

Anthony laughed deep in his throat. "Umm-hmm, I'll settle for that."

"It'll be good to be far away in another world for a while." Though she didn't mention the trials or Ike, Anthony seemed to be reading her mind.

"I've never seen Uncle Ike look defeated before." Anthony's eyes clouded with sorrow. "It hurts to see him suffering in spite of all the wrong he's done. I feel like I've lost two fathers."

"I'm sorry it had to end the way it did."

Anthony searched her eyes and found only sincere sadness. "You really mean that."

Michelle caressed the dark, tight curls of hair at his temples. "Losing someone you love is horrible. What hurts you, hurts me."

The sorrow melted away, replaced by a soft, loving smile. "Having you means I can face anything. Nothing and no one will ever come between us again. Lady, you're stuck with me," he teased.

Michelle felt a quiet joy. The future opened before her like a beautiful flower, a future shared with this magnificent man. She lifted her mouth to his. "I wouldn't have it any other way," she murmured.

About the Author

Margaret Emery Hubbard, writing as Lynn Emery, is a native of Baton Rouge, Louisiana. She lives with her artist husband. Ms. Hubbard is by profession a social worker. Having earned a BA in psychology and a Master's degree in social work, she has worked in the field for twenty years.

Look for these upcoming Arabesque titles:

December 1996

EMERALD'S FIRE by Eboni Snoe
NIGHTFALL by Loure Jackson
SILVER BELLS, an Arabesque Holiday Collection

January 1997

ALL THE LOVE by Bette Ford
SENSATION by Shelby Lewis
ONLY YOU by Angela Winters

February, 1997

INCOGNITO by Francis Ray
WHITE LIGHTNING by Candice Poarch
LOVE LETTERS, Valentine collection

TIMELESS LOVE

Look for these historical romances in the Arabesque line:

BLACK PEARL by Francine Craft (0236-0, $4.99)

CLARA'S PROMISE by Shirley Hailstock (0147-X, $4.99)

MIDNIGHT MOON by Mildred Riley (0200-X; $4.99)

SUNSHINE AND SHADOWS by Roberta Gayle (0136-4, $4.99)

ROMANCES ABOUT AFRICAN-AMERICANS!
YOU'LL FALL IN LOVE
WITH ARABESQUE BOOKS FROM PINNACLE

SERENADE   (0024, $4.99)
by Sandra Kitt
Alexandra Morrow was too young and naive when she first fell
in love with musician, Parker Harrison—and vowed never to be
so vulnerable again. Now Parker is back and although she tries
to resist him, he strolls back into her life as smoothly as the jazz
rhapsodies for which he is known. Though not the dreamy innocent she was before, Alexandra finds her defenses quickly crum-
bling and her mind, body and soul slowly opening up to her one
and only love, who shows her that dreams do come true.

FOREVER YOURS   (0025, $4.50)
by Francis Ray
Victoria Chandler must find a husband quickly or her grandpar-
ents will call in the loans that support her chain of lingerie bou-
tiques. She arranges a mock marriage to tall, dark and handsome
ranch owner Kane Taggart. The marriage will only last one year,
and her business will be secure, and Kane will be able to walk
away with no strings attached. The only problem is that Kane has
other plans for Victoria. He'll cast a spell that will make her his
forever after.

A SWEET REFRAIN   (0041, $4.99)
by Margie Walker
Fifteen years before, jazz musician Nathaniel Padell walked out
on Jenine to seek fame and fortune in New York City. But now
the handsome widower is back with a baby girl in tow. Jenine is
still irresistibly attracted to Nat and enchanted by his daughter.
Yet even as love is rekindled, an unexpected danger threatens Nat's
child. Now, Jenine must fight for Nat before someone stops the
music forever!

*Available wherever paperbacks are sold, or order direct from the
Publisher. Send cover price plus 50¢ per copy for mailing and
handling to Penguin USA, P.O. Box 999, c/o Dept. 17109,
Bergenfield, NJ 07621. Residents of New York and Tennessee
must include sales tax. DO NOT SEND CASH.*

IF ROMANCE BE THE FRUIT OF LIFE—
READ ON—
BREATH-QUICKENING HISTORICALS FROM PINNACLE

WILDCAT (722, $4.99)
by Rochelle Wayne

No man alive could break Diana Preston's fiery spirit . . . until seductive Vince Gannon galloped onto Diana's sprawling family ranch. Vince, a man with dark secrets, would sweep her into his world of danger and desire. And Diana couldn't deny the powerful yearnings that branded her as his own, for all time!

THE HIGHWAY MAN (765, $4.50)
by Nadine Crenshaw

When a trumped-up murder charge forced beautiful Jane Fitzpatrick to flee her home, she was found and sheltered by the highwayman—a man as dark and dangerous as the secrets that haunted him. As their hiding place became a place of shared dreams—and soaring desires—Jane knew she'd found the love she'd been yearning for!

SILKEN SPURS (756, $4.99)
by Jane Archer

Beautiful Harmony Harper, leader of a notorious outlaw gang, rode the desert plains of New Mexico in search of justice and vengeance. Now she has captured powerful and privileged Thor Clarke-Jargon, who is everything Harmony has ever hated—and all she will ever want. And after Harmony has taken the handsome adventurer hostage, she herself has become a captive—of her own desires!

WYOMING ECSTASY (740, $4.50)
by Gina Robins

Feisty criminal investigator, July MacKenzie, solicits the partnership of the legendary half-breed gunslinger-detective Nacona Blue. After being turned down, July—never one to accept the meaning of the word no—finds a way to convince Nacona to be her partner . . . first in business—then in passion. Across the wilds of Wyoming, and always one step ahead of trouble, July surrenders to passion's searing demands!

Available wherever paperbacks are sold, or order direct from the Publisher. Send cover price plus 50¢ per copy for mailing and handling to Penguin USA, P.O. Box 999, c/o Dept. 17109, Bergenfield, NJ 07621. Residents of New York and Tennessee must include sales tax. DO NOT SEND CASH.

PUT SOME FANTASY IN YOUR LIFE—
FANTASTIC ROMANCES FROM PINNACLE

TIME STORM   (728, $4.99)
by Rosalyn Alsobrook
Modern-day Pennsylvanian physician JoAnn Griffin only believed what
she could feel with her five senses. But when, during a freak storm, a
blinding flash of lightning sent her back in time to 1889, JoAnn realized
she had somehow crossed the threshold into another century and was
now gazing into the smoldering eyes of a startlingly handsome stranger.
JoAnn had stumbled through a rip in time . . . and into a love affair so
intense, it carried her to a point of no return!

SEA TREASURE   (790, $4.50)
by Johanna Hailey
When Michael, a dashing sea captain, is rescued from drowning by a
beautiful sea siren—he does not know yet that she's actually a mermaid.
But her breathtaking beauty stirred irresistible yearnings in Michael.
And soon fate would drive them across the treacherous Caribbean, toss-
ing them on surging tides of passion that transcended two worlds!

ONCE UPON FOREVER   (883, $4.99)
by Becky Lee Weyrich
A moonstone necklace and a mysterious diary written over a century
ago were Clair Summerland's only clue to her true identity. Two men
loved her—one, a dashing civil war hero . . . the other, a daring jet pilot.
Now Clair must risk her past and future for a passion that spans two
worlds—and a love that is stronger than time itself.

SHADOWS IN TIME   (892, $4.50)
by Cherlyn Jac
Driving through the sultry New Orleans night, one moment Tori's car
spins out of control; the next she is in a horse-drawn carriage with the
handsomest man she has ever seen—who calls her wife—but whose
eyes blaze with fury. Sent back in time one hundred years, Tori is falling
in love with the man she is apparently trying to kill. Now she must race
against time to change the tragic past and claim her future with the man
she will love through all eternity!

*Available wherever paperbacks are sold, or order direct from the
Publisher. Send cover price plus 50¢ per copy for mailing and
handling to Penguin USA, P.O. Box 999, c/o Dept. 17109,
Bergenfield, NJ 07621. Residents of New York and Tennessee
must include sales tax. DO NOT SEND CASH.*

HISTORICAL ROMANCE FROM PINNACLE BOOKS

LOVE'S RAGING TIDE (381, $4.50)
by Patricia Matthews

Melissa stood on the veranda and looked over the sweeping acres of Great Oaks that had been her family's home for two generations, and her eyes burned with anger and humiliation. Today her home would go beneath the auctioneer's hammer and be lost to her forever. Two men eagerly awaited the auction: Simon Crouse and Luke Devereaux. Both would try to have her, but they would have to contend with the anger and pride of girl turned woman . . .

CASTLE OF DREAMS (334, $4.50)
by Flora M. Speer

Meredith would never forget the moment she first saw the baron of Afoncaer, with his armor glistening and blue eyes shining honest and true. Though she knew she should hate this Norman intruder, she could only admire the lean strength of his body, the golden hue of his face. And the innocent Welsh maiden realized that she had lost her heart to one she could only call enemy.

LOVE'S DARING DREAM (372, $4.50)
by Patricia Matthews

Maggie's escape from the poverty of her family's bleak existence gives fire to her dream of happiness in the arms of a true, loving man. But the men she encounters on her tempestuous journey are men of wealth, greed, and lust. To survive in their world she must control her newly awakened desires, as her beautiful body threatens to betray her at every turn.

Available wherever paperbacks are sold, or order direct from the Publisher. Send cover price plus 50¢ per copy for mailing and handling to Penguin USA, P.O. Box 999, c/o Dept. 17109, Bergenfield, NJ 07621. Residents of New York and Tennessee must include sales tax. DO NOT SEND CASH.